GW00598321

Seeds of Anger

In this vivid successor to THE WHITE LOCUSTS, James Ambrose Brown continues the saga of two families whose lives affected both Boer and Uitlander in that turbulent decade which founded Johannesburg.

Penlynne and his ambitious society wife, Dorothy, are caught up in imperialist ambitions. The gold heiress, Katherine escapes from her unhappy marriage and finds love at last. And Christiaan Smit, the brilliant young Boer lawyer, helps to quell attempts to foment a revolution which would have turned his republic into a capitalist-dominated country.

Threaded through these lives is the threat of German imperialistic ambitions and all is set against the backdrop of a raw, undeveloped and still half savage South Africa.

Skilfully blending fact and fiction, SEEDS OF ANGER brings to life an epoch that is almost forgotten – a time when violent revolution seemed the only solution.

**Also by the same author,
and available from NEL:**

The White Locusts

About the Author

South African author, James Ambrose Brown,
has many years of successful writing behind
him, including work for radio, television and
the theatre. He has written plays for both
adults and children which have been translated
into several languages and won many awards.
His novels, including THE RETURN and THE
ISLAND OF THE BIRD, as well as THE WHITE
LOCUSTS, have also won awards, including
the Republic Prize for English Prose.

James Ambrose Brown was commissioned to
write volumes 2 and 4 of the Official History of
the South African Forces in World War II: A
GATHERING OF EAGLES and EAGLES'
STRIKE. He lives and works in Cape Town.

Seeds of Anger

James Ambrose Brown

NEW ENGLISH LIBRARY
in association with
Southern Book Publishers (Pty) Ltd

*The characters and situations in
this book are entirely imaginary
and bear no relation to any real
person or actual happening.*

First published in South Africa
by Southern Book Publishers
(Pty) Ltd in 1987

NEL Paperback edition 1988

British Library C.I.P.

Brown, James Ambrose,
1919–
Seeds of anger.
I. Title
823

ISBN 0-450-48487-4

Printed and bound in Great Britain
for Hodder and Stoughton
Paperbacks, a division of Hodder
and Stoughton Ltd., Mill Road,
Dunton Green, Sevenoaks, Kent
TN13 2YA (Editorial Office: 47
Bedford Square, London WC1B
3DP) by Richard Clay Ltd.,
Bungay, Suffolk.

Prologue to Book Two

Hooters on the mines were calling the day shift. In the silence of the great house Muriel Rawlinson sat with the body of her husband. She was listening for the sound of carriage wheels on the drive announcing the arrival of Katherine. She looked at the gold watch hanging from her neck. The up-mail from Natal should be in by now. Katherine would not be long.

There it was! The crunch of wheels and clatter of hooves. Awed and silent servants opened the front door. She heard the quick rush of Katherine's feet on the stairs, the rustle of her dress. A child's voice was raised and hushed and the older woman saw the pale beauty of Katherine, paler now in the shock of her father's death. She was still in the light clothing of Durban's humid summer.

The young woman took her hands and they embraced. Walter Gardiner and Spencer stood in the doorway of the bedroom, the boy, wide-eyed, trailing his sailor's straw hat by the ribbons. He held his father's hand. He was well aware of some tremendous event.

Muriel Rawlinson rose to remove the boy. 'You'll want to be alone wi' your father, Kathy. Come Spencer.' The boy evaded her. He darted to his mother's side and stood staring at his grandfather.

'Is grandpa sleeping?', his blue eyes taking in every detail, his face half-hidden in his mother's skirts but the bold gaze missing nothing. He was already headstrong.

'How long ago was it?' Walter asked in low tones, his eyes on the figure on the bed.

'Two hours ago ... just as the hooters went for the day shift.'

'A stroke?'

'Aye.'

As Gardiner looked at the figure of his father-in-law he heard Muriel say: 'You'll make the arrangements, if you please Mr

1

Gardiner.' She had never been able to address him by his first name. Even though she was now Rawlinson's widow it seemed an undue familiarity. The servant woman who had married her master!

'If you wish … certainly, Lady Rawlinson.'

She was probably hearing the title used for the first time and not unaware of the irony. Within twelve hours of being knighted by the queen the man was dead.

The big American lifted his son and carried him downstairs. He had always thought of Muriel Rawlinson as coarse. But he had never underestimated her shrewdness and force of character. They had each other's measure.

He set the boy down at the fish pond. Together they watched the golden carp finning among the roots of water lilies. The child plunged his arm among them, snatching at the gleam of scales. The man tightened his arm about him. My boy, he thought. Wilful, obstinate Spencer. He felt possessive about him, something he had never expected to experience at his age.

'Grandpa's dead,' the boy said.

'Yes.'

'He was very old.'

Good God, the man was in his mid-fifties! How many had achieved so much in that time?

Katherine sat with her father. He had been many fathers to her. The first she remembered was the man who put her up on his horse at the river diggings on the Vaal, safe against his body, the tremendous voice booming out greetings and orders. From the beginning he had meant authority to her, and safety. When she was budding out of childhood he had been sharp with her, even harsh at times. She knew now it was the concern of a widower for a girl among so many men.

Tears flowed. This was the man who used to remind her, as if to impress it on her, 'It's for you, Kathy. It's all for you. Why would I work like this? I could have given up that time in Kimberley when Rhodes and Beit tried to do me in … everything I worked for wiped out in a night. Everyone I trusted bought over … or sold me out. I came near to shooting myself. Yes, my girl … I would've done it if I hadn't come to your room that night … it was in my pocket, the pistol. You were lying there. I thought

2

you were asleep … your pretty hair on the pillow. I knelt down to kiss you.'

There was a sad sweetness in Katherine's tears.

'And then your arms came out of the covers and round my neck. It broke my heart. I pitched the pistol down the well and went over to Beit's office. You never knew that, did you? They all say it was Beit gave me a fresh start … called it generosity. More likely guilty conscience! It was my dear girl saved me.'

Katherine saw the white stubble breaking through the marble of his face. Hard lines of mouth were relaxed, as if cut by a sculptor who did not have bitter memories of the man.

Muriel Rawlinson had drawn the dark red curtains. The brightness outside gave the death chamber a glow that lent the corpse a spurious warmth. He might have been asleep. Katherine touched his hand and recoiled. It was icy. Someone would have to remove the thumb ring. She had always hated it. What a contradiction of a man. Emotional. Hard as flint. Bullying and insecure. Why else had he married his housekeeper? Muriel's was a voice he had come to trust in a world of enemies.

Katherine overcame her repugnance to kiss his forehead. Silently she left the room. A fly settled on the face of the dead man. In a moment it disappeared into a nostril.

Downstairs the doorbell was ringing. They were beginning to arrive. Friends and enemies. One could not tell them apart. Today solemnity would cover all. The young woman straightened her back and composed her face.

An heiress might weep in private. Never in public.

Chapter One

Leonard Penlynne called up to his coachman. 'Pull up at the gates of *Bloukoppen*, Williams.' The man grinned. He knew the house well.

'The big gate's padlocked, Sir ... been that way for months. You'll 'ave to use the small gate.'

Penlynne passed the peeling sign – For Sale – and walked through the rank, overgrown garden. The soil beneath the magnolia tree was heady with fallen blossoms. He opened the front door. Hot, stale air of a long-closed house enveloped him. When Kitty had lived here the house had always had a rich, warm odour; a combination of her clothes and her perfumes, male odours of cigars and liquor. It had been the most stimulating place one could imagine. Music and lights ... lights everywhere. And loud laughter.

He returned his latch key to his waistcoat pocket. Absurd to have kept it. He had no desire to renew the affair. Regrets?

Yes, my God, how could a man completely put her from mind. A woman whose physical ardour and joie de vivre had so exactly matched his own at that moment of his life when to possess her had seemed the due reward of his astuteness. It was up there, at the head of the stairs, he last saw her, raging in her indignation. 'Get out you bastard ... you Jew bastard!' The silverbacked hairbrush! How often he'd lain in bed watching her drawing it through the shoulderlength red hair. It had clattered at his feet. 'Take it ... take everything!'

The impulse to see the house again had come upon him suddenly. He was depressed. He was entertaining visitors from Europe, men of wealth and influence. Big investors. But before they had been in the city a week they were talking evasively. Capital was afraid of Johannesburg. Kruger's politics were going to kill it. He made no secret of his hostility. 'God gave the Boers this land ... Satan brought the English, the *uitlanders*. I will tax

5

them till they bleed to death … play Pharaoh to their Moses.'

The old fear gripped Penlynne. It seemed often to reassert itself these days. A dread of losing everything; as in Kimberley. An act of pure superstition had brought him here to relive that time of confidence. It was growing dark. He struck a match, startled by the image of himself in the huge gilded mirror. This was not the face he showed Johannesburg. Dark, saturnine, brooding. The expression of a man who feared something in the shadows behind him.

The inner man looking at the outer man … finding him less, much less, than the tailored clothing suggested. Was it the heat … or the stale air? He had broken out in a sweat. He felt it trickle from his armpits, run from the chest hair to his belly. He went slowly up the stairs. Avoiding the bedroom, he opened the door of Kitty's sitting-room and walked to the window. Through the shutters he saw the farflung twinkle of lights that marked the reef. Stars at the top of headgears and the red glow of furnaces; sparks from tall chimneys. Could it be taken away? Brought to a standstill? The veld grow back over the hills of broken rock? Could all this be wrested from him?

He rested his hand on the door of Kitty's bedroom. In better times the house and everything in it would have been sold long ago. Today there was a mood of uncertainty; no one was buying. He turned away and went slowly downstairs. He was about to let himself out when he heard voices and footsteps on the gravel. It was an embarrassing situation. He had no choice but to brazen it out.

He fumbled for a switch. The chandelier in the hall blazed into brilliant light. Everything was just as she had left it – the gilt chairs, mirrors, carpets. And that damned ridiculous black-amoor in the gilded turban still holding the silver tray for visiting cards that never came. No one had broken in. There was nowhere to dispose of such goods in a town of this size.

Two men entered; Baron de la Roche and Carl Marloth. Their astonishment matched his own but he recovered first. 'Carl!' he cried with genuine enthusiasm. Marloth had built *Bloukoppen* and lost it in a debt to Alfred Beit's company, at that time being managed by Penlynne. The great-fleshed German with his cheerful meaty face had walked out without rancour. Always restless, Penlynne had last heard of him prospecting the windswept beaches at the Orange River. Diamonds there were unlikely. But that was Marloth, always the pursuer of mad ideas. Hunter, mapmaker, explorer, horticulturist, optimist and loser. Also an amateur geologist with skill enough to have made the first charted references to minerals as far north as Lobengula's country. And beyond. Germany's new possession in the north-east, Tanganyika, was now admitted as the German Kaiser's sphere of interest. The vast hinterland had come under his Imperial Charter of Protection.

Marloth embraced Penlynne.

'You made changes, hein!' He was visibly astonished at the decor. From the solid black Bavarian of his taste, shipped out from home in enormous crates, he was gaping at the gilded frivolity of the Rue de la Concorde.

'So *Bloukoppen's* for sale,' Marloth said.

'Are you thinking of buying it back?' Penlynne smiled.

Carl had gone into the wilds before Penlynne installed Kitty and he was somewhat reluctant to go into further details or explain why he had been so eager to take over the house at that time.

'It belongs to a woman friend.'

'The famous Miss Loftus,' said de la Roche. 'Where did Kitty develop a taste for Third Empire? Amusing upstairs too, eh, Penlynne? We must look around, Carl. You'll have no objections, Penlynne?' He preened. 'I have the honour to be appointed Honorary Consul for Turkey ... I am instructed to find a suitable consulate.'

Elegant boots, laundry gleaming, clothing by Italian tailors and the glitter of white teeth matching the insolence of his diamond cufflinks, he was undeniably foreign; and yet, not entirely. Penlynne knew the man was shrewd; damned shrewd. He was not honorary consul for love of the sickly old man of Europe, Sultan Suliman on his decaying throne at the mouth of the Bosphorus, presiding over his harem and an empire in which the Germans were showing unusual solicitude.

It shocked Penlynne. These two did not belong together. He liked Marloth as much as he disliked de la Roche. The pleasant German, bluff, gruff and travel-stained in corduroys and veldschoen, informal to the point of being disreputable. The dubious Frenchman with the dubious title. Why was Marloth with the arch-foe of the mining industry? With most of Kruger's Raad in his pocket, he had become an intimate of those known as the Hollander Group or the German Group – all of them expert at wrangling rights and concessions from the Government in Pretoria.

One damnable thing about de la Roche, he had a sense of humour and a disarming candour that made him a social favourite. Especially with the large, overdressed Peruvian females with their excruciating, lisping Lithuanian Yiddish … low-bred wives of men who had the mining stores concessions in their pockets and were ruining black labour, on the side, with rotgut liquor supplied by de la Roche. He was not to be trusted an inch.

'What price is Miss Loftus asking?' The baron offered a cigar-case already engraved with the crescent moon and star of Turkey.

'It cost me fifteen thousand to build,' grunted Marloth.

'In today's market … maybe six,' said de la Roche speculatively.

'Not a penny less than twenty.' Penlynne could feel blood burning in his face and his heart pounding with extravagant exuberance. He knew he was being mocked.

'Will you negotiate on her behalf?'

'Certainly not … the sale is none of my concern.'

De la Roche turned away with a knowing smile. At times like this Penlynne cursed his open liaison with Kitty. Recklessness had made him scorn the opinion of others. But he would not see her robbed.

'Tell me Carl … what are you doing in such exalted company … consuls forsooth. I took you for an honest fossicker. I should avoid a game of cards with His Excellency … a man like you, with a weakness for gambling.'

Marloth laughed exuberantly and embraced him. He smelled of snuff, sweat and woodsmoke. An honest smell, Penlynne thought. They parted with expressions of mutual esteem. As he went down the drive, Penlynne threw the latch key into the shrubbery. He could hear the trampling of his pair and impatient jingle of harnesses. Above the islands of brightness that were the few gaslit streets, he could see the dark tower of his own offices. He had a sudden sense of urgency.

'Back to the office, Williams,' he ordered. The former army ostler had a dash of cheek in him that Penlynne could appreciate.

'There's guests tonight, guv'nor, and the 'orses is cold.'

'You'll get your nosebag,' Penlynne laughed. 'Make haste.'

The Zulu nightwatchman sprang to 'bayete' with prancings and loyal demonstrations. 'Nkos ... lord!' Penlynne strode into the dark of the splendidly appointed foyer and went aloft in the first elevator in the city. He knew enough of his office to lay his hands on the file on Marloth. Genial, blundering Marloth, butt of a hundred jokes. So obliging with maps and information about mineral deposits that he had nothing for himself except an amateur's pleasure. Was it possible that everything Marloth had done by way of exploration, his tracing of the Orange River to its mouth in Namaqualand, for example, had been in the service of the German Kaiser? Where had he been since he handed the keys of *Bloukoppen* to Penlynne? Without a trace of regret. His maps and reports could have been the very ones which had brought the grey hulls of the warships now standing close inshore at Luderitzbucht.

What about Marloth's travels in East Africa? From the Umba River in the south to the Rovumba in the north it was all German. All done in the name of suppressing the slave trade so much abhorred by the Christian conscience.

The newspapers Penlynne got from home were full of it ... the scandal of German warships at anchor in ports where British influence had been dominant. There had been nothing covert about Marloth's membership of the German Africa Society. It was a branch of the respected International Association for Exploration and Civilization of Africa. Penlynne was in complete agreement with its aims; exploitation of the interior, the opening of an untapped wealth of labour.

Was it just coincidence? Marloth turning up at the very moment de la Roche had been appointed Turkish Consul ... de la Roche with his strong friends in Pretoria? Pretoria with its hatred of Johannesburg. Hollanders, Germans, Boers and the French, united in hatred and contempt of everything British. Penlynne had worked for his wealth. 'Here I sit, a millionaire at forty-five, employing thousands. Creating a city. Bringing the culture of the world's most advanced civilization to a plateau six thousand feet up in the African emptiness. Respected, my

9

opinion sought. President of the Mining Chamber. Chairman of companies and committees. Leader of the English community.' He was seeing something for the first time. Money alone was powerless. He worked twelve, often sixteen hours a day, and fell into bed beside Dorothy, too stimulated to sleep. Turning over the day's problems while she slept like a child beside him. He was a babe politically.

He closed the file. Was it too far-fetched to imagine that he might have to defend his possessions? He had fought with his bare hands to make what he had ... slaved harder than most and outwitted some of the sharpest. You thought you were there ... the distant mountain seemed ever closer. In fact it had receded. If this were a newspaper cartoon the words Krugerism and Germany would be printed between the figure marked Penlynne and the mountain peak.

Stephen Yeatsman had finished writing his obituary column on Josiah Rawlinson. He routed out a printer's devil. 'Take this proof over to Mr Penlynne's office and wait for it.'

As Stephen walked back from the stone to his editor's cubby-hole in the clattering shed that was the Works Department of *The Oracle* he received cheerful nods. His compositors were men who could set a column of type by hand as fast as he could pen it. And their spelling was more accurate.

Some words he could never get right. Cemetery was twice mis-spelt in his obituary. The community was doing the Old Buc-caneer proud, as they said in the printing trade. Rawlinson's own paper was running every page with a black border and all the advertisers were in profoundest mourning. Columns of In Memoriams, each more fulsome than the last. Suddenly the man had nothing but sincere and grieving friends. All mourned his passing. *Sic transit gloria*. The extravagance of their praise would soon stop. Yet, whatever they privately thought, a giant had fallen. And the ground had shaken. Some were seeing Rawlin-son's exit as a portent of disaster. Drape the Mining Chamber in black and close the Stock Exchange for the day! For the first time in years nobody was shouting prices between the chains in Simmonds Street.

Shirt-sleeved, Leonard Penlynne looked down on the streets. He would be going to the funeral – frock coat and tall hat –

Dorothy insisted. Rumour was around that the Rawlinson family could not agree where he was to be buried ... at the Langlaagte plot or at his estate in a white marble mausoleum still to be built. In the meantime he lay in frozen state at home. The ice factory was taking no more orders for the time being. Drinks in the club were going to be lukewarm till Rawlinson was underground. There seemed to be more genuine discomfort at that thought than about an industry dominated by the man who had made more out of the ground here than an Indian prince.

Penlynne sat down with Yeatsman's leading article. Who will forget the majestic figure in the white helmet? The legendary helmet in which he claimed to have panned the Reef's first gold, this man who seized opportunity when others scoffed.

Without his vision (and greed, thought Penlynne) it would be fact to say that the great gold-mining industry of the Witwatersrand might never have come into existence. His was a vision of territory open to all but guided by British principles of justice and fair play.

Penlynne poised his pen over the last line. What did Rawlinson know of justice and fair play! Still ... why not a truce? At least till the man was underground. He owed it to himself. Someday they would be writing his obituary. As if a catalogue of a man's achievements counted for truth. The thought depressed him. There were already streaks of grey in his dark, curling beard. He used tweezers to remove them. One could not deceive oneself indefinitely. Sooner or later one had to accept the marks of time, the sign of what was called distinction and achievement.

Rawlinson had had the best years and the easiest pickings ... not that he had lacked vision and guts. From now it would take more than hard-headedness and scant concern for the rights of others.

Walter Gardiner hurled aside the newspaper report. *The bereaved Lady Rawlinson was supported at the graveside by Mrs Walter Gardiner (neé Rawlinson) and Mr Walter Gardiner the eminent American engineer ...*

He crushed an ember that had sparked out onto the leopardskin rug. There was a stench of scorching fur. He had driven away with Katherine and Muriel Rawlinson. Muriel did not wish to return to the mansion in Doornfontein. She and Katherine held hands.

'I'll be better in the auld hoose,' she assured Katherine. 'That's where I started wi' him.' In her late forties, the thick black hair streaked with grey, her stubborn face was set and pale behind the heavy veil. No tears. She went into the shuttered house and closed the door.

Walter drove on with Katherine. He put his arm about her and he could feel her tremble with emotion held in check. She would not break down, he knew that. The boy watched them silently.

'My father was greatly misunderstood,' she said. 'He was good and brave ... and generous.'

'Of course,' he replied. 'You knew him better than anyone.'

It had been hard on Katherine. When Gardiner left her father to go over into partnership with Penlynne she had kept the family connection open in the face of the old man's anger. Old Rawlinson had doted on Spencer. Gardiner did not doubt that Katherine would inherit it all. Yet as Katherine's husband he would have total control and it was not too soon to think of that.

The possibilities were immense ... he was already working on a project to make the Rand look smalltime. The less said about that at this stage the better. Penlynne did not approve. He would have to go it alone.

That night Gardiner had been prepared to respect Katherine's privacy and grief so he was gratified to find her clinging to him with a kind of desperate passion he had never had from her before. She held him as if deep emotions were loosened. Then she turned away and curled up alone.

Later the sobbing began. When he touched her she shook him off. It had been neither love nor passion but instinct filling the void left by death. He lay awake, slowly becoming aware how offended he felt.

Condolence cards arrived in avalanches. Front door draped in crepe. Curtains drawn, shutters closed. Servants crept about. Never a voice was raised or a door slammed. Katherine in deepest mourning from head to toe, blonde hair severely dressed. Visits from company officials and their wives. Solemn and ill at ease.

'Keeping on the right side,' Gardiner told himself, cynically amused that they approached Katherine as heiress. He could stand to one side for the moment. This was her hour. His was to come.

It surprised Penlynne how often Dorothy was ahead of him in her intuitions. As chatelaine of *Far Horizons* she had the hostess's gift of seeming to favour each of her guests. More valuably, she had developed a knack of encouraging confidences. Men, in particular, blurted out their plans during the strolls she took with them in the gardens, arm in arm. A parasol shielding her fine skin, she was as exquisite in manner as in dress. Although she did not solicit confidences, they came to her and she was often able to anticipate some crisis.

'I think there's going to be a fearful rumpus about Josiah Rawlinson's estate ... don't you think?' She was going through the coming week's engagements when she paused, turning from the escritoire. She liked to work there at her ease in negligee, free to plan without the pressures of the household. Penlynne was already in bed, looking with admiration at her shapely back and shoulders, at the way her dark hair curled at the nape of her neck. How pretty her feet were! It seemed incredible that it had taken him so long to discover all this. He had been lying there, waiting for her to slip in beside him, his mind on the funeral that morning, trying to imagine Muriel Rawlinson with the Rawlinson fortune.

He sat up. 'The man marries his housekeeper ... he dies. She inherits. It's hard on Katherine perhaps, but Gardiner's a wealthy man and no doubt her father has made adequate provision for her ... and his grandchildren.'

'He didn't make a will,' she said calmly.

'No will?' Penlynne was incredulous.

'Arthur Crawley came up to me at the funeral.'

'Oh, come now, Dorothy. I wouldn't believe a word Crawley said. A man like Rawlinson has disposed of his goods down to the last collar stud.'

'No, I believe not.'

'Gardiner would have told me. No ... no, it's preposterous.'

'Well, I'd ask him ...'

'I certainly shall.'

'Crawley was standing with Emery.'

'The company lawyer?'

13

'Yes.'

'What did he say exactly?'

' "Can you imagine it, Mrs Penlynne ... intestate!" Emery confirmed it.'

'Rawlinson intestate!'

My God, Penlynne was thinking, a man like Crawley trying to fill Rawlinson's boots. For all the dead man's faults he had been a restraining influence on Kruger. Crawley had never been more than a rubber stamp. Trust an arsehole like that to blurt it out at the funeral.

'There will be chaos in the Rawlinson camp.'

'And opportunity,' she said unruffled.

'For whom, pray?'

'Gardiner, surely! Won't he contest the inheritance in favour of Katherine?'

'I prefer not to believe it ... at least, until it's official.'

Without Rawlinson's bullying management the empire could fall apart between officials and directors manoeuvring for control.

Dorothy eased into bed beside him, the glowing warmth of her skin fragrant from the bath. The pregnancy they had hoped for had still not eventuated. At this moment it seemed more important than ever. He was astounded at Rawlinson's folly. Dead men spoke through their wills. Suppose this were deliberate? Could it be Rawlinson's last gesture of contempt for others? As if he were saying from the grave – without me no one can prosper. He could have been capable of that ... the last resentment. He was a man who had tolerated no one out-achieving him.

Penlynne slipped from her side, 'I won't be long.'

In his study he lifted the telephone. 'Connect me with Mr Walter Gardiner's residence.' It was late. He imagined the bell ringing in the silent house where the funeral meats had been served that afternoon. The Rawlinson fortune was the greatest made so far in South Africa, at least as great as that of Rhodes and Beit. Ten times what Penlynne owned so far in mines, land and mineral rights. If Gardiner had not fallen out with the old man, would things have been different?

Rawlinson was a shrewd judge of men. After Walter left him to join Penlynne, he had written the engineer off as an opportunist. Yes, there was an instability in Gardiner. As he grew older it might lead to recklessness. A genius engineer, he was not a man to be charged with heavy financial judgements. Could it be the old man's hesitation about finalizing his will had been due to his assessment of his son-in-law's character? A reluctance to hand over his assets to the control of a man he mistrusted? For, of course, Katherine's husband would be the effective user of the Rawlinson fortune.

'Gardiner here.' He sounded short.

'What's this I hear Walter, can it be true?'

'What are you talking about?'

'The old man died intestate … That's the story.'

There was a long silence. 'Walter?'

'Where the hell did you hear that?'

'Is it true?'

'It's the first I've heard of it.'

Penlynne had a sharp ear for nuances, for the hesitation that indicated a playing for time and a defensive stance. He heard none of this in Gardiner's voice. More like the silence of a man who had heard the bell tolling.

'I hope I haven't dismayed you, Walter.'

'Hold on!' The American's voice was oddly indistinct. 'I'm pouring a drink.'

Penlynne was aware that Gardiner had been working for months on the development of a new theory. Penlynne himself considered it quite outlandish; not as sound as the deep levels had been. If it were correct at all, it was twenty years too soon. There was enough to do raising capital to develop the deeper mines without new adventures.

'Are you there, Walter?'

'Where did you get this?' Gardiner came back.

'Crawley let it drop at the funeral.'

'He's acting chairman … it would be just his style to gloat over a situation like this … if it's true. He's always been arrogant to directors, bootlicking the big man. But by Christ, if it's true, it must have been a rare moment for him when he offered his condolences to Katherine … and me! Crafty little shit.'

Gardiner had never doubted that Katherine would inherit. When he put Spencer up front on his saddle, he knew in his guts that his boy would be the inheritor of it all. But first it would be

15

in his own hands ... he'd be free of Penlynne's growing caution in their association.

'Give him a ring at once, Walter.'

It was in Gardiner's mind to shake up a groom and ride over to Crawley's place. 'I'll look into it.' He hung up the instrument and stood, contemplating the future. It seemed imperative to get to his work table in spite of the late hour. Pinned over the multi-coloured Government surveyor's charts of farm lands were his tracings showing the topographical features. His theory would be proven there. A mosaic of barren, rocky outcrops and un-productive land. With the Boers, space counted more than sub-stance ... they had neither the capital nor the incentive of markets to improve what they owned. The extension of the reef, that fabulous reef, was his personal devil. He admitted it. An ob-session. But then, so were the deep levels before he proved them. It could take years to prove his new theory ... years and a fortune.

Rawlinson intestate! Could it be possible?

He did not wake Katherine but as he passed by her room he looked in. She lay like a beautiful effigy on her pillows, her hair spread. Her grief had not marked her. As he stood there, mar-velling at her serenity, she stirred and moaned, turned on her side and was suddenly awake.

'What is it?'

'It'll keep,' he said, leaving her reluctantly. He told her at breakfast. She took the news quietly, apparently more absorbed in Spencer. The boy burst in from the garden with a chameleon. 'Look mother ... a dragon!'

'Take that damned thing off the table,' Gardiner ordered. He noted how Katherine drew the boy to her, running her fingers through his curls. Spencer shrugged off the caress with a scowl. Gardiner smiled. He approved the boy's spirit. A bit of me ... bit of Rawlinson. His mother's eyes though. The same deep brown. Soon he'd go to the States for schooling.

'Kath,' he urged. 'Consider the implications. If there is no will it means, as I understand it, that Muriel will inherit your father's fortune. It's inconceivable, but if it's true ... it means his promises to you were worthless.'

She caught fire at that and flashed at him: 'Don't speak like that ... you have no right.'

16

Gardiner controlled his impatience. 'I don't think you understand.'

'I don't want to know about these things,' she said stonily. 'Not now.'

'We shall have to contest it. I shall insist on doing that. On your behalf. It will be nothing less than my duty, as your husband.'

'Father's barely in his grave,' she said, her eyes filling with tears.

'Katherine, there are millions involved. Rightly yours.' He knelt at her side and put his arms around her, smiling. She looked into the blue eyes, bluer now that his crisply curling hair had turned grey at the temples and still startling in his weathered face with its thin line of lip and deeply clefted chin. Far too good-looking, she sometimes thought. Often cruel; often thoughtless.

'I've no quarrel with Muriel ... I'm really quite fond of her. Don't do anything yet,' she appealed, touching his face. 'Wait a little.'

'As your husband, I must. Think of Spencer. It is his birthright. For myself ... I don't care. What I can't stand is injustice and spite.' He rushed on incautiously. 'I believe he did this to get back at me, because I broke with him.'

'He was never petty.' She was rising agitatedly, skirts brushing aside the child's playthings, unaware that she had chosen the very word the world used to describe him.

Gardiner had spared her the knowledge of how notorious her father had become in his later years. Some newspapers, spiteful but accurate, had lampooned him without mercy. One had pointed readers to a grave by the side of the Main Reef Road. Among a jumble of broken tools and abandoned machinery an obituary was scrawled on a gravestone of slate. *Here lies Jake Honeycomb. First his legs then his life.*

The story was he'd been refused compensation and died of drink. His last wish was quoted with relish. 'Bury me where that bastard can't miss seeing me every time he goes to the Star.'

Rawlinson had removed it many times but someone always stood it up again, so the story went.

'Walter!' Katherine turned from the mantelpiece and he saw a flash of the old man. 'I want to respect his wishes. He would never have done anything to hurt me.'

17

'You must leave it to me, Katherine,' he insisted. 'I respect your grief but the matter cannot rest.'

Muriel Rawlinson had never imagined that any of Josiah Rawlinson's goods would belong to her. He had never treated her as if they shared equally. What was his was his.

She had gained the upper hand of him in the last months of his life but never believed that all – or any – of his possessions could come to her. Listening to Arthur Crawley, vice-chairman of Rawlinson Holdings, she sat composed, her large hands in the lap of the severe black dress, her face veiled. She looked at Crawley with his high whiskey complexion and pomaded hair, his frock coat and high collar with flowing cravat and gold pin. She still regarded him as a lackey of her husband ... a pompous man, unused to real authority. The lawyer Philip Emery was a stranger. And evidently not to be trusted ... why else had Josiah sent his will to London for scrutiny? Mind you, he had faith in no one.

It's a fine room, she was thinking. Rich woods and fine carpets. Josiah never spared a penny when it came to his own comforts. She avoided the gaze directed at her from the oil painting behind the chairman's vacant seat. Rawlinson's brutally direct stare still dominated the room. Crawley, for all his assumption of control, had not yet occupied the green leather chair.

She sensed that Crawley was being over-deferential. No doubt he would be like that until he knew exactly where he stood with her. She was well aware that it seemed incredible to Crawley that Josiah had married her, and even more improbable that he had done so in community of property. She had not understood the details of the marriage contract.

'Just sign there, Muriel, that's it. Good!'

To her, marriage was the joining of two hands. With Rab, her first husband, a sharing of nothing had seemed reasonable enough. With Josiah she had never believed she was actually acquiring more than the status of bedfellow-housekeeper. Now there was this business of the unsigned will. Intestate was the word.

'It seems, Lady Rawlinson, that the late Sir Josiah intended to leave his entire estate to his daughter ... but under the law of the Republic, the surviving spouse is, *ipso facto*, entitled to half of the joint estate. Very fortunate indeed for you, if I may say so.

His signature would have deprived you of everything.' A thin smile. 'I congratulate you.'

Emery handed her a sheaf of papers. The listed possessions of her late husband. It seemed endless. Crawley was saying, 'Of course, you may leave everything to us ... be assured, we shall think only of your interests.'

As she drove away in her carriage nothing seemed real except the clothes on her back and the plain gold band on her finger. She was thinking, 'I maun tak' a grip on mysel'. They'll mak' a fool o' me if they can.'

Until today she had lived with the expectation of being told it was time for her to pack her bags and go back to where she came from. In her sewing room, busy with her hands at her millinery, she had made her own weeds from the black bombazine dress that had been her uniform as housekeeper. Now she was slowly realizing that everything around her was hers.

No one could take it from her. No one could tell her to go. She could buy anything she wanted. Anything in the world. Wasn't it strange that she could not think of a thing except erecting a decent stone in the cemetery?

That evening she drew the curtains and lit the lamps in the office of the good stone house Josiah had built at Langlaagte in 1885, the first on the barren flat lands of the Reef. It was here she had come as a widow to be his housekeeper. He had always been a secretive man, trusting no one. Not even his lawyers. She believed that what she was looking for would be in the safe or in one of the pigeonholes of the rolltop desk. He still kept clothing in this house and it shocked her now, even though she had every right, to go through his pockets and to open drawers that had been forbidden to her. She was looking for the envelope marked O.H.M.S. She once saw it, early on in her service with him. She had been lifting papers from pigeonholes to dust them and had paused to read his handwriting. It was the Last Will and Testament of Josiah Rawlinson, dated 1865.

She read a few words ... *to my dear wife Sheilah, the balance of my estate* ... Katherine's mother had died of camp fever when the girl was an infant. It startled and touched her to see that he had kept the document so long after Sheilah's death.

'What's that you're doing?' She turned, startled. There was no one there. The words Josiah had challenged her with on that occasion were still in her consciousness. In the warm, eerie emptiness of the room it was as if he were still there.

'You are never to touch the desk,' he had said, standing there immense in the doorway, one hand drawing back the green velvet hanging, the other grasping his riding crop. There was no sign of a later will. In any case, it was not what she was looking for.

She opened a drawer. It contained a revolver, some loose rounds of ammunition and the tarnished gold of his captain's epaulets ... the same he wore in the portrait above his desk. She had a feeling there was more here. A click ... and a small panel sprang open. It startled her to see the words 'War Office'. The letter confirmed Rab Ferguson missing, believed dead. The document had come from London in answer to Josiah's enquiry before he had asked for her hand. Suppose Rab had never died? The implication shocked her. He might still turn up on her doorstep ... now that Josiah was gone.

'An' can I have a word wi' her ladyship,' she'd hear him say. 'Tell her it's an auld acquaintance turned up like a bad penny.'

She sat on in the study in Langlaagte, listening to the metal roof creaking and groaning as it cooled. To have come so far as this! She took up the War Office letter and went into the kitchen.

She thrust it into the empty blackness of the stove, her hands firm as she set a match to it. She waited to see the fragments curl and fall into ash. For a long time she stood watching the wind in the flue stirring the grey heap. From now on she would never see a workman humping his gear or a transport driver flogging his mules but she would wonder. And if a whiskery down-and-out came knocking she would look twice before opening.

With Rawlinson's death Christiaan Smit knew his last link with Johannesburg was broken. He owed the place no further loyalty. On his return from Holland with the law degree Rawlinson had paid for, he had worked for the magnate for some time and felt an obligation to sympathize with the *uitlanders*. He had admired their industry. They had transformed a barren and windswept highveld, a place of poor farms and wandering *kaffirs*. Emptiness and desolation had given way to gardens and plantations of pines and eucalyptus. Along a ridge of sixty miles where nothing had stirred, Christiaan had seen a city grow with mining villages and the beginning of industry. The continentals and the English had established a culture that was unmistakably foreign. Educated in Holland himself, thanks to Rawlinson, he did not mind that. What dismayed him was to see his own people waking too late to protect what was theirs.

Rawlinson had always rationalized his vast holdings. 'It's to the benefit of the Republic ... not just us, Christiaan. Think of the children!'

Looking at these *uitlanders* round the grave, the evidence of wealth and ostentation they could not conceal, even at a time like this, he had felt anger. There were Boers like himself who had come to see the truth. The land was slipping from their grasp.

At the graveside he had spoken to Katherine Gardiner.

'Thank you for coming, Mr Smit,' she had said, her black-gloved hand in his.

'I felt it my duty to be here ... I sincerely admired your father. His independent spirit, his identification with the Republic ... no truly, a son of this land.'

He glanced at the assembly of frock-coated financiers and mine owners. Faces often seen in Pretoria. Demanding, bribing, grasping.

'Thank you for saying that,' Katherine's eyes were bright with tears behind the mourning veil. 'He had many friends among your people.'

'He gave me my chance, Mrs Gardiner.'

Among the fashionable crowd (he would not have called them mourners) he saw Leonard Penlynne's face; sombre today. Even at this distance and dressed in the anonymity of dark clothing, he stood out. A man to be watched.

'How is Anna?' Katherine asked.

'Thank you ... well.'

'The little one?'

'We lost her.'

'I'm so sorry. That was sad for you.'

He felt sincerity in her tone. The infant was buried here. He and Anna came less often now that they lived in Pretoria. So many children in the cemetery. More infants than adults. He watched the floral tributes heaped on the red earth, the undertaker retrieving black-edged cards. Stewart MacDonald came over. Christiaan had come to respect the Scots doctor. Their wives had been friendly but Anna had not wished to remain in the town after losing the child.

Stewart MacDonald had sat on by the bedside of the child until dawn ... watching the small life ebb away.

'There is nothing I can do, Christiaan.' The infant body was like a doll in its waxen immobility. 'One day we'll have the answer to diphtheria ... it's a cruel disease, rampant in summer months in a place like this.' Christiaan was touched that MacDonald could share their grief, their sense of helplessness. To his mind, Katherine Gardiner's loss did not compare with Anna's. Her grief was ritual, Anna's was deep and inconsolable.

'I can't live here any longer,' she had told him. At that time he had an office in Simmonds Street Chambers. Briefs were scarce, even though it was well known he had won Rawlinson's case against African Gold Recovery. What Johannesburg remembered was that Penlynne had still got the better of Rawlinson. In a typical Johannesburg manipulation of the stock market, Penlynne had turned what should have been a crushing loss into a killing.

No, they were adroit these *uitlanders*; French, German, English ... so many of them Jews. They despised the real owners of the land.

'Our people are suffering here,' Anna often said. Personal grief had made her bitter and aware. She had been in the market and met Afrikaners begging, a woman and her children searching for wasted food. 'I know we were poor as children. We had little enough ... but, at any rate we had the farm. Things have changed for the worse now. These poor creatures have nothing and have nowhere to go in this Babylon.'

Christiaan listened to the final funeral oration. It disgusted him ... 'what this man achieved for South Africa and all its people will be remembered. He brought richness and opportunity ...' Christiaan heard words like 'backwardness', 'ignorance', 'unfitted to this modern age'. Even here the English took their opportunity to insult his people.

On the train back to Pretoria that afternoon he shared a compartment with a number of men. Their ignorance of Transvaal affairs would have amused him had it not been so one-sided.

'I see they've got this nigger Magato at last,' said one. 'He held out long enough. Seems he was being advised by a Scotsman!'

'He must have run out of whiskey!'

'He's in the Pretoria *tronk*.'

'God help him ... it's a hellhole.'

'You've been there!' They laughed boisterously.

'I've smelled it in passing.'

The talk turned to Transvaal justice.

'One law for us ... another for them. None for the *kaffirs* ... a judiciary that takes its orders direct from Kruger.'

'That is not so, sir,' Christiaan interrupted. 'The judiciary is free.'

They laughed. 'The papers are full of cases ... perverted justice, always against the English, naturally. Fines, imprisonment ... I never heard of our people getting off.'

'Until you people came here we had no need of jails for white men.' Christiaan was holding onto his control. 'Today we haven't enough to accommodate vagabonds, thieves and drunkards. Murderers, gentlemen, mostly your countrymen. The real scoundrels will probably never be behind bars ... though I would like to put them there. As for Magato, he has had a long run, but he will have a fair trial.'

'Perhaps you will be on the bench?' They were not so much hostile as amused. A scrawny Afrikaner with a yellow rag of beard and an ill-fitting suit, rawhide shoes and a stained grey hat. And yet, the shrewd eyes were coldly appraising.

'Not on the bench, sir,' said Christiaan. 'I am Assistant Attorney-General.'

'Is that so?'

One of them leaned forward. 'Your Honour must not take my friends seriously. Do you perhaps know His Excellency the President?'

'I have that honour.'

'Would it be possible for Your Honour to arrange a meeting for us?'

'That is not my function,' said Christiaan coldly.

Chapter Two

Owen Davyd closed the door of the lean-to he hired as an office for the General Mining and Trades Union. He shouted into the reek of the smithy. Pungent with horse-shoeing, urine and dung, it was a pestilence of flies, and the din of clanging metal gave him perpetual headaches.

'Key's over the door ... be back soon,' he shouted over the clangour, tucking an empty sleeve into his coat pocket. Last time he walked this way it was to see the funeral of the great Rawlinson. Boilermakers, fitters, shaft timbermen, stopers and developers, pumpmen and winding engine drivers ... they were all at the master's funeral. Black suits, black hats.

The Rawlinson Star alone employed twelve thousand, most of them *kaffirs*. They'd had few *indunas* there too ... last respects to the Great White Father. Every cab in town had headed Braamfontein way and you couldn't get a ricksha or a seat in a tram. Owen Davyd had walked. At home, in Wales, he'd walked further underground to get to the work face.

He'd have liked the chance to say a few words at the funeral; nothing they'd like to hear, from a man who'd lost his arm in one of the Star's drives for tonnage. But he'd been lucky. He knew all the graveyards from Springs to Randfontein and a good number of places in between. The earliest miners had been buried near petered-out strikes and abandoned shafts. Names scratched on slates and scrawled on ant-eaten wooden slats. Cousin Jacks, Geordies ... hardcase Jocks from north of the Tweed. Coalminers and copperminers. Rockfalls, misfiring charges. And now, this lung sickness. Hammerboys and machine drillers ... it hit them worst. You could spot a man with rockdrill fever; staring eyes in a face turned to stone. Already enough of them buried to fill a small town at home. Bright-faced lads he'd come out with on *The American*, six years back ... he'd seen them blue and gasping but still optimistic ... 'all I need is a bit of a sea breeze!'

Sir Josiah Rawlinson and owners – Rhodes and Barnato and Penlynne – they'd given them six feet of red earth and no compensation for widows and orphans. Take the hat round for a coffin made of packing cases. Union Jack. Brass band from the mine. High tea and a night of heavy drinking. That's how they went.

They had slow-marched old Rawlinson to his grave; heavy drumstrokes, footsteps in time to Dead March in Saul. Going like a bloody king, he was, through streets lined with crowds. Black-plumed horses and the high-glassed hearse a shop window for the angel of death. Shops closed. Not that they'd closed down the mine for half a shift. The drive was on for tonnage.

At the funeral he saw a face he hadn't seen for months. Doctor Stewart MacDonald was getting down from a cab with ... yes, the pretty Mary, broadened now. She'd borne two since he'd lived with them in the mine house, recovering from the amputation. Stewart had come up in the world since then ... no longer the mine doctor. He was the one who'd taken his arm that night when the hanging wall collapsed in the Star's Number 2 Shaft. Stewart the immigrant doctor ... his comrade aboard *The American*.

Owen pushed through the crowd, amazingly silent for cosmopolitan Johannesburg. Blacks with their eyes like saucers, Peruvians still pushing their trade ... jostling with their trays of trinkets, pimping for French Town. He could hear the thump of the band ahead and the clatter of hooves.

'Stewart ... Doctor Mac!' He got within a few feet of the doctor. Stewart MacDonald turned. He'd lost some of his Scots high colour. He had the look of a man deeply preoccupied. He was the Rawlinson family doctor. Brought Katherine Gardiner's children into the world. What time had he for miners now!

'Stewart ... a word with you, mun.'

Stewart gave him a wave and called out. 'Come to my rooms later.' The press of bodies carried him through the gates and into the family circle of the Rawlinsons.

The following day as Stewart MacDonald locked his consulting rooms in Jeppe Street, he became aware of the short, dark-haired Welshman at his elbow. Yesterday he had noticed the shabbiness of the man's clothing. Stewart was tired and low-spirited. It had been a hell of a day. There was diphtheria among the poor Boers in Ferreirastown – the *witseerkeel* that strangled the children. It had already turned dusk and Stewart longed to take off his boots and feel Mary's cheek against his.

'How are you, Owen?' He was mustering patience for the little Welshman with his empty sleeve and his bitterness against the mine owners. Stewart felt in no mood for another of Owen's trade unionist tirades.

'I'm just now back from Kimberley,' the small man began. 'They're treating our men like dogs there. But never mind ... that's an old story. I'm here because of Davis ... Peter Davis. Remember him, doctor mun ... on *The American?* Cornishman. Tin miner. A fine baritone ...'

'Aye,' Stewart remembered, 'singing on the foredeck of the immigrants' quarters.'

'That's right, Stewart mun. For old times sake, see him. He's in bed, in a bad way with his lungs. I wouldn't have known about it if I didn't get this note. It came to my place with a coloured lad ... said he was Davis's son.'

Stewart unlocked the door again. They went in. 'Sit down, Owen,' he said taking the letter from him. Painfully illiterate. On cheap paper.

I'm on hard times Owen, he read, *and not complaining, it's the lungs. Not much singing these days mostly it's coughing but as I say not complaining if there's a whip round the pub with the hat the boys will get me home yet. Come and see your old mate and bring a halfjack of the good stuff.*

'Have you seen him, Owen?' The Welshman nodded.

'I'm organizing a whip around but he's not the only one, Stewart. If you've been in cemetery lately you'll be aware of that. They're telling us it's the drink and pneumonia and I don't know what the hell else ... never what it is. You'll have seen my letters in the *Standard and Diggers' News* ... responsibility of owners ... duty to the workers. Managers don't give a damn. Plenty more fodder.'

'I must get on home now, Owen ... Mary's expecting me. Come along and have a bite of dinner.'

'Thanks Stewart, no. I've a meeting at the Oddfellow's Hall. I thought mebbe you'd see Peter Davis for old time's sake.'

'I will,' said Stewart. 'I'll find time.'

'Thanks mun, I knew you would.' The Welshman's eyes were feverish and he had lost weight.

'There's so much to be done,' he rushed on angrily. 'You heard about Kimberley then? Locked the union men out and when we marched on the yard management and scabs, hiding in boilers and scrap, opened fire. Case dismissed ... word of the union men not worth a damn. Two dead, three bad hurt.' The Welsh lilt was still there but the tone was bitter.

The thin figure disappeared into the shadows, passed under a gas lamp, lit a smoke and hurried on. Stewart stood with the torn scrap of letter, pencilled on the back of a waybill from Tarry's Iron Foundry.

Soaking in the galvanised tub, Mary scrubbing his back and the smell of good dinner coming from the kitchen, Stewart barely heard her talk of the day. He was watching the play of lamplight on her features, her absorption in a pleasurable task. In the past it had led to lovemaking.

His status had improved but she was not keen to leave the wood and iron house. Their child had died here of meningitis. Sometimes he'd put it to her gently, 'We can afford something better. Perhaps in a year or so.' She seemed to have a horror of the place being swept aside by spec builders, the yard where the child had played built over. He had turned down offers already. For one who had been so full of the peasant vitality she had brought from her father's Ayrshire farm, Mary had quietened, her eyes often shadowed. He blamed himself. He could not be with her more. They spoke of another child, but none came. All her affection was now lavished on their remaining child. Little Ruth had somehow been strong enough to resist the infection that had carried off so many. Stewart saw that when Mary played the piano these days, it was more likely to be some hymn tune of the kind played on the parlour harmonium of her girlhood. The melancholy would lift, as it had now, while she soaped his shoulders and ran her fingers through his wet hair. Ruth was already asleep in the next room. It was just another night when he had got home too late to carry her to bed and there were dried tears on her cheeks.

In the Brickfield Camp, Stewart MacDonald was known for his quick walk. He carried his head forward as if brushing aside obstructions in his way, black bag dragging at his arm. His boots were red with dust or clay. He put on a clean overall every morning but never had time to change it on his rounds of the camps. Mary sometimes scolded, 'You look more like a vet than a doctor. I should hope you'll tak' the overall off when you make house calls in Jeppe.'

He'd slip off the stained overall and put on his black coat before he called on patients behind lace curtains. But at the camps and shanties he was greeted on all sides. He could have worked the whole day there but now there was his upper-town practice and the mine hospital twice a week. Other doctors had much the same routine. His thick blonde hair had bleached and his face was sun-reddened. His eyes had a startling blueness.

'Doctor ... doctor, sir!' He turned to the yellow-skinned boy. A Griqua with a head of tight *korreltjies* and the blue eyes of a Cornish father.

'Peter!' The boy nodded. 'Take me to your papa.' Children of all ages and shades of skin ran ahead of him, whooping and tugging at his arm, offering to carry his bag.

Peter Davis was living with the Griqua mother in a shanty of wooden crates and rusted iron sheets. Stewart found it at the end of a huddle of similar dwellings reached by muddy, garbage-strewn tracks. The air was blue with the reek of dung fires. Washing hung wherever there was room and women boiling clothes in paraffin tins still strove after the decencies.

The Johannesburg press credited the camp with 'a murder a night'. It was bad, Stewart knew, but it was better than the dark, stinking slums of the Gorbals in Glasgow where he'd worked in his student days. The difference was that this place had an expectancy of better things. Against all the odds the sounds from it were cheerful.

He found a white man sitting in the sun in a broken chair. He looked to Stewart to be about fifty but he knew Davis was still in his thirties. Clothing hung on him. He had been thickset, with powerful shoulders. Now he laboured for breath. As Stewart approached he lifted a hand in welcome. A spasm of coughing turned his face blue. His eyes stared in mute appeal. There was panic in his expression. He brushed the Griqua aside and began a gasping monologue.

'I was butty of that Welshman … him that lost his arm in the old Star and you done the job yourself, Doctor. Aye, I was a driller … machine driller and before that, hand driller. What they call hammerman … Cornish, where the miners come from.' He fell into a fit of coughing. The mouth gasped for air. Stewart noted a rigidity of the chest and the shoulders that did not rise. The expression was anxious. Through the stethoscope on his back, Stewart heard the wavy, lagging respiration … extremely harsh. There was no more resonance from these lungs than from a stone.

In the first years of his work on the mines Stewart saw the development of the machine drill. It was more efficient but a change for the worse for the drillers. The drill bit slogged into the rock, spurting back clouds of rock dust, to mingle with the fumes of explosives and the unsettled reek of the last shift's work.

'Stone, Doctor … me lungs 'ave turned to stone.' Davis attempted a blue-mouthed grin. 'The rockdrill fever … carries us all off. All I'm asking … get me home to die.'

'Cornwall?'

'Aye. Middlemuch.'

'What about your wife and boy?'

'She's a good girl. Her and the boy can stay. But I must die there, it's my home. All I'm asking from my mates is the price of my ticket.'

'What was your last mine?'

'The Star … old man Rawlinson.'

'Mr Rawlinson is dead.'

'Aye … a bit from his daughter then … her that got it all.'

'Mr Davis, I'm going to find a hospital bed for you.'

'No bed … it's home or nothing.' Davis gripped Stewart's arm with the fading strength of a man who had slammed drills into the reef with a ten-pound hammer.

The Griqua woman was one of the pretty ones with high cheekbones and a small rounded head. Her peppercorn hair was teased into twists. She dressed like a white woman and wore a wedding ring. 'He wants to go home, Master,' she said timidly. She was offering him Davis's blasting certificate. The pay-off slip from the Star. He read the tattered documents.

She looked at him trustingly. 'I'll do what I can,' he told her, knowing that the next document with the name Peter Davis would be the death certificate.

Kitty Loftus was walking across a field in the Essex countryside. The toddler with her stopped every now and then to pick a flowering weed and hold it up to her. It was a sultry day. The cottage pointed out to her by the stationmaster seemed never to come any nearer as she passed by crofts and vegetable gardens. The place was only ten miles from London. Yet to Kitty it might as well have been in a foreign country.

The heat made her dizzy. The whirr of mowers seemed to come from far off. She must get this over quickly. A foster mother had been arranged from a frowsty office up a stair in Brewers Lane, off Charing Cross, and the gas lights in White-chapel Road were still burning at ten in the morning. Outside, a line of rain-bedraggled sandwichmen stood in the lane waiting for hire. They advertised anything and everything; play bills, where to get a good cheap dinner, flight from the wrath to come. The melancholy parade of headdown men, trudging in all weathers, was part of her childhood.

Nothing in London seemed changed. In the years she had been in South Africa it had become grimier and noisier. Her ears had become unaccustomed to the harsh accents of the streets. Her clothes drew stares and nudges from slatternly women lounging in doorways or shrieking from windows. Fifty pounds a year for the boy's care; 'fostering' the agent woman called it.

Kitty carried a small wooden horse, a ball and a parcel of clothing. The boy had his mother's colouring, the same striking red hair. And yet, there was a look of Penlynne about him, the same dark eyes set off by his mother's white skin. He was a strong and healthy child.

'Come Laurie!' She urged him from his examination of a tangle of brambles. She'd called him Lawrence. He sat down to squash purple berries into his mouth.

'Plenty of time for that,' Kitty said, lifting him in her arms.

She carried the child up the path to the low-roofed brick house. The battered green half-door stood open. She smelt honeysuckle and her skirts were dragging at lavender and mignonette. A squall of barefooted children came out to meet them. She was struck by the reek of smoke, the mucky green puddle with ducks. Hens running in and out.

A big woman suckling an infant tucked a breast into her bodice and brushing a wisp of hair from her face, greeted Kitty.

'You'll be missus Loftus ... brung the boy. 'E'll do a'right here, Missus, never worry your head. Vi'let! There's a little boy come to stay! She's good with 'em.'

A girl in a patched pinafore, about eight years old, appeared with a child at each hand. Laurie went to her without much protest and as Kitty retraced her steps across the field she did not hear him cry. She felt empty and light-headed.

Issy was waiting for her at the station, looking at his watch. 'You've been gone forty minutes ... we missed the 2.40.'

'Aw, shut your face,' she came at him. He offered her a hand-kerchief. Issy dressed too sharp for a gentleman. But then he wasn't a gentleman.

'A lot you care ...'

'I'm not 'is old man. C'mon ... we'll have a night at the Crystal Palace. Don't you want to see where you used to be the big hit?'

The train fussed in. Isadore Isaacs opened the door of a first-class compartment, gave the stationmaster a cigar and put his gleaming brown boots up on the seat. 'Forget it ... that's it! You had bad luck ... You've done your best, the kid's left with a good mother.' Tears rolled down Kitty's cheeks.

'Aw, come on,' he coaxed. 'His father's paying ... you got nothing to worry about.'

To remind her of her child, Kitty had a lock of his hair and the mother-of-pearl and ivory-and-silver teething ring Penlynne had bought for him. She was a fool to keep it, but it made her feel less like she'd given the child away. She began to sob quietly.

'The bastard,' she moaned.

He put his arm about her and tried to make free with her bodice but she pushed him off. Penlynne had insisted the boy be taken home. Too embarrassing for him for the child to remain in Johannesburg. 'Make arrangements ... I'll pay for everything,' he had insisted. 'The passage home for both of you, of course, and everything the child needs. If you decide not to return, I'll have *Bloukoppen* sold ... see you get a decent price. When he's older we'll see about some education. And for yourself, my dear ...' His smile had been as of old; charming, friendly, not quite sincere. 'A prudent investment will give you some income ... not that I believe you'll be lonely for long, Kitty.'

'I'll never come back here ... that's for sure.'

'Very wise.'

Of course, that's what he wanted. By the time she sailed for England the child was toddling. She had a first-class cabin. A stewardess took charge of Laurie. A prudence she had never quite relinquished even in the heady days of *Bloukoppen* warned her to go carefully with her money, to make her clothes last and to take modest lodgings.

She'd hardly sat down in the ship's saloon when this curly-headed Jew ... a real Joh'burg sharper, came right over and introduced himself. 'Isadore Isaacs ... and I think I know your face.'

She called herself Mrs Osborne ... name of a character in a play she'd been in when she'd tried to return to the stage. He was sure they'd met before. More like he'd seen her behind the footlights of *The Globe*.

Her last months in Johannesburg had been hell. To be inconspicuous – that must be wonderful – not to turn the heads of men, nor draw the condemning stares of women. There were times after Penlynne left her when she saw herself as something hateful. It took an effort to complete her toilette. The mirror threw back a Kitty Loftus she didn't know. Or knew too well. She felt she could not venture into the street. Some nights she was in such a sweat of nerves that she had to turn to the gin for courage.

The anguish and terror she had lived through as a child in London returned in recurring nightmares. She was in a line of shabby women; a small child holding onto her mother's skirt, she was shuffling into a woman's shelter – White Chapel.

There was a driving rain outside. How lucky they'd been to get admitted to the warmth where damp clothes and leaky boots steamed. There was a struggle between two stenches ... dirty bodies in wet clothes, and Lysol. The narrow rows of boxes were like coffins. Women of all ages groaned or lay inert, unable to reach out and touch each other. Painted on the wall were words she never forgot: Are you ready to die? The terror was that you'd get no bed. The grim woman pointing them to left or right would say: too late! It would be the alley for them if Kitty's mother did not have tuppence or they came too late and it was full.

In those first weeks on her own she'd woken in her hotel room to hear the night sounds of Johannesburg. She got to know the nightsoil carters banging their buckets, the creak and strain of the iron roof cooling from the day's heat, the battering of rain that turned streets into red rivers, and from the camps, the howling of dogs and thumping of drums. She'd had offers. When she took up with Penlynne she'd never expected to be kept. When he took her to that huge empty house – Carl Marloth's mansion in Doornfontein – she was astonished. It was Penlynne she fancied. Anywhere would have been good enough. He'd really behaved like a gentleman, treating her as if there was no difference between them. It was Penlynne who wanted the good times and the actress in her responded. She'd never thought herself a beauty till men told her and Penlynne dressed her up.

The dismay she felt now was not so much that he'd thrown her over, her and the child, but that she'd been so infatuated.

There was something of Penlynne in this Isaacs; the same energy, the same confidence and openhandedness. He put up lavish prizes for the ship's games. She heard one gentleman murmur, 'Trying to outdo Barnato, isn't he?'

'There's money in rotgut,' sneered his companion. 'He's got a string of *kaffir* canteens from Springs to Randfontein.'

When Isadore talked of his sister, Kitty felt soft towards him. He described the dark-haired girl with such genuine affection. 'Not like me ... she's educated, religious. She don't like my style. Got high principles ... orthodox. She'll marry a poor man and no regrets. Me ... I don't believe in nuthin' ... only myself.' There was such energy in the small, stunted body, vitality in his gestures, his features, his eyes. Yes, she could see him as the stowaway of ten years ago with passage money only enough for Rebecca.

'An' me ... perishing of cold in a lifeboat and praying to die. Know who it was who paid me landing *geld* ... they was goin' to send me back on the next boat. Penlynne ... yes him.'

Kitty bit back hot words.

'Know who else was on that ship? The Scotch doctor, Mac-Donald ... going steerage. They had this outbreak of typhoid ...

quarantine. Also that bastard de la Roche. You've heard of him – shipping out girls from home ... picking them up in job lots in Spain and Italy as friends for lonely miners. Poxed to the eyes the lot of them. That's why every second quack in Joh'burg's in the siff trade.'

'Leonard Penlynne,' Issy rushed on. 'He's made his millions. Seems to me like half of Joh'burg was on that boat.'

He quickly saw that she did not want any physical familiarity. He did not press her or question her about her life on the Rand. He guessed her origins were not so unlike his own.

'I'll be going to have a look at the old Yard Court ... put a decent stone on my father's grave. You know Cheapside ... the East End? Limehouse, Bethnal Green ... White Chapel?' He was letting his voice take on the Cockney whine. 'Know the Watney Street Market ... Spread Eagle Yard? Many's the time ... Stephney, eh! Spital Fields ... Russians, Danes, Jews, Syrians, Gyppos, bloody Armenians, Chinks, Hindus, Irish ... oh yeah, Jews. Christ, what a mix ... but live, y'know, live! It's the same out there. I feel at 'ome in Joh'burg. Knows me way about, like.'

He was coming heavy with the accent and the wink.

They met a few times in London. He was always generous and well-mannered. He understood about Laurie though she said nothing of his father and she was glad when he offered to accompany her into the country to hand the boy over.

'Made up your mind what's next?'

'No, I'm thinking.'

'If you're short of money...I'm 'ere. I known what it is to be on your own.' She was grateful but held back. It's me face ... it's me body he's after. Friendship from a man. Not bloody likely!

One day he said he was going back. 'Booked me passage, First.' She experienced a sudden sense of panic.

'Why'nt you come back with me?' I'll see you get fixed up with something. I'd forgot the bloody weather. Strewth ... fog, rine. Summer on Monday!'

She had given him nothing to encourage him.

'I'm sailing Tuesday.'

'Not this time Issy, thanks.'

'Cost you nuffink,' he coaxed and she knew he meant it. His smile faded. 'I've been wondering myself if it's time to quit the drink trade. Get out of it before I get a bullet in me skull. Competition, see.' Then he laughed. 'You'll go back. Everybody goes back. There's nothing for us 'ere, is there?'

A few days later she saw him off and felt herself abandoned. A letter with the eagle coat of arms of the Transvaal Republic came to her digs. The sight and feel of it brought back the sound and smell of Johannesburg. Outside the grimy window of her room it was a rare London day. She had wakened to sunlight and the feeling that she ought to go out to the village and see her child. They'd walk the fields and she'd take him sweets and toys, a silver shilling and a sailor suit she'd seen in a window. H.M.S. Terror in gold letters on the straw hat. Laurie'd need new boots. And a little walking stick. She turned almost with reluctance to the letter. Letters never brought good news.

'I am instructed by my clients to inform you that the property *Bloukoppen* has been sold on your behalf by Messrs Highveld Trust and Estate under instructions from Leonard Penlynne, Esquire.' She began to weep and tremble, not knowing why. She could stay here now. But did she want that? The kid would soon forget her. She was lost in London now. She knew nobody. Men accosted her when she walked out. There were thousands of street-walkers. She recognized them as women of her own class, cheaply dressed, with the accents of her past. More than once when she had loitered on the pavement she had been challenged by a painted face, 'Git orf my beat!'

She sometimes saw women dragging at the arms of men, right outside her window, entering a closed cab or going up a dark stair. On a warm evening, the street lights glowing like golden fruit in the foliage of old, leafy trees, it didn't look all that bad. Some of the men looked decent. On the wet, cold nights and in the darkness of winter it was a hell of a trade. Some of them had kids too … you couldn't hardly blame them.

She felt like eating an extravagant meal in a posh hotel but at the door of her room she pulled the pins from her hat and read the letter again. She was afraid to go out with such a letter in her hand. Suppose she dropped it or someone stole it off her? She got up and changed her dress. She'd never know what she'd got for the house if she didn't go to this bank and get her money….

A week later she took a cabin on the *Sydney Star*. The ship was bound for Australia on its second voyage. Kitty was to disembark at Durban on the South African east coast. She assumed the manner of Mrs Osborne, the wealthy widow of the play. It made her seem something of a mystery.

It was thought she was going out to see the grave of her husband killed by Zulus at some place in Natal, Ulundi. ' ... she must have been much younger than him.'

'Her father, perhaps. Wasn't there a Colonel Osborne?'

'Of course, it's not finished yet in Zululand ... the tribes. Stubborn people ... they say there'll be risings again next year if the territory's turned over to Natal.'

Her silence about Mrs Osborne's past was respected. Sometimes she felt she was Mrs Osborne. When the ship was rolling it was hard to maintain the accents of Kensington. She had to grasp at something to stand upright. Toilet goods crashed from the shelf into the basin.

'For Chrissake!' she screamed as the cabin tilted and drawers shot open. The most frightening moments were when the ship seemed to go on rolling as if it would never stop.

'One of these times she ain't going to come back, ma'am,' said the stewardess. 'And I 'ear the smashing of dishes in the kitchen and storeroom is somethink awful ... and she's a new ship! You could speak to the captain, ma'am ... the officers tell us there's nothing to worry for. Some of us won't be on her next trip ...' She came closer to confide. 'My friend ... table steward in Second ... says she's top-heavy. It's all those decks. She's got one too many, he says. Not that I want to scare you, ma'am.'

After that Kitty could never get back to being Mrs Osborne with her stewardess and they could laugh when she assumed the role with her clothing.

'I'm an actress,' she admitted.

'Are you now? Oh, ma'am,' the woman exclaimed. 'I saw Sir Henry in *The Bells*. I'll never forget it.'

They talked theatre and music hall and it turned out that Pearl Archer had been a dresser in Manchester. 'If you could see your way ... I'd be obliged if you could find me something up there in Johannesburg.'

A dust storm was blowing. From the train window Kitty saw the whirling red cloud that hid the town and blotted out the sun. Grit rattled on the windows as the train groped forward the last half

36

mile. 'Welcome to Johannesburg!' she heard. Dust blew from the mine dumps in grey plumes. The air was stifling. The houses of Doornfontein and Jeppe were ghost houses. Closed doors and windows. Cabs with blinds down ... ricksha pullers prancing through the murk like black demons in some hell devised for the misery of Europeans. Red bath water ... red drinking water tasting of clay. Dust between sheets, in the seams of clothing, in the swollen pages of books. Dust gritted in bread. Dust filming the furniture and china. It was suffocating indoors, impossible outside. Dust whirled its way along the length of the Reef, gaining intensity with every mile. It passed over old open workings, lashed plantations of young bluegums. 'Good weather for the new brewery,' she heard. They hadn't forgotten how to laugh. She clutched at her hat and skirts, heard herself shouting 'Grand National' to a tout as she clambered into a cab. She should have been dismayed. Why did she feel this rising excitement?

She had been less than a week in Johannesburg when Isadore sent up his card. 'I heard you were back!' He came round next morning and handed her into a carriage, an open Victoria with red leather upholstery. A black coachman in green livery sat erect on the box. Silver fittings glittered. The high gloss of immaculate coach enamel showed little sign of dust. She smelled warm leather and the odour of hoseflesh mingled with the sharp whiff of *kaffir* sweat. She was impressed.

Isadore was clean-shaven, smelling of bay rum. Everything about him, from his boots to his waistcoat strung with a gold chain, looked expensive. He looked, she thought, like a man who had just been unpacked from a very expensive box. His dark eyes shone with excitement.

'Something to show you, Kitty,' he said, taking her hand in his yellow chamois gloves. He was so ugly, she thought, and yet she liked his vitality.

'Where are we going?' she asked.

'Surprise,' he smiled. The feel of his clothes and the luxury of the coach exhilarated her.

'Thought we'd take a turn out to the Orange Grove and have a chat. I missed you, Kitty, but I knew you'd be back. We all come back.'

'How have you been doing, Issy?'

'How do you think?' his eyes crinkling at the corners. 'Can't complain ... course I've got my problems, who hasn't?'

'Problems ... you?'

'The liquor business ain't all roses, Kitty.' He ordered the carriage to be stopped at the top of the ridge where the wagon road wound down to the dark green clump of orange trees. A warm breeze brought a heavy scent. 'Kitty, I'd like to be your friend,' he ventured. 'You're the kind of girl I like ... it's a hard town this and everybody needs a friend.'

'You are my friend, Issy,' she said. 'A good friend.'

Beyond the orange trees and the scatter of farm buildings the wagon-rutted track wound away to the east across empty veld. You had the feeling that if the town of Johannesburg wasn't at your back there would be nothing at all. Only the veld grass and the far, shimmering blue.

'Tell you what,' he smiled. She noticed the coachmen's backs, sweat trickling down below the silk hats and dark patches on the green livery. 'This road's a bit hard on the Victoria,' Issy said. 'I want to show you something I've bought.' The twinkle of brown eyes redeemed his features. He was not yet thirty and money was no object. There was something hard beneath the amiable exterior. 'I've had to fight every inch,' he'd told her in England. 'But I'm a soft touch ... to me friends, that is.'

'You married yet?' she'd asked in London.

'I've 'ad a look round ... seen nothing I fancy.'

'Some nice Jewish girl,' she'd said, thinking of dark, handsome girls, bold-eyed in second-hand shops and of the smells of strange cookings in alleyways where ringletted boys played hopscotch and old men pushed barrows. She'd recalled guttural shoutings and nasal singing.

'From Poland?' he mocked. 'Nah, it's not for me ... not yet a long time. I wouldn't want me kids to be orphans.'

The carriage pulled in through the gates of *Bloukoppen* and clopped smartly up the drive and around the circle to the front door. She realized his intention. Workmen were taking down boards from the windows.

'What the hell did you bring me here for?' she shouted.

'I've bought it.' He was handing her down, smiling.

She stepped into the hall. She had put her signature to the deed of sale without reading the document, taking the smiles and assurances of Penlynne's lawyer for granted. She had no idea and didn't care who the buyer might be. Dust sheets covered pieces of furniture still unsold. The lacquered blackamoor with the gilded turban stared insolently from the foot of the stairs. She saw Issy's pale face in the mirror across the hall. He had opened the door into the music room and lifted the lid of the piano. He struck a note on the keyboard. A crystal in the chandelier echoed the sound. She was aware of him behind her.

'Like it, Kitty?'

'I want to go back to the hotel. Now.'

'Oh, come on, Kitty,' he said softly and she felt his hands at her waist. 'We only just got here ... take your time and have a good look round. I've always lived in hotels myself so I don't know what's wanted.'

The dry stale air of the place was oppressive. Sunlight, released from the prison of boarding, poured shafts of heat on to the floor through motes of dust.

'Penlynne's old place,' she heard him say. She heard pride in his voice. Was it possible he had no idea she had lived here? There was nothing in his attitude to suggest that he did. It would seem that his lawyer had acted on his behalf just as Penlynne's had acted on hers. She could not believe that this generous little man would hurt and humiliate her intentionally.

'Don't you like it?'

'It's your house, Issy ... you're the one'll be living here. You'll 'ave to marry now, you know.' She went rushing on, trying to parry the words she saw were inevitable.

'No,' he said, 'take your time ... 'ave a good look around. You can change anything you want. Order what you fancy. I'm going to look over the coach-house. Have a look upstairs.' He walked outside, shouting for the coachman.

She walked from room to room. It was all too vivid: the day Penlynne first brought her here; her astonishment and disbelief at what he was saying. 'It's for you, Kitten. For us.'

With the stifling pressure of her breasts against tight lacing, Kitty felt anger rising. Almost against her will she went upstairs, turning left on the landing. There was Laurie's nursery. She didn't look in. Her bedroom stank of stale cosmetics. It was unchanged. Hardly able to breathe she tried to open the window but the sashes resisted. 'I gave twelve thousand for it, *voetstoots*'.

She heard his footsteps behind her, quiet on the carpet. For a moment she thought of accepting. How would Penn react to that!

She heard Issy sit down on the bed and throw his hat aside. He watched her, saying nothing, toying with his watch chain.

'I don't want to live here, Issy.'

'I thought you might ... we get along nicely.'

'Yes, I know ... but I wish you 'adn't bought it,' she said.

'In London,' he said, 'I thought we was real good friends ... maybe we could be more than friends one day. I never forced you or anything you didn't want, not so?'

'You've been a gentleman, Issy, a real gentleman, but I don't want to live here.'

She was remembering the last minutes in the house: the servants dismissed; waiting for a carter to pick up her baggage. She had looked in the mirror and seen a pale ghost of herself in a green velvet costume, her skin so white it seemed to let light through to her bones. She had felt abandoned and angry.

'Take me back to the hotel, Issy.'

'A'right, as you please.'

Nothing was said all the way back. At the hotel he handed her down onto the roadside, lifted his hat and curtly ordered the coachman to drive on.

Kitty hurried inside. Perhaps the day would come when she could explain her feelings to him. Her resolve never to be at any man's orders. There was no such thing as a man who did something for nothing. She'd have to be on the bones of her arse before she'd get herself under another man demanding his rights.

Chapter Three

Morning light struck through the shutters, gilding the plaster motif of fauns and nymphs around the bedroom walls, the work of Italian craftsmen. From Dorothy Penlynne's perspective, in bed, it had a look of classical purity. The same motif was repeated in the woven tapestry canopy and on the richly carved headboard. The drapes were of a heavy Florentine weave. She lay, arranging her social diary, on pillows of the finest Flemish lace. Dorothy was pregnant. The charming canvas of Firenze's *Madonna and Child* was Penlynne's gift to her when Stewart MacDonald had confirmed the pregnancy.

She was touched by his emotional offering. 'The little Mother of God will look after you this time, my dearest ... I'm superstitious, as you know.' He had smiled. 'You must be careful, Dotty,' he urged. 'You simply must cut down on your activities. This child means everything to us.'

'I'll try ... but how I can do it, I don't know. I have a full diary for weeks ahead and a houseful of guests.'

'We'll clear them all out!'

'You know that's not possible, even if I wanted. People we have invited months ago can't be diverted to an hotel in town, even if the hotels here were any good. Not the kind of people we know. And so many of them are important to you.'

'It's worth it to me to find other ways of entertaining.'

'In this town?'

He shrugged, conceding her point.

'You've waited a long time for this, Penny.' Her hands strayed through his strongly curling hair. The first streaks at his temples had only increased the look of strength and authority. He was young to be greying, and his eyes, black and challenging, often showed his deep concern. She would hear him groan in the night, unaware of it.

'Yes, it's been a long time, Dotty; I intend to look after you very well this time.'

'We'll keep it to ourselves a little longer,' she quietened him.

'My son will have everything,' he said.

Dorothy laughed, 'What makes you so certain it will be a boy?'

'How could it be otherwise!' She stroked his face.

'Yes, we've waited a long time,' he said more sombrely.

'That time in London ... those ghastly examinations and the operation ...'

'Don't, Dotty ...'

'It'll all be worth while ... you'll see,' she said.

She seated herself at her desk, her small feet showing below the hem of her nightdress. He kneeled beside her.

'You must go now,' she said with mock seriousness. 'Ring for Florence ... I have a household to attend to.' Dorothy had taken to the role of chatelaine, ordering every detail of the huge house with its full staff of European servants. Visitors were astonished. The guest book, he sometimes joked to her, read like *Debrett's* and the *Almanac de Gotha* with titles and compliments in half a dozen languages. He had made it possible, but how many women could have risen so well to the challenge? A dozen house guests and twenty or more round her table every night. No one of any significance came to Johannesburg without an invitation.

She kept her distance from the mining community of managers and their wives. This amused Penlynne, remembering her beginnings in Kimberley. But he respected her stance. It gave them a certain tone. She wanted nothing uncouth in their lives. When she drove through the town's mirey or dusty streets in shining equipage, attended by liveried servants, she could have been driving in the Bois de Boulogne.

It was on her return from a shopping expedition that she decided that something had to be done about animal welfare ... a special concern of hers.

Oxen often fell in their traces as they dragged crates of heavy equipment. The sound of the driver's shouts and the pistol crack of the twenty-foot whips were so common he no longer noted them. Starving curs scavenged and whelped in holes in the ground but the horses distressed him. Stamping, they were goaded by flies, as they dragged the city's hundreds of licensed cabs.

42

'I cannot bear it any longer, Penny,' she cried. 'It is so degrading, so unnecessary. I am ashamed of the impression made on our guests.'

'You are too sensitive, my dear,' he said. 'This is no time to take up another cause ... you have burdens enough.'

To raise funds, Dorothy arranged a garden party. Alas, a late afternoon rainstorm scattered the guests. *The Oracle* noted: *The garden party so graciously undertaken by Mrs Leonard Penlynne for the cause of domestic animals, was washed out but continued indoors, amid* Far Horizon's *rare collection of art treasures. Mrs Penlynne received guests in a toilette of white embroidered nin de soie mounted over satin ....*

Dorothy was partly mollified. To raise further funds it was decided to stage an evening of Gilbert and Sullivan in the ballroom. 'All right, I'll give it a go ... I'll sing,' said Penlynne reluctantly. 'But I had rather you didn't go on with this. If it's a question of a hundred or two, I'll write a cheque now.'

'It's a question of civic responsibility ... people must learn to care.' He saw that she meant it. Sometimes, he thought, it was as if, in her impatience for perfection, she could have banished every unwashed creature. It went back, he knew, to her ineradicable memories of Kimberley, and a deep inward shrinking from everything detestable.

She had the personal charm and power to encourage others but she could not persuade herself to forget those early years. They never spoke of them but Penlynne guessed that always at the back of her consciousness was the incident that had so disturbed the early days of their marriage and driven him out of her arms. Now, when he looked at this radiant woman in her late twenties, confident and beautiful, he found it hard to recall the shuddering, shrinking bride. Was anything uglier, more brutal than rape? Fortunately, the place where it happened, a ride in the Sachenwald, was now built over. The town had forgotten. Its volatile and ever-shifting population was indifferent. Newcomers had never heard of the incident. But Dorothy remembered.

Penlynne never drove past the Victoria Chambers in Pritchard Street but he saw the rapist hanging from its scaffolding ... the flushed and brutal face of the crowd.

On the night of the concert the crush of carriages on the

driveway up to *Far Horizons* reached back half a mile. Dorothy looked rather pale and as her maid put finishing touches to her dress, Penlynne was concerned. The door was already being opened for guests. 'I wish you had cancelled this affair tonight.' She was adjusting his black tie and he could see she was not her vigorous self. Knowing her as he did, she would go down to greet her guests as if perfectly well.

'Don't be silly, Penn, I feel quite all right.'

'I could tell them the tenor has laryngitis,' he joked.

'It's much too late. Do stop worrying.'

Stewart MacDonald had been called in the previous week when she had had a slight issue of blood. Stewart had urged her to rest for at least a couple of weeks. Dorothy had rested for two days, then continued with her preparations for the concert. Once she had the bit in her teeth there was no stopping her.

Penlynne went down to meet his guests. Dorothy's maid completed her mistress's toilette. Exquisitely dressed in a high-waisted brocade gown, her piled hair surmounted by a spray of osprey feathers, she wore no jewellery. Slowly she descended the stairs to the hum of the conversation below. Smilingly she greeted the elite of town society. While going from one to another she experienced the first stab of pain. No one would have guessed.

Penlynne watched her. A few moments later the curtain went up. She looked pale but composed, smiling in pleasurable anticipation. Perhaps his anxiety was unfounded.

Halfway through the concert he noticed Dorothy leave her seat and hurry from the room. Sullivan's jolly bouncing strains followed her up the stairs. She had felt the first severe contraction. She fell on her bed and rang for Florence. The maid did not respond. She heard laughter and applause and then another jingling chorus. Dorothy clutched the covers. Across the room Penlynne's gift seemed to mock her. Firenze's gentle mother smiled on the infant Jesus. Contraction followed contraction, and then a rush of hot fluid. Then Penlynne burst through the doorway. 'Dorothy!' she heard him cry.

'Don't say anything,' she gasped. 'Just send Florence ... I don't want anyone to know.'

'Oh, my poor darling. You're bleeding.' He was near panic.

She was deathly white. 'I'm losing your child again,' she moaned.

'I'll get MacDonald. He's here.'

'Get him,' she groaned. 'Don't make a scene. I could not bear it.'

It was interval. The audience was overflowing from the ballroom into the hall and out onto the evening terraces. Penlynne rushed down the stair for MacDonald. Brushing aside compliments and detaining hands he drew the doctor aside.

The concert agonized on. Speeches ... the playing of two national anthems. Congratulations. The society editor of *The Oracle* looking in vain for the hostess. Stewart MacDonald had spent some time alone with Dorothy by the time Penlynne was at the bedside. The frightening evidence had been removed.

'I'm so sorry ... so sorry, my dear,' she comforted.

'No, no,' he cried, his cheeks wet with tears.

'You'll have your heir,' she promised.

Next day Penlynne went direct to MacDonald's rooms in Jeppe Street. At the top of the hill near Von Brandis square there was an outspan. The slope looked east towards Bezuidenhout's farm, to the young willows and the meandering stream that some said was the beginnings of the Limpopo.

It was a bright day, everything gilded in brilliance; harness brasses, boots, fresh paint. Smoke from outspanned wagons drifted lazily, carrying a smell of meat and coffee. He felt terrible.

He had first met MacDonald on the voyage out. The red-cheeked, gangling young Scot, soft-spoken and embarrassed in company, had brought an outbreak of typhus on board under control while senior men panicked. In Johannesburg they were together on the Smallpox Committee organized to control the outbreak in the city. Death wagons trundled through the streets daily.

'It could have been due to excitement ... undue exertion,' MacDonald was saying. 'Some women are more prone to miscarry than others, especially those of a highly-strung disposition.' The analysis of his wife was what Penlynne had expected.

'What is to be done, Doctor?'

'She must have abundant rest and I suggest a thorough examination.' In the pause Penlynne found the word cancer in his throat ... Dorothy's fear.

'She has spoken of cancer.'

'I can understand that. The operations she had in Europe would predispose her to such fears. Do you know Dr Jameson?'

'He was my wife's doctor in Kimberley. Before our marriage.'

'He'll be in Johannesburg shortly for a conference on tropical diseases. He's been treating Lobengula ... the black king. We've persuaded him to join us in a Burns Nicht supper.'

'You Scots,' groaned Penlynne. 'Anything to get together over a dram and your instruments of torture.' He felt relief. Dorothy liked and trusted the merry, impulsive Scot. He had something of her own impetuous nature. The same quick changes of mood that made them both so charming and so unpredictable.

Dorothy's reaction was characteristic. 'Invite him to stay with us!'

About a month later Penlynne heard a voice he recognized in the card room of the Rand Club. Jameson was shirt-sleeved. He had a glass of whiskey at his elbow and the face of a man with a good hand.

'I heard you were in town, Starr,' Penlynne said. He didn't think much of the doctor's hand.

'I'm at the *Albion*'.

'Pack up ... we'd enjoy having your company at *Far Horizons*.'

Jameson played out the hand and lost. 'I'm easily bluffed,' he laughed, reaching for his coat.

'That's poker,' said Penlynne.

'It's how you play them,' said Jameson amiably.

On the drive up the curving road to *Far Horizons* Penlynne pulled up the trap to cool the horses. Jameson looked out over the valley towards the far off Magaliesberg. 'Rhodes has a great admiration for you,' he said.

Penlynne was conscious of his sudden, direct gaze. The force of the man. 'Rhodes is the most inspiring man you'll ever meet. It's his vision ... his incredible ability to make events turn his way. When that man looks you in the face and says "Go forth"! My God, Penlynne! It makes a shiver go down your spine. I've been very close to him in recent months. We must talk, you and I.' As he spoke, he took a small penknife from his pocket and made an incision in the thorny arm of an aloe, drawing out a plug. He squeezed out the bitter juice between finger and thumb. 'It's a harsh purgative,' he said, almost mystically. 'You've had children?'

'Not so far.' Penlynne spoke of the miscarriages.

'I remember her ... Miss Orwell.'

'I'd be grateful if you'd examine her.'

'I've given up medicine for politics.'

'You treated Lobengula.'

'That was diplomacy. It's one thing treating a gouty, irascible old savage surrounded by wives, tipsy most of the day ... quite another a woman like Mrs Penlynne. I believe I did warn her ... years ago, that some operative treatment might be necessary.'

'She spent two years in London and the Continent.'

Jameson laid a sympathetic hand on Penlynne's arm. He was, when looked at closely, insignificant. Except for the lustrous eyes. There was something unusual there. This man could consume himself if what he believed seemed just.

He was the perfect house guest: bright and entertaining, and a favourite with the women. He made an examination of Dorothy. 'In my opinion you might still have a child.'

Dorothy was at her desk at the usual hour she set aside for correspondence. In the period of depression following the miscarriage she had not been up to answering a letter from her mother in Stutterheim. It struck her as she read that it was quite unlike the writer's usual querulous tone. Could it have been dictated by Robert? She was longing to see her daughter again.

Doctor here is very pleased with my health, it ended cryptically. Dorothy turned over the last page. In her brother's hand she read: *Mother has been sober for two months. I believe she is cured. Do please give her a chance and invite her for a visit. I would bring her up from the Cape myself and guarantee her behaviour.*

Penlynne made no comment. 'I can find something for your brother ... I daresay,' he said.

'You've been more than generous to him already.'

'He'll find his feet.'

'He's failed everything so far. I would have to make a

bedroom and sitting room available for mother ... she is not always presentable.'

Penlynne laughed. 'Her indisposition, as she calls it, is not always noticed by strangers.'

'She'll bribe the servants to bring her liquor. There simply isn't room for them.'

'Fifteen bedrooms?' said Penlynne dryly.

'It would be a prolonged stay ... a misery.'

'You have nothing to fear, my dear. You are another woman. I have no regrets that I met you in Kimberley, in that little wood and iron house with the din of the location over the road.'

'Please,' she objected, rising.

'Nothing can touch you now, Dorothy. And if anything should happen to me, you'd be well provided for.'

She clung to him. 'Don't talk like that ... I need you. Everyone needs you.' He was astonished and touched by the vehemence of her feelings; there was no sign of the assured society woman, the imperious creature who could silence a dinner table with a gesture.

A few days later she was talking animatedly about a dinner she was planning. 'It's to be a Mad Hatter's Tea Party. There will be croquet on the lawn,' she wrote to those invited. 'But not with flamingoes and hedgehogs if I can help it!'

'You will come as the King of Hearts,' she enthused to Penlynne.

'I shall come as the Mad Hatter,' he said gravely.

'I wonder if I could persuade President Kruger to come as the Mock Turtle,' she went on. 'Shedding oceans of tears for his poor burghers ... quite drowning us all.'

He understood that her flippancy covered a very real anxiety about the future. Only that day he had written to his partner Julius Wernher in London. *There have been disgraceful scenes here. The President met the British High Commissioner at the station and the carriage was stormed by the worst kind of jingo fanatics. They draped it with the Union Jack and uncoupled the horses, leaving the old man sitting alone in the carriage while they roared Rule Britannia and chaired Sir Henry ... to his considerable embarrassment. He had come up to talk reason to Kruger about our disadvantages, taxes, etc. and this was the way we showed him our reasonableness. I apologized to the President in person but the Afrikaner community is seething with rage. The irony is that we cannot be loyal to a state that refuses us representation and Kruger cannot give us equal rights without being voted out of power. One must proceed, my dear Julius, with delicacy and diplomacy.*

And yet, even as he wrote, sitting in shirtsleeves, a carafe of ice water at his elbow, the handmade cigarettes he favoured sending coils of smoke to the ceiling, he was aware of deep unease. He added a footnote:

I am enclosing a pamphlet by the National Union. They are pressing for our rights here. I have subscribed a thousand to them. It is a useful forum to keep Kruger aware of uitlander *wishes. And a safety valve for some of our hotheads.*

He laid down his pen as his secretary entered.

'Look down there, Mr Penlynne.'

Penlynne saw a cluster of Boer horsemen riding through. About forty of them, armed with rifles. Men came out of saloons to stare. Some shouted after them. The clatter of hooves came up. The Boers rode with a slouching, casual arrogance he did not remember seeing before.

'Ring our managers on the West Rand,' he said calmly. 'Warn them ... the men must not offer provocation. I believe it is nothing much ... a show of force.' He returned to his desk to add a postscript.

I sometimes envy your isolation in London where you can see everything in perspective. Here we are either in a frenzy of excitement or in a sweat of despair – or playing the fool as if there will never be a day of reckoning.

He was glad of Dorothy's Mad Hatter's Party. It had made a welcome diversion from politics in the daily press. There was too much inflamed journalism for his taste. And yet, what was printed was a pretty fair reflection of emotions.

Some nights later he was pushing his cycle up the road to the gates of *Far Horizons*. Cycling was a fashionable fad. It was pitch dark except for the circle of light thrown from the bullseye lantern. He could hear the hiss of carbide gas and the tick-tick of the Sturmey-Archer 3-speed gear. Ahead of him the house blazed with light. The sound of the generator came reassuringly. Thump-thump-thump! Like a steady heart beating away in the warm darkness. Dorothy had gone to much trouble to restore

49

the damage done to the koppie by blasting, bringing in aloes and cycads; strange and prehistoric.

He often paused to draw breath at this point. As he leaned on the Raleigh, looking down at the miles of twinkling lights that marked the east-west sprawl of the mines, it seemed to him incredible how much had been achieved since 1886. He moved on, well satisfied, and yet, impatient.

At that moment there was a flash off to one side. Something hummed past his ear, struck the rock and whanged away. A gash appeared on the back of his hand. Dazed by the hammer of concussion so close, he stood, stupidly licking the graze. That anyone could have fired on him seemed beyond belief. He could not accept it.

'What the hell are you playing at!' he shouted, almost expecting some oaf with a hunting rifle to come out of the dark, apologizing. He had potted a leopard himself not long ago on this same koppie. Silence. Then stones rolling on the hillside. Only then did he fully grasp he had been shot at. The graze from a chip of flying rock was slight. He explained it away to Dorothy. 'A skid on the gravel ...' He lay awake for a long time. For the first time he was aware that he was not immortal. He reached out to touch her. 'Is Jameson coming to the party?' She was already asleep.

Chapter Four

Walter Gardiner thrust out his long legs irritably, one foot on the window ledge of the lawyer's office. Jacob Esselyn waited for another outburst from the American, ponderously stuffing his meerschaum with tobacco. '*Ja-nee,*' he said complacently. 'As the law stands, the heir *ab intestato* is your wife Katherine. But in our Roman-Dutch law, this does not cut out the surviving spouse. It's a very interesting law ... derived from an ordinance in Holland in 1580 ...'

Gardiner scowled. 'So?'

'It means, in effect, that the estate of the late Rawlinson will be divided in equal parts.'

Gardiner sat up. 'Do I understand that this servant woman is entitled to half ... half the Rawlinson estate!'

'That is the way it stands, Mynheer Gardiner.' Esselyn went on with infuriating legalistic complacency. 'The interesting thing will be the division of the estate between the heirs.'

'Muriel Ferguson ... his housekeeper! She married him in his dotage! Entitled to a sum of money like that. Half the Rawlinson Star ... never mind the rest of it! Are you telling me she'll end up with power ... substantial power in the Rawlinson companies?'

'Ja ... she, or whomever she appoints as her administrator.'

'Katherine will never accept it. Her father always told her it was all for her.'

'No doubt it was his intention, Mynheer Gardiner. A pity he did not leave the drawing up of the will to his company lawyer.'

'There must be some way of contesting it.'

'Not as long as Roman-Dutch law applies here.'

'You mean, under British law it would not count?'

'Perhaps he was attempting to arrange something when he died ... a transfer of his assets to England.' Esselyn watched the American, his eyes half-closed to the heavy smoke. The greed of his clients did not amaze him nor cause him to make moral judgements. To him it was all a game of wits and the very imprecision of the law only increased his satisfaction with it. 'As I said, it's in the who-takes-what that the elements of bargaining will lie. Your wife may take her father's house … and see it burned down next day! Shares Lady Rawlinson's lawyer may advise, strong now, maybe worthless next year. Fascinating, not so … and most unusual in an estate of this size.'

'How long will it take?'

'Years.'

'Good God!' cried Gardiner. He could have kicked the lawyer, grinning through his haze of vile, homegrown tobacco smoke.

'Of course, the company will go on … Sir Josiah's interests are in capable hands. It will not affect your wife's living in any way.'

Gardiner walked slowly across town. He paused to light a cigar and put his boots forward for a bootblack. He saw the red dust flicked away with a kind of disinterest that seemed to focus on trivialities … on the flies that swarmed round the black child's eyes, on his sing-song whining: 'Baas will give me shilling for good job.' Old Rawlinson had had the last laugh. He'd never been able to stomach Gardiner's leaving him to join Penlynne after he'd been brought out to the Rand to advise Rawlinson on the pyrites problem. Marrying the daughter, he'd sometimes thought, had been part of the old man's strategy to keep him here in Africa. In any case, he knew now he'd waited too late to marry. The years of bachelorhood had made it impossible to accept the restrictions of family life. Gardiner did not see himself as selfish. It had never crossed his mind. But now there was a will more powerful than his own, frustrating his purposes.

Katherine was curiously inert. She would not be drawn on to the subject of the estate. She had gone into heavy mourning, unaware that she was as striking in black as in any other colour. 'Your father did this on purpose, Katherine,' he argued with her. 'To make quite certain that I wouldn't use Rawlinson assets to develop the Southern Deeps.'

She turned to him with lifted chin, very pale and aristocratic.

'Surely it is Penlynne's business to find capital for that?'

'In today's climate of distrust it can't be raised. Dammit Katherine, I proved the deep levels and I can prove them again … and far beyond the Southern Deeps. I know what I'm doing.'

'Surely we have enough?'

'Spoken like a woman,' he thought, 'one who'd never thought where money came from, who had always been sure of it.'

'It's not the money.' How could he make her understand that money was a tool? For him the fascination of mining was not its rewards. He felt a pang of envy every time a prospector came into Penlynne's office and dumped down a parcel of ore, opening his maps to show where he'd sampled it. 'All I want is a stake to go back there and prove it, Mr Penlynne!' Gold from Lobengula's country … tin, zinc, lead, nickel and chrome. And bloodred hematite of iron found in the age-old Bantu workings with the broken tools of metal workers, long gone. Fascinating. Challenging. Beckoning. For months now he had been working on this theory ….

The gold reef they were working was only the rim of a saucer. Somewhere to the east lay the other rim. He was convinced of this. On a clear day he could see as far as the hills of Heidelberg, a smudge of blue eighty miles away. That was where it would surface. 'Look over there, Penlynne,' he'd said more than once. 'That will make your Rand look like beginner's luck.'

'Geology's an imprecise science, I believe,' Penlynne said dryly. 'Ninety percent guesswork. We've got enough on our hands developing what we've got. If you'd been with me in Pretoria you'd know that talking to Kruger about development is like talking to someone out of the Book of Deuteronomy. And you come to me talking of a million sterling for a dream – and so far we haven't seen a penny from the deeps. That old man is making it impossible for me to raise it. I told him the gold mines are his only salvation ….'

'What did he say to that?'

'The Scriptures say: put not your trust in riches.'

'You've always raised capital in the past.'

'Capital's frightened. What we need here is stability … a sense of permanence to create confidence. Kruger thinks the mines can't last long … he'll milk us dry and when it's gone, he'll have his pastoral republic again. Of course, he's too late for that. They tried for years to keep us out … finding gold was a capital offence here. Did you know that!'

Gardiner laughed. 'We can declare our own republic and the hell with them.'

'Don't think I haven't thought of it,' said Penlynne. 'And don't think they haven't thought of it. They're not fools. They're as scared as we are ... different reasons, that's all. No, Walter, I'm convinced they're out to close us down ... to empty Johannesburg. Maybe run what's left in their own way. But first ... ruin us. I was told the other day there are people among them ... extremists, who talk of destroying the mines.'

'We'd fight before that, surely?'

'Against ten thousand well-armed burghers ... with what, pray?'

'We can bring in arms, turn Joh'burg into an armed camp.'

'That's crazy talk, Walter ... you know the kind we've got here, tradesmen and chancers ... hardly fighting material. Besides, they've got no stake in it. Why should they risk their skins ... for me? For the mine owners? No, they'd have to be convinced they were doing it for something more important than keeping the Peruvians in business.'

'Patriotism ...?'

'Turks, Lithuanians, Greeks, Cypriots, Germans?'

'What then? ... I can see you've something in mind.'

'Go north ... into Lobengula's territory.'

'You mean begin again!'

'There are no Boers up there. Not yet.'

'Abandon everything here?'

'Of course not, but perhaps it's time to think of alternatives. There's gold up there. We know it's the site of ancient Ophir. Solomon used its gold to sheath the temple in Jerusalem. Powder the hair of his charioteers with gold dust. S'fact, not just stories. Samples for assay have been coming back for years. Imagine another Rand. Without the Boers!'

'Who would you send?'

'You. Take a couple of months off.' Penlynne could see Gardiner was both startled and stimulated. 'Well?'

'It's a bad time for me, Penlynne. I'm about to contest Rawlinson's will. Can you imagine Muriel Ferguson inheriting ... and by default! So far all we can get from her lawyers is that the old man had the documents drawn up here and had sent them to his London solicitors for approval. And dropped dead before they came back for a signature.'

'What does Esselyn say?'

'It's going to be an interminable wrangle. Years of it.'

'There might be nothing if the Boers have their way.'

Even amid the luxury of leather, fine woods and carpets – all the appurtenances of wealth – both men were aware of unease; the unease of a jerrybuilt city built by chance. Built on rock, but there had never been a moment when men did not feel a sense of impermanence. As they sat in silence, smoking, the building shook. A giant fist had taken it by the foundations. The chandelier tinkled. Dust fell on Penlynne's documents. Underground there was swirling dust and splintered timber, and flesh ground into broken rock.

'Pressure burst,' said Penlynne. Gardiner nodded.

The problems for the engineer were increasing. The deeper they dug and blasted, the greater the risk of pressure and heat. There was only crude ventilation to carry off fumes of explosives. These were stark facts. Penlynne looked across the room at his associate. 'Walter, I can tell you we haven't got all the time in the world.' Normally so articulate, so persuasive, he found it hard to put his thoughts into words. So far, it was only a vague apprehension of interests greater than his own beginning to manoeuvre and manipulate.

He had felt it strongly over there in Pretoria ... something uncoiling. Kruger put on this front of naivety but from his actions – and if what one read in *Die Patriot* was an indication – there was a bigger game afoot.

It was nothing less than a Boer ambition to sweep the English out of South Africa. They wanted a Dutch hegemony with its foot on the neck of a million blacks. The rural atmosphere and the blue haze of jacaranda trees in the capital did not conceal its hostility.

'Damned if I'm ready to let it go,' said Gardiner.

'There are others who feel the same ... make no mistake.' Penlynne had always forced his way, turned mountains of rubble into green pastures. He would not be defeated now. 'By the way,' he broke the silence.

Gardiner expected him to press for a decision but enigmatic as ever, the man was tilting his chair back, throwing over a quick sketch. 'If I am ever to be knighted,' he said, 'my coat of arms will be a stamp battery flanked by leopards. Motto: *I have what I hold*. In Latin, of course.'

'Bully for you,' said Gardiner dryly.

Mrs Orwell's telegram arrived just as Dorothy's arrangements for the dinner party were complete. Her mother and Robert were due by the Kimberley train.

'Send the coachman,' said Penlynne. He was sensitive to her apprehension of the station platform and its crowds, to the vulgar and the curious. 'I can send Williams, if you prefer. I won't be needing him.'

'The Press will be there ... everyone.'

'Shall I go?' he offered. But she did not seem to hear.

'I can only hope that Robert has been as good as his word and that mother is cured. It's all so inconvenient. One thing I will insist on. She will not be mingling with my guests. I shall make quite certain she is kept upstairs in the west wing until she goes.'

She was unusually pale, and was bracing herself for an ordeal. She had not been at Park Halt since that night two years ago when she had returned unexpectedly from England. The whole town was at a ball Penlynne had given at the Wanderer's Sporting Club. The stationmaster had found her a cab and she'd driven to *Bloukoppen*, cold with apprehension. She had never lived there and Penlynne had been rather evasive about his acquisition of it.

The moment she entered she was aware of a woman's presence. It was dawn before Penlynne came in. He was with a young redhaired beauty. Noisy companions were calling for champagne and breakfast. She never passed the station now without an inward shrinking. Today would be a special ordeal. She stiffened her face and ordered the closed cab.

Dorothy awaited the train's arrival with that air of aloofness she had learned to put on as an armour against the curious. Johannesburg knew that face and respected it. No one knows, she thought, how vulnerable I am. Keeping my back straight is the only thing that prevents disintegration.

The train was on time but no Mrs Orwell appeared. The greetings and excitement of others flowed past as she stood aside. Carriage doors slammed. Steam and stench and noise; the always frightening jostling of *kaffirs*, ... the panic-arousing acridity of sweating flesh. Suddenly, the hissings, the clangour of metal and the yellings of hotel touts all ebbed away. She saw her brother Robert. He gave her a disarming smile.

'Where is she ... mother?' she demanded.

'Have you got a cab?' he countered. He was in a brown suit, rather baggy, with a look of *dorp* store about it. His goodlooking young face had an expression of strained eagerness. 'She's in the last coach ... I'll get a porter.' He seemed eager to be gone.

'I have the carriage,' Dorothy said.

'She's taken rather queer ... it's just nerves ... the excitement, you know.'

Dorothy found Mrs Orwell propped up in the corner of the compartment, smelling strongly of eau de cologne. Her lips were purple from chewing cachous. She roused herself with tipsy regality to greet her daughter, exclaiming in a loud voice how amazed she was. What a change in her little girl!

'Not now, mother ... please not now,' cried Dorothy.

At the door of the vehicle Mrs Orwell insisted that she could mount without help.

'Honestly, I don't know where she got it,' said Robert.

'Through the carriage window, of course,' gritted Dorothy.

'I didn't give her money ... I didn't have any.'

'You will take her back just as soon as I can arrange it.'

'You might tell them it's the thin air up here,' he grinned. 'I mean ... if there are questions.'

'The visit is greatly inconvenient,' she said.

He was looking out with excitement. 'What a town! I say, what a town! Leonard said he'd make a place for me somewhere.'

'What can you do?' she said coldly.

'Things haven't been too good, I'll admit. I say, what's that tower?'

'The telephone exchange.'

Mrs Orwell mumbled and nodded as the carriage rocked, raising her powdery face now and then to cast a benevolent smile on nothing in particular.

'My husband gets thousands of requests from young men with proper qualifications. He can pick and choose.'

'I'll find something,' he assured her cheerfully. 'I couldn't help it if the damned sheep pegged out. Farming's hopeless ... everything dies.'

Mrs Orwell was assisted up the steps into *Far Horizons* and hustled away to the rooms Dorothy had prepared for her, along corridors and up a wooden stairway into quarters designed for a governess. 'I shall rest and bathe and be ready for supper.' Mrs Orwell sank down among her cases and bundles, loose hair straying from beneath her bonnet, her grip firm on a wicker basket that clinked.

'In the meantime you will be dining here, mother,' said Dorothy firmly.

To Robert she warned: 'I shall put you on your honour not to supply her with drink.'

'Am I eating up here, too?' he said with a flash of heat.

'Have you a dress suit?'

'It's a little small.'

'You'll have to see Leonard's tailor at once. You are really quite a goodlooking young man.' It touched her to see he had the same eyes as her father, rather gentle and contemplative. When he smiled he showed excellent teeth, not yet stained by tobacco. She hoped that what she had taken for weakness at first glance would turn out to be immaturity. Penlynne at his age was managing diamond diggings for Rawlinson. Her own father had been a dreamer and a failure, ill equipped for the mad scramble that was Kimberley at that time. Robert had barely lived there. Boarding school in the eastern Cape had been Mrs Orwell's idea of preparing him for the life of a gentleman. It had prepared him for nothing.

Dorothy laid table for thirty on the evening of the Mad Hatter's Party. It was a six-course meal beginning with *Consommé a la Portugaise*, served from a silver tureen by the butler and brought to the table by liveried manservants.

'Ah, soup of the Portuguese!' cried Jameson merrily down the table. 'Now if it were stew of the Portuguese ... or the pickle of the Portuguese!' Everyone paused. Eyes turned expectantly. It was common knowledge that the Portuguese were making a mess of things up there at Beira where the great muddy Pungwe flowed into the Indian Ocean.

'Pray do tell, Doctor,' responded Dorothy, imperious in costume as the Red Queen but with one eye on the butler ensuring that he did not spoil the *Ris d'Agneau avec petit pois* by bringing it in from the servery too soon.

Jameson had the voice, mannerisms and ebullience of a sixth form schoolboy. He had been upbraided by a guest for abandoning his patients for politics. 'Ah madame,' he replied. 'The map of Africa is in dire need of surgery.' Now, as silence fell on the table, it seemed to Penlynne that the Mad Hatter's Party had been a childish whim. Jameson had not dressed for it and Penlynne had set aside, as soon as possible, the top hat with label: 'this style 10/6'.

Jameson, realizing that his remark had drawn serious attention, began to talk about the new territories to the north. The immense prospects for development. 'It is, above all, a land marvellously suited to white colonization. I understand from ladies in the pioneer column who took rose cuttings, that our English flowers flourish like weeds in its soil ... soil, which up to now has been used for nothing better than pumpkins and kaffir corn.'

He spoke with such urgency Dorothy felt he might abruptly rise and dab his lips with his napkin. 'Excuse me, dear lady ... I have some unfinished business for Her Majesty in Katanga ... or Lake Nyasa. I'll finish my anecdote about Mr Rhodes when I get back.' Then he began to talk gallantries to the ladies, the table relaxed. Dorothy unclenched her hands. The dinner was going to succeed after all.

A croquet match had been arranged in the ballroom. Everyone gasped. Pots of red and white roses had turned it into a royal garden by Tenniel. The warm air was heavy with scent. The croquet match was an hilarious diversion with loud cries of 'Off with his head ... off with her head!' It was hot work in costume with the languid fans churning the heat. There were frequent pauses for fruit punch laced with chilled *Veuve Cliquot*. The french doors were opened wide. Guests strayed onto the moonlit terrace where marble forms gleamed palely.

Dorothy moved among them. Katherine Gardiner was in close conversation, smiling readily with a tall, slender young man with sandy sideburns and the look of a soldier about him. He had put a shawl about her naked shoulders and received a grateful look. He was so altered that for a moment she did not recognize him as Lord Charles Warewood. She knew better than to interrupt a moment that had the appearance of more than a social gesture. There had been talk that Katherine had been courted by him in England and that he had followed her out just in time to send a wedding gift. Penlynne had invited him and she had placed him next to Katherine at table, calculatedly and watchfully. Gardiner did not appear to notice.

At that moment, Dorothy was called away by the house-keeper. She saw at once that the woman was in a panic. 'Oh, madame,' she said, trying to keep her dismay from the guests. 'I can't find Mrs Orwell ... she's not in her room.'

Dorothy looked around for Robert. Penlynne and Jameson had left the ballroom and there were other male faces missing. The headdress suddenly pressed heavily. She felt ludicrous, as if about to be exposed. Women were so alert to recognize unease in a hostess.

'My brother ... find Mr Robert.'

'He went with Mr Penlynne and the other gentlemen.'

At that moment Mrs Orwell appeared in the ballroom. She was in a gown Dorothy recognized as the relic of one she had worn in her young married life and had sometimes brought out in Kimberley to emphasize the kind of company she had been accustomed to. Her mother came forward among the guests with tipsy regality, like some tattered queen, fanning herself vigor-ously. Dorothy stood petrified. None of the guests had any inkling that this was Mrs Penlynne's mother. Mrs Orwell sig-nalled a footman and drank thirstily from a glass of *Dom Perignon*, moved among the guests and seated herself.

'Shall I remove her, ma'am?' said the housekeeper.

To Dorothy that seemed even more risky than introducing her. She feared another outburst: 'See how my daughter treats me ... ashamed of her mother! I am not even allowed to appear at the dinner table.' In the short time she had been at *Far Horizons* she had already complained of servants stealing her trinkets. Somehow she had got liquor.

'Can I help?' George Borchard's pale blonde looks were well suited to his get-up as the White Rabbit. He had designed *Far Horizons*. Dorothy regarded him as a genius and she included him in most of her affairs. She had plans for his talents in the future ... though not what he wished. His attentions were flatter-ing but it was irritating to have him constantly worshipping. He was sometimes useful as a confidant and she would vary her aloofness with the small gestures that he accepted as the limit of her affection. She had told him her mother was a permanent in-valid and a trial.

'Do see if you can persuade her to go upstairs, George.'

'I'll manage her,' he said cheerfully and she saw him bow, introduce himself and sit down. Mrs Orwell condescended. Shortly afterwards she moved through the ballroom on his arm, pausing only to lift a glass from a tray. Dorothy breathed more easily.

It was after midnight before the carriage guests were gone and the house guests settled. Dorothy waited for Penlynne's usual light tap on her door as he passed to his room. Twice she heard the muffled chiming of the grandfather clock in the hall. It was an Addison piece made for the Cape. On its painted face three merchant ships in a gale tick-tocked against Table Mountain. There! It was striking the quarter again! She checked an impulse to go down to the smoking room.

Penlynne had been constrained with her. Since the night he had been wounded he'd been reluctant to talk about the episode. At first he insisted he had fallen from his cycle. The wound was slight and he had come in with a handkerchief about it, rather pale and had poured a stiffish drink. That was unusual for him. Days later he admitted lightly, 'I believe I was shot at … yes, deliberately.'

'Where, for heaven's sake?'

'Just outside the lodge gates.'

'But why? Who would have done that?'

'Some disgruntled mine employee. I've been threatened before now. That trade union fellow … the Welshman. Owen Davyd.'

'You might have been killed.'

'It had occurred to me,' he smiled.

'Was it, do you think … political?'

'I don't think a Boer would have missed!'

'A warning … a threat?'

'That's possible.'

'Please don't keep these things from me again. I have a right to know.'

'Of course you have, my dear …'

There was his footstep now. She could hear him open the cabinet and the whirr of the mechanism as he reset the weights. She rose and half-opened the door.

'Still awake!' He was in an exalted mood, his dark cheeks flushed.

'Is Jameson still up?' she asked.

'No, he's turned in. The others are long gone.'

'What on earth have you been talking about?'

It had been the most extraordinary evening of Penlynne's life. The vivid little Scot had put a spell on his listeners, standing back to the fire, occasionally turning to deliver a kick to a dying log. His hearers were long stripped of jackets and collars, and the English sporting prints clouded in a haze of cigar smoke. It had all been unpremeditated. Or so it had seemed. Or had Jameson accepted their hospitality to gain Penlynne's private ear? There was no saying ... except that he had held them spellbound for hours.

Jameson was some ten years older than his host and Penlynne had seen his eyes moving over his possessions, neither critically nor enviously. More as if he had been appraising their value in terms of a catastrophe yet to come. Then he had asked for a copy of the new map of Africa by Stanfords of London.

'Look here,' he lectured. 'English influence is already as far north as the borders of the Congo Free State. Nyasaland's our Protectorate. Rhodes's Chartered Company is occupying a huge territory in what we're now calling British Central Africa. Forts are established at Salisbury in Mashonaland and at Bulawayo in Matabeleland. Bechuanaland will soon be a Protectorate. Indeed, there is only this obdurate old man in Pretoria blocking the way to the next map being printed red – from Cape Town to the Congo.'

He laid a ruler on the scale of miles. 'Damn near five thousand miles of unexploited territory ... an unending reservoir of labour that must learn to earn money and spend it on British manufactured goods. The Germans?' He turned grave.

'The Germans are already into all this territory along the southwestern coast from ... look at it! ... the 18th parallel south to the mouth of the Orange River. To the north they're in Tanganyika. Does it seem likely that England will allow Kruger to sit in Pretoria forever ... blocking our way!' His enthusiasm had risen, infecting his hearers. They gazed fascinated at the immense territory he was brushing with his hand ... almost casually, in gestures that dismissed the realities, the hazards of occupying and subduing it.

He seemed to Penlynne to sing down his nose. 'I believe it's our moral duty to develop that benighted land ... groaning under native tyrants with dangerous, unbroken armies thirsty for blood. Any blood. It is even more our duty to spread our civilizing influence there before Kruger. So far, gentlemen, there is nothing but our outposts ... a wagon road from the Limpopo River. Totally undeveloped ... teeming with game ... untapped mineral resources. *El Dorado*, my friends!'

Penlynne lay down and put his head on Dorothy's lap.

'I have had a profound experience,' he said. 'But one must see this in perspective. There is an element of the buccaneer in Starr Jameson that gives one pause. But my god, Dorothy! What is there to prevent it all happening? On the other hand ... why be reckless? Then again ... if we do not move to protect our interests and our future in Africa, we may lose everything.'

For some time he lay in silence, his fingers sliding from her flesh to the silk of her nightgown, quite unaware of its effect on her. He got up and strode about.

'There is a very real danger of Kruger introducing repressive legislation ... measures to prevent the *uitlanders* from buying up the whole country and ousting the Boer. I have no desire for political rights ... all I wish for is good, honest, intelligent government. I have always hoped that a better, more enlightened element would emerge. So far ... no sign of it. Jameson has urged me to go down to Cape Town and talk to Rhodes.'

'Is this known to others?'

'There are few secrets in this place.'

'Will you see Rhodes?'

'I should certainly incur the most virulent revenge from the Kruger regime. And perhaps justly. In any case, would I be wise to listen to his advice? I have always been my own man, Dorothy. Made my own decisions.' He stroked her hair. 'Rhodes is, after all, in competition with me. Why should I do him any favours? Except ... except those which are in my interest. One thing I will say, Dorothy ... I have come too far and flown too high to hand everything over to that old peasant in Pretoria.'

He looked splendid, standing in his purple robe. Like a Judaean king in a fragment of pottery she'd admired in the British Museum ... the same jutting beard, the same stance of authority. How far he has come, she thought. And I can match his ambitions all the way.

'Don't cut me out of your thinking,' she urged. 'I may have qualities you do not suspect.'

'I know your qualities,' he said admiringly and drew her into his embrace.

Chapter Five

Muriel Rawlinson had never managed to break the daily routine. She'd established it as Josiah's housekeeper. He was a man who rose at first light and wanted his shaving water standing hot at his hand. While she prepared his breakfast, she could hear the lick-lack of his razor whetting on the leather strop. Sometimes she fancied she still heard his heavy tread on the *stoep*, the crash of the flyscreen door. The man's presence was still here. The sprawl of the Star workings had grown around the house. Over there were the mine manager's new house in acres of lawn, with fruit trees and tennis courts and rows of semi-detached cottages for foremen artisans. Behind high iron fencing were compounds for the blacks. Muriel hardly heard the crash of shunting locomotives, the clang of blacksmith shops and the screech of machinery.

She was glad she had chosen to return to Langlaagte. At the Doornfontein mansion where he had died, the white servants had been dismissed. The house was locked up and the furniture sheeted until the matter of the estate was finalized. She had allowed life to contract. She had no sense of possessions. The title 'Lady Rawlinson' startled her and she would barely answer to it. She was getting a substantial cheque every month. It was an embarrassment. Often she had not cashed the last one. Her time with Josiah had been too short to acquire the need for high living. He had entertained little at home, and frugally at that. He was always scornful of the high style of Leonard Penlynne and particularly of Walter Gardiner with his French chef.

'Small eating and high thinking, Muriel!'

She looked forward to visits from Katherine and her children. Spencer was the image of his father. In Sarah she saw the likeness of Josiah's first wife ... her that died of the camp fever.

'Kathy,' she said one morning, picking away at the material of a garment she was making over. 'There's nae doubt that Josiah, your father, meant for you to inherit. And I've nae quarrel wi' that. I'd be well satisfied with this hoose and enought to keep it up.'

Katherine sent the children outside.

'What is it, lass?' the older woman said. 'Is all well at hame?' Katherine's eyes suddenly enlarged. She scattered tears furiously aside.

'It would not matter to Walter if I ceased to exist.'

'You're the mother of his bairns.'

The girl laughed scornfully. 'Yes, at least I have them.'

'Is it another woman?'

'There have always been other women.'

'What is it then? ... It isna money.'

'I'm no more than a piece of Rawlinson property to him. Dividing the estate has become an obsession. There are so many quarrels ... he has debts, frightening debts.'

'How can that be? Josiah complained he was the highest paid engineer he'd ever hired.'

'Gambling ... the stock exchange. Reckless investments. It's a nightmare.'

The older woman hesitated, then spoke quietly. 'He's been here, Kathy. Him and that Crawley. On at me to sign papers. I've no head for it and so far, I've agreed to naething. If it'll make it easier for you, Kathy ... I've never felt I've any right to it. I'll do as they ask.'

'No, please, do nothing without a lawyer. Let me find you a lawyer.' She threw her arms about the older woman and felt her hard body; the strength of years of domestic work, hands that had never recovered from the buckets of scalding water and the soda, the horny nails.

'Against your ain man, lass!' They laughed. The Scots woman grew sober. 'They're telling me your father made mistakes in his last years ... that there's no accounting for things he did ... papers missing, no records of this and that ... moneys transferred and can't be traced. He was unfit ... past it all.'

'I don't believe a word of it, Muriel. My father often told me he could carry every detail of his business in his head. No one could trip him up.'

The room shuddered. A locomotive clanked past, whistle screaming. They were changing shift at the No. 2 Shaft. A swarm of blanketed *kaffirs* straggled by, grey with rock dust, shouted on towards the gates of the compound by indunas in old military tunics. Teacups rattled. In the silence that followed, flies buzzed around the ceiling. A smell of sweat and dust penetrated the screen door, pungent and somehow disturbing. Katherine remembered her girlhood visit to Charles Warewood's estate in Sussex. Meadows and forest land, deep rotted leaves and the summer scents of mowing. Dust in her nostrils touched off a memory of unused rooms in Warewood, musty portraits in the gallery, endless corridors and a deep sense of things unchanged.

'I'm thinking of gaun hame,' she heard Muriel say, snapping a thread with her teeth.

'What ... to Scotland?' Katherine's dismay was evident.

'There's nae a monumental mason here fit to raise a stane to Josiah.' From a catalogue she pointed out a grim edifice in black granite. 'A proper mausoleum, shipped oot, stanes an' all.'

'When are you thinking of leaving?'

'Soon as I'm able ... there's the bottling.' They laughed.

'Josiah would never let the fruit lie on the ground, Kathy. And when I come back, they'll have it a' sorted out, the estate. These things only make for bad blood. I've nae ambitions to be a leddy.'

Katherine went out onto the back *stoep*. Muriel watched her gather her children to her skirts in a movement of possession. When she returned she took the older woman's hands.

'I shall miss you more than you can imagine.'

Emotion flowed between them. 'I have such a strong feeling,' Katherine said. 'If you go, you will never come back.' It had come over her like the touch of a cobweb across her face. She shivered. 'Must you go?'

'I've been dreaming these past nights,' said the older woman.

'Wait till it's all settled and we'll go together,' Katherine urged.

'I canna explain it, lass.' It was a dream of hedgerows white with hawthorn. She felt the wind that blew off the Irish Sea and came blustering over Arran and the isles, rain dappling the dark waters of the Firth of Clyde ... in over the Heads of Ayr, tangy and moist. She smelled kelp and heard the washing snapping and billowing on the green. It twisted strangely at the heart.

'I smell the May ... May blossom.' She lifted her head, her

severe features moved by some inner joy.

On the *stoep*, eddies of dry dust swirled. With the wind came the reek of cyanide tanks, bitter and squeezing at the nose and throat.

'I feel I maun go, Kathy.' She put out her hand to stroke the blonde head as the young woman lifted troubled brown eyes. 'It will come right,' she said.

Katherine shook her head. 'Oh, what a fool I was,' she said bitterly.

'Aye, you were nothing but a lass.'

The Indian Ocean port of Durban had increased in size and importance since Muriel Rawlinson last saw it. In 1881 most shipping lay outside, beyond the sand bar. Passengers and cargo came ashore by lighters. There were many sailing ships riding out there on the indigo swells. Muriel was to join the *Sydney Star* today. It lay alongside a stone dock with the green, tropical ridge of the Bluff above its masts. There was a brisk wind blowing off the slopes of the Berea ... a momentary illusion of the hills of Clydeside ... but this wind was hot and humid. Aye, she was a handsome ship. Brand new from the yards of Burns and MacIntyre, Clydeside. She had a black hull and white upperworks. Smoke lazed up from a red funnel. Winches were busy and hatches were taking in cargo of hides. A steady procession of Zulus were coming aboard, chanting under sacks of coal. Coal dust was blowing in gritty clouds. The decks stank of hides and wattlebark.

Muriel found her cabin an improvement on her last, fifteen years previously on Her Majesty's Troopship *Calcutta*, bound for South Africa with Rab, a trooper in the Inniskillings. They'd been five years in India. She was in her early twenties, with the lumpy figure of a servant woman. She'd been glad to get the life of the cantonment behind her. One good memory was the spreading banyan tree in the married quarters where the wives gossiped at sundown. The dry heat of the plains had soon faded the roses in her cheeks. Beyond the barracks and the parade ground there rose the walls of the native town with its bazaars, and its shuttered houses with peeling walls ... ochre, yellow and blue ... its sounds of jangling music and the crying of pi-dogs. The bugles and the shouted commands of the barracks came back to her with the gleam of brass and white paint.

Walter Gardiner had been courtesy itself when it came to goodbyes. 'Believe me, Lady Rawlinson, we shall have the estate all settled by the time you return ... these things take time.'

'I'm no' impatient,' she said briskly. When he called her 'lady' she always felt a note of mockery. She embraced Katherine's children with a wrenching sensation of loss. Beautiful bairns ... they'd never want for anything. Katherine's eyes were moist behind the veil.

From the deck Muriel watched them diminish, the children still waving. She was hardly at sea when she regretted her passage was booked in the name Rawlinson. She received deference due to her rank but was shrewdly aware of looks and whispered comment. Can that odd creature be the widow of Josiah Rawlinson? Is it true she's worth millions? It put her on her mettle to be herself; plain and unvarnished. She lapsed deliberately into her Scots brogue.

Away from Johannesburg and its pressures, she felt an unusual perceptiveness. As if she had been suddenly gifted with an instinct for coming events. Her mother had been fey – so it did not surprise her. She believed all Scots had the gift to some degree. She felt prompted to write a letter. The kind of letter that would be found among her personal things.

In the event of my death I want all my share of the estate to go to Katherine Gardiner, maiden name Rawlinson.

Things looked sharper. She wondered if it was the approach of fever. One thing that was not imagination was the odd set of the water level in the bath. Higher one side than the other. Water in the jug sloped too ... not much, but sufficient to be obvious.

'It's nothing unusual, ma'am,' said the taciturn stewardess.

Muriel accepted this. Something to do with the mysteries of ships. Then she heard talk of a passenger who'd left the ship in Durban. 'She's top heavy,' went the word. At Muriel's table the Second Officer snorted: 'A ship like this! Clyde-built with reciprocal quadruple-expansion engines. A speed of 13 knots. Passed A-1 by the Board of Trade, by Lloyds ... a 10,000 tonner carrying over 200 souls. Lifeboat accommodation for 660. Liferafts and lifebelts!'

Beneath them was the reassuring thudding of great engines. The thump of screws as the vessel, running into southerly winds, lifted her stern and buried her bows. Next evening in the lounge, while the orchestra dispensed light music, Muriel heard talk of difficulties in stowing the cargo, first at Sydney, and then at Durban. Coal had been stacked on the forward deck. Two hundred and fifty tons of it! Had Lady Rawlinson noticed how slow the ship was to recover from a roll? 'Sometimes, it looks as if she'll never come upright.' And why would a man who had paid passage to England leave the ship halfway home at Durban?

She liked to walk the deck, well-wrapped. It was mid-July. She had not forgotten how icy the winds could be, winds that swept up from the southern seas. Six thousand feet up in Johannesburg the same wind froze the fish pond. The dried autumn grass was stiff with frost till the sun rose. Sometimes at Langlaagte a dead *kaffir* had been found lying in the veld, stiff as salted fish. 'Tropicals,' Josiah told her. 'No stamina.' Then he had cursed the drink peddlers and the liquor canteens run by that Peruvian, Isadore Isaacs. It was on her return from an evening of whist on the third day out of Durban that Muriel had a strange experience. She entered her cabin to feel the presence of a woman with staring eyes and floating hair. She knew with sudden insight that she had drowned. The strange thing was that she felt no fear. She turned on the light. There was no one there. The wardrobe door was swinging on its hinges. It must have been her own image she had seen in the mirror. Her sense of apprehension, quickened by the talk at the tables, had created the presence.

The stewardess entered soon after and closed the steel shutter over the porthole. She was not disposed to answer questions. 'Nothing to worry about, ma'am. The weather's getting up … nothing unusual in these parts. Ring if you need me.'

Muriel composed herself to write to Katherine, intending to post it at Cape Town. The notepaper kept slipping across the desk and the inkwell was on the verge of spilling. She dated it July 14 and wrote only a few lines before it came to her that it was pointless to go on. The letter would never be posted. 'Well then,' she thought, 'that will take care of many problems.' No need to torment oneself with the sharing of Josiah's goods. Katherine would take care of Josiah's memorial. She picked up the pen again and signed the letter: *Your affectionate step-*

mother and friend. She had never presumed herself in that role. But now it seemed right. *You will find your happiness, never fear,* she added in the stiff, careful writing that betrayed her near-illiteracy. But even as she wrote she thought, 'There's nae joy in wealth … only anxiety.' Having sealed the envelope she put on her nightdress and said her prayers. The usual prayers … a pattering repetition of phrases learned in childhood. Other words kept creeping in. 'O, hear us when we cry to thee for those in peril on the sea.'

She lay composed, hands folded. In her practical mind repeating, 'there's naething a body can do ….'

At 8.24 p.m. *Sydney Star's* bridge logged: *Further shift of cargo in forward hold. Ship listing 30 degrees starboard. Speed reduced to 8 knots. Wind south-east approx 30 knots. Heavy swells following one another at half-minute intervals. Effort being made to relocate coal hampered by heavy seas.*

At 8.43 the officer noted: *Coal on forward deck shifted. Heavy seas breaking over starboard bow. Captain informed.*

At 9.27 *Sydney Star* laboured to the peak of an enormous hill of water that flashed its white crest at a level higher than the bridge windows. She shuddered and toppled forward. She slid down a glissade of black water, fathomless to those who felt her rushing descent. Ahead of her bows, the massive shape of another wave reared up, high as the mast top. *Sydney Star* ploughed her bows into the base of the rising mass. The immense crest curled downwards and fell on the vessel. The forward hatches tore away. A seething monster of water swallowed the ship. Her hull plunged deeper into the belly of the wave and the mast-top lights vanished.

At 9.28 the procession of waves continued. They passed as if nothing had been in their path: *Sydney Star's* last logged position was 330S by 280 53 E.

A month of rumours and almost daily new versions of the *Sydney Star's* disappearance had passed, each wilder than the last. Walter Gardiner arranged a meeting with Arthur Crawley and the company lawyer. Subject: the probability of Muriel Rawlinson's death. Both men were cheerful. They awaited the arrival of Advocate Armstrong. Crawley had all the press cuttings in order. Instability was the recurrent theme. There was also the unusual violence of the storm the day following the last reported sighting of the vessel. A deck chair washed ashore near the Bashee River mouth was reported. It was said to have the name of a passenger on it. A seaman reported seeing an explosion ... flames shooting high into the night sky, then suddenly blotted out. 'I believe her bunkers blew up ... she must have went down like a stone.' The mate of a coastal trader had logged what looked like floating bodies. 'Sharks in unusual numbers,' he noted.

Crawley received Armstrong with excessive politeness. It had always made Gardiner wary of the man. Armstrong would not be hustled. 'Gentlemen, I can't speak for Roman-Dutch law. And that is the law here.' He laid down an armful of legal works, slips of paper at relevant pages. 'In our law ... that is at home, if nothing is heard of a person for seven years, a presumption of death arises.'

'Seven years!' said Gardiner. 'What about here, man?'

'I understand that in Roman-Dutch law there is no fixed period. The missing person is not presumed dead. Death is not lightly accepted, gentlemen. There is a case on record of a person missing for thirty years. The court did not grant an order.' Armstrong seemed to relish the law's obstinacy.

Crawley looked bleakly at Gardiner.

'Must you be so pessimistic, Armstrong?'

'We might make application to the Supreme Court in Pretoria,' went on Armstrong. 'But as I say, gentlemen, a judge will require all the relevant facts. Given these, he might grant an order to presume Lady Rawlinson dead.'

'Damn it all, man ... we have no facts. Only rumours.'

'Exactly, gentlemen. Of course, had the vessel been seen to go down, the court might ... *might* agree that the probability of death was strong enough. But she simply disappeared.'

'What about an appeal to English law?'

'I looked into that, Mr Gardiner.'

'Well?'

'Lady Rawlinson was resident in the Transvaal ... only the Supreme Court here can make a pronouncement on the possibility of her death.'

'Make an application to the court, Armstrong,' insisted

Crawley, twisting away at the waxen tips of his moustaches.

'It will not succeed, Mr Crawley.'

'We may have definite proof by then.'

'Very well, gentlemen. I'm sorry I can offer so little encouragement.'

'The old bitch never did like me,' said Gardiner.

Chapter Six

Beneath the slowly churning fan Penlynne, shirt-sleeved, read the latest letter from Julius Wernher. It had come from London in the special bag marked for his personal and private information.

... in conversations with the Colonial Office, I learn that German economic penetration of the Transvaal is closely linked to Berlin's political ambitions in Southern Africa. The Kruger regime is more than sympathetic. You will be shocked, as I am, to learn that the Nederlands Railway Company's high tariffs are aimed at crippling the entry of British goods into the Transvaal. It is German-owned. The Dutch holding is a mere front. German banks, encouraged by the State, have majority holdings. We know now that the German interest in overseas investment is closely linked to territorial ambitions. The aim is to counter British trade interests. Lord Salisbury tells me that Berliner Handelsgeselschaft has invested several millions of marks in this railway system that is holding you to ransom. The total German investment in the Rand is already some 500 million marks. The German ambassador to England, Hatzfeld, told me with a smile that there are already some 15,000 Germans working in the Transvaal Republic.

Germany now holds 23.5 percent of the South African market. Up from a mere 14 percent two years ago. The bulk of it on the Rand.

Penlynne read the letter with a sense of confirmation. Wernher was not an alarmist. He had an uncanny gift for interpreting the monetary scene. He was kept informed by agents all over Europe. He was astute and level-headed ... much less a prey to his emotions than Penlynne. Ten years older than his partner in Johannesburg, Wernher was on intimate terms with the power-brokers on the Continent and in England. He was sounding the alarm.

He read on, almost reluctantly. *German banks, of course,*

adhere to the Gold Standard and have to admit the power of the Bank of England as the seat of the world's monetary stability. England's strength today is based on Rand gold ... from our mines, Leonard. If the Germans succeed in coercing the Boers, it will be German gold from the Rand that will dictate terms from Berlin. The effect on England will be cataclysmic. I have no doubt, and Salisbury has no doubt, that their ultimate intention is world economic domination – through the Rand's gold.

Penlynne walked to the window and looked out. It was a scene he thought of as a crossroads of the world. Strident, brash, cosmopolitan. Jostling with every kind of wheeled vehicle drawn by horse, ox or man. He had read recently that the new petrol-driven Daimler would function well at this altitude.

Across the glitter of unpainted metal roofs rose the growing dumps of mine rubble. Some were already higher than a two-storey building. From the north window he could see *Far Horizons'* copper-sheathed dome. The homes of men less wealthy were already encroaching on its isolation. At forty-three a man should have no doubts. Gardiner must go north without delay. Penlynne was not accustomed to being deflected from his purpose. He had a growing intolerance of time squandered. Impatiently he sent for the American.

'Sit down, Walter!' The flush of enthusiasm darkened his cheeks. He seemed to have cast off his desk-bound role and become the Penlynne of his twenties. 'Look here, it'll be months before you can presume Rawlinson's widow dead. You said you'd go north for me if the opportunity came. Here it is!'

Gardiner's heavy bulk was slumped in the green leather chair. He had deteriorated, Penlynne thought. Good living, the hospitality of his table, his penchant for French cuisine, rich sauces, the best wines of France and Germany ... to say nothing of his relentless pursuit of pleasure after dark in a city that offered much, all these had put the first marks of deterioration on the man. Skilled tailoring could not conceal it. He was tall enough to appear as powerful as before. And there was no denying the attraction of his person. His reputation as a mining engineer had never stood higher. He was the right man, indeed the only man Penlynne would trust with an exploratory mission to Lobengula's country. The Gardiner of five years ago would have jumped at it.

'Look here, Walter,' he urged. 'Not a day passes but I have evidence of German influences on Kruger ... word that they are looking to Lobengula's country. If they persuade the old savage to revoke his mining concessions to Rhodes in favour of German and Boer interests ... we are sunk. We shall have the enemy on our doorstep. All we've achieved will fall into German hands. There are forces at work against us, believe me.'

He held up Wernher's letter. The American said nothing.

'It's not just a matter of our own interests here, Walter. It's far bigger than that. It's the right of the fittest to rule ... that's the root of Rhodes's vision.'

'So you've seen him.'

'I had a meeting with him.'

'I had no idea you were such an idealist.'

'Maturity brings responsibility. One must have the wider view.'

'Forgive me if I'm cynical about that. I thought it was gold you were after up there.'

'The real gold is land, population, markets. The Germans know that.'

'Trousers, muskets and gin.'

'Crudely put.'

'I'm no missionary.'

'I'll put it bluntly, Walter.' Penlynne could feel his temper rising but he strove to remain persuasive. 'If the Huns prevail they will have everything ... including the Rand. It's them or us, Walter. It's either going to be unparalleled disaster or unparalleled opportunity; the greatest chance ever offered to you and me. Think of it ... that whole vast black and benighted continent. Look what you Americans achieved ... the great surge of energy and conquest. We began it here. We must see it through.'

'I didn't suspect you were such a patriot.'

'Patriotism be damned, man. This ... this ... all this! To hand it over.'

'It's the Boer's country ... speaking as an American.'

'What about the Rawlinson interests ... your own now?'

'Why don't you go yourself?' said Gardiner, red in the face.

'What's got into you, Walter?' We've been partners up to now ... achieved much.' He still attempted a conciliatory tone.

'True.'

76

'Walter?'

'It doesn't suit me to go now.'

Penlynne found his hand on the whiskey decanter was trembling, his fingers moist. 'I see,' he said, splashing liquor into two tumblers. 'It's a woman.' He said it with a whimsical twitch of the lip … one man to another.

'She must be rather special.'

'That's my business.'

'You'd only be gone two months … can't she keep?'

'You've said enough, Penlynne.'

'I respect your privacy.'

'Keep it that way.'

Then it surged out of Penlynne. 'It won't be private for long, Joh'burg being what it is.'

'You ought to know about that.' Gardiner extinguished his cigar in the whiskey and rose.

'What do you mean by that?' said Penlynne. And then he understood. He was thunderstruck. 'Kitty Loftus … she's taken up with you.'

'If it's any of your damned business.'

'Walter … listen to me. I'll admit her attractions. But I never allowed her to come between myself and opportunity. And when the time was right I put her aside as a mistake.' Looking at Walter's flushed face he wondered if what he saw there was what others had seen in his when he had been infatuated by the woman. What was it that got into a man's blood? She'd been like a drug. Her power to draw him back had been like some damnable sickness … at the end.

'Don't be a bloody fool, Walter.'

Gardiner's heart was pounding. Blood thundered in his ears. He wanted to smash the dark Levantine face with its swarthy good looks, the black curling beard concealing a hard mouth.

'I'm not going north for you, Penlynne … you can leave it to Rhodes or anyone else. I don't give a damn!'

'Walter … we're partners.'

'Go to hell!'

Penlynne sat on for some time among his papers, sick at heart. Correspondence from London and Paris demanded his attention as did board meetings, a luncheon, an urgent problem over surface rights on the West Rand. He could not fall out with

Walter at a time like this ... he was dismayed at the paralysis of will he had seen in the man. Yet he would not go crawling to him.

Walter Gardiner signed the documents which made him master of *Bloukoppen*, shook hands with Isadore Isaacs and called a cab. He had bought the house *voetstoots*, and sight unseen. He drove to it, his heart pounding with an excitement he had not experienced in years. He had imagined all that behind him. It had not been as easy as he thought. Kitty was no longer the disingenuous girl who had coloured up when he lifted his hat to her in the street ... way back when she was still with Penlynne.

'I'm broke,' she admitted the day he visited her in her hotel room which struck him, even as a man, as being tasteless. He had looked about him for evidence of patronage and could hardly keep his eyes off the bed as she toyed restlessly with a collection of Japanese dolls.

'I'm sorry to hear it, Kitty.' Attempting to sound concerned but not paternal, and conscious for the first time of his habit of sitting with his legs wide apart to accommodate the *embonpoint* his French chef encouraged. He had found her in her dressing-gown and barefooted, her mass of red hair pillow-loosened, and for a moment he had thought, 'Do I want her that much?'

'I was told it was a good investment ... turned out to be rubbish.'

'A mining venture ... shares? Too bad.'

He watched her, thinking how delightfully voluptuous she was. A little heavier since the bearing of Penlynne's child and her fine English skin touched by tiny lines at the corners of her eyes. 'You're looking wonderful. Better than ever.' He was waiting for her reserve to crumble but she sat on the chaise as if to compel him to remain where he was.

'I'd like to help you,' he offered casually.

She looked at him with those lustrous cat's eyes, shrewdly.

'I won't rush you ... think about it.'

She nodded, fingering the doll's kimono. He noticed then that it wore its hair geisha style. Did Kitty understand what it represented, the chalkwhite face? At the desk, on the way out, he asked for her account and paid it. He went out into bright sunlight, an exhilarating sense of possession in his stride.

The house was almost exactly the way he remembered it from

the days of Penlynne's parties. He went upstairs and examined the bedroom she'd used. There'd be suppers up here ... her nakedness in that setting, undressing her ... carrying her to this bed. He'd paid Isaacs a hefty price, the bold Jewish eyes probing, aware of his intention. Making the price hurt, shrugging: 'I only 'ad it six months ... it didn't suit me.'

'It's pricey.'

'That kind of 'ouse ... they don' come cheap.' The implication – a gentleman didn't quibble about price for a woman he fancied. 'All right ... I throw in the furniture ... cost a fortune.' Gardiner had no idea that Isaacs had bought the house for the same purpose. And for the same woman, and Isaacs had no idea that this man had the same idea. Had he known, he might not have sold so readily. But he was ready enough to accept that Kitty was one of the world's vulnerable women. He could not see her in the role of harlot. In the Cheapside alley where he had run as a barefoot boy, his father's pieties about loose women had prickled his mind.

He could not read Hebrew but his father's warning about the dart that pierced the liver stayed with him. It was only years later that he found the passage in the English translation and read it with a strange sense of excitement. *Come let us take our fill of love until the morning*. Then came that bit about the strange woman's lips...*that drop as an honeycomb* and the mouth smoother than oil and how she would catch a man by the hand. *I have perfumed my bed with myrrh, aloes and cinnamon*. All right, he could believe that about Kitty, but not that bit about the dart in the liver.

'Stop here!' Kitty Loftus gave the cabby twice what he asked, her hands shaking as she fumbled with silver. The Lithuanian grinned and looked her over with leering curiosity. 'So, sweet lady ... stories I could tell you yet from this house!'

In the hall she stood where she had first seen Dorothy Penlynne, the morning after the costume ball at the Wanderers, standing just there at the door of the music room. She had known then that Penlynne would put her aside; this woman would be too strong. Again she felt anger rising. She would make it hard for Walter Gardiner. 'It'll be on my terms,' she had told him.

'I accept that,' he said, sliding his arm about her. She had evaded him, drawing the brush through the heavy red hair, looking at him in the mirror as he withdrew, watching her.

'It'll have to be done over … refurnished.'

'Sure … whatever you want.' Again he approached her and leaning over her from behind raised her heavy breasts in his hands and put his face in her hair. 'You're a very beautiful woman … I always thought so.'

'You better go now … you 'ear!'

Flushed and breathing heavily, he accepted the order.

'Don't keep me waiting too long,' he said.

So now she was here again. She sat down on the stairs and loosened her hair, kicked off her shoes. With Penlynne it had been parties, music, wild gambling. Every moment filled with gaiety, gifts and flowers. Money of no account. Waste, extravagance. This time? 'I expect I'm a whore,' she thought. 'I never thought of myself that way but I reckon it's the truth, so if I'm a whore I'm going to have a whore's wages.' She'd give or deny as it suited her, reduce him to begging, pleadings, and at last … rage. No one would ever humiliate her again.

She walked slowly from room to room. She was not aware that the style of furnishings she had insisted on from Penlynne had been an echo of that house in Jermyn Street, London. Almost a copy of the ornate decoration; the rich, airless hangings, the pieces of statuary and the paintings that had shocked, the music, the rouged faces, and gleaming chandeliers. And upstairs, that bed. The mirrored ceiling where she'd wakened from a drugged sleep to see a naked woman staring at her from the ceiling. Blood on the sheets. Shocking but strangely pleasing, arousing senses she had never been aware of. Then … drugged and shipped out like a whore by de la Roche. Only one man had ever treated her decently. Stewart MacDonald. If he had taken to her, would she be sitting here now? A doctor's wife or a millionaire's tart? Some'd say she'd played her cards right. The cards she'd been dealt.

She turned to feel, rather than hear, footsteps on the stair carpet behind her, descending. He'd been drinking, she could see that. And he'd been waiting.

'You've kept me waiting a long time,' he said. He was pulling her against him, drawing her towards him with his hands

80

grasping her buttocks, bruisingly. 'I always meant to have you here ... on this carpet. Penlynne's precious Aubusson. I'm surprised he left it.'

'Not here,' she pleaded. 'I'm not to be handled any way you like.' She broke away. He knew he had gone too far but his eyes were like stones, burning stones.

He looked around at the furnishings, Penlynne's stuff, his anger growing as he walked from room to room. Instinctively she knew that he was sensitive to the opinion of his intimates.

'Everythings's to go!' He lifted the blackamoor with its gilded turban, inlaid eyes, ruby lips and grinning ivory teeth. It had never seemed so grotesque as now. He hurled it through the french doors onto the terrace. The head broke off and went rolling into a flower bed where the veld grasses were already contending with a tangle of roses. The lacquered black face stared up from among them.

Chapter Seven

Katherine Gardiner reined in the pony trap. It had taken an hour to reach the Klip River Valley where her father had put extensive acres under cultivation. The river was one of the 'white water' streams that gave the Wit Waters Rand its name. Bordered with young oaks and willows and green pastures it had been a favourite picnic place for Katherine and her father.

She had driven out of town to think things through, taking the old wagon track to Vereeniging, turning off along the stream at *Eikenhof*. She let the horse take its own pace.

The lands were hers by inheritance yet she had no sense of ownership. She felt drained of all sensation. Last night Walter had come to her bed in his liquor. She lay beneath his weight, crushed and revolted. She was aware these days of being irritated by trifles. She was either unnecessarily harsh or weak with her children, with Spencer in particular, either scolding or embracing him, tears in her eyes. She wandered about the great house in her gown, daring the maids to lift their eyes to hers.

Without being aware of it, she was experiencing the same sensations that as a girl in Kimberley had driven her to gallop her horses to a standstill and then to pull up, panting, under a thorn tree to gaze with a kind of dull anguish at the featureless landscape ... dust in her hair, her breasts sweating and between her thighs the wild sensation that shamed and nauseated but never satisfied. And now, in her marriage, there was a resurgence of the same rebellion of her flesh ... so intense that it was painful. As a girl her legs had been covered by floor-brushing garments, her breasts subdued and her hair drawn tightly back, knotted and pinned down. In this way she had learned to control her feelings.

Now, as she stood by the shallow stream, listening to its soothing fall of sound, she found herself unbuttoning her blouse to let wind and sun caress her breasts. Fronds of willow blew across her face. She shivered as if touched by an unseen hand. Her nipples rose, hard, involuntarily. She drove on along the broken track, charmed and soothed by the wildness, the unsubdued grasses.

There was more cultivation than she remembered. Suddenly she saw the old Boer house her father had given his farm manager. Around it was a maze of sub-divisions. It had all been broken up into small fields. How was it she knew nothing of the change? She sat in a state of barely controlled anger.

A young man appeared. He was short and thickset with vigorous black hair framing eyes the colour and shape of almonds. His arms and neck were dark with sun. He was astonished to see her, as she was to see him. He carried a hoe and was turning water from one furrow to the next, clear water purling over his broad feet.

'Good day, lady,' he said in Portuguese. She saw with inward shock that the blue shirt was open to the navel, that black hair rioted on his nakedness. She saw the knotted red rag at his throat, black with sweat. He pointed to the land. Young corn was rustling waist high, and beyond, on a rise, she saw the oblong whitewash of a windowless house and a scatter of hens.

She was seized with panic. It was almost as if he had reached out and touched her, intimately. Shame flooded her face as she turned the horse's head and set it back the way she had come, flogging it to go faster along the track. She was furious with herself, without knowing why, certain that he still stood there in the field, his thin ankles splashed with red mud, like blood run from a wound in his groin.

She challenged Walter that night.

'You didn't tell me you'd sold the Klip River farm.'

'I can't account to you for everything,' he returned mildly.

'I believe it's time you did.'

'You do not understand these matters,' he replied, talking as to a child.

'You have made sure that I have been kept uninformed. You … and Arthur Crawley.'

'Are you questioning my judgement, Katherine?'

'Why was the farm sold? What else has been sold?'

'It was necessary. I am not prepared to discuss my handling of the estate's affairs with you.' He saw that he had shocked her.

He became at once conciliatory, rising and putting an arm about her. She stiffened at the contact.

'I am going to insist on an accounting of your disposal of my property, of Spencer's inheritance. I am not a child, Walter.'

He smiled. 'You are in the eyes of the law.'

'I shall look into that,' she cried.

'Do ... by all means. It will only confirm what I say.'

'Are you saying you can fritter away my inheritance and there is nothing I can do about it?'

'I guess that's about the truth of it. But why take this attitude? Let me tell you something. Your father made mistakes in the last years of his life. He had this obsession about being his own man. Others were forming groups ... syndicates. Others saw that this damned reef here is going to take a brutal amount of capital to develop. And capital is not forthcoming. Europe won't touch us till we get a breakthrough. There are thousands idle ... you've seen it. The old days of easy pickings are gone. The deep level values are still low, damned low. It'll take fortunes to get a reasonable return for money.'

'So, you're selling off everything?'

'Disposing of worthless assets, yes.'

'The Star ... worthless?'

'It's played out. Oh, there are a few years in it yet but it's costing more than it's worth. Dammit Katherine, do you take me for a fool?'

'It's this new reef you've been talking about. You need money for that.'

His face for a moment turned almost visionary.

'I've assayed values there as high as 98.5 pennyweights. Unheard of! The Star's giving five pennyweights today. There's never been anything like this ... never. Of course I need capital. We'll raise half a million in ten pound shares. It'll be no problem once the news is out. It'll be the biggest boom yet ... anywhere. You'll see ten pound shares change hands at a hundred. So Crawley says ... Penlynne's not in it. He's lost his nerve.'

He laughed, getting very red in the face. 'Of course, we'll retain a substantial shareholding ... developers' rights. You'll be a very rich woman, Katherine.'

'I had sufficient ... more than sufficient.'

He began to shout. 'In a few years you'd have had nothing.

Goddammit, Katherine, don't question my judgement.' He regretted his outburst and shrugged. 'I admit finance is not my strong card, Katherine … that's Crawley's pigeon. Please trust me.'

'I seem to have no other alternative,' she said.

Later, as she walked in the garden, half-hearing her small daughter's chatter, she was aware that Walter was more disturbed than he knew. She did not question his knowledge. As a mining engineer he was the best. She did question his state of mind and Arthur Crawley's influence over him. She heard, almost as if he was actually there, her father's warning, 'Arthur Crawley's a snake but he has his uses. He does what he's told.'

She had forgotten the occasion but the words rang clear in her head. She paused at the end of the walk and sat down beneath the wisteria arbor, again conscious of the hot smell of freshly turned earth. She instantly dismissed the image it evoked; of bare feet in running water and the inexplicable churning in her loins, of the heat of the sun beating on her head and shoulders. Almost fainting, she saw Sarah come running with a fistful of mulberry leaves for her silkworms. She clasped the child to her fiercely, hardly hearing the cries of protest.

She had come to the end of her passive acceptance. Walter had to be challenged. There had to be some way to demand an account of moneys used … to challenge his misuse of it. She was realizing that she was as ignorant as her child … that she knew nothing of the terms of the marriage contract.

There had to be someone to whom she could turn.

Arthur Crawley rose from behind her father's desk, immaculate in frock coat and silk cravat, white carnation in buttonhole. It was a shock to see him behind her father's desk. The man was of slight build. His fair moustache was waxed at its tips. His blue eyes gave an impression of evasiveness. The portrait of her father was gone.

'See we are not disturbed,' Crawley was saying. 'Now, my dear Katherine.' He was evidently prepared for a confrontation but he was smoothness itself … small talk about wife and children, the rose show. Katherine felt her heart pounding.

'Mr Crawley, I have come to demand an accounting of my father's affairs.'

His lips turned back in a smile that showed a gold-capped tooth. 'Why, Katherine,' he said, 'the Chairman's Report is open to you ... to anyone. You are a major shareholder, you know we have nothing to conceal. Our affairs are regularly reported in the Press. Our shareholders attend meetings. We have their approval of our decisions.'

'Decisions I knew nothing of have been taken.'

'My dear, I am so pleased to see you taking an interest in your affairs. Until now, of course, your husband has seen to matters. You do know that we are forming a new company and liquidating Rawlinson Holdings.'

'I know nothing of it.'

'It has been in the pipeline for some time ... surely Walter told you?'

'Walter tells me nothing.'   •

She could feel herself trembling and knew that she had gone deathly pale but her anger was mounting. 'You are very well aware that this has been taking place behind my back.'

'With your husband's full approval.'

'Have I no rights in my affairs ... nothing to say about this dismantling of all my father created?'

'Your father was injudicious in his later years.'

'I don't believe it.'

Crawley smiled pityingly. 'There are auditor's reports going back, if you care to examine them, some six years. A legacy of disaster, my dear. I think an interview with the auditors would convince you ... and I must say, Katherine ...' in a voice softly chiding, 'that I am dismayed. Yes, dismayed. I stood at your father's right hand for many years, enjoyed his confidence. But he was a headstrong man ... a man of impulse.'

She knew there was some truth in that and knew that unless she resisted he would quickly overcome her. 'Mr Crawley, I shall insist on an examination of the company's affairs.' At that his face hardened. He opened a file at his hand.

'You were married in community, Katherine. Your father evidently believed that Mr Gardiner was a fit man to assist you with your affairs.'

'He did not foresee this.'

Crawley was forcing his eyes on her now. She had a sensation of paralysis. His voice was softly insistent, even soothing.

'Where husband and wife are married in community, the husband, by virtue of the *jus mariti*, can dispose of the estate without the consent of, and without consulting the wife in any way. That is the law.'

'I will not leave it at this,' she said in a voice she hardly recognized as her own.

'The law is the law,' he said with a smile. '*Loci contractur* ... the law of the place where the contract was made. And women, being the weaker vessel as the Scriptures remind us, are subject to their husbands.'

'You are saying that there is no way ... no way that I can have a say in my affairs.'

'The law is for your protection.'

She saw that he smiled no longer. He believed the law was just and reasonable. 'Of course ... if you were to be widowed there would be no conflict. Now, a cup of tea?' He had slipped into the role of pleasant host as easily as if there had been no tension. Talk turned to a garden party, a new rose he had cultivated.

'With your permission,' he smiled and coming round the desk he took her gloved hand. 'I would like to name it Mrs Walter Gardiner.'

'That would be most unsuitable,' she said coldly.

The mirror in the descending lift showed her a Katherine she did not know. Features stiff and drained of colour. Widowed? The possibility dismayed her only by its improbability. She came out into the glare of noon. Perhaps it was the crudity of the street and crowds of idle workmen, the dismaying atmosphere of an unfinished town that had lost its impetus, but she had an intuition of impending disaster.

Gardiner left a note to say he'd gone down to Durban. For weeks he had been cursing the delays. No progress had been made in the matter of the *Sydney Star's* disappearance. In West Street he spoke to an English businessman who had quit the ship there. He was a florid-faced, beefeating type on his way home from Australia, his passage to England fully paid. Gardiner met him in the Planter's Club. 'Bernard Partridge,' he heard. 'Importer of wattle bark.'

'Walter Gardiner ... engineer.'

'Yes,' said Partridge after a drink, 'I decided to leave her the

87

moment she came to port. Unstable! When she rolled, it was frightening, frightening. We had heavy winds all the way from Sydney and with that topheavy superstructure it was a nightmare.'

'What's your theory?'

'She turned turtle.'

'Why have searchers found nothing ... no debris?'

'I'm not a nervous man,' said Partridge, wiping his brow. 'It was the dreams that did it. I used to wake up in a cold sweat. I was always walking on the passenger deck. There were others there, playing games. Suddenly the sea would open ... and a man appear, waving his arms and shouting ... pointing at me, as if trying to tell me something. No one else saw him. I would make for the bridge to tell an officer ... but always, just when my foot was on the first step the figure would vanish. The captain laughed at me ... said I was not to alarm other passengers.'

'How often did you dream this?'

'Three nights in a row.'

'Do you think they'll find anything?'

'I watched her sail from here. They laughed at me when I left her. She was painted black. I never liked that.'

'Did you meet a Lady Rawlinson ... a Scotch woman?'

'I believe she got on at Durban. I never saw her.'

'She married my wife's father, Sir Josiah Rawlinson.'

'The mining magnate ... then of course you've good reason to want to know what happened.' He leaned forward, sweat gathering in the folds of his chin. 'May I advise you ... the shipping company will do its best to obscure the facts. I will be there, Mr Gardiner, at the Board of Trade Enquiry in London. I shall have something to tell their Lordships.'

'You were a lucky man,' said Gardiner, rising. He took a ricksha to the top of the Bluff and stood looking out to where *Sydney Star* had last been seen, dipping below the horizon, her smoke smudging sea and sky. It angered him that Katherine was one of those who would not accept that the ship had gone down. She grasped at every straw of rumour. When search vessels returned, she refused to accept that Muriel Rawlinson was dead with the rest of them. She insisted on sending a cheque for a hundred pounds, a public subscription, to charter another search vessel.

'What is the point of further delays, Katherine?'

'I love Muriel,' she said, passing him the cheque for his signature.

'You are doing it to get back at me,' he said, signing.

Charles Warewood had been coming to the house. Katherine had reason to think it was more than a social call ... though he never failed to ask after Walter. When she saw him coming up the drive, erect in the saddle, she made certain she was in the hall to meet him. He was in her thoughts more than she cared to admit. Sometimes she thought wildly, 'I'll take the children and live in the Park Lane house.' When she rose from her bath to warm towels and the sight of her body in the mirrored walls, she seemed to be observing a woman who never was. She would touch her breasts and find the nipples hard. As her mirror showed her the fullness of her hips and the blonde curl of hair on the *mons veneris*, she was almost certain of a man's hand on her ... sometimes so vividly that she would turn. In the heat of the bathroom, in the scented air and the languor of her senses, she longed to feel his arms go round her ... feel the hardness, the maleness of his embrace.

When she felt physical pain to match the pain in her heart, then she would call for her horse and ride hard over the veld, risking their necks over fences and dongas.

Once when Charles held her hand in a moment of mutual admission of what was happening, she almost fainted. When he turned away she understood that his sense of honour had prevailed. 'I expect you'll be glad to get away up north on this errand for Leonard Penlynne,' she cut at him.

'I'll be sorry to be away.'

'I find that hard to believe.'

'It will give me a chance to think,' he said. He was pale.

'Think?'

'Of us.'

He would have embraced her then had Mildred not entered. Katherine was in a fever for hours after. When she could stand it no longer she sat down and wrote him a note, asking him to meet her at the Eikenhof store. Mildred knew what she was going through. Her silence seemed to the distracted Katherine to be complicity, if not approval.

'No answer is required,' Katherine told her. He would turn up at the rendezvous. Or not. The night passed in a fever, in a state between sleeplessness and dreaming. Nothing need happen, she assured herself. All sensuality had fled from her mind. She was going to this thing with fear and trembling. As she rode she sweated, her leg crooked over the horn of the saddle. Midsummer heat rose suffocatingly from waist high grasses. The din of insects thrummed on her ears. Turn back, she kept hearing, but she rode on.

Below the last ridge lay the cultivated lands, the small river glinted among the willows. She saw red walls of adobe, and flat iron roofs pinned down with river stones. Smoke rose over a scene of rural simplicity. She heard the distant voices of children; black and Portuguese, a *kaffir* calling another from a distant hill, voices carrying. She felt as if she were riding to her execution. Her mouth was dry … dry as earth. She got down and drank thirstily; water cupped in her trembling hands spilled down her blouse. Her horse whinnied. She raised her head as Charles came riding towards her. She tried to rise but could not move, could only watch his approach. The water seemed to rush past with increasing speed and noise. Would she hear him if he spoke?

'Katherine!' He crossed the stream and tethered his horse in the shade. It was all going on with a kind of irreversible momentum. Every twig, leaf and thorn seemed to have a special sharpness and definition of its own. Charles came to her from behind, his arms going about her waist. He turned her towards him. She felt her knees give way and her mouth open. His hands were opening her blouse, finding her breast. Sensations never guessed at coursed through her. She was aware of the smell of him … of tobacco, gun oil and musk.

'Oh my sweet Katherine, my love,' he was crying. Again she heard the stream and the sharp tearing of grasses by their horses, the jingling of bits. In his mouth, tobacco and wine … words she could not put sense to. She felt a loosening of every fibre of her being. Grasping at the curls of his head, their cries … his and hers … were followed by a sudden darkness and then a quietness. The roots of a tree hurt against her naked back.

It had happened as she hoped. She was content.

Penlynne still used the letter book when writing to Julius Wernher in London. It made a copy. *For your information, J. I am thinking of increasing pecuniary assistance (without our name appearing as sponsors) to the National Union. It has been agitating in a feeble kind of way for constitutional reform. I think it deserves some support. And if it makes enough noise it will suit our purpose. I have taken some options to acquire a concession for tin in Swaziland. Some samples washed carry about 10 percent. The king's personal concession is the one the samples came from. So we have a friend there ....*

He turned to the door in irritation. 'What is it, Chilvers?'

His secretary entered, his face adjusted judiciously. The door opened and de la Roche pushed in.

'His Excellency, the Turkish Consul,' said Chilvers lamely.

De la Roche showed his teeth and offered his hand.

'To what am I indebted for this visit, Baron?'

'I will not deceive you.'

'That is very civil.'

'I am here to do you a favour.'

'That seems unlikely.'

'In these times one needs friends ... one needs to know that one's interests ... and one's life, are secure.' The man gave Penlynne a glance so peculiar that for an instant he relived that moment in the driveway, the whine of bullet off rock, the burning sensation across the hand. Involuntarily he covered the scar. It occurred to him that the man was an opium eater. Or more likely with the Turkish connection, a hashish smoker. Certainly he did not look normal.

'So you have come to offer me protection.' The last time he had spoken to this man had been in Bloukoppen when de la Roche turned up with Marloth ... the German explorer and the Turkish Consul. Turks were not so numerous on the Rand that they required consular protection.

'I have come to remind you that where our interests have coincided we have worked well, to our mutual advantage. I am empowered to offer you a substantial interest in cement. And I need hardly tell you what the future offers there.'

Penlynne needed a moment to grasp at the offer. The audacity of it took his breath away. So far the cement concession granted to this man had produced no cement. The factory erected was non-functional. What the devil was this?

'Your factory's concession is about to expire? Correct?' De la Roche nodded.

'It is only a front. What you sell comes from England. You put it into bags and increase the price five-fold to the mining industry. You know that my company has fought concessions tooth and nail. Dynamite to the German group ... transport to the Hollanders ... liquor to Lewis and Marks ... waterworks, electricity! The Transvaal runs on concessions to its friends ...'

'I agree ... a pernicious system, especially for those who do not hold concessions.' The man was all suavity and insolent confidence. 'I have applied for renewal of the cement concession ... costly ... but I'll get it.'

'How do I come into this?'

'This time we will have to produce cement.'

'That will be a novelty!'

De la Roche screwed a Turkish cigarette into its holder.

'Government wants your involvement, Penlynne.'

'Government has done everything in its power to obstruct me.'

'Government respects efficiency.'

'Why should Government suddenly decide to produce honest quality cement?'

'Government has use for it. Government will pay well.'

'You are saying that if I invest in your company there will be substantial, guaranteed contracts?'

'Correct.'

'Forgive me if I am wondering why you come to me and not one of my German or Dutch competitors. Surely being English is against me in this ... my antagonism to Government.'

'I will be frank. We ... Government ... the Boer cause, need friends.'

'Money buys friends?'

'Cement at a tenth of the price assures the mines of profits. You will never bring in the new deep levels, profitably, at today's prices. If you do not develop the deeps it is all over anyway! You know that. Gardiner must have warned you.' De la Roche rose coolly and poured himself a drink, sipped and commented on its quality.

'It was not made by Sammy Marks or Isadore Isaacs,' said

Penlynne dryly. They both laughed.

'Think about it, Penlynne. The concession is due for renewal a month from now.' De la Roche watched the ash fall from his cigarette. His kid leather boot ground it slowly into the Turkey carpet; his expression did not alter. 'There would be no objection to a new flotation with your holding at fifty-one percent.'

'You offer this to me ... why not Rhodes?'

'Rhodes has his interests ... his Imperial loyalties.'

'You are saying that such an offer would hardly deflect Rhodes from his ... shall we say ... particular ambitions. What do you know of my ambitions ... or where my loyalties stand?'

'To your company ... your interests and what you've made here.'

'The danger to my life you hinted at?'

De la Roche shrugged. 'You and I know that the smart thing is not to lose. There will be enormous developments in Transvaal in the next few years ... powerful elements involved.'

'Back the right horse, is that it?'

De la Roche left behind him an odour of cologne that irritated Penlynne. From the window he saw the man cross the street between rickshas and cabs. It came to him slowly that the man was out to protect his own interests ... would it be against the German group? Did their interests perhaps coincide? The sense of achievement and power the view always gave him seemed trivialized. He had been threatened. He had long been aware of forces marshalling against him but this abrupt confrontation was unexpected. He gulped at a glass of water. No one could say for certain what the next years would bring. He might see streets deserted, buildings shuttered and the sound of the stamp batteries silenced. He might see the street names in German. Damn it, he thought, I like Carl Marloth ... genial, ungrudging Carl. One of the better kind. 'I'm going out,' Penlynne told his secretary.

He found Walter at the long bar in his club. Walter Gardiner had always had a knack of dismissing apparent disaster with a kind of shrugging disclaimer. 'Look here, Walter,' he smiled. 'I spoke out of turn. If what I said seemed to imply criticism ... please accept my apology. You must do as you please.'

'Damn right I will,' said Gardiner but he took Penlynne's hand and leaned on him with an emotion that was either genuine or the result of an afternoon's drinking. It was hard to say with Gardiner but if he started to talk about his exploits on the purdah train from Rajahstan ... when he had a coachful of Hindu wives for a journey of eight hundred miles, then it would be all right.

Chapter Eight

Penlynne had been talking in a perfectly conversational way, without heightened expression. He sipped a cup of hot chocolate by the bedroom fire, his bare feet thrust out to the burning logs. Dorothy, completing her toilette, was noting, not for the first time, the signs of a premature maturity, even sadness, on the dark face.

'It is a distinct possibility,' he was saying, 'that when our appeals for justice and our demands for equal rights have been refused, they will force an occasion on us ... a provocation. I find it useful to have one of our companies selling them cement for fortifications.' He smiled.

'How on earth did that come about?'

'One has interests in many things. Not all of them to one's liking. As a matter of fact, we took shares in the company to prevent its being completely under the control of de la Roche. Actually, he made the offer.'

'How extraordinary.'

'I intend to make it public ... it was a bribe.'

'But whatever for?'

'To throw dust in my eyes ... to persuade me to turn a blind eye to what is going on. I shall accuse him directly of complicity in a Boer-German plot to oust British interests from Transvaal ... to ruin us.'

'Oh, my dear. Is that wise?'

'Not wise ... expedient.'

She was suddenly seized with a sensation of exaltation. The fire fell in. The bright glow enlivened the plaster relief of nymphs and fauns with a sensuous life she had barely noticed before. The figures, cold and remote as Grecian marbles, seemed to move and beckon ... join us while there is still time. His gown had fallen open and she saw the long-boned legs, thighs dark with hair. 'Like Esau, I am an hairy man,' he had once quoted. She bestrode him, aware of the power of this man as never before.

The Oracle was now in a two-storey building with imported presses and had a large share of the town's commercial printing as well as its advertising. Penlynne thought Steven Yeatsman still had more the look of an academic than the lean and hungry aspect of newspapermen. No doubt it was the Oxford background. Not yet thirty, he was already drawing his scanty blonde strands over a pink-domed head. Shirt-sleeved, he was busy with page proofs of the afternoon edition when Penlynne entered.

'I can't print this letter of yours, Mr Penlynne,' he said at once.

'You will print it, if you please, Stephen.'

'I would not be in this chair if I did not support your view, Mr Penlynne. I am all for the rights of the industry ... the *uitlander* cause, but this goes too far.'

'I believe I know what I'm doing, Stephen. The attack is justified.'

'Can we prove it?'

'It will find wide support.'

'But Mr Penlynne, you have directly accused Baron de la Roche, admittedly a more than somewhat shady character – but a man of powerful interests here.'

'Hand in glove with Government ... a monopolist ... corrupt.'

'Accused him of complicity in a plot to overthrow British interests in the Transvaal and beyond ... of being in league with powers abroad....'

'Germany ... Germany's imperial interests. The Colonial Office is most concerned.'

'Sir, the Anglo-German Colonial Agreement! Germany gave up many of her claims in East Africa in exchange for Heligoland ... a useless rock in the North Sea. The *Times* called it a striking demonstration of Germany's conciliation towards England ... even a purchase of goodwill.'

'Germany is looking elsewhere!' Penlynne saw by the bewildered look on Yeatsman's face that his editor wanted only reassurance. How could he explain to him that he had little to go on beyond his instincts and Wernher's letter. A man became very sharp when his interests and his life were threatened ... very sensitive to events and skilled at reading between the lines.

'The Germans and the Boers have one thing in common,

Stephen. Hatred of us. Through his concessions and monopolies, de la Roche has the ear of eager German industrialists. We know that. This article is to warn: we are onto your game!'

'We will be sued, Sir. Depend on it.'

'Print it, Yeatsman ... there's a good fellow.'

It had been a wet summer on the highveld. For miles around Johannesburg the veld was sodden by cloudbursts. Draft animals for sale were in a wretched condition, dying in scores. The Penlynne expedition to Rhodesia was taking an interminable time to equip. Penlynne thought it best to go fully prepared.

'Take firearms, gifts, liquor, tinned goods, sacks of meal and sugar, and medical supplies for dysentery, fever and ague.' Reports from the north said the Shasi River was still fordable. The trip had to be made now or abandoned until winter.

Walter Gardiner had come to respect Charles Warewood's judgement when it came to equipment. So the day the Englishman came to report the wagon road to Pretoria was impassable to oxen, Gardiner was ready to forget the whole thing. 'They're off-loading wagons at every drift, floating stuff across. At Six Mile Spruit they're floating wagons and swimming the bullocks and horses. It's a week's trek to Pretoria!'

'That about settles in then,' Gardiner said.

'I suggest we rail our supplies to Pretoria and take a Cape cart from there. We can get to the Sashi in two weeks going through Nylstroom and Warmbad, passing through the Waterberg ... over the Crocodile at the junction of the Notwani and into Bamangwato country.' Spoken like a soldier. His enthusiasm was shared by Penlynne.

'I wish I were going with you,' he said, almost wistfully.

'Charles ... I'd like a word with Walter.' Warewood went out.

'He's a good fellow,' Penlynne said.

'For an Englishman ... a lord.'

'He's the kind we need.'

'Katherine thinks well of him,' said Gardiner dryly.

'He's resigned his commission.'

'What does an out-of-work soldier do?'

Penlynne shrugged it aside, conscious of some unspoken friction. He handed Gardiner the printed proof of a letter. *'The Oracle's* to print this ... I'd like an opinion.'

Gardiner read and handed it back. 'Why man, that's a pretty outspoken piece. What proof have you? He won't take that lying down.'

'The man had the audacity to stand there and warn me my life was in danger.'

'A threat?'

'What else?'

'The German fraternity … there's muscle there.'

'There is also complicity.'

'Political dynamite, you realize that?'

'That's what I intend.'

'Reckless?'

'A calculated risk.'

'Burn it, Leonard. Unless you are prepared to go all the way.'

'I am.'

'You're saying there's Boer-German collusion to bar English ambitions in Africa … it's a reckless statement.'

'It's true … they're out to block our way.'

'You'll be sued for all you've got.'

'I'll risk that.'

'When did you make this decision?'

'When de la Roche came to offer me a controlling interest in the cement industry.'

'You've turned it down?'

'Certainly not … but I do know what it implied. I have been asked to take sides … to turn a blind eye to the Boer-German conspiracy.'

'This letter is to expose it.'

'To make public that we are not a pack of idiots … we are alert to the game.'

'Forget it.'

'And then what?'

'Take up the offer.' The American gave him a shrewd sidelong glance. 'If you haven't already done so.'

The writ for defamation was on Penlynne's desk within twenty-four hours.

'… my client the Baron Claude de la Roche, will claim that the article in *The Oracle* is calculated to bring him into hatred, ridicule or contempt … makes false imputations on his character and has damaged him in the sum of ten thousand sterling. Its slanderous accusations have caused him grievous injury in his personal esteem and public humiliation by reason of its false and unjustified assertions ...'

Stephen Yeatsman telephoned him almost simultaneously.

'This has certainly done it, Sir ... our own lawyer advises the only course is to compromise and pay. If it goes to court de la Roche will undoubtedly win his case and get full damages. *The Oracle* has not got ten thousand and I need hardly tell you what effect our losing the case would have to our cause ... to Rhodes. It will damage the British government and help Germany and Kruger.' There followed a long silence.

'Are you there, Mr Penlynne?' From the other end he heard a throaty laugh.

The man Penlynne called 'the estimable Esselyn' was methodically stuffing his yellow-stained meerschaum with the coarse black Magaliesberg *twak* he favoured above the adulterated blends of imported tobacco. He had never become part of Penlynn'e organization. 'Still holding onto your independence!' Penlynne used to twit him. He knew Esselyn for incorruptible in a profession that in Johannesburg swarmed with chancers, many of them unfamiliar with Roman-Dutch law. He was a tenacious lawyer with a flair for pulling out the unexpected and telling point and for having the last word.

'You haven't got a dog's chance in this case, my friend. I am not going to ask what on earth got into you ... I know you always have your reasons. But this is libel!' He shoved the newspaper cutting over to Penlynne. Yes, Penlynne thought, how remarkably libellous it does look in what is called 'cold print'.

'What are your instructions, Mr Penlynne?' Esselyn, mechanically stoking his furnace, sucking and drawing, and expectorating into the wastepaper basket.

'We will defend the suit ... oh yes. Let him have no doubt of that.'

'With what, pray?'

'With luck,' said Penlynne with a short laugh. 'Have we notice of what date the case is set down for?'

'Not yet ... he's expecting you to admit libel and talk settlement terms.'

'Tell him that it would be in his best interest to withdraw the suit.'

'He won't do that.'

'I know … but tell him. It will give him pause.'

'You mean,' smiled Esselyn taking advantage of long association, 'You mean, it will give you time to think of something and give him the impression that you have facts … strong facts, demonstrable facts. Preferably well documented. We have a few weeks before the sessions. And you may be sure that whoever is on the bench will not be impartial.'

In the course of the next few days Penlynne was to become aware that the article had not just stirred up murky waters but had created a climate of near panic in some quarters. On the share market prices fell. He was accused of using the matter for his financial advantage.

Wherever Penlynne went in town he was stopped. 'How does it look … the case?' Those hostile to his interests assured him he had 'put his foot in it this time'. He made cheerful, vague replies. Any arguments he had to make must be kept for his defence of the suit.

'De la Roche is suing us … suing the paper for defamation,' he told Dorothy.

'The letter?' She was aghast.

'A matter of ten thousand … the nerve of it. We shall fight, of course.'

'Can you prove your allegations?'

'Not sufficiently to satisfy a court … especially a court packed with his friends. I nearly said accomplices. It's what will come out that matters – or perhaps even more potently – what they will try to hush up at all costs. Indeed, I think he has been quite reckless in challenging me.'

'You expected this?' Accustomed as she was to the sudden twists, the feats of agility by which he escaped the apparent noose, the turning of defeat into victory by holding the hidden trump, she was apprehensive.

'It may force their hand.' His face fairly burned at the idea. 'Imagine Dottie … an end of Krugerism … an effective slam of the door on German ambitions.'

'You have no proof?'

'They cannot conceal their ambitions in open court.'

'Surely they know that?'

'De la Roche is impulsive … some think a little mad. There is a rumour that he has, shall we call it, the same extravagant turn of mind as Randolph Churchill. And for the same reason, if you'll forgive me.'

'A man like that to have so much influence!'

'Kings have been crazy before today.'

'I believe you don't despise him.'

'Should I? If I despised everyone who deserves it in this town I'd have precious few people to deal with. It's all a game, Dottie, and he plays it well. But I shall bring him down with this one, if he persists.'

He rose, and coming to her side, kissed her. 'Don't wait up for me.' It was going to be one of those nights when sleep fled till the first streaks of dawn and he woke in his chaise.

'I am glad you spoke out.' Dorothy looked splendid standing there in the stately room she had created with his money. She had become indispensable.

'Thank you for that, my dear.'

'I believe I may be pregnant again,' she said quietly.

He crossed the room and put his arms about her. 'This time we must be very careful. I think perhaps it is time to take a place in the Cape. St James, near Muizenberg. It looks across False Bay to the Hottentots Holland range. The same scoured mountains as one sees in Greece … and an astonishing sea. You'd have tranquillity there.'

'And die of boredom.'

'There must be no undue exertion … no uncalled for excitements.'

She burst out laughing. 'Are you serious … in this household.'

'Rhodes has a cottage there.' He said it as an afterthought but it sounded significant to the woman. Penlynne never did anything without a purpose.

A son? Yes, he still hoped for a son by Dorothy. The child of his maturity. He had not yet reached the point where he could honestly say that all this had been for an heir. Wealth had been its own incentive. It had given him authority. He had tasted the pleasure of power over other men. If, from head and shoulders above the ruck one saw a wider landscape, the distant mountains loomed more menacing. For a long time he sat inactive at his desk. What if Dorothy's child were not a boy? Suppose there were no other male of his blood than Kitty's child? He winced at the word 'bastard'. It was true, nonetheless. Dorothy had said: 'He will have a claim on you. Did you not think of that?'

These days he thought of his affair with Kitty not so much with dismay as with disbelief. Had it really happened? How had something which had been so compulsive, so irresistible, become so remote? At the height of his infatuation he had seen her in every woman. She was always hovering in his thoughts. It had delighted him to please her. How could one feel so distanced from such a passion? It might never have existed.

The boy was real. He had left it to Kitty. There was nothing unusual in Europe about the child of a demi-mondaine being suckled by a countrywoman. Rural England was no stranger to gentlemen's bastards being kept in ignorance and squalor by some slattern peasant for a few shillings a week.

He groaned inwardly. Something would have to be done about the boy.

'For God's sake,' he said aloud, 'I don't even know his name.' The thought of his son being brought up in squalor and ignorance was repulsive. Bastard children were no rare thing in Johannesburg. Blue-eyed blonde children clutching at the skirts of coloured women. It still jolted him. Even after so many years on the diggings. What became of them? What would become of the black children sired on white women? No wonder the Boers looked on in disgust.

How many men with whom he dealt were patrons of the ladies of 'Frenchfontein'. Every house in an area of eight city blocks was bedecked with half-dressed females, soliciting from windows and verandahs. They left their calling cards in bars ... some brazenly advertising their specialities; some as prim as the vicar's wife. Already there was a movement among churchmen and the authorities in Pretoria to eradicate what *The Standard and Diggers News* called 'this open sore'. No decent woman was safe in that part of the town bounded by Bree and Anderson Streets in the north and south and Kruis and Sauer in the east and west.

Why this rush of moral censure, he asked himself? It is because your possessions and your integrity are threatened by a man who began his public career in Johannesburg by pimping for an establishment still run by the town's most notorious madame, Mrs Henrietta Brisbane. For God's sake, the man could be laughed out of court!

In her cold, south-facing room overlooking the coachyard, stables and servants' quarters Mrs Orwell had made a decision. She was not going to suffer further humiliation at the hands of Dorothy. She would not be allowed to appear at dinner again tonight. Her room was cramped. 'A maid's room!' It had a dormer window and low ceiling at the end of a long passage and steep wooden stairway. It was uncarpeted. All around were water tanks and cisterns. She had had better quarters before ... on the second floor, but Dorothy had found it too accessible to servants ready to supply her mother with liquor.

Sometimes Robert came up to see her and she would plead with him to soften his sister. The young man frequently found her in a peculiar state of vagueness, her eyes enlarged and her speech ponderous. 'Where are you getting it, mother?' he pleaded.

'I have not the slightest idea ... to what you are alluding.' Alluding was a word she used with unfortunate vocal complications. Often he found her in her dressing gown. There were times when she hurled trays of food down into the stableyard, appearing at the window wild-haired and vociferous to the considerable amusement of Zulu grooms.

She wrote notes to her daughter and pressed them on the servants. 'Take this to your mistress at once!' The white maids who changed her linen and carried off her laundry and chamber knew better than face Mrs Penlynne with demands from 'that daft old biddy'.

Mrs Orwell always knew when there was a dinner party. The door to the stairway was locked. She longed to be allowed down to the company to regale Dorothy's guests with stories of the past. She had known everyone who counted in Kimberley. Barnato was a koppie walloper buying stolen diamonds. Rhodes ran an ice factory in a tin shanty and Penlynne was nothing better than a common digger who'd failed to make a strike. These were things they'd all like to forget.

It was growing dark. From the high window she could see the arrival of carriages and hear the clatter in the yard. Robert had promised to come up ... so handsome in evening clothes. 'Yes, I'll bring you something, mother ... just this once.'

Presently she heard the key in the lock. Robert appeared in his dark suit ... an echo of his father at that age. He sat down reluctantly, noting the open wardrobe and scattered garments. She was rummaging among her toilet articles for some piece of jewellery still unbartered for liquor ... finding nothing. A clink of empties.

'You may tell my daughter that mother will be down for dinner. I know the company will be pleased to meet Mrs Penlynne's mother at last. Questions have been asked, you know, and I have had invitations to *soirees* from numerous quarters. I don't seem to find my blue silk ... the one I wore to the governor's ball. I think they will recognize a lady when they see one.'

She was becoming increasingly irascible as she hunted. Pins fell out of her hair. 'Go down,' she panted, 'and tell your sister to come upstairs at once ... and to bring my blue silk.'

'I'll tell her, mother,' he said, glad to escape. Mrs Orwell sat down with regal dignity, holding her head up. Her mouth quivered and the thin hands gripped the chair to prevent their shaking. It grew dark. Robert did not return. Dorothy did not come up with the blue silk. She went down the passage and tried the door. She beat on it. No one came. She returned to her room and unscrewed the top of the paraffin lamp, splashed oil on the curtains and searched for matches. They'd open the door soon enough when the curtains were on fire. See if they kept her locked in after that!

Walter Gardiner had not expected the request. 'A favour, Walter,' Penlynne said as they knocked the balls about on the snooker table before dinner. 'I'd like you to take Dorothy's brother along with you ... up there. He's a personable youngster but doesn't know what he wants at this stage. Dorothy's not too keen to have him knocking about town ... if you take my point. My wife believes he has a certain sensibility ... I think he needs a bit of roughing up. Make him sweat a bit. I'll find something for him if he shapes up.'

Gardiner eyed the scowling young man. 'I hear you want to come north with me.'

'It's Leonard's idea,' Robert replied, lifting his coattails to the fireplace, a touch of mockery about the corners of his mouth.

'What have you done?'

'I had a shot at chicken farming … the brutes all died.'

'I expect you did it from the *stoep*.'

'It wasn't my ideal.'

'What is your idea?'

'I'm looking around.'

'How old are you?'

'Twenty-two.'

'Rhodes was a millionaire at twenty-one.'

Robert flushed and looked away.

'I hear you like life in Johannesburg.'

'Did Dorothy tell you that? I rather think it's my business, don't you?'

'Can you shoot?'

'Of course.'

'Get yourself kitted out.'

'I didn't say I was going.' He was swinging a signet ring at the end of his watch chain.

'Frankly, boy, I don't give a damn what you do,' said Gardiner.

Dorothy's dinner party was by way of a farewell to Gardiner and Lord Charles. It was smaller and less formal than usual.

'Almost family,' she joked as the footmen served lobster Newberg. An excellent chilled Johannisberger foamed into cut glass. She looked radiant. The food and wine had been served faultlessly. She had seated Lord Charles with Katherine Gardiner and noted his attentiveness, the sidelong glances she sometimes stole at him and the sharing of some private joke. Gardiner paid his wife no attention. He was in high form, full of amusing stories and constantly signalling for the replenishing of his glass. Some of his stories were verging on the risque.

To keep the conversation elevated was Dorothy's concern … to keep the mining camp out! She was usually able to persuade herself that beyond these walls, the rich hangings and the glow of rosy light on glass, silver and exquisite napery there was a city worthy of *Far Horizons*. And not as it was, a crude and often disgusting town. She watched Robert with a calculating eye. He was already flushed. She signalled the butler with a look. Pay less attention to Mr Robert's glass.

Mary MacDonald, the doctor's wife, looked frequently across the table at her husband and drank only Vichy water; she seemed uneasy away from her husband's side and unaccustomed to the array of cutlery. But she was a sweet young woman and she had agreed to sing Scots ballads later on. 'Songs of Mrs MacDonald's native heath,' said Dorothy, somewhat unctuously. She managed to have a few words with Stewart MacDonald who looked frequently at his watch and eventually excused himself, going round the table to kiss his wife. Not a woman at the table but felt the unselfconscious charm of the act. Mary bent her head in confusion, then looked up at him, her eyes suddenly brilliant.

Conversation languished ... dread of every hostess.

It was a silence measurably and nervously prolonged, as if each person at the table was taking stock of a life partner and finding the other inadequate. 'An angel passing by,' said Dorothy and was about to assume command when Robert laughed out loud. He held out his glass to the butler with a gesture not unlike his sister's.

'Talking of angels ... the burgundy please, Henry ... I saw one today. A most stunning woman. Like something out of that painting by Tintoretto in the hall ... the *Anunciation*, I think. She was getting out of her carriage.'

'Some trouble with her wings, perhaps,' said Penlynne winking broadly.

'No, with the footman ... a clumsy brute. A German. It was bright yellow and so highly varnished you could see your face in it ... not the German ... the carriage. The man was slow about letting down the step.'

'So you stepped up smartly and let it down!'

Laughter and expectation of more.

'Yes, I handed her down.'

'Did she wear gloves?'

'Of course ... lilac. I think they were lilac. She rather took my breath away.'

'She'd probably have taken your money as well if you'd given her half a chance,' said Penlynne gaily, ignoring a glance from Dorothy. The dinner was going well. Tomorrow they'd be off to the north. He had drunk more than usual and for the moment the old illusions were restored. He was still young ... no one could injure him.

'She thanked me,' Robert persisted, 'and asked me to visit her some time.'

'Visit!' said Gardiner with sudden loudness.

'At her house … she had quite amazing red hair. She seemed to know where I lived.'

'That is enough, please Robert,' said Dorothy. Suddenly the atmosphere was icy and deathly silent, as if there was no way of postponing the inevitable. 'I think,' said Dorothy rising, 'it is time for the ladies to withdraw.'

Gardiner had pushed back his chair, his eyes fixed on the young man who rushed on unconscious of the hiatus. 'And what was this lady's name?' demanded the American.

'I don't know … I didn't ask. She said she lived at … *Bloukoppen*.' He broke off, his tipsy enthusiasm slowly chilling. All at once he seemed to be sitting at the table, alone. Mary MacDonald's voice came faintly from the music room. Robert got up and pushed open the french doors. The cold air would refresh him, he thought. Perspiration was icy on his brow. Gardiner had looked as if he would like to kill him. Dorothy had gone white and Penlynne's gaiety had evaporated. Christ! It must have been some clanger!

How long he remained outside he could not have said. Part of his thoughts were with the pressure of the woman's hand as he handed her down; and the invitation of her smile, as if it had been kept especially for him. But another part of his mind was grappling feebly with his failure to do anything effective. Even the clothes on his back were courtesy of his brother-in-law. He had gambling debts that were going to catch up with him and Penlynne would have to pay. He leaned against the terrace wall, his back to the town lights and looked up at the great stone house. What now? Gardiner would never take him on the expedition.

Something above caught his eye. For a moment he could not believe what he was seeing. A woman was standing at the window, three storeys high, her arms upright in the sheath of flame. The room behind her had turned scarlet.

In the moment of paralysis he seemed to be seeing some kind of religious effigy. The curtains she clutched at disintegrated around her and as they fell, the fire suddenly roared out from shattered panes of glass. He could hear the tinkle of fragments on the bricked yard. Grooms suddenly ran out shouting.

Drivers of visiting carriages were running to calm their horses.

Robert stood. He was dimly aware that no one inside the house knew what was happening. His mother's room was up a back stair and facing the courtyard. At that moment the front door opened. The Penlynnes were taking leave of their guests. He ran towards them, aware of startling white dress shirts. The group on the steps seemed to freeze into a tableau.

Penlynne ran forward and instantly took command. Someone pointed. A woman screamed. The figure in the window aperture toppled forward ... falling like a bird in a veld fire. The thump of her fall on the bricked yard was hideous. Robert knew he was seeing something he would never eradicate from his inner eye ... yet, curiously, he did not see it as his mother ... merely a scorched creature writhing among the glowing embers of grass roots to be killed with a pitying blow. He began to run ...

Chapter Nine

The Press had spoken respectfully of 'the shocking accident at *Far Horizons* ... tragic death ... mother of popular hostess.' Dorothy read the accounts with relief. No one had suggested that Mrs Orwell had been confined. An accident ... the spilling of an oil lamp.

Robert had come to her, very pale and tense.

'Compose yourself,' she said. 'No one is to blame.'

'She asked me again and again to take her away. But how could I? What could I have done? You might have let her come down. That would have been enough for her.'

'That was impossible ... you know her habit.'

'Just now and then ... would that have hurt you?'

'She should never have left Kimberley. I didn't invite her.'

'Or me,' he said bitterly.

'You will have to make something of your life, Robbie,' she said, not without feeling for him.

'I'm not like you, Dottie ... you've always had such go. Everything I touch seems to fall apart ... school ... dentistry ... the chicken farm. I thought of editing father's notes on Cape flora. I'm keen on that. I've some notes of my own ... and sketches.'

She saw that the loss of his mother, whatever their relationship, had left him with a sense of being painfully severed – not so much from a tyranny, as from a feeling of being of worth to someone. She had always assured him he was a gentleman.

'Show me your sketches,' he heard his sister say.

'They're not awfully good.'

They were good. Actually very good. Dorothy was pleased enough to take him to the library where she and Penlynne had begun a collection of rare books, mostly European. She unlocked a case.

'You should look at these ... *Specimens of the Flora of South Africa, by A Lady*.' He was charmed. His comments were informed. Good heavens, she thought. He has talent after all.

'I shall do birds, too,' he enthused, 'and grasses.'

How strange, she thought. It had taken the ghastly death of their mother to discover her brother's tastes matched her own. Suppose she were to send him to Europe to be trained? He was really quite a prepossessing young man, slender, with fine eyes and a sensitive mouth, the soft beginnings of moustache. It would fulfil something in herself. She had already begun to collect pictures for the city art gallery that was to come. A nucleus of what would be The Dorothy Penlynne Bequest. She had never shown these to Robert. It had simply never occurred to her that he would find them interesting.

Robert found no merit in them. 'Why did you buy that ... particularly?' he queried, looking at a painting of the storming of the Bastille. Women with bursting bodices and burning eyes, the glint of steel in their hands.

'The spirit of it!' she exclaimed, a little miffed.

'It's old-fashioned.'

'It cost five hundred guineas.'

That would have cleared my gambling debts, he thought.

'I think I could get you a place in the Kensington School of Art ... my friend Mr Bourne-Jones would put in a word. Does that appeal to you?'

'I like Johannesburg.' He walked to the window with a possessive swagger.

'I hope you're not taking up with that woman.'

'What woman?'

'You know perfectly well.'

'I don't know what you're talking about.'

'Thompson tells me the gig has been out till all hours.'

'Good lord ... what a liar,' he said uneasily.

'People are not blind, Robert. As long as you live here you must consider our position in society ... my husband's reputation. And mine. This is a vicious, small-minded town. Besides, you must think of the girl you will marry one day. There are grave risks, Robert. She is a loose woman.'

'I'm not a child,' he flared.

'Promise me you'll not see her again.'

'I can't do that, Dorothy ... have a heart.'

'Are you aware she is a kept woman? How else do you think

she maintains a house like that?'

'I really don't care,' he said defiantly.

'It does not bother you that Mr Gardiner is her patron?'

'Gardiner? I had no idea.'

'Keep away from her, Robert.'

'I run my own life, Dorothy.'

She had turned pale. 'Not while you are under my roof.'

'I say, shall I fetch your smelling salts?'

'I am perfectly composed.'

'I'll get out if you like.'

'And where to ... may I ask?'

'Take a room. I'm sick of being ordered about.'

She had the last word. 'If it comes to living by your wits, Robert, you won't survive long in Johannesburg.'

The first time he had visited Kitty she had been rather formal. Tea had been served. 'I wondered if you really meant it ... about my coming to see you,' he ventured, balancing his teacup.

'One lump or two,' she said in the accents of Mrs Osborne.

'I hope you did not think me too forward, Robert. Have you lived long in Johannesburg ... I mean, I have not seen you at the races or the theatre.'

'Mr Penlynne's my brother-in-law ... I'm living at his place.'

'I know,' she said primly. The teacup spilled into his saucer. She reached for it ... their hands collided.

'I'm so clumsy,' he said. The scent of her hair almost suffocated him.

'Not your fault, I'm sure ... clumsy of me.' They sat silent.

'Do you like music?' Rising, she took his hand and led him to the music room.

'Do you play?' he asked, taken aback by the Steinway grand and the gilt chairs, the huge mirror that threw him back at himself ... pale and ineffectual, he thought.

'No, I sing,' she laughed. 'I thought mebbe you play. You've got artist's hands. I always say you can tell by the hands ... right off, don't you think?' She took his hand and turned it palm up, studied it intently, her head bent forward. He could see the swell of her breasts and again the scent of her came at him, overwhelmingly. Her cool fingers traced the palm lines.

'You got a good life line ... but I don't see money here. A lot of broken hearts ... oh yes, plenty of them.'

He was delighted by the flattery. 'That's very clever, Miss Loftus.'

'My friends call me Kitty.'

At the door she held out her hand. 'Please come again some time. I'm on me own at present.'

He turned at the foot of the drive but she had gone inside. He stood looking at the closed door, his heart hammering. My God, he thought, I'm in love.

The second time he arrived unannounced. She kept him waiting some time before making an appearance. She was cold.

'I've tickets for the circus,' he said. 'I thought you might like to come with me.'

'No thanks,' she said. She didn't offer tea and he left reluctantly. He had not so much as touched her hand. She was in a loose gown, her hair on her shoulders, as if she had just been wakened from sleep. He had a horrible feeling that she was not alone. As he mounted he saw the blur of her at a window and raised his hand. She waved back and his spirits soared. He went straight to the Barnato Bank, took a loan of fifty pounds and bought shares to the value of five hundred from a broker selling over the chains at Simmonds Street. Two hours later he sold them with a profit of a hundred and eighty.

Intoxicated by his success ... he had not so much as seen the script, he sent a bottle of French champagne and a bouquet to *Bloukoppen*. It had been easy. So easy. Penlynne could teach him nothing.

With his luck in he walked to a house in Ophir Street and knocked on the shutters. He asked for Idel Judelsohn. Dark, aggressive, about his own age, Judelsohn admitted him to a game of blackjack. The players had been at it all night by the look of them. 'I'm locking up,' Judelsohn said with a bleary yawn. 'Come back tonight and I'll fix you up with a game and some sport if you fancy it.'

There was a calculating glint in his eyes that he concealed by a grin ... an expansive wave of the hand. 'No limit here.'

Robert was dressing for dinner when Penlynne knocked and came in. 'I've found something for you, Robert. I want someone I can trust to keep an eye on things in Pretoria ... you'd learn the cement business and make reports to me.'

112

'I don't know much about cement, Leonard.'

'You'll learn. You shall have a hundred a month … more when you're useful.'

There was no refusing. 'When would I have to start?'

'At once.'

'I'll think it over.'

'It's settled!'

From Dorothy's expression at dinner he saw that she was behind it. He ate smoked Scotch salmon and a pheasant pâté. With a sullen expression gulping at a Chateau Mouton '79.

'That's no way to drink good wine, Robert,' Penlynne reproved. Robert left the table in a sulk and took a cab to Ophir Street. By the time he left he had run up a debt of over a hundred.

'No trouble,' he was assured by Idel Judelsohn. 'Better luck next time.' Robert turned away thinking: he's not a bad sort, really. They say the Judelsohns … Idel, his brother Simon and their father … are pretty hard but he took my note of hand without question. They know a gentleman when they see one.

As the door was shuttered behind him Idel Judelsohn grinned wolfishly. 'Know who that pigeon is … Leonard Penlynne's brother-in-law. Give him plenty of rope … much as he wants.'

Robert got down from a cab at *Bloukoppen*.

'Where have you been?' Kitty reproached. 'I got your flowers. Ta very much. Come in then. I've a friend here but he's going now. Issy … this is my friend Robert I was telling you about.' Her hand was plump and warm as she led him to a small man with heavily Semitic features. He was really quite startling in his ugliness. He looked at Robert without a flicker of expression.

'E's going to draw me, Issy,' Kitty said. 'Isn't that right, Robbie?'

'If it's any good I'll buy it for my saloon.'

She pouted. 'See how good he is, Robbie.'

'*Missugah*, you mean.' Isadore Isaacs took his leave.

'Who's he?' said the boy jealously.

'He's my friend … my best friend. He's the only decent man I know. He'd do anything for me but I won't let 'im. He's got to find himself a nice Jewish girl … that's what I tell him. He's a Londoner … same as me.' She came at him. 'You're jealous, aren't you?'

'Certainly not.'

'Oh, go on! You are.' Brushing against him. 'You will draw me, won't you. I'll sit ever so still and won't say a word. Tomorrow. Meantime, sit here. Beside me.' Patting the couch. 'You're really a very goodlooking boy. Did you know that? Will I do for a picture … I mean, a proper one with oil paints?'

She seemed to have fallen back on the couch, her lips slightly parted, her eyes on him were greenly vacant. 'I can't seem to breeve,' she said. 'Loosen me, Robbie.' Against the fallen swirl of titian hair the whiteness of her neck ran downwards to the rising swell of her breasts. His hands were shaking.

'There!' she sighed as her breasts burst from confinement. 'Kiss them Robbie … kiss them.'

Later he heard her murmur, 'undress me, love.'

'There are hooks and things.'

'Shall I 'elp you?' she mocked, taking his hand and guiding it among the garments to encounter the textures of soft materials, obstructions of stiffening and then a smoothness unimaginable. A sudden encounter with the flesh of her inner thigh … his fingers seemed to penetrate a hot, wet territory of coiling hair and parting flesh. Her hands were unbuttoning him. In a daze he heard her admonition, 'don't come now.'

That was the first night he did not go back to *Far Horizons*.

'Stay … stay,' she urged him in the morning.

'Dorothy will go mad.'

'Fuck Dorothy!' Reaching out to him from the bed's disorder. 'Stay wiv me, Robbie … you don't know what it's like by me'self. It's bloody awful knowing he's coming back.'

'I don't want to hear about it.' He dressed and went quickly out, pulling on his coat, one part of his mind busy with lies to placate Dorothy, another bursting with elation at his luck. As he sank into the cab he put his hands over his face and inhaled the intoxicating odour of their intimacy.

It was two days before he managed to return. He'd been to Pretoria to look over the cement factory. She was as cold and remote as if she had never seen him before, chattered on about the servants, shouted at her maid and finally burst into a storm of weeping.

'What is it?' he implored. 'I'll do anything.'

'You better go now.'

114

'I love you … I love you.'
'Don't be sich a fool.'

For Walter Gardiner, what had seemed desirable in the city began to fade. In the good life of the open veld, shooting for the pot, yarning around the campfires of sun-bleached wood torn down by elephant, he felt himself shedding years. To wake in some sunlit glade in the morning to the clamour of birdsong and find the spoor of predators around the camp, to smell coffee brewing … it had been like going back to times when life had been uncomplicated. Sometimes he groaned. Where was he heading, anyway? He was shocked by his loss of control over Kitty, and tried unsuccessfully to forget that last ugly incident.

'I want the truth, Kitty … this business with Robert Orwell. Who said you could invite him here behind my back? A fine damn fool I looked when he came out with it at the dinner table.'

'I don't know no Robert Orwell.'

'He described you … and the yellow carriage. Red hair!'

'Coloured girls use henna … the light ones.'

'Coloured girls in a yellow carriage!'

'Why not … they got their blokes.'

He had hit her then. She lay on the carpet, tense with anger and heard him swishing soda into a tumbler. He came back and stood over her with his leather gaiters and powerful legs. She could hear his heavy breathing.

'I'm going away and I don't want any damn fooling around while I'm gone.' She looked up at that and he saw the trickle of blood from her nose. Instantly he was contrite. He kneeled and fondled her foot.

'Get away from me,' she hissed, recoiling from his touch.

He got up and stood, irresolute. She had never looked more beautiful. Pale, with a strange, almost inward stillness, as if she had stopped breathing and turned to marble. The streak of blood shocked him but he could not unbend to her again. He dropped a handkerchief at her feet and went out. She sat there for a long time tracing patterns of blood on the white marble till the smears dried.

Gardiner was beginning to like Charles Warewood, his almost silent companion. Warewood would listen to Gardiner's ac-

115

counts of mining in South America, in Malaya and India with a faint smile on his lips and would occasionally cap a hunting story with one of his own. He gave an impression of having hidden resources. He'd go off with the shotgun and come back with a brace of pheasant or partridge, gun in the crook of his arm, as if strolling over his own estates. With the full moustache on his upper lip and the cool blue eyes, he was, Gardiner thought, the model British cavalry officer.

'Seen any action, Charles?' he once asked.

'Nothing worth speaking of ... some pig-sticking in India and a lot of polo. All a bit of a bore, really.' He would not be drawn. Perhaps there was nothing to add as he smoked his Engligh tobacco mixture, stretched his *veldschoen* to the fire and gazed into the flames.

Joseph Ogilvy was something different. Gardiner had taken him on in Robert Orwell's place. He looked a typical English drifter, sunburnt to a painful brick red and light grey eyes with that unflinching stare Gardiner knew for the sign of a liar. He knew the country. Or said he did. He had a fund of stories about 'them niggers' in Mashonaland and Matabeleland.

'I'll tell you about this Ben Gully,' he volunteered one night before they reached the Shashi River.

'Nothing tasteful, I daresay,' said Charles shortly.

'Seen it with my own eyes ... up there in '89. Know what this Ben Gully does to this soldier. They brung him afore the king for drinking a calabash of the king's royal beer. It's a hanging job up there. Only they don't hang them civilized. Pore bugger falls down in front of the king. Ho, sez 'is 'ighness ... so you bin drinking the royal beer, tasting it with that tongue of yourn. You won't be needing it no more. 'So you bin smellin' the king's beer ... you won't be needin' that nose, no more.'

'That'll be enough of that,' said Charles in disgust.

'Hang on then, captain ... you're going up there.'

Ogilvy grinned. 'What about them eyes then ... that seen the king's beer.'

'I said "enough"!' Charles rose.

'Bloody 'eathens,' Ogilvy spat. 'Turned the poor bugger loose to be et by hyenas. Pore shrieking bastid. Mind you, they got respect for the white man s'long as 'e don't interfere in 'is customs. I seen things I kin tell you. Now the wimmin ... they'll sell a gel

116

for an old musket … fine big strapping gels, nothing on 'em but a string of beads and a bag of charms … muti they calls it. Did I say somethin' to upset you, captain?'

As the journey went on Gardiner noted the increasing savagery of the landscape, the numbers of wretched, half-starved creatures who cringed away from them, or raised skinny arms, pleading for scraps of food. It was obvious that they had reached an area where law had broken down. There were ominous signs of raiding parties; burnt huts and ravaged fields. Empty bottles, tins and spent cartridges marked the camping sites of Europeans who had gone ahead of them. But most of the signs were weeks old already.

Two days after crossing the Shashi they outspanned on the banks of the Limpopo, a place of tall fever trees of sulphurous colour and thick tropical vegetation that included wild bananas.

White water rushed over rocks and tree roots and sunlight slanted into groves paradisal with tree ferns. Gardiner went out with the shotgun. On the trunk of a huge wild fig, loud with the buzzing of bees, he saw a carved inscription. The bark was freshly peeled. *C. King's Rest – fever*. The grave was piled with river stones. The dead man's bush hat was nailed above his name.

The atmosphere was miasmic, heat and haze rising from the heavy reeds. The high scream of a fish eagle startled Gardiner from thoughts of blackwater fever.

Ogilvy reported the river too high to cross so they decided to push on along its banks towards Tuli and cross there, perhaps finding it dry except for stagnant pools. Next day they met blacks who came to them, trembling, warning them not to go on. Some showed the scars of half-healed wounds and begged for medicine.

That night Charles Warewood went down with sudden and virulent fever. He shuddered and shook beneath the piled blankets as the rigors seized him. He was soon delirious. Ogilvy looked at his sweated face and staring eyes.

'E'll snuff it,' he said without pity.

'Damned if he will,' said Gardiner forcing quinine between the clenched jaws and holding him down as Charles tried to rise.

'Blackwater,' said Ogilvy. 'E'll snuff it. I come through Potgieter's Rust last month. First farm I come to I knock. No answer. I goes in ... it's stinking. 'Ole family dead in their beds. The same next farm. The *kaffirs*'d run for it. This is bad country, mister. 'Orse fever and dysentery ... sleepy sickness. Malaria and tsetse fly. Nobody would live 'ere if it warn't for Ben Gully's soldiers ... wetting the spears they call it ... knocking orf the corn as soon's ripe and the same wif the gels.' Showing his yellow teeth.

Gardiner sat by Charles Warewood, revolving many things. His association with Penlynne and Rand Mining Enterprises and Finance would be severed when the Rawlinson will was settled. He had his own theories to prove and exploit. Being second man to anyone, even of Penlynne's brilliance, did not suit him. He did not have patience or the flair for negotiation and intrigue. So what was he doing here by a campfire with a sick man and a drunkard of a guide who had passed out on Cape Smoke?

He stirred the embers and threw on more wood. The flare-up lit the clearing. Katherine ... the kids? He missed them. Kitty Loftus? A man could make a fool of himself there. Yet the thought of her softened him. He'd make it up to her.

'I want to go back to the stage,' she'd told him.

'Like hell you will,' he answered.

'I got no friends,' she burst out. 'I sit here all day doing nothing. Penny used to take me to the races ... the theatre. I might as well be buried alive.'

'Take the carriage ... go downtown. Buy yourself something.'

He had promised to have the place done over. In the end he'd done nothing.

Suddenly Charles Warewood sat bolt upright in his blankets. His eyes stared beyond the glare of the fire. 'Lie down, boy,' Gardiner ordered. The Englishman resisted. 'What is it ... what are you staring at? Lie down!' He forced him back. Warewood lay muttering and tossing and presently was silent. Gardiner wiped his streaming face and piled on another kaross. He had watched Warewood's infatuation with Katherine with amused tolerance, knowing that years back he had hoped to marry her. Could a man hang on for years ... for nothing? Was there something between these two?

Damnation, he thought. I like the man. He's a guy you could trust at your back when things were getting sticky. His kind, once committed to a loyalty, never wavered.

118

Charles was rational in the morning. 'Hope I haven't been too much trouble,' he murmured. 'I'll be fit to move as soon as you're ready.' Gardiner felt a pang of compassion. In the strong light of morning, the campfire a heap of grey ashes, another man's passion for his wife seemed not only improbable, but pitiable. He had never doubted Katherine as a woman of principle; a wife and mother. It was her inability to kindle a flame in him, or his in her, that had turned him elsewhere. Looking at the face of Charles Warewood, his blonde hair sweated to his scalp, his blue eyes looking out of deep pits, he suspected that he might be looking at the better man of the two.

He was turning over a mess of reed buck kidneys in the frying pan when he saw Ogilvy hurrying across the glade. The man had gone out earlier to try for guinea fowl before they left their roosts and took to the grass with their scurrying run. No shots had followed.

The man was looking over his shoulder as he ran. 'Over there,' he panted, 'alf a mile orf … a wagon outspanned. The lot of em done for … the Matabele done it.'

'Are you sure they're dead?'

'Acked to pieces, guv'nor.' He gave a frightened glance around. 'We got to move … git out of 'ere.'

Gardiner picked up his rifle.

From a hundred yards off the wagon seemed untouched. It was outspanned under a giant wild fig tree and as he came closer he could hear the loud humming of bees in the branches. Then he came on scattered goods; camp stools and broken dishes, an overturned table. With a growing sense of horror he advanced. Two men in ripped khaki lay face down in pools of dried blood. Flies swarmed up as he approached and turned over the nearest corpse.

He was a middle-aged Boer, grey-bearded, light grey eyes staring. Tumbled over the corpse was the body of a younger man, straw-bearded, somehow Germanic in appearance. They'd evidently been eating supper when their killers came out of the long grass. The wagon had the name of a Pretoria builder he recognized. The oxen had been driven off towards the river.

He began to search among the scattered papers and books for the identity of the two men. Dutch and German newspapers. A *Heilige Bybel* and some technical manuals in German. There was a reek of liquor broached from a broken barrel. Everything was sharply delineated in the harsh sunlight, so bright he could see fresh blood painting the sharp edge of a grass blade. In the hot stillness a troop of gazelle wandered into the clearing and stopped, dead still.

Gardiner was suddenly overcome with fear. He had to force himself not to bolt. Identity? Who were these men? In the Bible he found a name. Francois Jacobus Uys. It had a faint ring of recognition for him but he could not place it. In a book of flower paintings – it appeared to be a botanist's manual on flora of Southern Africa by George Dionysio Ehret – he found the name Carl Marloth. Was this object, its skull stove in by a *kierie* blow and the eyes fallen into the emptiness, genial Carl, geologist and wanderer? Map-maker, gambler, the ever-likeable, song-singing Carl? The man who built *Bloukoppen*?

By midday Gardiner and Ogilvy had buried the two men. He knew nothing of Uys but it struck him as pathetic that a man of Marloth's ability had finished up like this, buried like any tramp adventurer in an unmarked grave. He took the Bible and the flower book as proof of their identities and was coming away when Ogilvy gave a shout. He'd been scrounging in the wagon. He tossed out a briefcase. It was stamped with the eagle coat-of-arms of the South African Republic.

Gardiner opened it. It contained maps and documents in German. A sealed envelope was addressed to Lobengula. 'Pen-lynne will want this,' he said aloud.

'Let's get to 'ell out of 'ere, guv'nor,' pleaded Ogilvy.

Something had miscarried. The dead German and the dead Boer had been emissaries from Kruger to the black potentate. By some quirk of fate they had been killed by one of Lobengula's raiding parties. Perhaps it meant war. A rising against European ambitions. Gardiner had kept out of politics but now he seemed to hear Penlynne's assessment of the Boer.

'When you have made every allowance for their mental attitude and their methods ... when you have remembered their outstanding courage, their small numbers in an ocean of barbarians ... their obstinate and slow-moving ways, their reluctance to face change; when you have considered all these aspects you also have to take into account their secrecy, their duplicity and their blind persistency in gaining their objectives. Nothing will divert them from their intention.

'They are as unyielding as Africa itself and as cunning as the natives they have overcome. Oh yes, products of a savage land. And yet, one cannot help admiring them even in their deviousness and in their hostility to everything British. They share this with their German cousins. They will do everything to block our ambitions to the north ... yes, even to fomenting black revolt.'

Gardiner considered; was there any point in pressing on into Mashonaland with a guide ready to quit and a companion too ill to be of use? This was warning enough not to go further into a territory notorious for not allowing white men in ... but once they were in, making it even more difficult for them to get out.

'What about the wagon, guv'nor?'

'Burn it!'

Standing there in the clearing, the sun directly overhead in a blazing silence, Gardiner had a sense of turning back towards something bigger than he knew, of being involved in spite of his intentions to stay clear. He stood back from the burning wagon. He had plans other than the affairs of England's empire. Yet he could not but feel that this briefcase might affect the lives of thousands, not excluding himself and his ambitions.

Had he the right to break the seal of a letter addressed to the king of the Matabele? What the hell ... he was only a nigger.

'What's it say, Mr Gardiner?'

Gardiner ignored him. He read Kruger's words ... when an Englishman once has your property in his hand then he is like a monkey that has its hands full of pumpkin seeds. If you don't beat him to death, he will never let go.

A fortnight passed before Penlynne had the translation of the documents recovered by Gardiner from the site of the massacre. A young Jewess had done the work. 'Miss Isaacs,' he said as he received the papers, 'I am relying on your discretion.'

Hers was a pale, intelligent face. The dark eyes framed by pitchy hair had a certain melancholy earnestness. It gave him confidence to see that she understood.

'I have spoken to no one, sir. I would be afraid.'

'Your face is familiar to me.'

'Is it, sir?'

'Where have we met?'

'No sir, we have not met before.' She assumed that he had confused her with some other young woman in the flood of Jewish immigration.

'Where did you learn languages, Miss Isaacs?'

'In Cape Town ... at the Jewish Cultural Centre.'

'You were recommended to me by Advocate Esselyn.'

'I have done work for him.'

'Nothing like this?'

'Nothing political, sir.' The word seemed uneasy in her mouth.

She sat in his study at *Far Horizons,* hands folded, waiting for the signal of dismissal. He was remembering Esselyn's reaction. 'A Government dispatch case ... you're tampering with what amounts to a diplomatic mission. You realize ...?'

'Certainly I realize!' The whole thing had such an atmosphere of improbability; even this girl sitting in front of him.

'When did you come to South Africa, Miss Isaacs?'

'In January of 1891 I arrived ... on the ship *The American.*'

'I was on that ship myself.' He was remembering now. There had been a young Jewish stowaway and his sister. He had guaranteed their landing money and paid the boy's passage to prevent his deportation. It was done on impulse. He had heard the story at breakfast before going ashore. In his own elation and certainty of success he had done it as a gesture to fortune.

He saw that she gripped the arms of the chair. He did not mean to probe further or embarrass her with the revelation. But how strange. Under the circumstances, he pressed her further. 'What became of your brother ... was it Isadore?'

'He is here, sir ... in Johannesburg.'

'Is he doing all right?'

Her face tightened and she did not reply. Then, 'I do not see anything of my brother, sir.' He made a mental note to enquire further of the man. The name had a faintly disturbing resonance. He found himself repeating: 'I am relying on your discretion, Miss Isaacs.'

He wrote out a cheque and saw her to the waiting cab. He returned to his study and gave orders that he was not to be disturbed or called to the telephone.

The contents of the dispatch case and the papers of Marloth were in his safe, the translations were before him. Almost with reluctance he took up the papers, the image of Marloth kept intruding. Marloth handing him the keys of *Bloukoppen,* amiably disclaiming further interest in it. 'I am going on my travels again,' he had shrugged and had shown Penlynne a sample of asbestos ore from the Zoutpansberg. 'Interesting, hein!' This was a man obsessed by Africa. He seemed to Penlynne to stand outside personal greed. Dispassionate, scholarly, his studies had included weather, agriculture, geology, tribal boundaries and customs.

He had an omnivorous fascination for everything African. Even its strange and grotesque art. The native masks and ritual images he had brought from the Cameroons and the Congo had been hung among his heavy Bavarian furniture, equally black and carved with the hobgoblins of European fancy. Kitty had insisted on his burning them. Instead he had taken them down and had them stored, realizing their value as an art form doomed to extinction.

He groaned inwardly as he began to read. He had always thought of Marloth as the better part of himself. Incorruptible, a man without envy or desire for possessions, unburdened by the lust of the flesh or money. The eternal fossicker, driven on by a restless curiosity.

And now ... God, this! Everything in front of him confirmed that Marloth was the man who for years had been supplying the German Government with its information on Africa. The letters in his spidery Gothic hand were attached to smallscale maps; geological notes on minerals. The Witwatersrand was shown as the key centre of a German South Africa. There were careful drawings of Delagoa Bay, with soundings for depth; also for the estuary at St Lucia and the mouth of the Zambezi at Beira. On the west coast he had shown every possible site for a landing by troopships, Walvis Bay in particular.

'For us the Boer States,' Marloth had written, 'with the coasts that are their due, signify great possibility. Their absorption into the British empire would mean the blocking of our last road towards an independent agricultural colony in a temperate zone. It is my conclusion that South Africa would be the ideal colony for us, more desirable than Brazil. We must wrest it out of British hands with the help of the Boers.'

Penlynne was shocked. A spurt of anger went through him.

123

The papers trembled in his hand. He rose and walked about. He must read on, calmly, dispassionately. Marloth, the genial Carl, his image of the man had become distorted by the description he had been given by Gardiner ... the caved-in skull, the detached eyeballs, horrific wounds of the deepstabbing blades, the hands mutilated by grasping at the sharpened iron. What dismayed Penlynne was the realization that beneath that jolly round face, the ruddy cheeks and the blue eyes was German ambition, a military professionalism that was elevated almost to a religion as the massed bands crashed and the eagles dipped in salute. *Hoch der Kaiser!*

'It is a land,' the translation went on in Miss Isaacs's neat hand, 'which can receive an unlimited number of white immigrants. In South Africa we can secure the supremacy of the Teuton race. The greater part of the population is of Low German origin. We must stimulate their hatred against Anglo-Saxondom. No doubt the Boers will, with characteristic German tenacity, retake their former possessions from the English by combining slimness with force. In this attempt they can count on the assistance of the German brother nation ...'

For some hours he went through all Marloth's notes and memoranda. Marloth visualized a German colony that stretched across the continent from the Atlantic to the Indian Ocean, swallowed the immensity of the Belgian Congo and usurped the weakly held Portuguese possessions.

'This will effectively shatter the dream of a British colonial empire from the Cape to Cairo. The key to all this is in our support of the Boers. Without Low Germanism we cannot succeed. The German capitalists and mining magnates on the Rand will fall in with us.'

Penlynne felt his flesh grow cold. At the Mining Chamber he had cordial relationships with German mining magnates. They shared his concern for high costs, exorbitant taxation and official inefficiency. Was he to believe that men like George Albu and Adolph Goerz of Deutsche Bank would be prepared to seize the assets of British firms? It was inconceivable. But then, so was Marloth's perfidy.

The final words in Marloth's memorandum to the German Colonial Office were stark. 'We must stimulate and encourage a deadly hatred for England among the Dutch-Boers.' Attached to it was a note in Miss Isaacs's hand: 'See original document No 14 page 3. Final paragraph indecipherable.'

Penlynne turned to the original in Marloth's spidery Gothic hand. From the incompleted sentence he sensed that the ink had still been wet when Marloth looked up to see his death.

He began to jot down his thoughts, his pen stabbing the paper in his urgency. The economic rulers of the Transvaal must become its political rulers. British Capitalism had to triumph. Not just because it was good for the shareholders, but because it was right. Before the coming of the *uitlanders* Kruger did not have a gold sovereign in his treasury. Legend put it at twelve shillings and sixpence! Today the man had a million and a half sterling a year to spend. And where was it going? On Krupps cannon and Mausers.

The sky was growing pale when he rose at last to lock it all away. Strangely, he could find no place in his heart for bitterness against Marloth. The discovery of the name de la Roche was another story.

Tired though he was physically, his brain was singularly alert. He saw that it would be fatal to England's interests to face de la Roche in open court with evidence that would crush the man's case. The irony was that he had wanted facts. Now he was overwhelmed by them.

He walked on the terrace in the fresh morning air. There was a heavy dew on the lawn and the last of the season's roses were hanging on. The mid-summer rose unfurled its petals too fast to last. These splendid late blooms would open slowly to a perfection of maturity. Inhaling the heavy scent as the sun rose he made his decision: he would let the world think that his attack on de la Roche had been a gesture of spite. Hasty and ill considered. He would send his personal cheque for ten thousand pounds to the man's lawyers today. The Marloth papers would go to Rhodes in Cape Town and from him to the Foreign Office in London.

Chapter Ten

The Cape Mail clanked out of Park Halt. Johannesburg fell behind. Stephen Yeatsman sank back on the seat of the First Class coach. Slum yards and the disorder of industry pursued for some distance, then open veld followed, hardly less dismaying. What a country, this Transvaal. Why had he left England for this? Leafy July, tinkle of teacups on a shaded lawn and not so far off the thwack of willow on leather. Spatter of applause. 'Well held, sir!'

He hated Johannesburg. Endless turmoil and dispute. Arrogance and greed. Dregs of humanity of all races. Yet, he had to admit that since his arrival it had begun to sort itself into a pattern of recognizable development.

The wretched condition of the poor, landless Boers in slummy encampments of wagons and tents, these were depressing. They had sold their land to the syndicates or been driven off it by the cattle sickness and locust. He saw no future here for them. There must be British rule, British capital and British justice.

He was smarting with humiliation. Publishing a prominent apology to de la Roche had been harder for him than it had been for Penlynne who'd paid damages of ten thousand. He'd resigned. Penlynne had pleaded. 'I'm not accepting, Stephen.'

'I believed we were going to fight the action...stand by our article.'

'We printed the truth, Stephen.'

'Then why...why have we backed down?'

'It is no longer politic to stand by our assertion.'

'What are our readers to make of our *volte-face*?'

'I admire your indignation, Stephen...and share it.'

'Spare me the platitudes, Mr Penlynne.'

'There are times when one must retreat to advance.' Penlynne laid his hand on the shoulder of the younger man and looked at him with eyes not only compelling and appealing but curiously vulnerable. 'I don't like to appear a liar, Stephen. Facts are, I now have certain information...it has turned what was a matter of business into a political emergency...I'm talking of our country now, Stephen. England and our colonies.'

'I'm being mocked.'

'Shrug it off.'

'De la Roche read me a lecture in the club...it was galling.'

Yeatsman winced, remembering the incident, the insolence of the tall, dark foreigner with his curiously hybrid accent. He was celebrating his triumph over Penlynne and *The Oracle*. His cronies cheered when he read out Yeatsman's front page apology. He lingered on some lines...*entirely without substance...deeply regret any imputation that may have reflected on the integrity of Baron Claude de la Roche, His Excellency the Turkish Consul.*

The young editor had stood his ground. He had friends here too and they pressed to his side.

'I hear *The Oracle* is up for sale, Yeatsman...bankrupt.'

'Not true.'

'In future steer clear of politics, my boy. Stick to reports on church bazaars and weddings and funerals. The busy doings of Madame Penlynne will fill pages.' His expression turned the remark to innuendo and received a gratifying titter.

'Take care, Baron.' Yeatsman shouldered his way to the bar and ordered.

'Take care, is it!' de la Roche laughed. 'It's somewhat late for taking care.' In the sudden silence Stephen heard him go on. 'Next time I will seek damages my own way...as a gentleman.' He summoned a man who put a polished wooden box on the bar counter. 'Open it,' he invited Stephen.

The weapon was brand new of a type unknown to the onlookers. It had an unusual square section in front of the trigger, and a cocking mechanism that no one had seen before. The cold gun metal looked new and unused. 'In these days of provocation a man must be ready, don't you agree?' De la Roche took a metal clip of cartridges from a side pocket and slipped it into the broomhandle butt.

'*Waffenfabriek Mauser*...the new design by Peter Paul Mauser, my good friend in Obersdorf. Gentlemen, you are looking at a weapon that will have much to say for itself...perfected only this year. Herr Mauser assures me the British have nothing to match it. You can tell that to your friends, Mr Yeatsman.'

He clipped an extension onto the butt. The handgun had become a carbine to fit a saddle holster. 'Ingenious…and accurate up to two hundred yards. An interesting item for your paper, Mr Yeatsman…I give you leave to mention it.'

Recounting the affair to Penlynne, Yeatsman was surprised by his cool response. 'A bit of sabre-rattling, Stephen, by way of a threat. His indiscretion is typical of the man. If such weapons are indeed being purchased by the Transvaal he should know better than advertise the fact.' Then with disgust and disdain. 'The man's ill…'

'You mean…not responsible.'

'Syphilitic.'

'Good God!'

'One can expect the irrational behaviour.'

'Is it known…I mean to Government. To the officials he deals with?'

'I doubt it matters to them as long as his behaviour is hostile to my interests, our national interests. Say nothing of it, please.'

'Of course…but his connections in armaments, in cement, in the liquor trade, in continental finance…are they aware of it?'

'Who knows. The man has a tremendous flair for corruption and intrigue. Still, I do not discount his…you could call it genius. In some men syphilis…' He broke off as if it demeaned him to speak of it further. 'With his background, are you surprised!'

For a moment Yeatsman had a feeling that Penlynne was actually sorry he had spoken about it; something had darkened his brow. 'I believe he was involved in an attempt to kill me.'

'What!'

'Yes, some months ago.' He showed the scar on his hand. 'Then he turned up in my office and warned me my life was in danger.'

'Rather contradictory, would you say?'

'His background is English, you know. A good impulse, quite irrational. Men sometimes do such things. A sudden impulse…throwing out a lifeline.'

'For you?'

'For himself.'

'How did you know his background...he gives out he's French.'

'I despise the man,' Penlynne said abruptly, but that moment he was thinking of himself, of Gardiner and the Rawlinson fortune. The man had turned flabby, obsessive about rediscovering the reef at Heidelberg...eighty bloody miles away! That's why he'd sold the Rawlinson Star. Crazy! He turned from the young man to prevent a smile. How long, he wondered, would it be before Gardiner really understood the extent of his mistake and who had been the buyer of the Star. With the man's name so near his lips he had to use it.

'Gardiner...Walter. You know him, Stephen. He's going to Cape Town for a high level conference on the *Sydney Star*. It might be worth your attention...make a good article.'

'Thank you, I will go down.'

Penlynne felt himself absolved. The boy's eagerness was so genuine. He fed him a little more to whet his appetite. 'If the ship is declared lost with all souls, Gardiner will have what he wants.'

'Presumption of Lady Rawlinson's death.'

'Exactly.' He did not add that Gardiner was not the man to handle it. Brilliant in his field ... after all, the deep level mining had been his intuition, but a fool with money. And women.

Yeatsman felt a spurt of enthusiasm. Anything to escape humiliation here. The Rand soon forgot. Penlynne shook his hand. 'Oh, you might take a package for me...by hand. For Mr Rhodes. Something of mutual interest.'

'Certainly, sir.'

'To tell the truth, Stephen, I dont trust the postal authorities. Everything is opened these days.' Penlynne produced the package, already sealed. 'Do you know Cape Town? No? You'll find it civilized.' He gave Yeatsman names and addresses of useful contacts. And went so far as to see him off at the station. He did not care whether Yeatsman reported on the *Sydney Star* conference or not. He was an unquestioning messenger. Rhodes would use him, of course, as he used everyone. Except, Penlynne told himself, except those who were one jump ahead. As I am. Oh yes, I'll make the most of the connection.

He stayed late at the office to write to Julius Wernher.

The truth is, at this stage we no longer care whether Kruger gives the uitlander *the vote or not. We must obtain power. Without it,*

129

capitalism is toothless. But do not be alarmed, I shall do nothing on my own. A formal deputation will call on the President with a petition signed by twenty thousand. It will make reasonable demands, remind His Excellency of the state's dependence on capitalism and it will come away empty-handed! With that old man crying: it is not the vote you want, it is my country. And, of course, he will be right. But what other option have we with German ambition to colonize Africa and the gold mines its richest prize?

No, my dear Julius, I have come a long way. When we have sufficient provocation we will act.

As he addressed the envelope it struck him – Wernher is German-born. Yes, but a capitalist. An internationalist at heart. A man with no frontiers. The movement of capital across regional boundaries concerned him more than loyalty to any flag. The Paris Bourse and the London Stock Exchange were his real country. And will be mine. He would use patriotism, shout the accepted slogans, even feel a degree of passion for the cause of empire. But it was not his personal goal. He had not created all this to have it snatched away.

Walter Gardiner had not planned the arrangement. It had never been his intention to travel to Cape Town in the same train as Katherine and the children with their nurse. Her arrangements to sail in *The Saxon* had been made before his return from the Shashi River expedition. He had found the change in her quite striking. It was like returning to a house to find it occupied by a different woman.

This new Katherine had a hauteur, a remoteness and a confidence he had never seen before. She seemed in command of herself, her servants and her children. No sign of the uncertain girl and the yielding wife.

'You didn't tell me you were planning to go to England,' he challenged. What's got into you?' He raised her face to meet his demand, a gesture that had always reduced her to his will. She broke from him, almost with disdain.

'You are leading your life...I have mine. I am going to London to make arrangements for a memorial.'

'For your father?'

'It was Muriel's intention...now it is mine.'

'It can be made here, surely?'

'But not what she had in mind.'

'Something grand?'

'Something worthy of him.'

He bit back the thought: plenty around here would say a hole in the ground was good enough for Josiah Rawlinson. Some would have dumped him down the shaft of the Star.

'It was his wish. He often spoke of it.'

'It will cost a packet.'

'It is his money,' she said coldly.

'What's got into you, Katherine?'

'Shall you be living at home...or elsewhere?' she returned.

'This is Joh'burg, honey,' he said flippantly.

She gave him a momentary look of scorn then left the room. He was intrigued and more than a little nettled by her composure. He had thought of taking Kitty to the Cape with him by way of making up, but Katherine's decision changed his mind. He'd have to play the family man. It would look damned odd to read in the newspaper's 'Departures' that Mrs Walter Gardiner, children and nurse had travelled in one compartment and Miss Kitty Loftus and Mr Walter Gardiner in another.

He bathed and changed, impatient to get over to *Bloukoppen*. He could have phoned but he wanted to surprise her. The clouds were mounting for a thunderstorm, piling and wreathing against a blue-black sky. As he turned the trap into the driveway the first thick drops were striking the dry earth, instantly evaporating. The air crackled with electricity. Light had turned a bilious yellow that gave every growing thing an ugly unfamiliarity. How would she receive him? It dismayed him to realize that it mattered.

In the empty stable yard he shouted for a groom. Nobody came. He pulled at the lionshead bell pull and heard the bell ringing far back in the house. No one came. Sweating, he used his latch key.

'Kitty!' He stood in the hall, heart beating hard. His shout seemed to mock him from the emptiness. Everything was in perfect order. By God, he'd shake her for this. 'Kitty!' He charged at the stairs, flung open the bedroom door and stared across the white carpeting to the bed. It was disordered, the covers slidden to the floor. Imprint of two heads on the pillows.

The smell of her cosmetics had always aroused him…now he was sickened and weak at the knees.

He went from room to room, some with the shutters closed, others distorted by the sulphurous sky. Where in hell was she? Finally he came to the door to the attics. It was locked. He put his shoulder to it and went up the uncarpeted steps which smelled of dust and dryness. Attic windows let in light from the roof. He saw a carpet and a green velvet chair. An artist's easel. Colour was still wet on the canvas. He was looking at nakedness, flaring red hair and ivory flesh. Her gaze…her whole attitude was voluptuous.

He stepped back astonished. He had seen the mock-classical pose in a hundred bars and cathouses from Golden Gate to Hong Kong. Yet this was more than that. It was less skilled but it said much more. It was like intruding on secret passion. He could have killed her. It was like being stabbed in the belly. Christ, it hurt! How could she do this to him?

Something moved at the far end of the attic. Kitty came forward in a gown of some flimsy material. Behind her he saw the pale face of Robert Orwell.

'I didn't know you was back,' she said with a toss of the head.

'Just stand aside…I want a word with the artist.'

'Don't touch 'im,' she cried.

He was aware of Kitty yelling and holding him back…of the satisfaction he felt in striking. The boy kept getting up. The easel had fallen. 'My painting…my painting,' the boy was saying.

'Get to hell out of here,' Gardiner shouted.

At the door Robert turned and gave a wild look in the direction of the canvas. He never looked at Kitty…then he ran down the attic stairs and after a moment the front door crashed.

'So much for young love,' said Gardiner. It was absurd to feel such anguish and impossible to rationalize the pain in his heart. It's my age, he thought. How else could she have gotten at me like this?

At the Orange River halt the Gardiner family walked on the platform. They greeted people they knew also waiting for the Cape train to make connection with the Transvaal coaches. Mrs Gardiner had raised her parasol. The children walked with nanny. Stephen Yeatsman thought they made a handsome group...the kind of family the country needed. Gardiner gave him a nod but did not stop. At the station buffet everyone mingled. Mothers Katherine recognized were taking their children to England to boarding school. Spencer was old enough but she did not want to lose him yet to the system that made men of them. Everyone said so. Gardiner still threatened schooling in America. 'Democratic,' he called it. 'No goddam snobbery.'

'No doubt in a log cabin,' she retorted. She saw both Gardiner and her father in the boy. Tall for six, his blonde baby hair had darkened. He was quick and impetuous, forever darting from her side. At Kimberley he disappeared for an hour. She was frantic. As the locomotive was whistling he turned up. He'd run all the way to De Beers to see the Big Hole.

'Grandfather made it,' he enthused.

'Pick up any diamonds?' smiled Gardiner.

'There wasn't time...the train whistled. One day I'll go back and buy it from Mr De Beers...Grandfather said it was stolen from him...he found the very first diamond there. He did! He told me so. He had it on his ring.'

She brushed the wayward lock that fell over his clear brow.

'If that's what you want,' she smiled.

Katherine was surprised that Sarah went so readily to her father. He was going out of his way to please her and the child responded, curling into his lap to listen to his watch. 'Is it very, very valuable?' the boy insisted.

'Enormously,' Gardiner said and opened the back to show him.

Close to the railway line ran the old coach road. Walter pointed it out to Spencer. 'Your grandfather sent a coach all the way to Beaufort West to pick up your mother...that's when I got to know her.'

'Was I there, father?'

'I was,' the girl said confidently.

Gardiner laughed. 'Not yet.'

The veld slid by mile after mile, unvarying in its monotony. The children dozed. Katherine read a novel called *The Soul of Daphne* by the Marchioness of Carmarthen. Daphne and the young poet were lost together in a snowstorm. *'There can be no death when we are together,'* he assured her. *'A new joy may await us in another world...here we have exhausted happiness. Why should we hesitate...? I will never believe that love like ours is finite.'*

Katherine put it firmly aside. Did Walter regret the way things had turned out, she wondered. Did he guess that she intended to stay in England for some time and that some of it would be at Warewood Hall? He gave no sign of knowing the change in her relationship with Charles. Or how unbearable it had been for her since he left, going through the motions of a domestic harmony that did not exist and giving no sign of an inner anguish. It was especially hard when she was with friends in their circle, with people who had their emotions under control and the talk was of children, money and mutual friends. She longed to be away from it all. The decision to go to London was quite sudden. She sent orders to the staff to air the Park Lane house and she wrote to friends. The season would be in full swing. She would recover her spirits.

The train rattled on south. Nothing moved but the dust devils swirling across the emptiness. Sometimes a span of twenty or thirty oxen went by, trudging northwards, dragging transport wagons. She thought of the coach journey north with Walter at her side, of his male odours, the touch of his hand and pressure of his thigh against her as the vehicle swayed...the strange mixture of fear and excitement. Was he remembering now, taking nips from the silver flask? Yes, she despised him now. For the rest of her life she would be at the mercy of his ambitions. He could do what he pleased with her father's fortune...and there was nothing, nothing she could do to prevent it.

Gardiner was in high spirits. He was certain the *Sydney Star* enquiry would be cleared up in a week or two. 'I'll keep you informed, Katherine. You'll want to know at once. I've no doubt we'll be able to petition the Supreme Court for a presumption of the woman's death.'

'She was my friend,' Katherine retorted. A vision of the Scots woman on her knees, mouth full of pins, hemming up the wedding dress. Calling her 'my lass'. Her eyes filled with tears. He changed his tone.

'I know you were fond of her...it really is too bad it had to be this way.'

'I don't believe you care a damn. The money is all you care for.'

134

'The children have ears, Katherine.'

Suddenly he changed his tone again. Almost casual. 'I got to know your friend Charles quite well on the Shashi trip. I kind of took to him. I think he's still sweet on you, Katherine.'

Blood burned in her cheeks.

'Not like the usual Englishman out here...bums, remittance men.' She did not trust herself to reply. That night she lay awake in her rocking bunk, the train lights moving across the low brush of karroo bush. From the darkness the eyes of an animal would be lit as if by an inner fire. What did she know of Charles? Public school and the army. The languid style that concealed a streak of steel. He was the kind, she thought, who'd charged the Turk guns at Balaclava and never said a word about it afterwards, merely hung up his swords, put on an old jacket and slouched into the woods with a shotgun. He had a way with horses and dogs and was a man who spoke to his tenants without condescension. *Noblesse oblige,* wasn't that the phrase?

Sarah cried out and sat up. Katherine took the child in beside her and soon the small limbs relaxed, she sighed and resumed the swift breathing of childhood. Utterly at peace. My baby, she thought. Nothing shall hurt you.

Chapter Eleven

Walter Gardiner turned quickly away from the Cape Town docks. He had waited long enough to see *The Saxon* leave and the crowd disperse. He shouldered his way through vendors, porters and seamen and hailed a Malay cabbie. It had been touch and go whether *The Saxon* would sail. A fullscale south-easter was blowing. He had seen Katherine and the children to their cabin on the promenade deck and brought them gifts and flowers. The children did not understand this would be a prolonged separation. He and Katherine kept up the pretence.

As she took off her hat in the cabin, he appraised her. She was a fine-looking woman not yet out of her twenties. Strands of hair fell from her pins and curled seductively on her neck. She had greeted friends with an animation she never showed him. The age gap, he thought. Once it would have amused him. He had taken her as a girl. Now she was a woman, cool and unemotional about their parting.

'You'll cable me as soon as you arrive.'

'Of course.' She had no illusions that he had made the journey to see her off and seemed impatient to have him gone.

'Did I see Charles Warewood on the docks?' he suddenly shot at her. 'Come to see you off.'

'Really...he may be going home. I didn't see him.'

'I expect he's recovered.'

She seemed preoccupied.

He would have thought nothing of it before. Why now?

He was going down the gangway when he knocked into Warewood following his servant and his bags. The man was still sallow from fever and seemed astonished to knock into Gardiner.

'Gardiner,' he said in a friendly way. 'Seeing someone off?'

'My wife.' Warewood did not react. 'Are you recovered?'

'Quite. Going home to get a bit of Africa out of my blood.

Fever knocks a man about. The Penlynnes were very kind but one has to get home to shake it off...change of soil, you know. I'll spend summer at Warewood...all very peaceful.'

'Coming back?'

Gardiner thought he evaded answering. Then in a low voice he replied, 'I'm looking up one or two people for Penlynne.'

'Business?'

'You might call it that...if you take my drift.'

'It's blowing that way, is it?'

'Yes, it looks like it.'

'A show of force or the real thing?'

'There's only one way, Gardiner.'

'This year?'

'When we're ready. Keep it under your hat.' He pushed on up the gangway. No one would suspect that this was the same man who'd dug for water in the bed of the Shashi but the look of a soldier was unmistakable. His easy assumption of authority was of one born to it; expecting nothing less. He assumed the right of the British to take what they pleased. Cool, damned cool. You never could tell what they were really thinking.

'Keep an eye on Katherine for me!' he shouted after Warewood. Warewood did not look back. Gardiner turned away. Penlynne had gone further than he had let on. Didn't he trust him? Maybe he thought it was no business for an American. And he was damn right. Keep out of their revolution!

It was blowing hard when the cab dropped him at the top of Long Street, gusting as if to tear the clothing off him. A cataract of white cloud poured over the cliff face of Table Mountain, like a tidal wave, he thought. Something immense...something as overwhelming had fallen on the *Sydney Star*. If her engines had failed, as they said, it would have caught her on the beam as she drifted and rolled her over...twin screws churning the air. Then gone.

On a brass plate he read the name of the Red Funnel Line's agent in Cape Town. Geoffrey Beasley. The office was in a Georgian building a century old with a single palm tree next door. It was a mosque with a notice on the half door in Arabic script. From nearby came the nasal chanting: 'There is no God but God and Mohammed is his prophet.' Red fezzes of men hurrying to prayer went by. It was unexpected here in a city so strongly English in its style … so civilized when compared with that tin-shanty city up there on the Transvaal highveld. And between them were a thousand miles of wilderness broken only by a few crude villages, inns and the wagon road he'd taken north with Katherine. But now only two days away by train. He'd come to solve an engineering problem. And he'd stayed. Maybe too long already.

He'd made and spent a fortune and was looking for another. No way he'd leave his investment now, pushing fifty and if he listened to Penlynne he'd be seventy before his partner would listen to his plan to rediscover the reef. It was too late to move on now. Not with the Rawlinson fortune for the taking.

Kitty and that damned painting. She'd had the nerve to face him, up there in the attic.

'You can pack your bags and get to hell out of here!'

'See if I don't then.'

He had followed her downstairs, so aware of her scent, her nakedness, the swish of her gown. His anger quickly cooled. 'All right, let's not do anything crazy.'

'I got a right to a friend,' she replied, shaking off his hand.

'Take it easy, Kitty.'

'Don't bloody Kitty me.'

'Listen…' He tried to restrain her. 'I'm going to Cape Town. Katherine's going to England. She'll be gone for months. I promise it'll be different. We'll have some fun…go to the races, the theatre. Whatever pleases you. Kitty?'

Her expression changed to an angelic smile. She looked over her naked shoulder. 'I want the 'ouse in my name then.'

'It's yours.'

Foot on the stair he shook his head at her audacity. He'd give her any damn thing she wanted and she knew it. Just where he'd raise the money for the house was something else. Christ! Katherine'd spend more on a mausoleum for a dead man.

Geoffrey Beasley was short to the point of rudeness. Coldly efficient among the files, heaps of correspondence and cables, he was the focus of every enquiry aimed at the Red Funnel Line. Every hour he was tackled by someone wanting an answer. Relatives demanded the latest information about the search. Reporters hoped for his comments on the bizarre theories of cranks. He was in no mood to be questioned by Gardiner. He was due to represent the company at a meeting in the office of the Prime Minister, the Naval Commander in Chief would be there, the Governor of Cape Colony and captains who'd searched for the missing ship.

'I had a relative on board...'

'There's nothing I can tell you, sir. Nothing I can add to what's been made public.' He was rising.

'This hearing today...I take it it's open to the public.'

'On the contrary.'

'I'm representing my wife...daughter of the late Sir Josiah Rawlinson. Lady Rawlinson was on board and I intend to be at this meeting, sir.'

'The meeting's in camera.'

'Behind closed doors?'

'This is not the enquiry, Mr Gardiner.'

'What then?'

'It's to make a decision...to abandon the search or go on.'

'What do you mean, go on! The ship sank in July. This is September. Last week it was reported they'd found a deck chair marked SS *Sydney Star* ... picked up at Coffee Bay, between Port St. John's and East London.'

He noted Beasley's thin smile of superior knowledge. 'Against the Agulhas current ... impossible.'

'You actually believe she's still afloat?'

'Certainly...a splendid vessel. The latest design. Her captain has been thirty years in company service. I have letters here from passengers on her maiden voyage to Australia...everyone of them praising her. I have the reports of Lloyds' experts and the Board of Trade proclaiming her seaworthy.'

'Adrift for two months?'

'She has sufficient water and provisions to last eighteen months. Oh yes, Mr Gardiner, I believe she's still afloat. She will be found. About here, I hazard a guess.' Beasley put his finger on a spot in the middle of the South Atlantic. 'The isle of St. Paul...30S by 80E.'

'Two thousand miles!'

'You may smile, Mr Gardiner. In 1885...last year, the steamship *Lysidias* broke down a hundred miles from Agulhas. She drifted one hundred days...twenty miles a day into the Roaring Forties.'

'So you're sending a search ship to St. Paul's.'

'Mr Gardiner, if you imagined that the purpose of this meeting is to declare the vessel lost, you are to be pitied. Only a full Board of Trade enquiry is competent to do that. In London. At Caxton Hall, Westminster.'

'Your confidence amazes me, Mr Beasley. Three months ago I was in Durban. I talked with a Mr Samuel Partridge. He left the ship there in fear of his life.'

Again the thin smile, thinner than ever. 'The so-called clairvoyant. Yes, we have his account...the dream! Mr Partridge is hardly likely to give expert testimony.'

'He dreamed he saw the ship turn turtle.'

'Very graphic and a damned lie.'

'He dreamed it, Mr Beasley, the night before she was last reported seen...the 27th July.'

'Did you know that Mr Partridge is under medical care in England...a disease of the nervous system?' The man laughed outright. Gardiner blurted back at him. 'He's alive ... thanks to his nervous system.'

'Forgive me, Mr Gardiner...relations, both for personal and financial reasons, have an interest in the ship being lost. Lady Rawlinson's estate was considerable...the gold-mining fortune.'

'I want the matter cleared up ... settled, that's all.'

Beasley put a whiskey bottle on the table. 'This was picked up by a fishing vessel...longitude 43E.' From a drawer he produced a folded scrap of paper. Gardiner read: *Will the finder please inform Mrs Ethel Volbrecht, 27 Almsbury Court, East London that all well aboard* Sydney Star. *Message dropped on August 24. Keep up your spirits. Due to engine failure.*

Gardiner scowled at the crude handwriting, the illegible signature. 'You base your optimism on this?'

'Certainly not. However, it is somewhat more substantial than a dream, wouldn't you agree?'

'You know what I think, Mr Beasley? The company's stalling. The day the *Sydney Star's* confirmed lost the owners of Red Funnel Line will be out of business.'

'Forty years in shipping!'

'They keep the search going...hold up the enquiry.'

'The legatees will have to be patient, won't they,' said Beasley putting on his hat. As a parting gesture he gave the American a brochure. It showed the *Sydney Star* under full steam, cleaving great seas with majestic indifference.

'She looks top heavy to me,' said Gardiner. Now he understood the extraordinary calculation made for him by Partridge at their meeting in Durban. On the back of an envelope of the Planter's Club he had scribbled the figures, talking nervously all the time. 'We were still a few days out of Durban, Mr Gardiner. I was watching from the hurricane deck the way she ploughed into the waves...not rising, you see, but ploughing through them. I made this calculation. If the sea broke over her and the forward well filled there would be about half a million tons of water aboard. She would never recover. That night I had the first dream.'

'Dream ... of disaster?'

'I saw a man coming half out of the waves. He had a sword in his left hand and in the other, a rag covered with blood. At breakfast I mentioned it to a Miss Hay, who remarked, "How horrid!" '

'Did you mention this to any officer?'

'No. My steward...he said it was a warning and some of the crew were talking of leaving ship at Cape Town. I wired my wife from Durban.' Partridge consulted a notebook. *Sydney Star* top heavy. Cancelled passage home. Will take next mailship.

'What date was that?'

'August 4th.'

'But you landed on July 25th.'

'That's so.'

'And she sailed next day?'

'Yes ... and I dreamed again on the 27th. The same dream.'

'Why did you wait so long to cable your wife?'

'I hope you are not suggesting I am making this up, Mr Gardiner.' Partridge rose huffily and left the club. Of course the man could have made it up when the ship was reported missing from Cape Town with Miss Hay and the frightened steward both dead. It was the kind of story one heard in mining. The apparition that warned of the cave-in told by the man who didn't go on shift that day. It was bullshit. Bullshit!

Any hope of a quick decision was out of the question. Good God...the British Board of Trade would have to get depositions from seamen, former passengers and experts scattered all over the world…subpoena them to appear or make sworn statements before consular officials in places as remote as China and South America.

He groaned, remembering how long it had taken to assemble the experts for the case against African Gold Recovery, the cyanide case Rawlinson had brought against Penlynne. A year? Two years? The short solution was to get drunk; very drunk.

There it was again. The unmistakable sound of a hen scratching and clucking, then the crow of a rooster and the beating of wings. Where in hell was he anyway? Gardiner lifted his head and a bolt of lightning went through it. For a moment there he'd thought himself back in childhood, woodchopping and morning chores to be done. He was mother naked. Next to him was a black-haired girl, skin the colour of apricots. He had no recollection of anything. The girl turned over lazily. She had mango breasts. Eastern? Sumatra…Java? He had an uncanny feeling of having regressed in time. Time? What day was it? The girl said it was Sunday. He'd been here since Friday.

'You got the *babbelas*, darling!'

'I sure as hell got something.'

He stood up, groaned and pushed open the shutters. He looked onto a small yard stacked with empties. He saw a huddle of walls, rooms without windows, rusty iron roofs. Church bells were ringing with iron strokes. The Cape sunlight was blinding.

'Get me a drink,' he ordered. The girl went out of the room without a stitch on her. He heard a gabble and clinking. She came back with a bottle and glass and sat on his knee. She told him he'd come in a cab with seamen. Gardiner gulped raw spirits and felt better. A small dark man in a red fez looked in. Cheerfully garrulous, he shaved Gardiner with swift strokes of an open razor. Suliman shaved all the gentlemen. Gardiner gulped two raw eggs in a tumbler of brandy.

'Get me a cab.' The fat madame had pressed his suit and ironed his shirt. Smiles…all smiles. Evidently he had paid. The house was old with many rooms and creaking floor boards. It reeked of curries, booze and cheap perfume. The girl's name was Victoria and she pouted, pretended to cry. Said she loved him and begged him to come back quickly.

On the stoep he tripped over a seaman's boot. Hoots of laughter followed him to the cab. 'Where to, master?'

'The harbour.' In fragments it was coming back…Fish Lane.

Through the smoke of a tavern in Fish Lane he could see the bay. Waves were slamming against the jetty, boats dancing. Yesterday's newspaper told him that the search for *Sydney Star* would go on. The paper was critical about the cost. 'Why charter a ship to sail south into Antarctic waters when three warships of the British fleet had given up the search.' They were going to give it three more months.

Voices were raised among a group of seamen. 'I tell you, I seen her with my own eyes. Floating face down. She was that near the bilges was spilling on her…a little girl in a red gown, all spread out on the water. She had bare knees and black stockings.' The speaker was a seaman in reefer jacket with brass buttons, white canvas trousers, dark blue jersey with SS *Tantallon* in red letters; a man with iron-grey hair and hands like teak. 'Ten or twelve years old she was…'

The bar was suddenly quiet. 'I called the second mate. He seen her, too. 'Bout an hour after I see another body floating by real slow, just under the surface. There was a white sheet over it. Arms open…like this!'

Someone broke in. 'You ever see a sunfish?'

'It was bodies. We was twenty-five miles south of East London … August eleventh. Ten days after she sailed.'

Gardiner shouldered his way to the seaman and drew him away from the bar. 'Did you report what you saw in Cape Town?'

'We was under orders to say nothing…captain's orders.'

'Why did he say that?'

'Said he didn't want no enquiry wasting his time…owner's time.'

'He wanted it kept quiet, is that it?'

'That's it, mister.' His voice dropped. 'The navy come aboard at Cape Town…sent a cutter with an officer. You seen anything of *Sydney Star* he asks the skipper. I see the agent give the old man a look. "Nuthin", says the old man. I kept my mouth shut.'

'Did the skipper log your report?'

'Sure … whale offal…blubber from the whaling station.'

'What about the second mate?'

'He said the same.'

'Anybody else see it?'

'Job Day...prentice.'

Gardiner pushed a sovereign over the table. 'Let's find him.' After a bar to bar search and much drinking they found Day in an argument in the Crown and Anchor. 'That's him,' said the *Tantallon's* man...'and that's Ewart Evans ...the chief officer. And a bloody Welsh liar!' The argument was raging and tempers high.

'I'll tell you what you saw, boy,' Evans was shouting. 'A skate ... a big skate and a few pieces of blubber. Captain put ship about and spent a good hour looking for bodies...time lost for nothing.'

'It were bodies, sir,' the apprentice protested. 'One of them had an albatross on it.'

Gardiner's friend piped up. 'We sailed through the stuff for two hours...the sharks was busy and I seen this girl in the red cape.'

'S'true as God, sir,' echoed the youngster.

'Just a minute,' Gardiner said. 'I want these two men to make depositions to a Justice of the Peace.'

The chief officer turned on him. 'Who the hell are you, mister? And you two ... get aboard if you know what's good for you. Keep out of our business, Yankee.'

Gardiner's punch took Evans on the side of a head that felt like teak. He grunted but he didn't fall. After that Gardiner didn't remember much. The room was circling and whether it was Evans's fist or his knee he was never sure. He had a vague recollection of a cab ride...being helped up steps by someone. More liquor...noisy music and shrieks of girls. The cabby was pulling up his horse.

'The harbour, master ... what ship?'

'*Tantallon.*'

'She sail a'ready, master.'

Gardiner felt in his pocket for his wallet, found two depositions. Day and Noble ... the man in the *Tantallon* jersey. Sworn before a Justice of the Peace.

He had not the faintest memory of it.

144

Chapter Twelve

Christiaan Smit thought it better to tell his wife at once. Anna was a direct person. They were spending Easter at the small-holding he had bought since his appointment as Assistant Attorney General. He needed a place like this for contemplation and the redirection of his mental energies. Politics? That might come yet.

They had driven out to the farmhouse directly after the *nagmaal* service attended by the President. Many of the Volksraad and representatives of foreign states were present. It was a sombre, black-coated occasion, a Good Friday on which the betrayal and execution of Jesus Christ seemed peculiarly relevant. Done to death by a foreign invader of his land by a Governor with Rome's authority. A world empire at his back. It was all he could think of...the parallel. He had gone through the ritual in a state of controlled anger.

'You are very quiet,' Anna said, bringing him coffee where he sat on the *stoep* looking out at the withering stalks in the autumn fields. 'We may have to return to Johannesburg,' he replied.

'I hope not, Christiaan. I hate that place.'

'So do I. So do we all. Unfortunately, it is there.'

She could not forgive it for the death of her infant son. The *witseerkeel* had caught him by the throat just as he was making his first steps. They said you could forget a dead child by having another quickly. It was not true for her. She had lost faith in a Jesus who let the little ones die in the choking, strangling horror of diphtheria.

'Why must we go back?' Her hands busy in a bowl of sweet potatoes.

'I have been given a special duty by the President. It is necessary. We have certain evidence that the smoke has turned to fire. Events are moving faster than we thought. They mean to have our country, nothing less. Sir Henry Loch is at the bottom of it.

He came over here to discuss the matter of the Englishmen who refused commando duty. You remember the uproar. All at once Pretoria was filled with angry *uitlanders* waving the Union Jack. A spontaneous gesture, Loch said. And he even managed to look embarrassed about the insult to the President. Uncoupling the horses from the President's coach and draping it with their damned flag....deeply regretted, he said. Two days later he had secret talks in Johannesburg with Mr Leonard Penlynne and others. What was agreed on there we now know. Certain letters are in our hands ... enough to hang Mr Penlynne for high treason.'

He limped the length of the *stoep*, his slender body taut with anger. His intensity of feeling no longer amazed her as it had in the early days. The limp from his war wound was more evident.

'Where will it all lead?' she said.

'The pot is coming to the boil, Anna. Every day we are offered more provocation by the English press...gross insults to our nation. The word 'Krugerism' has become synonymous with tyranny. It's as well we have friends abroad. Germany will not stand aside and see England swallow our *volk*. Our German citizens did not refuse military duty.'

'There will be war,' she said quietly.

Christiaan looked out across the lands, his grey eyes narrowed against the glare and she was remembering him as he had been, a boy on her uncle's farm. Her brothers had mocked his eagerness for education ... thrown his books in the dust. He had risen from every brawl more determined. The intensity of his gaze had become more piercing and intimidating. She remembered him as he had been brought back after the Magato campaign, unconscious in a wagon. He had told her since: 'When you nursed me in that room I was convinced it was an angel sponging my wounds and sometimes, my darling wife, weeping over me in the small hours.'

'I have loved you all my life,' she told him when he asked her to marry him that day in the schoolroom while the children gaped and giggled as he limped with her to the shade of the old marula tree. He had waited seven years to ask her while he studied in Europe. She knew that she would never match him in education but she could match him in quality of mind and spirit...she could still heal his wounds.

'I'll come with you, of course,' she said.

'I can't go without you, Anna,' he said. 'You are my courage. Without you I am just raw anger and frustration.' He looked at her gratefully and put on his hat. He would return with veld grasses and strange plants. This time it would be more than that. He would know exactly how he intended to act in the situation.

When he returned with his grasses he said quietly, 'We are invited to the official reception to celebrate Kaiser Wilhelm's birthday. I believe the President is to make an important speech. They will all be there...the foreign community ... Dutch, German, Portuguese and English. The English will expect the President to yield to pressures on him to give the *uitlanders* the vote, and give Germany a snub ....'

'Will he do that?'

He smiled and said nothing.

Officials of Government, diplomats and trade commissioners mingled with leading figures of commerce and mining. There was an air of expectancy as the old President rose to propose a toast to the German emperor. Anna's hand groped for Christiaan's and felt his arm go about her waist.

'I am convinced,' said Kruger in his strong, guttural accents, 'that the German Kaiser's aim is to strengthen ties between our South African Republic and his own great country ... as for my German burghers, I have found them ever loyal and willing to obey the laws of the land ... they are not involved in the incitement of Transvaalers against our laws, as are certain subjects of Her Britannic Majesty who turn to England in times of difficulty.'

Anna saw English faces go stiff and cold. Kruger went on in his ponderous way. He became strangely playful. 'When we asked Her Majesty's Government for bigger clothes for this growing child, they said: "Eh,eh! What's this?" They could not see we had outgrown our swaddling clothes. I feel certain that when the time comes for the Republic to free its limbs you Germans will have done much to bring it about.'

The toast to Kaiser Wilhelm was drunk with fervour, faces flushed and eyes bright with enthusiasm. The English hardly touched their glasses to their lips. Later she asked Christiaan: 'Is it wise to encourage the Germans...do we want them here?'

'Only to rid us of the English.'

147

'Why can't they leave us alone,' she said passionately.

A few days later Christiaan had to go over to Johannesburg. He found himself in the same compartment as Leonard Penlynne. Unless someone else got in at the Irene Halt, he would have an hour in the company of this brilliant half-Jew. He sensed a chance to feel him out, to get the measure of the man face to face. Encapsulated as they were, things might be said that would otherwise remain unsaid. A railway carriage was peculiarly suited to indiscretions and confidences.

Penlynne recognized Smit at once and extended a friendly hand. 'I don't believe we've spoken since your brilliant handling of Rawlinson versus African Gold Recovery. I hear you are now Assistant Attorney General. Congratulations and commiserations.'

He offered a cigar. Christiaan declined, taking in the man with his well-tailored suit, rose in buttonhole and expensive footwear. Signet rings on well-kept hands. Beard greying. He had a face marked by the realities of wealth and power yet capable of being charmingly persuasive. An open-minded man, incapable of deception. He could have deceived me until a few days ago, Christiaan thought.

The coaches of the Nederlands Railway Company rattled on briskly across a landscape of prospering farms and homesteads. There was an illusion of settled peace ... *Kaffirs* driving cattle and spans of oxen hauling firewood and produce to market on the Great North Road as some called the rutted track to Johannesburg. The ripened veld grass, noisy with finches, moved in waves of gold, now dark, now light as the wind and sun played over it. Christiaan felt a deep sense of possession.

'Are you going over for the Agricultural Show, Advocate Smit, or more serious business? Several progressive Boer farmers will be exhibiting. This country can be made to bear fruit. Do you farm?'

'No.'

'I thought every Boer was a farmer. At least at heart. My company has made extensive purchases in the Lowveld where we plan to grow first-class timber for the mines, and probably citrus for export.'

The complacency of the man's tone, his assumption that his money could buy anything – the whole country if he wanted –

was galling to the Afrikaner. There was a long silence. Penlynne opened a briefcase, then he looked up with an almost whimsical smile. 'You and I should work together, Advocate Smit.'

'To what purpose, Mr Penlynne?'

'Why, to make this country great.'

'Is that the reason why you've been buying the so-called Liberals in the Volksraad? They will take your money, Penlynne, but they will never unseat the President. There are too many loyal Boers.'

Penlynne rose to it. 'There are plenty of Boers to whom Krugerism is anathema. That old man has feathered his own nest very adroitly for favours granted...concessions *etcetera*. Why don't you turn your talents to forking over that dunghill of corruption in Pretoria ... some ugly creatures may slither out.'

'A symposium on the degrees of moral corruption might be instructive. For myself, I reserve my contempt for those who bite the hand that feeds them.'

'Spare me the Kruger parable.'

Christiaan smiled. 'An Englishman, Penlynne, is like a monkey with his hand in a calabash of pumpkin seeds. He is too greedy to let go when the farmer comes with his gun.'

My God, thought Penlynne. Where have I heard that before? Yes, of course. In the sealed letter addressed to Lobengula. A striking simile, not easily forgotten. Was this its author? They were speaking without heat, almost bantering, each man with control of his feelings, smilingly, as men of the world can smile while they measure one another, daggers still sheathed.

'I was sorry to hear of Marloth's death.' Penlynne said it watching Smit's face. 'I liked him ... for a German.' He saw with a sense of elation that this was either the first Smit had heard of it or he was a consummate actor. 'I expect he'd gone north on one of his explorations.'

'Where did you get this information?'

Penlynne shrugged as if it was of no account.

'No, I insist.'

'The astonishing thing about Africa, Smit ... it's so vast, there are only a handful of whites in it, yet there is always someone turning up with news about some mutual friend. We tend to use the same tracks, sit down on the same rocks and turn over the same stones. You knew him, of course.'

'Only by hearsay.'

'I found him amusing but erratic. A generous fellow with information others made use of. But unpredictable.'

'Where did it happen ... was it fever?'

'On the banks of the Shashi ... assegais. So I was told.'

'By whom, may I ask?' The pale blue-grey eyes probing.

'I believe I heard it in the club,' said Penlynne with assumed indifference and turned again to his papers. They journeyed on in silence until the outskirts of the city appeared. 'Perhaps you would care to be my guest at the opening of the Agricultural Show.'

'Thank you ... I shall be in His Excellency's party.'

'I trust there will be no bad-mannered incidents,' said Penlynne.

'That is entirely up to the English press and the mobs it takes such pleasure to incite.'

'Good day, Advocate Smit.'

The slim, almost meagre figure with its suggestion of a lean, muscular body, limped into the station crowd. Penlynne saw him met by a man with thick moustaches and the bulk of a policeman. By now he regretted his impulse to mention Marloth. It had slipped out in his mood of depression after a day of shocks.

As he related it to Dorothy that evening: 'Dr Leyds...the Secretary of State, coolly informed me that he could do nothing to lower the price of dynamite...or put the concession into other hands. He told me with a smile that it would alienate good friends in Europe, powerful supporters of their independence.'

'You mean it's in German hands?'

'Of course. *Dynamit Actien-Gesellschaft*...and behind it German banks...and behind them, the German State. Can you see Kruger cancelling such a concession to his friends? Or should one already call them allies?'

'What will you do?'

'I must write to Sir Henry tonight.'

Dorothy sat stiffly erect, her hands clenching the damask arms of her chair. 'Then it will come to the worst,' she said. He rose and went over to her. Kneeling, he took both her hands.

'There is an alternative.'

'Go on,' she said calmly. The ormulu clock on the mantelpiece

150

tinkled the hour, its gilded figures circling, the filigree hands together at twelve. He waited.

'Loch and I have been corresponding. We met twice after the incident in Pretoria...in secret. He told me he could make the Transvaal British by raising a hand. He asked me how many rifles we had in Johannesburg. I said I had no idea...mostly sporting guns. He said he intended to enlarge the British garrison in the Cape at once to five thousand men and to station troops at Mafeking, near the Transvaal border.'

'Please go on.'

'What can we do here, in Johannesburg, I said.'

There was a knock at the door. Penlynne sprang from Dorothy's side as Robert looked in. 'Oh, I beg pardon,' he said. 'I was on my way upstairs and saw the light.' He backed out as if embarrassed. Penlynne went to the door and turned the key. She gave him a glance as if to say: has it come to that!

'Loch told me that if we could assure him that we had an adequate supply of arms he would guarantee military assistance. I asked what arms he would consider adequate. "Maxims are the thing," he said. "Rhodes took Rhodesia with the machine gun." I reminded him that we would not be fighting Matebele with assegais and oxhide shields. He said, "could you hold out for six days until help arrived." '

There was a long silence. In it, the sound of the stamp batteries seemed to rise from an unheard murmur to a roar that might have been sustained gunfire. 'The wind has changed to the south,' Penlynne said involuntarily. 'We shall have rain tomorrow.' He was looking through the french doors at the Florentine statuary he loved, its pale marble mysterious against a sky lavished with stars. Cypresses sighed in the wind. 'It will be cold,' he said. 'Come to bed.'

'What did you answer him?' Dorothy persisted.

'I said I'd look into it.'

'How did he take that?'

'He said, "I propose to re-annex the Transvaal and go on from there to a federation of all South Africa under the British flag." '

'How splendid!' she cried. 'To see an end of that uncouth old barbarian in Pretoria with his cunning little eyes, his greasy frock coat and antiquated top hat ... his Scriptural quotations. And misquotations to suit his purpose.'

Penlynne began to laugh immoderately. 'My dear,' he said, 'he is to be your guest of honour at the show on Saturday.'

'I shall be icily civil,' she assured him.

As they went upstairs he paused at the door of his study. 'I must write Sir Henry tonight...forgive me.'

She had hardly dismissed her maid and turned out the light when he burst in.

'What is it?' she said, sitting up.

'The Loch correspondence...it's gone from my desk.'

'Surely you took it to the office.'

'I particularly didn't do that.'

'You've been under strain...'

'Who could have taken it...and why?'

'I hope you're mistaken.'

'Thank God I sent the Marloth papers to Rhodes with Yeatsman. Yes, by hand. At least they didn't get those.'

'It will turn up,' she reassured him. 'Your secretary has misplaced it.'

'No,' he said with a short, bitter laugh. 'An enemy hath done this thing...if an *uitlander* may be permitted to quote the Scriptures.'

He said nothing more but he thought: the day is already here when we will not know whom to trust. His mind shrank from the organization that would be necessary. The acquiring of arms would be the least of it. They could be brought in in crates marked 'machinery' for the mines. To get Johannesburg to the point where a rising would be like a spark to tinder...how was that to be done?

It was freezing in the wood and iron bungalow in Bree Street. Bitter August winds swept the town. Christiaan Smit got to his office early, striding through deserted streets. He sometimes found the water in the horse trough frozen over. The keen south wind had shrivelled foliage. On his desk the police dockets were gritty with mine dust. He'd shake a sleepy constable to rouse up and bawl for the *kaffir* to make coffee. The mudbrick cells behind the office were crammed with drunks and petty malefactors. A sour stink permeated the building, an odour he subconsciously connected with crime. He'd been sent to investigate the corruptive effect of illicit liquor selling on the police force. But he had noted much more. Prostitution – rampant. Illicit gold dealing – rampant. Public disorder – frequent. Drunkenness – endemic. He had sympathy for police dealing with such a population. Greeks, Cypriots, Germans, Hollanders, Americans, Armenians, Belgians, Turks, Russian Jews. Swarming blacks of a score of tribes, Coloureds and Indians. And, of course, the raw, immigrant Englishman in all his ignorance and arrogance.

To keep order was difficult enough without it being bedevilled by political strife...but that was coming. There was no loyalty here. No gratitude for the golden opportunity. Only abuse of his government and leaders. Christiaan did not know he had become a man who seldom smiled. He seemed to see through people with his pale grey-blue eyes. Older men standing before him felt ill at ease. He seemed to repress a driving energy with difficulty. His very self-control had the appearance of coldness.

'I am not much liked,' he knew. When he put a pot of cacti on the window sill to catch the wintry sun, nobody commented or shared with him the plant's slow blossoming into scarlet flowers. He saw it as a parable. Out of the bitter flesh had come this radiance. One morning he came in to find the pot shattered on the floor. He gathered the pieces, his silence more ominous than an outburst.

The Loch-Penlynne correspondence had first shocked, then elated him. It brought the blood to his pale, thin cheeks to think he was onto the conspiracy. 'Drop everything else,' Dr Leyds told him. 'You have my full support.'

Here was the first hard evidence they had of *uitlander* treason and Imperial perfidy. He examined the signatures of Loch and Penlynne side by side as if to read the deepest secrets of their characters. Somehow these papers had to be returned. The channel of information kept open.

He kept nothing from Anna. 'How did they come into our hands?' she queried. They were sharing their body warmth in the icy house in Jeppe. The rainwater tank would be frozen in the morning. Going out in that wind to the pit toilet was an ordeal he made himself enjoy for its Spartan virtue. It was not the deep penetrating cold of Holland where he'd studied, but *hemel!* This was Africa!

Their proximity, her warmth, the smell of her hair, was arousing him. 'No, tell me,' she insisted. 'First tell me.'

'Afterwards,' he whispered ardently. He loved her with a passion his colleagues could never have imagined from 'that cold fish'. She gave in to him, willingly, lovingly. 'You know,' he said later, stroking her gently, 'a man in love will do anything. And if he is also in debt...well, it's a compelling combination.'

'No philosophy, please...facts.'

'Penlynne's young brother-in-law took them. He has gambling debts to Yudelsohn. When we knew that, we put pressure on Yudelsohn to demand payment from Penlynne. Young Robert was in a panic. One day he was rooting through Penlynne's papers, hoping to intercept a letter from the Jew. He came on the Loch letters. The boy's infatuated by this Loftus woman ... the so-called actress. There was the notorious affair with Penlynne some years back at *Bloukoppen*. Anyway, Robert told Loftus about the letters, possibly not realizing their significance ... perhaps just a titbit of gossip about a man she hates. He abandoned her with a child, you know.'

He felt Anna's instinctive sympathy.

'No need to feel sorry for her.'

'Not her...the child.' Her response touched him deeply. She had thought of his own fatherless childhood and her girlhood love of him, of the bushveld grave where his mother lay under a cairn of stones and an anteaten cross. 'Well, one day this fellow Isadore Isaacs walked in and asked to see me. We have a dossier on him for illegal liquor dealings. One of the worst. He knows we are after his skin so he came, offering to make a trade of the letters for immunity.'

'How did he get the letters?'

'His friendship with the Loftus woman. She told him about the letters and he saw the possibility of making use of them. They put Robert up to removing them from Penlynne's office.'

'What a contemptible young man.'

'Weak...he'll be useful.'

'In what way?'

'Return the letters before they're missed.'

'But will he...the risk?'

'He has no option. In return we'll take care of his debts from the Secret Fund for as long as he's useful. As I said, a man in love with that kind of woman will do anything.'

He felt her hand grope for his. 'Must we do these things?'

'Believe me, this is only a beginning. Unless the English back down and give us full independence there will be such a struggle ... some of our people hate the *uitlanders* so much that nothing will appease them except the end of Johannesburg. Yes, abandoned ... the veld grass covering the scars.'

'Surely that's not what you want?'

'There are extremists among us ... just as there are among them. I never see a trainload of dynamite shunting in the Braamfontein yards without thinking: if that went up!' A mighty, rushing wind would sweep the veld clean.

They lay silently looking up at the ornamental tin ceiling with its manufactured imitation of skilled stucco. Bogus, like everything else in this town. False facades of sundried brick. Tin roofs on houses with pretensions to being mansions. An imitation Europe. You could imagine it as such until you saw a span of twenty-four oxen drawing a wagon or saw a mounted Boer threading his way among hansom cabs and carriages.

Then you knew: this is Africa. My Africa.

Christiaan was up at his usual hour. He read his portion of Scripture and bowed his head briefly. Anna came with coffee and *beskuit*. She put down the cup among the notes he kept on grasses, each with the Latin name he had suggested for species still unclassified by the botanical world. That was when she noticed the old Bible.

'I've never seen this before, Christiaan.' She opened it. In Dutch and printed in 1864. 'Where did you get it?'

'It belonged to Oom Francis...Colonel Uys, you remember him.'

'Why is it here?'

'He's dead. It was sent to me by Mynheer Penlynne.'

'How did he come to have it?'

'If I knew the answer to that I would know a great deal. In his account of it some of his people found the bodies of Oom Francis and Carl Marloth near the Shashi River...murdered by Matebele.'

'You don't believe that, evidently.'

'Dr Leyds believes ... and so do I ... that our emissary to Lobengula was murdered at the instigation of Cecil Rhodes. And, of course, of Leonard Penlynne and his friends.'

'Why would he send the Bible to you?'

'A gesture … a man as devious as that could have had many reasons. Perhaps even genuine regret. What he did not send back is far more significant.'

Chapter Thirteen

A knocking on his window woke Stewart MacDonald. He was long accustomed to the midnight summons, some ashen-faced man or woman standing at his door, lantern in hand. How many times had he slipped out from Mary's side, groped into his clothes and let himself out to the waiting trap, trying to clear his brain in the cold air, not knowing where he was going or to what emergency – an appendectomy on a kitchen table…an intestinal obstruction…once even to a marriage bed where a girl was bleeding uncontrollably. His hopes of finding time to make a systematic study of the diseases of the community had come to nothing more than a few notes.

'Who's that at the window?' Mary rose on one arm. These nights there were often disturbances, shots in the distance and galloping hooves. She dreaded finding some man on the stoep with a gunshot wound.

Stewart threw up the sash to see Owen Davyd, a muffler at his throat, the empty sleeve tucked into the pocket. Behind him was a hand cart, a tarpaulin thrown over it and a black man pushing it. 'It's Peter Davis, doctor,' Owen said. He threw back the tarpaulin. Stewart saw the Cornishman he'd last seen in Ferreira's camp.

'There's nothing I can do for him, Owen.'

Owen Davyd gripped his arm. 'Listen to me, Stewart. It's his wish. You're to do a post mortem, make a report. You know the owners. They won't listen. Men dying like flies and all we get from them "it's not our problem". Plenty more where they came from.'

'You can't bring me a corpse on a hand cart and demand a post mortem, Owen. I've no authority. Who's written the death certificate? I've no responsibility for this man.'

'He thought well of you, Stewart, taking trouble to see him.'

'Who attended him when he died?'

'I was there. Me and his wife. It was his wish. Make some use of me, he said.'

'You must take him back…arrange for his burial.'

'He gave me a note.'

Written in an illiterate hand on cheap paper it begged pardon for trouble given and hereby donated his body to science and hoping it would be useful to understand the rockdrill fever. Signed, *Yr obed.servant, Peter Davis.*

There was no precedent for post mortems and no facilities. Today's dead were buried tomorrow. Death certificates were perfunctory, causes arbitrary. Bodies went unidentified. Tomorrow Davis would be in a hole in the red earth. His death would not even make a statistic.

'I'll get dressed,' he said, both reluctant and excited. In the dissecting room at Glasgow Infirmary old Andrew Carnegie demonstrated the swift slash from sternum to abdomen, laying open the viscera. He remembered gas lamps flaring and wavering in that icy vault of a basement and how his hand shook as Carnegie pressed the scalpel into his grasp: 'What are you scared of, lad. He won't bite!'

Where could it be done? Theiler's laboratory. The Swiss would not refuse him. It was there he had dissected calves when he was struggling to perfect his vaccine to control the smallpox outbreak two years back. 'Take him to Theiler's lab,' he ordered. I'll get some clothes on.'

As the hand cart creaked away into the darkness he turned to Mary. He patted her reassuringly. 'Fetch me Fowler's *The Human Body*…the red book on my bookshelf.'

'At this hour?'

'Aye, hurry.'

'Is it an emergency?' Her instinct told her, that and his excitement, that he was embarking on something he might have cause to regret.

'I've been waiting for this chance, Mary. It's not to be missed.'

'A post mortem?'

'Aye…rock drilling.' She had heard him many times on the subject, berating himself and his colleagues for ignorance. She had seen patients sitting in the waiting room, gaunt, grey-faced miners, their clothing hanging on them, had heard their struggle for breath. She had seen Stewart's face when he made up bottles in the dispensary. 'Useless syrups!' When she remarked on the men's cheerfulness he groaned: 'Gallows courage...there's no' a one of them will be here next year.'

The mine hospitals had no remedy for lung diseases. The men themselves were fatally footloose, moving from mine to mine as long as they could work, finally dying in some bachelor's digs sitting upright to breathe the last struggling breaths, a whiskey bottle at the side. Married men left widows and young children. Anna felt a great sympathy for them. In the outfitter's window she'd turn quickly away from a ticket: *Widow's weeds, complete in 24 hours. Children also catered.* It was a grand place for black crepe ribbons. It seemed to her that death on the Rand was always brutal, sudden or cruel. You did not have to drive far into the veld to see empty rib cages and scattered bones of draught animals. The gibbering laugh of the hyena was not all that unusual. A mile from town at the ridge they called Vulture's Head, the great birds soared the cliffs on the summer wind and were often seen circling above the market.

In the barren red-earth cemeteries along the reef there were already enough to populate a town the size of the nearest market to her father's farm in Ayrshire. Oh, death was a busy partner here though the cypresses were young and the flowers withered in a morning. And on her child's grave it was the same. She felt the guilt of her neglect.

How many times had Stewart said: 'If I had known what I was in for ... I could have had an elegant practice in Edinburgh now. Frock coat and tile hat.'

'Not you, Stewart,' she'd say, always loyal to the ideals she believed worthy of him.

And now, this bizarre excursion in the middle of the night. She knew that look on his face. He'd go through with it whatever happened. He took the textbook from her, kissed her cold cheek and mounted his bicycle, the black bag secure on the carrier.

Getting knocked up in the middle of the night was nothing unusual to Arnold Theiler. By the time Stewart arrived Theiler and Owen Davyd had trundled the hand cart into the stable the veterinarian used as a laboratory. It was here Stewart had watched the Swiss, red to the elbows, doing post mortems on calves by lamplight in his search for the source of the *rinderpest*. Glass jars of specimens, block and tackle in the roof, the brassy glint of a microscope and racks of test tubes gave the place an atmosphere half-stable, half-laboratory. It stank of formalin and urine.

Theiler was enthusiastic. 'So, you bring one at last, doctor. One must seize the chance. Quickly now.' He closed the stable-door and shot the heavy bolts, turned up the hissing naphtha lamp to a brighter glare. He threw a rubber apron to Stewart. The cadaver was stripped and laid out on a cement slab with a drainage channel.

'Spread newspapers,' Theiler ordered Owen Davyd who stood awkwardly, already dismayed by what he had initiated. Dumbly he obeyed, with one eye watching the array of tools being laid out by Stewart.

'This is my first,' Stewart admitted. His face was pale.

'It is necessary...it is science,' Theiler assured him. He was standing with his sleeves rolled up, drawing on rubber gloves. 'I help ... the human body is also animal. It is the method that is different.' He handed Stewart the scalpel.

By the state of the body the miner had been dead some six or seven hours. There was a look of awesome serenity on Peter Davis's face, his head resting on a wooden block, the body laid out at a height that gave easy access to it. Stewart poised the scalpel hesitantly. There was a muffled thud behind. Theiler grunted and dragged Owen Davyd to one side.

'Begin, doctor,' he urged.

As he made the first incision beneath the chin and the flesh parted Stewart was remembering old Andrew Carnegie's cynical observation. 'Only the poor reach the post mortem tables ... we are studying only the diseases of the outcasts.'

It would be the same here.

Owen Davyd groaned and sat up. 'Make yourself useful or get out,' Theiler ordered. 'Fill buckets with water, we need plenty water.'

From his first incision to the removal of the lungs took Stewart over an hour of intense concentration. Andrew Carnegie had boasted that he could remove a brain in three minutes and examine an entire body – from preliminary incision to removal of the spinal cord – in less than twenty minutes. 'Six in a morning, gentlemen!'

Stewart no longer felt he was violating the body. He talked aloud as he worked: 'The lungs are discoloured and hard to the touch...gritty particles in the deeper layers of the visceral envelope...fibrous tissue...small gritty nodules.' He paused at intervals to scribble his observations in a notebook that lay at the dead man's hand, as if poor Peter Davis could have made the notes himself.

'Look here, Theiler!' he cried. 'There are fibrous changes round each focus of irritation...these air cells have coalesced to form patches of consolidation...solid. The man had only a section of lung tissue left for breathing. He literally choked to death.'

'Ja, the heart goes into syncope,' said Theiler.

'They go on working like this,' Stewart groaned. A miner he'd treated for shortness of breath and hacking cough (Stewart suspected tuberculosis) had died at his drill. Heart failure.

Lifting Davis's heart from the enamel basin he said almost to himself. 'I know nothing...nothing. And the cemetery's full of these fellows.' He was almost re-experiencing the dust-filled air, the reek of explosives that gave violent headaches, the heat and lack of ventilation to carry off fumes.

Theiler brought two large glass jars. He filled them with formaldehyde, dropped in the pair of lungs and stoppered both. 'Enough for tonight, doctor. Tomorrow we examine a section under microscope.'

The cadaver was packed with sawdust from the stable floor and stitched up with a packing needle and twine, dressed and returned to the hand cart.

'What killed him, Stewart?' said Owen humbly.

'I don't know. You're to say nothing about this to anyone. What we did may have been unlawful.'

'What about moral reasons then! What about owners' responsibility. Men dying...no compensation. You got to report what you found, Stewart. That's why I brought him. It's your duty, mun.'

'Owen, I found nothing I understand. So far, nothing.'

In the first grey streaks of dawn he mounted his bicycle. He rode fast in the coolness, glad to clear his lungs of the odour that would adhere to his hands for hours. In the brisk ride and as the mine headgears came into spidery relief against the light, he could not rid his mind of the calmness on the face of Peter Davis. The cold smile, as if he were thinking: 'What's all the fuss about

…I'm only a workman.'

Several days went by before Stewart was able to get an interview with Leonard Penlynne. The magnate received him cordially, reminding him of the time they had worked together on the smallpox committee.

'Theiler's a remarkable man,' Penlynne agreed. 'People here owe a lot to his vaccine, and your work with him, doctor.'

'I've come from his laboratory.'

'Still the stable?' Penlynne chatted on about the search for an effective vaccine against the horse sickness. 'He should be supported for that, don't you agree, doctor?'

'I believe the men are more important, Mr Penlynne.'

Penlynne's face turned to stone as Stewart spoke of the post mortem. 'By what authority was this performed, doctor? This could have dire consequences if it reaches Pretoria's ears. As for the effect on the black labour force. The mutilation of corpses has only one purpose for them…*muti.*'

'The opportunity came. Sooner or later we have to consider the appalling death toll from lung conditions. The Mining Chamber should require its members to keep simple statistics.'

'All accidents are reported to the Government Mining Department.'

'Statistics of lung diseases.'

'Mining is no paradise, doctor. Not here…not in Europe.'

'Sir, first statistics, then laws to improve conditions.'

'You can't lay tuberculosis at my door, doctor. Nor pneumonia. It's conditions…it's climate.'

'There's no proof that their deaths are due to either.'

Penlynne looked startled. 'We are not indifferent, you know. The fumes of poor quality dynamite has been suggested. Others put it down to rotgut liquor. Believe me, doctor, the white miner in this country is in clover. And what is more, it is the blacks who are doing his work.'

'Mr Penlynne, you astonish me.'

'It is hard to be sympathetic to a class of men who are, with few exceptions, reckless and irresponsible. Thirty percent of the workforce changes jobs every week. And you expect medical statistics!' He rose and came round his desk, putting his hand on Stewart's shoulder.

'Look here, I am not unsympathetic. One must be realistic.'

Stewart persisted. 'Lighter work could be found for a man in the early stages.'

'This is a problem of mining worldwide, Stewart.'

Stewart rose. He had been dismissed with a friendly wave. 'You might start a statistical record yourself, doctor. Begin with your patients. These things take time.' Stewart had reached the door when Penlynne spoke with every sign of sincerity. 'The industry has grave problems, doctor. Believe me they are considerably greater than the workmen's health. There may be no industry at all, if some have their way.' He smiled. 'Let me see a copy of your post mortem report.' Of course, he had thought of the need for a medical research centre. It would have to wait.

Almost at once his friendly expression altered to one of gravity. As he rang for his secretary his face had assumed the mask of authority. A rough estimate of the firearms owned on the mines and the reef villages was on his desk.

That night Stewart went again to Theiler's laboratory. What he saw in the microscope made him wince. Deeply embedded in tissue was a fleck of rock dust. A razor-edged saw of quartzite that required a microscope to see it.

'There is your killer, doctor,' he heard Theiler say.

Under Stewart's hand was a newspaper. A black-bordered advertisement proclaimed: *Myers and Brand, the leading undertakers. Official contractors to the Transvaal Police, Prison Department, the Government Mortuary and the Largest Reef Mines. Terms moderate.*

Stewart began to shake with silent laughter. 'We're in the wrong trade, Theiler,' he spluttered. 'The wrong trade altogether.'

Chapter Fourteen

The Saxon was still in tropical waters when the concert in aid of Seamen's Widows and Orphans was announced. Charles was sharing a cabin on the bridge deck with a Mr Richard Dives. The Durban merchant read Scriptures at night and morning and knelt by his bunk. Charles was embarrassed by his devotion. He would walk the deck until it was over. Church parades were the nearest he came to religion though he was not immune to blood-stirring phrases. God defend the Right. God save the Queen! Charles saw no reason why the Almighty should not be on the side of the best regiments, especially when it came to clobbering the heathen. He was still at school when elements of his regiment rode into Khartoum with Gordon and perished there. On an Arab scimitar hung in the Mess the inscription read: *Mohammed is the sword of God.* And no doubt the nignogs believed it. Charles thought the Almighty might change his mind if he'd ever seen an Islamic prison...

He was to sing at the concert and down for *Asleep in the Deep,* a ballad he had sung many times in the Mess and in drawing-rooms. Katherine had promised to accompany him. It was after one of their rehearsals, the piano still echoing the deep bass notes of his voice, when Mr Dives came over.

'I never hear that song without deep emotion,' he began ten-dentiously. Katherine rose at a nod from Charles. Mr Dives per-sisted, trotting alongside, determined to make his point.

'If they had listened to me, sir...it need never have happened. There are several of us aboard going to the public enquiry. I be-lieved it my duty to come forward and make a statement.' Katherine realized that he was talking about the Board of Trade enquiry into the *Sydney Star*. Mr Dives followed them to the palm court and sat down uninvited.

'I went down to the docks to see her,' he said with a look that invited a wider audience. 'I had a presentiment I would never

164

see her again.' Some teacups ceased to rattle. 'I was convinced she was top heavy and competent authorities confirmed me in this opinion. She'll turn turtle, I observed to one of them. Surely she should not be allowed to sail.'

'Do you often have premonitions, sir?' A stout, florid-faced man in his mid-sixties spoke up in a challenging manner and strong Scots accent.

'I had three premonitions in my family...of deaths.'

'Evidently you are clairvoyant, sir.'

'Well, I am a believer in divine inspiration and this was a divine inspiration. The vessel was too high above the waterline.'

'You are also an expert on ship design.'

'No sir, but I believe I was led by a Higher Hand to notice the construction of the bridge.' Mr Dives had become very red.

'My name is Tweedie,' said the Scot. 'I travelled in the *Sydney Star* on her first voyage. I have never been in a sounder ship ... or had a better voyage. I shall give evidence to that effect.'

Mr Dives rose triumphantly. 'Then where is she, sir, if my presentiment was false!'

'That I can't say ... not having the gift of clairvoyancy. Perhaps you will be able to tell the court after a look in your crystal ball.' Tweedie began to bawl with laughter.

Charles obeyed the appeal in Katherine's eyes. On deck he heard her anxiety. 'I hope this is not going to turn into a squalid affair.'

'The man's a crank.'

'Suppose there's no judgement ... the loss is unconfirmed?'

He knew what she hinted. It would take seven years to declare Muriel Rawlinson dead and finalize the estate in Katherine's name. His concern was for Katherine, nothing more. A deep concern not to compromise her among people who knew them both. Contact had been minimal ... even the contact of hand and eye. She was with her maid and the children's nanny. We must wait, he thought. He was startled when Katherine came to his cabin, ashen-faced.

'It's Spencer ... he gave nanny the slip.'

He took her hand as she swayed towards him. 'I know where he'll be ... where I'd be at his age.'

Spencer was right at the ship's prow, standing on a thick coil of rope and shouting as she dived into the approaching seas, spray hissing over the bulwarks. The boy turned, his face alight. 'Look!' he cried. 'Dolphin!' He broke away when Katherine scolded him and darted below.

'It was his grandfather standing there,' she marvelled. 'He's quite without fear.'

'Eton will discipline him,' he said.

'Why Eton?'

'That's where I went.'

'It's too soon to think of that,' she said evasively.

'Katherine ... tonight.' She turned quickly and gave him her lips. Sweet and salt. Then she was gone with a swish and a rustle.

In her stateroom the sounds of the ship were muted. He was aware only of the warmth and the scented pressure of her against him. The room was connected to the children's cabin by a door. She moved to listen and secure it with the bolt, then turned to him with flushed cheeks, pulling the pins from her hair so that the mass of bright golden tresses tumbled down her back. She was trembling as he began to undress her, seeing with excitement the white, inflowing curve of her back emerge in the mirror, the twin hemispheres of her naked buttocks startling in their erotic suggestion. She was leaning on him, as if she had lost all control of her legs and he had to help her from the clothing fallen about her ankles. 'Oh, my God! Katherine,' he heard himself groan, fumbling at his clothing with shaking hands.

'Let me help you.' Her fingers were so cool they seemed to burn him. Their naked bodies fell together, fused into an arc of enchantment. Eyes and mouths devoured each other, staring and tasting as if they would never be satisfied. Sounds of the ship returned and the ticking of the watch he had laid on the dressing table without being aware of it. In fact, he had laid it there with what had seemed, to her, an intolerable slowness.

In the days following he felt secure in her affection for the first time since they had met. She gave him the long, meaningful glances a woman shared only with a man for whom she felt a quickening passion. They were both oblivious of looks. Did it matter? Her marriage to Walter Gardiner was all but over. 'I shall never allow him to dictate to me how my father's money should be used. He has treated our marriage as a convenience. I have to break away from him. Even, my dear, if I had not met you. I was a child when he married me.'

'Will he agree?'

'Agree!' she cried. 'Johannesburg talks of nothing else but his infatuation with that woman.' He put an arm around her and she did not withdraw. 'What then?' he said, looking across the intense blue of tropical ocean to a silvery glitter of flying fish, their sudden freedom into another element concealing the jaws of the predator beneath.

'I shall live my life,' she said. He was too aware of her intensity of feeling to use the moment to press his claim. His being there was enough for her. He spoke of autumn at Warewood, of the falling leaves in the neglected forest where his mad uncle still hunted, of huge fires on the hearth and the glint of flames on old weapons. Katherine listened to his fond talk of ancestral lands, the crumbling mansion, the deserted cottages of tenants leaving the land for town and factory. It came to her with a pleasant shock that it had never crossed his mind to save his family estate by marriage.

Lying sleepless that night, the children asleep next door and the memory of his lips still on hers, she found herself thinking how good it must be to be loved for oneself in a marriage that demanded nothing; that had its obligations but did not turn them into rights. Was her marriage to Walter the norm among people of their society? Could one have great wealth and still enjoy one another for nothing more than something shared, something intangible? Suppose she was to lose everything her father had worked for in this war everyone said was certain to come? Would it matter? Would this man's loyalty to her be enough? She was her father's daughter after all.

Charles had told her, laughing: 'When I got to Johannesburg in time for your engagement party I thought it best to join an expedition to the north...as a trooper. All I got for it was malaria and I couldn't forget you.' He did not tell her of the pain of seeing her in the arms of Walter Gardiner. For two pins he could have shot himself that night as the American whirled her around in his triumph and old Rawlinson stood there receiving congratulations.

When she hinted at divorce he tried to conceal his hopes. Lady Warewood! What life she would bring to the old place. Then came a sudden sense of dread. There might be years more waiting while Katherine remained in an emotional limbo, still tied to Gardiner. Should he force the pace, man to man with Gardiner? No, he must wait for her. Wait as long as it might take. There would never be anyone else in his life. And she had already given him much. More than he had ever imagined possible.

However, he had not taken ship to England to meet Katherine by prearrangement. It had happened fortuitously. At first he had been dismayed that he had run into her at a time when he could not tell her of his purpose in England. He had spoken vaguely of the estate...the need to be there. He knew that she had not totally accepted this explanation and it stood like an ill-defined threat between them; a lack of openness that he regretted.

At the captain's table he listened to heated argument about affairs in the Transvaal. He offered no opinions. When he was pressed for a military solution he replied, 'I relinquished my commission some time ago...with regret, due to ill health.'

'If I were your age I'd be in the saddle,' said his questioner.

He was astonished when later that night the man introduced himself as a member of the National Union. 'You've heard of us.' Charles knew of them as a pressure group. Totally ineffective. 'You will, sir. It is our rights we are after but until we can win the big mine owners and influential people to our side, we can do nothing. So far, men like Penlynne are more concerned with their pockets. They will not commit themselves to reform.'

'Indeed,' said Charles with careful indifference. He had a sense of being tried out as if to discover how far he would commit himself. 'Do you agree that ultimately it will be a question of arms?' he heard himself asked, the man's eyes probingly on him.

'No doubt it will be settled,' Charles said. How little this man evidently knew of what was afoot, or was he trying to draw him? Was he, in fact, what he said he was, a member of the National Union? He claimed to be English, but was he? And if he were, there were numerous Englishmen who did not support *uitlander* demands.

The night before Tenerife he was cornered again. 'I have a feeling that you've been avoiding me,' the man said. 'I have something for you, a letter from a mutual friend. Don't open it here.'

In the envelope was a letter of introduction to the Birmingham Small Arms Company giving him complete authority to buy arms and munitions 'of his selection'. Also a blank cheque in the name of New Concession Syndicate. A typed instruction. 'You can be assured that preliminary arrangements have been made. Your signature on the cheque will be accepted, no questions asked. The goods are to be shipped to Kimberley, to De Beers, marked "mining and engineering stores".'

Charles never saw the man again. When he enquired of the purser he was told that the gentleman in question had left the ship at Tenerife. Preliminary arrangements had been made. That evidently meant that someone else had decided on what arms were required. Only his professional judgement of their quality was asked for. And the authority of his name. It was cool, damned cool of Penlynne to assume that he would agree.

'I don't say we're going to use them,' he'd said to Charles. 'But at the right moment we're certainly going to show we have them.'

When Katherine was last in England, her father had not yet bought the lease on Ludlow House in Park Lane. He had died before making any use of it. A servant opened its rooms for her inspection. She was seeing it for the first time but gave no sign of it.

'We're delighted to have you, ma'am.'

The three-storey building of white Portland stone was entered by a majestic hall of green marble pillars. It took her breath away. An electric lift in an elaborate wrought-iron cage moved noiselessly upwards between floors. In the drawing-room and reception rooms rich carpets were spread like gardens in some oriental paradise. Dust sheets still covered costly furnishings. About the entire house there was a hush that breathed the assurance of wealth.

'Is this our new house, mama?' Spencer's intelligent dark eyes darted to a lifesize portrait of her father in frock coat, posed against a background of mine dumps and headgears. She saw, with a pang, the original stone house at Langlaagte. The artist had caught his imperious air. One hand thrown out indicated the gesture with which he had brought all this into existence, in the other he toyed with a piece of quartzite veined with gold, as if calculating its worth to a pennyweight.

'Will you see the art gallery now, ma'am?'

Katherine knew that her father had been buying old masters of the 17th and 18th Century, Dutch and Italian schools as well as English and French. She was awed by the cathedral hush of the gallery. Tiled and marbled floors, soaring pillars and vaulted ceiling, like a wing of the Tate. Franz Hals, Rembrandt, Gainsborough. The eyes of famous figures followed her.

'Look mama, they're watching us!'

Whether he had bought them out of sheer acquisitiveness or actually admired them, she had no idea. There they were. Hers. She sat down on a velvet settle and looked up towards the huge crystal chandeliers and the glass dome that let in the pale English daylight. Spencer's voice echoed as he ran and slid on the marble floor.

Until now her father's fortune had been no more than figures on paper administered by others. For the first time she was aware of the meaning of wealth, great wealth. She understood Walter's impatience to lay hands on it. Once held, he would never let it out of his grasp ... this, and what it represented.

Suddenly Charles was coming towards her, smiling. She grasped his hand. 'I've made the enquiry,' he said. 'The Board of Trade will hear the case next month in Caxton Hall before a full board with members of the Admiralty present. All the experts. Until then,' he was softly pleading, 'why don't you and the children come down to Warewood? They'll enjoy it even if the weather is setting in for winter.'

'People will talk, my darling.'

'They're talking already, I believe.' Ruefully he added: 'I shall have to be away part of the time.' How different he looked here in England, she thought. The sea voyage had recovered him. He looked much as she remembered from their first meeting six years ago, a tall, slender young cavalry officer, red-cheeked and blue-eyed. She had met him during the year of her coming out, of her presentation to Her Majesty, of the round of the autumn social calendar so unusual for one from 'the Colonies'.

Now she was a beautiful woman. She knew it. Two children had matured her body. She was no longer the girl heiress besieged by many men, uncertain of her mind and afraid of her body. Johannesburg and Walter seemed never to have existed. The face she lifted to Charles had a newness about it. 'My God, Katherine,' she heard him say, 'How lovely you are.'

170

December 17th was a foul morning even by London standards. The gutters outside Caxton Hall were running full tilt and the grimed buildings of Westminster were all but obscured by sleet and rain. All London seemed black; black capes, black umbrellas, black skies, black moods. On Katherine's way from Ludlow House, the stream of carriages, drays and cabs had been held up. A great Clydesdale gelding had slipped on the cobblestones and had had to be shot. When she passed the place, blood ran mingled with rainwater. The horse lay under a tarpaulin as the mass of traffic moved on with a surge and a rumble.

The carriage was comfortable and warm. Katherine was veiled and was wearing a full-length sable against England's winter. The press of carriages outside Caxton Hall was so heavy that she had to walk before reaching the door. She saw that the hearing would be crowded and sensational. The Press had made the most of it: theories of the ship's loss and premonitions of clairvoyants were discussed with cranks; the anger of relatives hoping to sue the steamship line if the finding was negligence. The Press had been at her door but she had refused to see them. She was here to know with finality her position vis-à-vis her father's fortune.

An usher showed her to a seat in the front of the gallery. It looked down on a quadrangle of tables flanked by seats for witnesses. It was rather informal so far. Experts and lawyers came in and greeted each other. All this handshaking and geniality seemed a strange preamble. They were here to discuss how two hundred and eighty people had disappeared…their agony and terror. In her handbag Katherine had brought Muriel's last letter written in Durban. There were traces of a presentiment, not of disaster, but of something beyond her control. 'My folks are fey,' she wrote. 'I havna' the gift myself.' One paragraph stood out. 'I've never been afeared of the sea. In any case I don't want to put it off any longer. I dreamed my new hat blew off my head into the water. A gentleman said it was unlucky. I just thought, there's my guid hat and a' my trouble!'

Charles said it was better he did not attend the hearing. She missed him. He occupied most of her thoughts. She had reached a place in her emotions where she felt some strand of his being had been interwoven with hers. She knew when he was near. She looked up to see him with increasing delight. She had found herself listening intently if anyone used his name. It gave her pleasure when they spoke well of him. Strangely too, she found herself kissing or embracing the children in his presence. When he was near her she heard herself talking louder to remind him she was there.

The clatter and buzz below increased. She had seen him off to Birmingham from Euston station, her hand reluctantly letting his go as the train began to move. Under the echoing glass vault she was experiencing a pang of emptiness. Then the metallic clanging and hissing diminished. Only the stink of steam, smoke and oil remained…that, and the glittering curves of the rails that had taken him away. The piercing note of the guard's last whistle had sounded so final.

'At Warewood!' Charles shouted cheerfully.

The man who approached her said he was from one of the halfpenny daily papers. 'Mrs Gardiner, if I'm not mistaken,' he said familiarly, raising a disreputable hat. 'Over here for the hearing, not so?' He walked confidently beside her. 'Could you find a few minutes to give me a statement…how do you feel about Lady Rawlinson's sad death?'

Katherine walked on, ignoring him, her mind in a tumult, hurrying to where her coachman waited with a rug over his arm. As she mounted the rich smell of leather gave her a momentary illusion of safety. 'I'll be writing a neat little paragraph for *Causerie,*' she heard. 'The Rawlinson heiress was seen seeing off Captain the Lord Charles Warewood with a pretty demonstration of affection!'

'Drive on, Brixton,' she commanded and saw the hateful face fall back from the window. No doubt it would earn him half a guinea.

On the third day of the court proceedings she heard her husband's name called. 'Will Mr Walter Gardiner take the stand.' She was astonished. He had said nothing of his intention to come to the hearing. He came forward, bulking large over the usher. Suddenly all the focus of attention was on him. 'You have evidence relevant to this enquiry, Mr Gardiner?'

'Yes sir, I have the depositions of two seamen, sworn in Cape Town.'

'What is your interest in this enquiry, Mr Gardiner?'

'I am related by marriage to Lady Rawlinson.'

'Will you read the depositions to the court?'

Until her husband spoke the enquiry had been technical, stressing the owners' point of view. The vessel was entirely sea-worthy, incapable of turning turtle. No complaints had been made to the builders after her first voyage. Letters from the captain praised her performance. Suddenly the court was hearing of bodies in the sea, Gardiner reading in his commanding voice.

....I saw pieces of flesh floating...chunks of it...a little girl floating face down in a red cloak or dressing gown. She had bare knees and black stockings. The captain said it was whale offal from the whaling station and that's how he logged it, sir. But I seed it and my mates. She floated by close enough for the bilges to spill on her.

The deposition of Seaman Jack Noble went on to say that when his ship docked in Cape Town the captain gave orders to the crew to keep their mouths shut. They had seen nothing.

The deposition of Apprentice John Day described a body with an albatross perched on it...of sharks among the bodies and of steaming through chunks of white flesh for two hours.

Katherine listened, vainly trying to dissociate Muriel from the horrors so crudely recalled in the illiterate statements. She could see that Gardiner was relishing his grasp of the court's attention. 'I felt, sir, that in the interests of a true judgement the court should have these depositions.' He stood down in a buzz of speculation.

Katherine rose and went out. She felt nauseous and furiously resentful. Walter had made it so evident that he would not rest until he had the verdict he wanted. That afternoon he turned up at Ludlow House as if he owned it.

'Have you been busy, Katherine? Chosen the mausoleum for your father yet? You'll be able to add his wife's name to it while you're at it. There's no doubt of the verdict. I hear the ship owners have done their damnedest to suppress any evidence that the vessel was unseaworthy. Can you imagine what it will cost them. There's been some pretty chicanery. Did you know that the captain's reports of the trial voyage are missing, mysteriously? All the ship experts have been reassuring about the ship's qualities. Only the seamen and those with nothing to lose have given contrary evidence ... the others all had reputations to lose.' He laughed. 'It won't help them with those assessors – two admirals and a professor of marine engineering.'

It was the old, ebullient Gardiner smelling the kill from afar, his bold eyes taking in the splendid furnishings with the air of the proprietor, costing it in his head. 'We'll sell off the art collection right away. Madness to tie up a quarter million sterling. I might keep the Reubens. I like fleshy women about me.'

'My father spoke of giving them to the nation,' she flashed.

'He was too goddam tight for that.'

'They will hang here as long as I own the lease on Ludlow House.'

He laughed and came confidently towards her, reaching her from her chair to hold her against himself. 'It's been a long time, Katherine, and you're looking very beautiful.'

She broke indignantly from him.

'We ought to keep on good terms, Katherine. Don't you agree?'

He was so sure of himself, so infuriatingly certain that it was all in his grasp and that from now on he would have his way with her father's money. Six months ago she would have given in, not meekly but with her anger suppressed. In this house…hers by right of inheritance, she had felt the stirring of her father's blood. This place was, as it were, the summation of his achievement even more than the busy sprawl of the Rawlinson Star, his Johannesburg house and his enormous holdings in land. He had not slept a single night here yet it had an atmosphere of a life's work well done. It was a statement about the man. Here he had planned to sit down with princes and statesmen. She was his daughter, Spencer his grandson.

'Whatever the outcome of the enquiry, Walter,' she said. 'I intend to sue for divorce.'

'Have I given you grounds, Katherine?' he said whimsically.

'More than enough.'

'It would be a great scandal, don't you think?'

'I have thought of that.'

She was facing him with a cold self-assertion he could only admire. It had never occurred to him that she could ever think of divorce, let alone go through with it. A few soft words would be enough. 'My dear, I would not act in anything without your agreement. A husband's position is not entirely enviable.' He began to speak of carrying the burden for the woman…of the

174

skills needed to cope with the administration of wealth...of her duty to her children. 'Surely you can trust me, Katherine.' His tone conciliatory, dominating her with the sheer weight of his manhood.

She did not reply.

'A fortnight at sea seems to have done wonders for your colour and your confidence,' he said dryly. He was certain that the moment they had the outcome of the enquiry she would be overwhelmed by her responsibility and turn to him. She saw it on his face.

'I mean it, Walter,' she said. 'Our marriage is over.'

He paused at the door. 'I don't intend to part with you that easily, my dear Katherine.'

'Is that a threat, Walter?'

'No, just the way it is, that's all.'

Katherine did not go back to Caxton Hall. She followed the proceedings in the newspapers. Gardiner would sit in to the bitter end, he told her. The last time he spoke to her on the telephone he had recalled, with particular relish, a statement to the court by the lawyer appearing for some of the relatives.

'No, I did not brief the man myself, Katherine. I arrived too late for that, but he's a sound man. He shook them up yesterday. There was evidence, he said, that the captain had increased the ship's instability by...can you imagine it!...stacking the spar deck with coal taken on at Durban. He was out for a record trip and trying to save time. He took a chance on fine weather from Durban down that notorious coast, and ran into the worst storm in years. No, there's no doubt of the outcome...she capsized. Are you there, Katherine?'

'You disgust me,' she said and hung up the receiver.

Curiously enough, when the judgement came Katherine was calm. She had never wanted to believe that Muriel was dead or accept that she was now full heiress to the Rawlinson millions. How the Press rolled the phrase about! Now she read the report of the court's findings with relief that it was over.

It has been particularly trying, she read in the Times, *for relatives and friends to wait from week to week and month to month in hope. The court trusts that this very full enquiry will confirm public belief that there is no reasonable doubt, that whatever the cause, all the passengers and ship's company of the* Sydney Star *met their deaths at sea soon after she left Durban. The court regards it as the kindest course to emphasize this view in the strongest manner.*

One paragraph in the summing up gave her particular satisfaction. *The court dismissed the depositions of seamen who claimed to have seen bodies in the sea. The court is inclined to the ship captain's explanation of its being offal set adrift from the whaling station at Durban.*

That part of the verdict would enrage Walter. And this was likely to be the only satisfaction she would have. He was incontestably master of her father's fortune.

Chapter Fifteen

It was seven miles and a furlong or two from Swindon Beck to Warewood Hall. It all came back to Katherine as the carriage brought them closer to the great old house. First would come a glimpse of the stables and the small church in the grounds ... she was telling it for the children. 'We turn the corner at the little wood, pass over a bridge and there, you'll see it.'

'Is it very old?' Spencer asked. 'I mean...hundreds.'

'At least three hundred, Spence.'

It was a day of wintry sunlight. Warewood gleamed a pale red against acres of greensward. Square towers, gable ends, turrets and twisted chimneys rose against a backdrop of elms, now winter-naked. Some of the woods still held the last of autumn colours; russet, red and copper.

The carriage bowled under an archway beneath a crumbling coat of arms into the foursquare court where the ruddy brickwork was relieved by the greystone of mullioned windows. Katherine saw that only one stable was in use and the house had deteriorated further since she was last there. Closed upstairs windows looked as if they had not been opened in a century. She remembered its serenity in bright sunshine but now, in the fickle light of early December, the diamond panes were lifeless, the courtyard neglected.

The sky was leaden and the curious stillness of the atmosphere and the hush seemed a portent of change.

'There's going to be snow!' Charles welcoming them into the hall where a log fire blazed in an enormous hearth, taking her hands and drawing her in with a word to the children. In Africa he had seemed unsure of himself. Like so many Englishmen out there he looked alien, at odds with the land. How could he have ever thought to leave this house for the harshness and crudity of the Rand?

In the train down, she had felt herself rushing swiftly over a landscape from her past. She had made this journey so many times in her secret heart. Nothing had changed except herself.

That afternoon the first feathers of snow drifted earthwards, a thickening cloud that slowly obscured the landscape and muffled sound. Katherine watched it from her bedroom window. She realized with quickening heart they would be alone as never before. She would get to know this man. 'When I was Spencer's age,' he told her, 'I saw nothing of my mother. She was very beautiful, you know, and much sought after. I was brought up here by a tutor. My mother and father were wildly extravagant, with a house in Portland Square. I was very lonely, always begging my parents to visit me. They came down for the hunt and sometimes my father turned up with a buyer for one of the paintings. He had frightening debts. I know that more than once he gambled ten or twenty thousand pounds in a sitting of cards.

'I used to cut photographs of my mother from the illustrated magazines ... Lady Warewood in the Royal Box at Ascot...at Covent Garden. She had many admirers ... lovers, if I must be honest. I knew, of course, but I'd never admit it. My tutor fell in love with her. After that he had to go and I went to a private school that had entrée to Sandhurst. My father thought that I was so intensely stupid at school that I'd make a good cavalryman. "Always falling off on their heads," was his joke.

'Yes, I rode well and I had a room upstairs where I manoeuvred toy soldiers ... whole armies of them. On wet afternoons I used to refight Waterloo and the Crimea. My father used to say "with any luck you'll go out in a blaze of glory ... the last of the Warewoods. There will be nothing left here for you. Do you understand? The way I'm living is the way I am. A gentleman has no other choice." '

'Yes, I'm afraid it will all go one of these days. In my grandfather's time, of course, it was very different. Twenty or thirty guests at a weekend. A hundred house servants.'

'Are you sorry that's all gone?'

'Not a bit.'

They were walking along draughty corridors and he would open doors to display bare rooms, enormous empty fireplaces and what seemed like acres of creaking, uncarpeted boards. 'My father could not even afford two hundred pounds a year for my mounts. As a cavalry cadet we had to have four. Two for polo. It was sad for a man who'd raced under his own colours and been a member of the jockey club. In fact, he was overdrawn when he died.'

He spoke lightly, almost banteringly, and without drawing the comparison had made her aware of the difference between them. This house with its roots in English history and its fallen status; her own beginnings in the crudity of Kimberley and her present wealth. The contrast of crumbling and burgeoning fortunes.

'Shot himself...thought it was the right thing to do. Warewood's been on the market ever since. Funnily enough the last of the family money went on gold shares. The crash in Johannesburg wiped out father's last investment. You may remember the panic when Leonard Penlynne's company sent a flutter through the markets.'

'I remember. He saved his own skin though...got out in time.'

'I'd never believe that of him,' Charles said. 'I take him for a man of honour. I know him to be so. But I'm boring you.'

'Is that all?' she said. In the directness of her gaze he saw that she knew, or instinctively guessed, the truth of his journey to England. 'Do you really think, Charles, that no one is aware of what is going on? Mr Chamberlain is out to provoke a confrontation. He will do anything to forestall German interests on the Rand. I am a woman, but since my father died I have made every effort to understand everything that concerns my father's interests.'

He was astonished and could not conceal it.

'What Mr Penlynne and Mr Rhodes are doing is...shall I say it? Foolish. My father's companies will certainly not support them. Not if I can help it.' They had halted in the long dusty passage where the grey-white light bleached all colour from them so that he looked unusually grave; almost deathly. 'For my part,' he said without heat, 'I will do everything I can to overthrow that corrupt regime.'

'My father admired President Kruger,' she said looking down on the empty stable yard, the outbuildings and dairy and the evidence of a once-thriving establishment. What she saw was a warning that nothing lasted. Not even the riches and power that had built all this and enjoyed it in its heyday. Some gave the Rand only twenty years. Some less.

'I believe what we are doing is right,' he said quietly. 'Shall we go down for tea?'

Later, as he was showing Spencer old swords and pieces of armour, she saw that there was far more to his involvement in Transvaal politics than made sense to her. It had a different quality altogether from that of Penlynne and Rhodes. He believed in the right of the fittest to rule. It was an inbred conviction. 'You see Spencer, we British are destined to rule an empire we have not chosen to acquire…it is our destiny as a nation.'

'Why?' she asked. He shrugged it off. It was evidently something one believed but did not spout about. At that moment he looked to her like a boy, passionately doing something reckless. 'Have you considered how dangerous this is?' she asked.

He looked at her amazed. Outside snow was falling. At home, she thought, there are apricots and peaches in the garden. The nights are already hot. In this silence of snow and isolation she was as much an alien as he was in Johannesburg. She thought with sudden anger: what am I doing here with this stranger?

'Does it mean so much to you?' he said. She gave no answer. The old Rawlinson had rebelled. But Spencer was fascinated by Charles. 'Tell me about it…India. How you were fighting the Pathans. Were they very fierce?'

She had not known he'd fought on the north-western frontier. 'Why were you there?'

'Bringing order…protecting India.'

'From what?'

'Without us the hillmen would have long ago ravished the plains.'

'You really enjoyed it.'

He looked amused. 'They looked to us…to the Great White Mother, for protection.' She looked for signs of cynicism and saw none. Later he showed snapshots to Spencer. Charles in white topee on polo pony. Charles in spurred cavalry boots and whipcord jodhpurs. She listened to him explaining to the boy. Spencer was sitting very close to him, his blonde head against the man's arm.

'You see, old chap…we have to do it. It's up to us. Her Majesty expects us to do our best for her.'

How odd, she thought. His father is a stranger to him yet he follows this stranger about like a dog. In a room upstairs Charles showed Spencer the sets of toy soldiers he had played with. Grenadiers still marched and kneeled to fire volleys. Cavalrymen charged the guns. Dusty white tents marked the enemy camp. Tiny painted faces and brandished swords, pennants on lances and fallen horses on a dusty landscape. The boy stood awestruck by this mock panoply of war.

'Yesterday's battles,' Charles said quietly.

'That one's carrying the flag!' cried the child. 'He must never let it fall…isn't that so? If he does we shall lose.'

'Another will pick it up,' the man said.

'How splendid! Mother, how splendid!'

Katherine restrained a sudden, unreasoning urge to put her arms about the child, as if in some morbid anticipation of the future.

'Do the cannon really fire?'

'Rather!'

'Let's have a battle. Can I have the Guards, please.'

She watched them firing volleys into the ranks of the Imperial Guard. The blue-coated Frenchmen were drawn up on a hill to make their last stand for the Emperor. The Scots Greys were charging on their dappled mounts.

'Did it really happen like that, Charles?'

'Oh yes!'

It was the first time she had heard her son use her lover's name. She saw with a rush of feeling that he put his hand on the boy's curls.

'It's cold up here,' she heard her own voice. Neither appeared to hear. On the battlefield the front rank of the Imperial Guard went down before the dappled Greys.

That night she waited for his knock. Since the ship they had evaded sexual contact. The constraint was mutual, as if in some way the incident had been sufficient confirmation of their love. He had hesitated to invite her to Warewood. 'It will be compromising,' he warned.

'I don't care, Charles…frankly I don't care a damn.'

She lay watching the firelight play on the ceiling, shadows moving on the walls. She was alert for his footstep, restless and on the verge of anger. When he did not come she put on a dressing gown and sat by the fire. Then quite abruptly she went to his room.

'Yes, I wanted you to come to me,' he admitted afterwards. 'Not to take advantage.'

'And if I had not come?'

He laughed.

'Were you so confident?'

'I am confident of nothing,' he replied. Naked he walked to the fire and threw on wood. His back was scarred. She had not seen it before or been conscious of touching it. His limbs were long and lean, his body extremely white. The chalk whiteness of an English body...the white nakedness one saw in paintings, almost translucent. His face glinted with gold stubble of beard.

'Where were you wounded?'

'It's nothing...in India.'

She was thinking: other women have seen this scar and touched it. She rose and put her arms about him. 'Tell me.'

'Some day, perhaps.' His face had become serious, almost as if he had aged. She guessed that his mind had slid away to what was coming in the Transvaal.

'Everyone knows,' she said testingly.

'Knows what?' He was startled.

'The annexation ... it's common talk in financial circles.'

'What else do they say?'

'It's only a question of time ... and by whom.'

He said nothing.

'Would you advise me to sell up and get out?'

'Of course not. What Rhodes wants is a unified South Africa under the British flag. It has to come ... sooner or later.'

'They say the Boers will destroy the mines ... and Johannesburg.'

'Do they indeed! We have other ideas.'

'What do they expect from you?'

'I'm a soldier.'

'May I ask why you are doing this?'

'Surely you know it's us or Germany. There are German warships at Delagoa Bay. Been there for months. German marines could be in Pretoria in two days. Do you think they will care a straw for the Boers? It will be *hoch der kaiser* from the Limpopo to the Cape.'

He turned to her, his eyes ingenuously blue. 'We have to strike first ... raise the colours in Pretoria. Then we will talk. Then they'll see it is all for the best.'

What she saw in his face was an enthusiasm for something that had no reality for her. It had the same note as that song she had heard at a Smoking Concert on the ship ... piano thumping. A man's voice bawling: 'This is the song of the Saxon, of the race that rules the earth!' Prolonged cheers and clapping. They are brought up to believe it, she thought and a line of Houseman's poem came into her head: ... *the lads that will die in their glory and never be old.*

She turned away from him. 'You will not have my son for your empire.'

'Are we quarrelling?' he said quietly.

'Don't you see ... I'm afraid for you.'

'It will be over in twenty-four hours.'

'What, for God's sake?'

'The rising. We shall seize the arsenal in Pretoria and defend Johannesburg long enough for British forces to reach us. Oh yes, there will be arms enough and men to use them. The better sort of Boer will be glad to accept British rule, don't you know.'

'I see that I must go home,' she said.

'I'd rather you stayed on in England till this is over. Here, at Warewood. My home and yours, I hope, one day.'

As he spoke, it was as if she saw the grass growing in Pritchard Street. Shops boarded up. Market Square deserted. No more shouting share prices at the chains. Bands of ragged blacks on street corners and all the incredible, bustling activity of Johannesburg suddenly stilled. The great houses on the ridge deserted, coach houses empty, doors dragging on rusted hinges. On the mines the stamp batteries silenced. Corrugated iron sheds rusting and banging in the wind. Shafts flooding and timbering collapsing. It was so real that she shivered.

'Come back to bed,' he urged.

She drew back the curtains and looked out on the moonlit snowscape. Every shape had been obliterated. Nothing was what it appeared to be. Frost flowers sprang into shape when she breathed on the glass. Behind them the bed lay open and warm, pillows tumbled, sheets dragging. He had loved her with gentle ferocity, a controlled passion rousing an ardour in her that Gardiner would have envied. She had always known it was possible. 'I love him,' she thought. As he took her into his embrace again her fingers encountered the stiff ridge of the wound scar. It seemed an omen to her and long after he was asleep she lay awake.

Two days later she took the children back to a London filled with fresh alarms about Boer intransigence. Among telegrams from Johannesburg and messages to contact the London office as soon as she returned, was a newspaper clipping two weeks old. The halfpenny newspaper scribbler had kept his word. She could almost see him slapping his half guinea on the counter. Put the bitch in her place. She crumpled it contemptuously. In the light of the British agitation over Transvaal it was nothing. According to the Press Kruger had the golden goose by the throat. A newspaper cartoonist saw him as a plundering old ogre in a frock coat with a carving knife in his peasant fist. He had stopped all goods for the mines from crossing the drift on the Vaal River. Everything the mines needed was stranded on the far shore. On Rhodes's side.

In a month, wrote one journal, *he can bring gold production to a standstill. The effect on the share market will be catastrophic unless good sense prevails.*

The roar of London's ironshod traffic seemed to rise to a thunder. She did not for a moment hear her name spoken.

'Katherine!'

Gardiner stood there, massive and angry and overbearing. 'So you got back,' he said. 'Now you've managed to tear yourself away, you may be interested to know we have a first-rate crisis on our hands.'

'I'm well aware of it.'

'That's very accommodating of you.' He saw that it was impossible to browbeat her. He was looking at a new woman. Self awareness and confidence were in the poise of her head. Thick waves of corn-blonde hair were parted on either side of a brow, serene and white. The dark brown eyes were untroubled as they faced his. She sat there, turning her rings as if she were about to draw them off and toss them away. His eyes went to the fullness of her bosom and he felt his throat constrict at the image of Charles Warewood's head. Struck as he was by the signs of fulfilment, he found himself admiring the iron of her father in her jaw.

184

'We will have to stay on in London for some time, Katherine. Till this drifts business is settled. I expect that won't be entirely displeasing to you.'

'For what reason – if there is trouble at home?'

'Business. Your interests. You do understand that the forty percent share in the Rawlinson interests your father – in his wisdom – decided you should inherit, will be administered by your husband. I will be making all decisions, Katherine. I hope that will put your mind at rest. For the rest, please yourself. I have no objections to your amusing yourself with Charles Warewood. And I do not intend to change my own style of living.'

He turned at the door, smiling. She had the impression that he was about to administer some kind of *coup de grace*. 'Could you be available for luncheon with Arthur Crawley? Tomorrow.' A drizzle of sleet was falling as she watched him cross the road to a waiting cab. She stood in cold anger, tracing with one finger the slow slide of ice down the window pane. She was still there in the growing dusk. The figure of a lamplighter paused at the gate, thrust his glow-worm pole into the lamp and passed on, leaving a circle of light on the pavement outside Ludlow House.

The *maitre d'* bowed her to a table occupied by Arthur Crawley who rose to greet her. It was months since she had seen him, though as chairman of the board, his name had been frequently in the Johannesburg papers. He was as odious as ever. She could not forget their last meeting. He had made her position as a woman quite clear. He was still overdressed and over-barbered and she could have phrased the bogus chivalries before he opened his mouth.

The dining-room was fashionably crowded but Gardiner had not arrived. She took this as significant. Crawley was about to be persuasive.

'Good news for you,' he began. 'The new company has been granted a quotation on the London Stock Exchange. I need hardly tell you that the success of the deep levels, thanks to Walter, has become a focus of world attention. British, French and German capitalists are deeply committed to the Rand. At last South African shares are being actively traded here ... and in Paris, Berlin and Moscow. Even Constantinople and Cairo have caught the fever for "Kaffirs".'

She interrupted. 'What new company, Mr Crawley?'

'We are forming the new company with a capital of half a million with the power to issue debentures to the value of two million ...' He paused to replenish the glass she had not touched.

'Go on, please.'

'A holding company ... to control the interests of a number of mines. A new type of share ... it will have great appeal to the investing public. It offers safe investment.' He went on, flushed and enthusiastic. 'Deep level mining has at last caught the imagination of world finance. Our mines can be worked at a profit ... our resources are inexhaustible. There must be capital reconstruction of the older mining companies. Ours will be the largest group on the Rand ... indeed, the largest undertaking of its kind in the mining world.'

'What do you require of me, Mr Crawley?'

'A mere formality, my dear. Walter and I have taken care of the rest.'

'My signature.'

'This is the psychological moment, Mrs Gardiner.' How the name jarred. 'Gold is the sole basis of the western world's currency and credit. The riches of the Rand have been proved. The world's greatest gold field has been vindicated at the precise moment when gold is most needed to support the world's economic structure. You do agree? Yes, we are the envy of Europe. And we shall have our listing at a time when the gold market is booming as never before.'

A waiter slid a plate before her. The level of talk and music seemed to have risen to an appalling pitch. She lifted her fork. She understood with absolute clarity what was going to happen. England wanted the Transvaal to keep the Bank of England filled with Rand gold. So much for all the highflown, idealistic talk of a superior culture...the ultimate benefits of Empire, the indignation on behalf of the voteless *uitlanders*.

'You're smiling,' Crawley said.

'I'm listening.'

'Very well. Wernher, Beit and Company...Leonard Penlynne ... Rhodes, the Barnatos, Goerz, Neumann and the Albus ... all men with tremendous influence in the European markets, will follow our lead.'

She lifted the cut crystal to her lips and felt the invigorating tang of a very dry champagne, chilled to perfection. 'Pomeroy '76,' she heard Crawley murmur. 'Only the best, my dear Katherine.' She felt an extraordinary *frisson*, a thrilling of the flesh against her garments. It all seemed so right, so well deserved ... so much her due as her father's daughter.

'Where is my husband?' she said suddenly.

'I believe he is concluding some business ... we need all the capital we can raise. Ah, here he is.'

Gardiner's bulk seemed incongruous in the fragile gilt chair. He poured champagne and gulped. Then with a flash of his teeth beneath the greying line of moustache he dropped his bombshell.

'I got an offer of three hundred thousand guineas for the paintings ... minus the Reubens. I fancy that.'

He opened his pocketbook and laid the cheque on the table.

'It's Wernher's cheque ... he signed for Penlynne. A man of good taste, I must say. For the gallery Dorothy intends to build in Johannesburg. Nice to think your father was associated with it.'

Katherine reached across the table. She saw her fingers tearing the cheque into little pieces, heard Crawley's hiss of dismay and Gardiner's explosion of laughter.

'We'll manage without it, Katherine,' he said. 'If that's the way you prefer it.'

It was only later she realized that neither had said a word about the drifts crisis or its likely effect on the new flotation. They were buoyed up with the conviction that nothing they attempted could ever go wrong.

Chapter Sixteen

'I'm going to Europe, Yeatsman ... London.' Leonard Penlynne walked in the rose garden with the editor of *The Oracle*. Since the drifts crisis had blown up he had Yeatsman come up to the house every morning before going in to the office. The young Englishman brought with him the latest reports and cables from home. The rose garden was out of earshot of the house.

Penlynne fingered the blooms still tightly furled from the night's coolness. 'What a soil for roses, Stephen. The pity is, they'll be blown by noon. Everything we do here is the same. An hour of success ... then disaster.'

Heat from the valley rose dry and dusty. Already a hot wind buffeted the ridge. The sky was harshly blue, unclouded and the distant landscape hurtful to the eyes. It would be a foul day in town. He would have to face angry merchants crying ruin. Yesterday he had been jostled by a woman with a child in her arms, screaming abuse about her man out of work. 'What are the likes of you doing then!' He gave her a fiver before she was dragged away.

The incident rattled and grieved him. He was particularly sensitive because Dorothy was so close to her time. He had left her in the bedroom that looked out over the *koppies* towards the Magaliesberg. Her hair spread on the pillows, her maid laying out her clothes.

Approaching motherhood had dealt kindly with her. She had never looked better. He had promised to take her south to the Cape for her confinement. Now he doubted the wisdom of her making the journey over the disputed railway, even in the special coach Rhodes had promised him.

Penlynne had been down to the river where the line from the Cape connected with the Nederlands Railway Company's line to Johannesburg. He had seen for himself the chaos caused by Kruger's arbitrary racking up of the tariff of goods which crossed into Transvaal. Yeatsman had gone with him. The scene at the drift beggared description. Where ox wagon transport normally crossed the river at the old Free State wagon road, hundreds of mules and oxen were outspanned among stranded wagons in a confusion of angry men and bellowing animals.

'Did you ever see anything like it, Stephen?'

'It seems inconceivable that Kruger would cut his own throat,' said Yeatsman.

'Look over there ... that machinery is for us.' There lay the hoisting gear he needed for the new deep level mine at South Rand. Like so much litter on the veld. 'You know what that represents in lost revenue, Stephen?'

'I can imagine.'

Across the river, steam jetted from a locomotive arriving as an empty train pulled away into the Free State, its freight unloaded on the wrong side of the Vaal.

Yeatsman set up his camera. A Hollander in customs uniform came over and stood watching. '*Ja*, it make goot photograph.' Penlynne had to restrain himself from knocking the man down with his smug assurance that Kruger had won the day. Prices of everything had risen. The city was under siege.

Penlynne was too energetic to let it stay at that. He organized a wagon train from the Transvaal shore. It was the beginnings of this effort that he had come to watch. Night and day the wagons began to trundle over the hills. Campfires twinkled for forty miles between the drifts and the city. It was like 1886 again, the long uphill track winding between the *koppies*, dead oxen and mules, the whistling and yelling of *kaffirs* straining at unmoving wheels, rawhide whips flicking the flanks of beasts straining under the yokes, abandoned gear. It was primitive as hell. But for a time it worked.

Now Stephen brought the news. Kruger had refused to allow goods to cross the river into Transvaal. Everything was at a standstill.

'He's out to break Johannesburg, Stephen.'

'Well sir, they have a plausible cause. They blame Rhodes for demanding fifty percent of the tariff on goods from Cape Town to Johannesburg.'

'The truth is, Stephen, Kruger is responding to pressure from Germany ... German banks own his railway.'

Yeatsman showed his incredulity.

'They're out to squeeze us dry. German banks will own the whole Rand … it's as simple as that.'

They crossed the drift to the Free State side to see a crowd of immigrants detraining from Third Class coaches, putting down their gear and staring across the river. They looked haggard but still cheerful after two days and a night, crammed seventy-two to a coach for a thousand miles, without food or sanitary services except at halts. Blanketed *kaffirs* mingled with families of Europeans, without rancour. Immigrants were still coming off steamships at the Cape. Eight hundred at a time. All kinds. Tradesmen and clerks scraping up their last pounds to reach the *el dorado*.

'Just in time to see the shutters going up,' said Yeatsman noting with distaste the sour stink of coaches that reeked like cattle trucks.

'By God, Stephen,' cried Penlynne. 'We'll hold what we have. If promises made to me are kept.' Yeatsman did not ask him what he meant but on the return journey Penlynne told him of Sir Henry Loch's determination to overthrow the Kruger regime.

'For a start, Stephen, five thousand British soldiers at Mafeking. Loch assured me he could take the Transvaal with a snap of his fingers … ride into Pretoria and raise the flag. Now is the time, Stephen. Now or never.'

They got down from the train in Park Halt where a new covered platform was being erected. Penlynne looked at it with scorn.

'In time to welcome the Germans, perhaps.' Yeatsman detained him. He was looking at the rabble of unemployed, the street loungers and swarms of foreigners and blacks. His critical eye saw nothing but loafers, chancers and opportunists. 'Unlikely patriots,' he said. 'Don't you agree?'

'If Sir Henry keeps his word there will be enough good men.'

'And if the Liberal Government falls … as they say it will?'

'I don't doubt that the Conservatives will accept the Loch Plan. And act on it. At any rate I'm going over there to put our case to our sympathizers and to the Colonial Office.'

Yeatsman caught a tram from the station. Near Von Brandis Street it was held up. 'What is it?' he asked from the platform.

'They're moving the ladies from Frenchtown.'

The street was jammed with a carnival of open landaus,

hansoms and drays of furniture. The crowd cheered and whistled at women twirling parasols and fluttering handkerchiefs. Touts were moving among the crowd. A card given to Yeatsman offered French lessons from young ladies moving to their new address east of Government Square, a house called *Monte Carlo*.

It seemed that Christiaan Smit had begun the threatened 'moral crusade' with a threat to deport any woman who did not move to less fashionable quarters. He'd given them fourteen days.

Yeatsman thought it an odd time to worry about the morals of Johannesburg. He said so next morning as he walked on the terrace with Penlynne. 'Morality has nothing to do with it, Stephen.' He stopped suddenly and laid his hand on Yeatsman's arm.

'A consortium of German banks has raised a million to promote German ventures here ... and have appointed an agent.'

'De la Roche?'

'Who else!'

Penlynne seemed to Yeatsman to be completely sure of himself. A man who was seizing the initiative. He was impressed. 'Facts Stephen, facts. No room for weakness or sentiment. Do you realize that at this moment Johannesburg ... the Rand ... is at the centre of the world's finance. Last month our mines milled 194 764 ounces of gold. All of it will go straight to the Bank of England. London is the capital of the world. British securities were worth ten thousand million last year. The gold sovereign's the strongest money in existence. Can you imagine the effects on England if the stream of gold uncovered here in the last ten years was diverted elsewhere? To Germany! Our greatest trade rival!'

At that moment he was called away. He shook hands. 'We depend on you, Stephen. My office will send you over some facts and figures that will be helpful. Kruger must not be allowed to kill our gains. Oh, I'd like you to see me off at the station. Will you do that?'

Before Yeatsman could reply he had gone with his brisk step and the impression he left of unbridled energy. And yet, as always, he seemed curiously vulnerable. Friendship he had not offered before now. Was this friendship? Back in his office there were proofs for his attention. His eye caught a line: *His Honour, the State President, remained at home today, ill with dipteritis. It is hoped His Honour will be in good health for his 70th birthday* …. Then a paragraph from Angelica's Diary. She'd seen a wardrobe at Borthwicks and thought she must refurnish her bedroom with fumed oak.

My God, he thought. What trivialities we deal in. How long could it last? Yet one had only to walk into the nearest bar to sense the anger of the town. A climax was near. Any fool could see that. The irony was that South African shares were being quoted on the London 'Change at a hundred and fifty million sterling. Rhodes's Consolidated Goldfields had risen from 35 shillings to 397 in three years. Shares in his Rhodesian venture, Chartereds, were booming. *The Oracle's* financial page listed over three hundred mining and finance companies quoted on the Johannesburg Stock Exchange. Even before the prospectus of the Barnato Bank had been issued the £4 shares stood at £11. Madness.

For a year, frenzy had been the name of the game. Shares only remotely connected with gold mining were fought over in the wave of uncontrolled speculation sweeping the capitals of Europe. All of it centred on this town that might become abandoned as fast as it began. Yeatsman did not invest. Penlynne had recently given him shares in *The Oracle*. He had two rooms in a modest house. The frenzy of Johannesburg left him untouched except as a phenomenon to be recorded. He wrote much of the paper himself, five or six columns a day of close type. It did not give him much time for boozing or womanizing. His shorthand was precise. His eye for detail practiced. He sometimes thought fate had brought him here to witness something unique.

At the station Penlynne drew him into his compartment and handed him an envelope. 'This is the text of a speech I shall be giving two days after I arrive in England. Publish it on that date.' He spoke with unusual gravity, in a tone unlike his usual open manner, 'It will affect all our futures.' It was Yeatsman's impression that he was hesitant. 'I may not arrive,' Penlynne said quietly, his eyes moving over the crowd. Some pressed to the window to greet him. He chaffed lightheartedly … sorry he'd miss the sports meeting to honour the President's birthday. He waved and pulled down the sun blind.

'Some attempt may be made to prevent my giving the address.

Do make sure it is given prominence ... now, don't wait.'

That such a man imagined himself in danger seemed so inconsistent with the aura of strength he projected that Yeatsman stood until the train had disappeared. Suddenly he felt himself a focus. He hurried back to the office and put the envelope in a safe place. That night he went to the *Lyceum* to see a comedy by a London company. He was unable to laugh. Before the third act curtain he went back to the office and opened the envelope.

It was headed: *Casus Belli!*

The closing of the Vaal River drift is an act of deliberate provocation. It is the latest move in the Transvaal government's determination to oust the uitlander *community by ruining the mines. Machinery and material from Europe are being held up. Six weeks from now Kruger will have all gold production at a standstill. That is his intention.*

Not satisfied by withholding the vote, to denying our children education, to taxing beyond endurance those who have made his wretched little state wealthy, he has determined to break us. The people of Johannesburg have shown extraordinary patience but the time has come when we must look to England. This handful of obstinate people must be made to realize that it cannot ignore the inrushing tide of a superior culture. To attempt it is as pathetic as it is hopeless ....

Yeatsman's hand shook. This was it. When this address hit the presses in Europe the stock markets would go down like a house of cards. But if Kruger had his way, the closure of the gold mines would be a worse catastrophe. He had to approve Penlynne's strategy. He decided to have a cartoon drawn to go with it. It would show Kruger as King Canute, sitting on his rickety throne. The tide lapping round his skirts ... a tide of angry artisans and women with hungry children. The throne is toppling.

The Works Foreman beckoned in the din. A two column section of advertising was missing from the page one chase. 'What happened here?' Yeatsman shouted over the clatter of the press.

'Cancelled ... goods he ordered stuck on t'other side of the drift. And that's only the start, Mr Yeatsman.'

He walked home, the fresh newspaper under his arm. It was a moment he savoured every day. This was Johannesburg's life. Its gossip and its marketplace. Oxen for hire. Doctors' claims of wonder cures. Houses to let. Church services and moustache wax. Tobacco, liquor and death notices.

From an open hall he heard loud singing. Rule Britannia. The plasterwork insignia over the door identified the new Masonic Hall. It was a meeting of the Amalgamated Society of Carpenters and Joiners. A score of cycles were stacked outside. Across the street a ricksha boy sat waiting for custom, porcupine quills in his ear lobes. The song ended in a scraping of chairs and boots and clearing of throats.

Someone grasped his arm. 'Nothing worth a line in your paper, Mr Yeatsman. They've been talking half the night about a bloody smoking concert in the Transvaal Arms Hotel. No union affairs mentioned … no politics.'

'Good night then, Mr Davyd,' said Yeatsman. The one-armed man detained him with a firmer grip. 'They've got their pay, their booze, their fancy women and to hell with the rest. Listen to them,' he scorned. 'What did bloody England ever do for them … drive them out.'

He found a packet of fags and flipped it open, struck a light on the doorstep and inhaled deeply. Not much more than five foot two, his dark Welsh face was narrow as a fox beneath his cloth cap. All the force of the man was in his eyes. He wrote burning letters to the papers. He held meetings. He castigated the capitalist. He practically starved himself. There was little support for his General Workers Union. He turned away angrily, then stopped.

'Don't think the workers … the real workers, will do your dirty work for you, Mr Yeatsman.'

'What are you talking about?'

'I was at a meeting the other night … Coach and Wagon-makers invited masters to turn up and talk … problem of imported coaches. Men out of work. They sat like bloody sheep, mun … shuffling boots. Not a bloody master turned up. You think they'll support your revolution when jobs is threatened.'

'They don't support you either, Mr Davyd.'

'That day is coming, Mr Yeatsman. But the workers won't support your boss … tell him that. You see this road? Know where it goes? To Nob's Bloody Hill. Monopoly money building roads for the Penlynnes and the Rawlinsons. I'm opening their eyes. Telling them what's worth fighting for and it ain't millionaires' houses in Park Lane.'

'So you're busy breeding real grievances, Mr Davyd.'

The slight figure tossed the half-smoked cigarette to the crouching figure by the ricksha. 'What about the blacks, Mr Yeatsman? I read in your financial columns this new distillery across the Portuguese border is turning out a thousand gallons of 99 proof brandy ... every day. One million francs of French money invested. Got any share! It's a nice investment in dead men.'

Yeatsman tried to keep his temper. It was his business to listen. Words were his capital, especially words spoken in anger. 'Look here, Mr Davyd,' he said carefully. 'Your workmen don't show much concern for the *kaffirs* under them, do they. What's all this about workers' rights then? Read this ... no. I insist.'

Owen Davyd took the paper.

Page Two ... In Court.

William Twigg, a ganger on No.2 Shaft Rawlinson Star. Charge, breach of mining regulations. Allowed two natives to drill a hole for blasting while he read the paper. Drilled into unfired shot. Charge exploded. Mine Manager said no fault of accused. Fined £5 or ten days. Prosecutor asked bench to note: £2.10 per kaffir killed. Case dismissed.

Owen Davyd handed back the sheet. 'It's the system ... the system perverts decent men.' He hitched his narrow shoulders and walked off into the night. A defiant singing came back ... something to the tune of the Marseillaise.

At his lodgings Yeatsman opened the french doors onto the yard. There was a peach tree laden with ripening fruit. Over the iron fence were other trees and laundry drying. Sometimes he saw a woman washing her hair in a bucket of rainwater from the tank. Small things bound a man to a special place. He had despised and hated this Johannesburg but now, he thought, I am part of it and will not let go my share. He opened Burton's *Anatomy of Melancholy*. His reading of the classics had all but ceased but he still found solace in its humour, its pathos and its tolerant spirit. At this moment he needed its wide view of social and political reform, its deep understanding of the human animal.

Penlynne sank back in his seat as the Cape train gathered speed.

The campfires of wagoners at the Vaal drift disappeared into the darkness. Beyond the strip of light from the train the darkness was complete. At Vereeniging, where he changed trains to the Cape mail, he became certain that he was being watched. A Boer who left the train went into the telegraph office and did not rejoin the train. Penlynne concluded that if there were any threat it would come after the halt at Kimberley. He secured the door and turned in. He had retained his ability to discard anxiety as futile and energy-sapping. But he lay awake thinking of Dorothy. In these final days of her pregnancy her whole being had seemed to him transfigured. There was a radiance about her. Her eyes were soft and her skin glowed. The expectation of her fulfilment as a woman after so long and so much pain had touched him deeply. He had not imagined that this child could be so important to him. Was it an intimation of mortality, the subconscious need to be perpetuated in a situation that could lead to the disintegration of all he had worked for?

He had barely fallen into a sweated doze when the door rattled officiously. He had secured a single compartment on the crowded train with difficulty and the prospect of sharing annoyed him. Some baggage was brought in. He protested. He put his hand in his pocket ... to no avail. To his astonishment, the man who entered was Advocate Smit. The slender Boer arranged his things and offered his hand and his tobacco pouch.

'We seem fated to meet in railway carriages, Mr Penlynne.'

'No doubt these coincidences can be arranged, Advocate Smit.'

'A few hours together might be fruitful ... an exchange of ideas, perhaps even agreement on some matters.' Smit stretched his legs and drew on his pipe, his intense, pale eyes on Penlynne. 'You've seen the British newspapers, no doubt ... threats, sabre-rattling, insults. The *Times* says the Boer must be swept away. Mr Gladstone is being abused for handing back power to ... I quote, "the semi-civilized oligarchy ruling the richest country in the world." '

'I couldn't have put it better,' murmured Penlynne.

'It goes on to say the foreign population ... the *uitlanders*, have almost reached the limit of their patience. No mention is made of the Boer point of view. Still, we must have cool heads and not give way to impulses we might regret, not so?'

'Could we come to the point?'

'I am empowered by highest authority to make an appeal to you. Dissociate yourself from Mr Rhodes's ambitions ... throw in your lot with the republic as our German burghers have done. What has England done for you ... a Jew?'

'What have you in mind?' said Penlynne.

'When you arrive in London give a solemn public disavowal of British rights to intervene in Transvaal affairs. Invoke the London Convention in which England upheld our right of sovereignty.'

'Advocate Smit, you seem to forget that by closing the drifts your people have already broken the convention ... and made war a possibility. In any case, nothing I can say could stop the machinery Rhodes has set in motion.'

'I don't agree. What you say in London will carry great weight. For good or for ill.'

'I am a businessman, not a politician. I am for certain basic rights, nothing else. Free trade is one of them. England wants no more than fair play and treaties honoured.'

'Permit my scepticism. We both know what England wants.'

The train rattled on in the darkness. Occasionally they saw the bright glare of eyes, some beast near the line. The two men measured each other in silence. They were aware that they were adversaries in a deadly game. Strangely, there was no ill-will.

Penlynne uncapped a flask of brandy and offered it. The Boer drank and wiped the neck of the flask before returning it. They spoke of the prolonged drought. 'There were some clouds yesterday,' Smit said hopefully. They dozed and woke to stare. Once Penlynne found Smit smiling. He wondered what had amused this solemn, rarely smiling young man.

'Are you going far?' he asked, offering his flask again.

'Only as far as necessary.'

They laughed together and Smit enquired civilly after the health of Mrs Penlynne.

'I hope to return to find myself a father,' Penlynne said.

'Do you remember our last journey together? You said to me then that we should work together to make this country great.'

'I remember.'

'Well then ... can we shake hands this time?'

Penlynne was moved. The man's offer was obviously sincere.

There was an element in it of final appeal, as if beyond the offer there was a void. 'I hope we shall be able to shake hands some day, Advocate Smit.'

The hand was withdrawn. On Smit's face came an expression Penlynne would never forget. 'I hope to hang you one day, Mr Penlynne. Hang you as high as Hayman.'

'On what charge?'

'Treason.'

'Can I be treasonable to a country that refuses me my rights?'

Smit smiled and offered his pouch. 'Don't think I do not know the extent of your involvement. What you are doing will bring ruin to us all if you succeed. But in the end, we Boers will get what we want.'

'Well then,' said Penlynne calmly. 'We both know where we stand.'

At Kimberley they both got down for breakfast but did not eat together and when he returned to his compartment Penlynne found Smit's bag had been removed. There was a card on his floor: *reserved for Mr L Penlynne.* He thought it very civil of the State Attorney.

All day the train hurried along the straight line of track. The land was drought-seared with not a living thing moving. With nightfall came the Karroo, a desolation of flat hills. Nothing here worth fighting over. What he must do was unavoidable. Several times when he washed his face in tepid water he caught a glimpse of himself. The old, deadly fear of losing all still worked in his guts. The die was cast. In London, Wernher had already taken care of his end of the matter. Everything was ready for a bear operation. The market would crash from its crazy peak. It would be the greatest panic of all time. A man had to protect his interests. The Boers had made it necessary. The right kind of Boer would soon agree that it had been for the best.

First the crash. Then the expectation of a British take-over. Wernher was the quiet genius. Sell. Buy in. Reap. He was tense with anticipation. He was playing the cards dealt him. No more than that.

Sometime during the night he woke. The train stood hissing at an unmarked halt. He went out on the platform to breathe. The guard's lantern flashed green as a man mounted back there. The train moved. Shudder-shudder-clank. Metal grinding metal. An instinct warned. It will happen now. Smit had wired ahead. His man was waiting at this remote halt. The compartment was marked. So it had come to this? Why not? Smit was taking the best way out for his people. If it came to comparative moralities Smit's intentions were no more immoral than his own. Perhaps less. If an assassination might save his country, it was the right thing. Why have scruples? I justify my actions. He justifies his. His brain was icy clear. Wait for Smit's man here. Don't give him a moment ... catch him off balance. Open door ... push. No one would hear his death cry.

The man was approaching. Coach by coach. Penlynne could see his silhouette racing across the lighted ground alongside the speeding train. Window by window Penlynne could follow him. Now he was trying Penlynne's compartment, finding it unoccupied. Pausing. At that moment Penlynne was seized with violent stomach cramps. He threw open the door and waited. With a yell he hurled his weight at the man ... saw him grasp, topple. Penlynne saw his expression as he pitched backwards, features frozen in a reflex of astonishment. Then gone and only the rushing and clanking carriage ... the slam-slamming of the open door and the long line of lights turning, rising, as the train began to labour uphill. Sweat was cold on his face and body as the long, illuminated snake of lights began its downward plunge on the Cape side of the Sneeuberg.

Again the violent cramp seized him. Dorothy was giving birth.

Chapter Seventeen

An hour after the ship sailed, Africa had disappeared. Penlynne turned up his collar against a south-easter laced with icy spray. He had no inclination to join the crowd in the saloon. His time with Rhodes had been brief but long enough. How close the inevitable had come. They had walked together on the wooded slopes at *Groote Schuur*, the farmhouse he had restored as a prime ministerial residence. Rhodes pointed out the fallow deer he had introduced from England.

'They do well here. The climate's Mediterranean ... you'd never call the Cape Africa ... the real Africa lies beyond the mountain.'

He kept interrupting his monologue on African affairs to point out some bird or other. 'I've introduced our English varieties ... thrush, blackbird, chaffinch and starling. I miss the sound of our birds. African birds have no song, have you noticed?'

The man was obsessed to make an England. He dismissed the realities of Africa's harsh and unpredictable nature just as he dismissed the possibility of failure. 'The Rand will take up arms ... Kruger will run for it. British troops will occupy the Transvaal again. We'll have my southern African federation under the Union Jack. All it requires is determination. An effort by us all. They're behind us at home, every man jack. From Her Majesty to the man in the street they're for us!'

They returned from the mountain path to a plain English tea and that night an English dinner at the City Club in Queen Victoria Street where Penlynne signed the Visitors' Book.

Penlynne had realized the extent of his commitment. He and Rhodes had arrived penniless in Kimberley. Now they were coolly proposing to bring down the stock markets of Europe and overthrow a government. Rhodes, he realized, was a master at reducing huge undertakings to simplicity ... one skilful throw. 'It's a card game, Penlynne. And I hold all the trumps. England cannot afford to have its investment in Transvaal jeopardized. Neither can Europe. An enormous investment must be protected. The gold mines saved. Confidence restored.'

So simple! Penlynne had to laugh as he walked the darkening deck. Arm the rabble on the Rand, seize the arsenal in Pretoria and hope to God military assistance would come over the border in time. Secret drilling on the mines. Rifle clubs. The smuggling in of arms. 'Your man Warewood,' Rhodes had asked. 'Is he sound ... know his trade?'

Now it was happening this was a very different thing from the pumped up anger of the Press. Truth was, the average miner and tradesman didn't give a damn about the vote. The one thing they had in common was their contempt for the Boer.

'I should warn you,' Penlynne said to Rhodes. 'I am not a patriot.'

'Show me a patriot and I'll show you a fool,' was the reply.

'I'm in this to protect my own ... I'm angry.'

'Stay that way.' Rhodes poured another cup of tea.

'The Boers are not fools, you know,' Penlynne had persisted. 'They're arming.'

'Yes, British machine guns. Your man Warewood'll probably meet them in Birmingham.'

'They're building forts designed by German experts.'

'They won't be finished in time, I hear.'

'I don't think we can underestimate Krupps cannon, Creusot heavy guns and the latest Mauser rifles.'

Rhodes nodded heavily. 'A division of British troops embarked for India will be diverted here. The threat will do it, Penlynne. The empire's been built on bluff. I don't think we've lost a regiment in half a century. Imperial persuasion ... leaning on the wogs. We acquire colonies faster than a mongrel attracts fleas. You do your part ... I'll do mine. The time for reasoning is past.'

'What about Starr Jameson?'

'He'll do it again for me ... gallant fellow. The finest Englishman since Clive.'

'A Scot if I'm not mistaken,' said Penlynne dryly.

'Dash and daring will carry the day.'

Penlynne gripped the rail. He was chilled to the bone. His assailant on the train? Who might he have been? Some face he knew? It might be days before his body was found on that remote stretch of line. It might have been me, he thought. Survival gave him a sudden sense of elation yet he could not help a sudden pang for the unknown Boer. What a people! Ignorant and remote from world affairs, they had been thrust into the coming century against their will but they had learned the game ... even excelled at it. Death would be the penalty for losers. Of that he had no doubt.

As his man shaved him he watched the play of the razor. 'What do you think of this drifts business, Gibbs?'

'Impudence, sir.'

'What's the remedy?'

'A good thrashing, sir.'

His valet's confident ignorance gave him more assurance than he had felt from Rhodes's massive imperturbability. A leader was only in touch with the froth on the wave ... it was the weight of the tide that carried all before it.

A glance at the place card next to his at dinner gave the name Mrs Ormonde. It had a familiar ring but she did not turn up. 'Mrs Ormonde is under the weather, I gather,' he heard. It was two days before he encountered her. She was in a deck chair with several men paying her attention; Kitty, using one of her theatre pseudonyms. She turned vivaciously to her companions as he lifted his hat and passed on. He was taken aback by her beauty. More mature now, perhaps a trifle florid. Fleshiness of ripe peach. She reclined, her skirts showing the shapely thigh, her small feet and neat ankles. The mass of red hair was confined except where a stray tendril blew across her cheeks. She was rather too heavily rouged and her mouth was thickened richly with colour. Her laughter was more shrill than he remembered.

He asked the purser to move him to another table. As he took his seat he could not take his eyes from the white nape of her neck. The line of her chin as she turned her head seemed as fine as the Rodin marble of Miss Fairfax he had bought for the gallery.

What was she doing here? Had Gardiner given her up already? He heard that she was an invalid widow going to Switzerland to a clinic. It was hinted she was a consumptive. It was certainly a role she'd play, like Camille. Her presence reminded him that he was father of her child. Two sons now. Only one would inherit. He wondered, did Kitty even know where the boy was ... in whose hands he was being reared? It did not bear thinking of. One day ... perhaps. That business was far from settled.

He kept to his stateroom. It was not like him to crave isolation. He walked the deck at night, beset with anxieties and doubts. Would Johannesburg rise? Would the *coup de main* on the market have the effect required? Anger ... appeals to England. Demands for deliverance. It was so coldbloodedly simple that it chilled him. The moment his speech became public it would be too late for the average investor to escape the effect of huge blocks of shares being thrown on the market. Wernher had written: 'If we bear down far enough the whole of Europe will demand action ... Imperial intervention.' Wernher virtually controlled the holding of gold shares in Europe, especially in France. And the French were into it over their nostrils.

'Will they rise, Penlynne?' Rhodes had asked.

'If there's anger enough.'

'They must be goaded, Penlynne. Hunger makes angry men.'

That was the reasoning behind his demands on Kruger. And the drifts crisis had been the response he required. It was so calculated that Penlynne had been unprepared to see an emotive tremor in Rhodes's hand. The enormous eyes misted. The sullen mouth quivered.

'I shall make it up to them, never doubt it. Make it a land fit for kings.' What a contradiction of a man. Suppose, Penlynne thought, I don't go through with it? Suppose he never made his statement ... or watered it down. Too late. He'd given his word. In his isolation it was several days before he learned Barnato was on board, also keeping to his stateroom. He scribbled a reply to Barnato's note. 'Give that to your master.' He found Barnato lying up on a mass of pillows, his pince-nez askew and his hair tousled. He had thrown off the covers and despite the fans he was wet with sweat.

'I'm chucking it, Pen ... I've had enough of Africa. This last summer's been hell in Joh'burg. I'll never live in that house I built. Cost a fortune. Don't give a damn. I've my place in Lunnon. Spencer 'Ouse. Leased it from Lord Spencer till my own's up. I can run the 'ole show from Draper's Gardens. What brought you over in such a hurry?'

He shuffled some papers with studied casualness. Suddenly he let the pince-nez fall. 'Look here, Pen ... we're old associates. What the 'ell is going on with you and Rhodes? You and the rest of them, stirring up a hornet's nest. Rhodes is selling Chartereds. Been at it all summer. Needs cash in 'is hand ... needs it in a hurry. What the 'ell for? I don't trust 'im, Pen. Let 'im have his Rhodesia. Who cares, there's damn all there but niggers. But 'ands off Joh'burg. That's mine ... and yours.'

'Nice of you to share it, Barney.' They laughed.

'That's me, old cock!'

'How's the bank, Barney?' Steer him away. Too shrewd by half.

'As if you didn't fuckin' know. The first day securities were taken up, the price advanced a cool million. Barnato's Bank is in the pink. Johnnies are at an alltime high. There's confidence, Pen, bags of confidence. We 'ave our little setbacks but the show goes on.'

Colour had come into Barnato's face, his eyes gleamed behind glass. There was something too hectic in his manner, the kind of excitement that drained the strength of the consumptive. He lay back. 'Tell you somethin', Pen ... Rhodes'll get his bit of Khama's country ... run 'is bleedin' railway from Mafeking to Bulawayo ... get his machine guns up there to keep order. Tell you something e's forgot. The old Dutchman in Pretoria's no fool. I'm very sensitive to the market, Pen ... very sensitive, an' I've been feeling tremors.'

'I don't know about that, Barney.' Penlynne stared him down.

'I've a feeling there's going to be an unholy smash.'

'You've been overdoing it, Barney.'

'I'm on me toes, Pen ... you might just pass it on. Will I see you in Lunnon?'

'At the club, perhaps,' said Penlynne evasively.

'You know damn well they won't let a Jewboy over the doorstep. Even if the Lord Bloody Mayor's one of us.'

'You got into Kimberley Club.'

'Cost me millions!'

Penlynne laughed with him and moved to the door.

'Don't do nothin' stupid, Pen,' Barnato pleaded. 'I wouldn't want to see anybody get hurt ... especially me'self.'

Alone on the windswept deck Penlynne realized he was going into the maelstrom. He was going to be hated and reviled. He needed to be assured that he was right; that he had always been right. Once, there had been Kitty. Too late for that ... all passion spent. Would this thing pass so easily? He gazed out to sea. He had needed courage in the past. Now he would need more than courage. He became aware of someone at his side. Well wrapped in furs against the cold of the approaching northern seas.

'I hear you're a father, again.'

'Yes, a boy.'

'Don't forget you've a boy already.'

'There'll be a trust for him ... he'll be educated. Where are you keeping him, if I may ask?'

'As if you care. When he's old enough I'll tell him who 'is father is.'

'I told you he'd be taken care of, Kitty.'

'Men are all liars.'

She held the rail hard and stared down at the bright globules of phosphorescence churned up by the screw. It lit her features with pale intensity.

'It wasn't all bad times, Kitty.'

She pulled her fur tightly against her cheek. As suddenly as she appeared, she had gone, leaving an impression of warmth and perfume. Strange how all feeling between them had evaporated as if it had never been and they were linked only by this boy he would not recognize if he were to see him.

During the unending weeks of summer, Mary MacDonald had managed to keep her *stoep* plants alive, sharing her meagre bath water with geraniums and ferns. The garden was baked clay and shrunken shrubs. The young fruit trees had died back to sticks. At times the house was so airless she had to go out to breathe. All colour had been bleached from the landscape. The iron walls of the bungalow seared at a touch. And everywhere dust, dust, dust.

Plans had to be made for Christmas but was it worth it? Would they be here at all the way things were going. Stewart tried to keep the crisis from her but it was inescapable. You only had to watch the price of things going up. And the notices: no stocks – Sold out.

Stewart always said, 'no worries for nursing mothers. Think of the cows at Ferrygate ... ruminating.' Sometimes she did. At home in Scotland the first snows had already fallen. The harvest was safely in. Man and beast were settled for winter, the old greystone house half-banked up with drifts. Air clear and cold, her mother complaining of chilblains. There, nothing changed, nothing threatened.

Stewart urged her to take the children home to see the grandparents. He enthused about this so much she knew it was to get them out of Johannesburg. He'd manage fine, he said … and him with hardly time to sit down to his supper!

'Mrs Penlynne was here today,' she told him one evening as he sat down to unlace his boots and she poured his bath from what little was left in the rainwater tank.

'Whatever for? I saw her last week … the child's fine.'

'Asked me to join the women's revolver club.'

'She said nothing to me of this.'

'All the English women are joining. What do you think?'

'It's daft.'

'She said we'll have to stand by our men.'

'Damn the woman, I won't have it.'

'I told her no. She was put out … said I must speak to you.'

Law and order was breaking down. He saw evidence of it every day. Women were being molested in the street and in their homes. The crammed, unhygienic prison was full of prisoners awaiting trial. It stank of human flesh, disinfectant and faeces. A surface manifestation of worse. How much longer could the town contain its own corruption without bursting asunder?

Stewart had patients of every kind. The woman widowed by a rock fall. The merchant with a nervous stomach. He was a mine doctor, a private practitioner, a hospital consultant. A man who was stopped in the street for advice. He had standing in the community. He often thought: my God I'm only one small, ill-equipped man. How was it that this lassie with mild face and hidden strength could have been such a fool as to travel six thousand miles to share my life.

He watched her stir the water of his bath, lay out the towel and fresh linen. Her milk-swollen breasts wet the fabric of the dress and the odour of motherhood was on her, his child burping curds, small hands grasping at things invisible. He thought: and they would put a gun in this woman's hands.

Now his rare anger was roused, he spilled out something he

had meant to say nothing about. 'On one of the Penlynne mines,' he told her, 'there were men drilling. They said it was the sporting rifle club. In the machine shop they were stacking crates of spare parts. The foreman gave me the wink. Rifles sent out from England supposedly for Rhodesian police. I heard that machine guns were coming up from Kimberley in oil drums.'

'Why were you there?' She had turned pale.

'A man was crushed by a falling crate … it burst open. In the mine canteens they're bragging how they'll lick the Dutchmen in fine style.'

She moved tenderly towards him. So young, with the marks of his concern and his passion for duty already on his forehead. 'Och, my love, dinna fash yoursel'.

'I've as many Dutch friends as English … am I supposed to hold my tongue, pretend I see nothing. How can I invite Smit … Christiaan and his wife to my table and say nothing?'

'I haven't seen her lately,' she said slowly.

'People are taking sides.' There was a severing, a hardening.

Friendship with the Smits had begun through a chance meeting of the wives in the children's cemetery. 'Is your little one here?' Mary had put out a sympathetic hand. There were no shade trees as yet. The hard light glittered on white marble. Their children had been carried off by diphtheria. It seemed so natural when the Scots farm girl and the Boer mother joined hands and wept like sisters whose infants shared the same earth.

About the same time Stewart met Christiaan Smit in the line of duty. He was called to the police mortuary. 'I understand you've experience in post mortems, doctor,' Smit said. 'There's a young woman here, Daisy Melville.' He turned back the sheeting and Stewart saw the pale blonde corpse of a girl in a highnecked blouse. Her hair was curiously undisordered, he noted. Yet there was no composure in this death. It was a face he had seen on theatre posters … or was it in a handbill for French Town? Her name was often in the papers. Seen at suppers and the races. One of the pretty ones. There were traces of dried froth at the lips. The prussic acid had done its work swiftly. Dilated pupils. Clenched hands.

'Where did she get it, do you suppose?' Smit asked.

'A few pennyworth bought from a chemist … for photographic work.'

'Something will be done, doctor.'

'What I am wondering is … why did she do it?'

Daisy Melville lay in a reek of formaldehyde with black corpses and staring whites for company. 'I'd like to know who?' he said.

'It's a traffic that must be stamped out,' Smit said. He volunteered no more.

'It seems we both have impossible tasks,' Stewart said. They took to one another at once … perhaps it was the Calvinist heritage they shared. Stewart with his Covenanter background. His forefathers had stumbled across the moors and fallen to the sabres of the English dragoons, for their faith's sake. And for Christiaan, there had been the influence of Scottish preachers on his people trekking away from English rule. 'I can talk to you as a Scot, doctor,' he joked. They had drunk whiskey and thawed towards each other. Both their wives were heavy with child again.

Now there was this … not coldness. But a distancing. As if unconsciously they were choosing sides. 'Do I tell him what I know or pretend I never saw it?'

'What else have you heard then?'

'Wild talk.'

'I want to know, Stewart.'

'At the Phoenix I saw official mining regulations in Dutch and English … defaced. Someone had painted a skull and bones over it. And the name of the magistrate was scored out. They say the rifle clubs are for protection. I doubt it. I had a visitor the other night. He came to the dispensary.'

'Who was it?'

'A man I came out on the same boat with … de la Roche.'

'That man!'

For years de la Roche had represented everything that Stewart despised. In the gas light of the dispensary he looked ghastly. His normally immaculate figure was disordered. His speech was rapid, almost feverish.

'What is it you want with me?' Stewart asked him coldly. 'There are specialists for your condition in this town.'

'Alcohol and tobacco … doses of potassium iodine. Mercury and digitalis … all useless.'

'There's nothing I can do for you,' Stewart said.

If the man had already been prescribed mercury he would be near to the tertiary stage of syphilis. It was characterized by feverish energy, violent rages and distortion of judgement. Stewart looked at him with clinical coldness. He would be dead within a year, micro-organisms making their final attack on the central nervous system, the spinal cord and the brain. With it would come a total cessation of muscular activity ... paralysis, with the horror of total awareness of what was going on.

'I see you have made your diagnosis, doctor. The best in Europe can do nothing for me.'

'I repeat, why come to me?'

'I know you despise me.'

'Does the name Daisy Melville mean anything to you?'

The man started back as if struck. Stewart closed the door in his face. As he recalled the incident to Mary he asked her to fetch an envelope from his desk. It bore the seal of the Turkish Consulate.

'Read it,' he said.

'But this is madness,' she said as she read.

It was as if the man had embarked on an apocalyptic fantasy. A blast that would blow away this flimsy city. A giant puff of wind. A whirlwind of corrugated iron. And bodies ... a litter of corpses.

'What does it mean, Stewart?'

'The fantasy of a diseased mind.'

'Or a prophecy ... a warning,' she said intuitively.

'It crossed my mind,' he said. 'A warning of what?'

'Have you spoken to Christiaan? Maybe you should.'

Next day came the news of panic on the Paris Bourse. That evening the papers announced the collapse of the Banque Francais de l'Afrique de Sud. Stewart was called to police headquarters to inspect the body of a man who had put a pistol to his mouth. For a moment he thought it might be de la Roche.

'De la Roche was a director,' Smit said dryly. 'This was a shareholder.' As they drank bitter coffee Stewart thought to mention the letter he'd had from de la Roche, but said nothing. It was too extreme, too obviously the product of a disordered mind. More than that, there was a gulf between them that could not be breached. It was clammily hot in Smit's office. Flies buzzed and circled. Two noisy women in a cell tore off their clothes and stood there, naked and screeching.

'Whores,' said Smit wearily. 'Women like that were unknown here ten years ago. My men picked them up running naked in the streets. Doctor,' he said gravely, 'may I ask where your loyalty will be?'

'To my calling, I hope,' Stewart answered.

'Starr Jameson is also a doctor. Mr Rhodes's personal doctor.' Their eyes met.

'If you were a personal friend of Jameson, would you remind him some sicknesses should not be cured by ... shall we say, extreme purgatives.'

'I am not in Dr Jameson's confidence, Advocate Smit.'

They parted with reluctance. The handshake lingered. The grey eyes rested on Stewart. 'I'm advising friends ... and I count you among them, to send their families to the coast. A change of air.'

'It's pretty warm in Natal at Christmas,' Stewart smiled.

'It will be warmer here, doctor.'

As Stewart went out, a naked arm shot out of a cell grill. A whore began to scream. She was a loyal British subject. There was no justice. She demanded to see the British Agent.

He unhitched the pony trap and turned the pony's head towards Braamfontein. At the bottom of Von Brandis Street the road met the railway track. He was halted there by a goods train shunting. Trucks marked *explosives/springstof* shuddered and clanged as the locomotive pulled them past the huddle of shanties. When the track was clear he drove on over. He saw a spiral of red dust and rubbish rise on the hot wind and spin away between the dwellings. Everything in its path went up. Then the furious energy died as quickly as it had sprung to life.

For no reason that he knew, he whipped up the pony.

Chapter Eighteen

On the morning after his speech Penlynne slept late in his Savoy suite. It could have been the sleep of exhaustion but as he stirred he was realizing that it was more likely the sleep of evasion. A reluctance to face the stir. What had to be done was done.

In the street below, London shook and trembled to its traffic. He could hear the muted crying of the telephone. Its continual ringing had finally wakened him. A servant entered with a tray and the newspapers. It was the same cry in them all. The Transvaal millionaires had spoken. The gold magnates had had enough. Mr Leonard Penlynne had publicly identified himself with politics. *It can be taken,* crowed the *Times, that other financiers will now come forward and join the ranks of the Reformers. The capitalist has revolted. Capital, as Mr Penlynne observed, is always on the side of good law and order. Such must be achieved if Britain's vast investment is to be protected. We note that Mr Penlynne's statement is fully supported by the Transvaal Mining Chamber.*

The stock exchange would not be open yet. By eleven the market would have reacted. He bathed, breakfasted and asked Cartier's to send round a man. He meant to choose a diamond piece for Dorothy. His son was already ten days old, a fine boy, and Dorothy was well.

Wernher had met him at Tilbury docks. 'Congratulations, Leonard. You have an heir!'

They shook hands and travelled up to the city together in a private compartment. 'Everything is ready, Leonard ... our nominees are waiting for the signal.'

'The speech is ready, Julius.'

Wernher offered his cigar case. Penlynne noted the well-kept hands, the fleshy pads of his fingers on the green morocco. How different was this return to London. Last time he had come back Third Class. Defeated. One of those who had not made it in

211

Kimberley. This smiling, soft-spoken Jew had saved his skin then. Given him his start in Johannesburg. They were collaborators now!

With Cartier's man gone, he drove to Wernher's offices, remembering the first time he had gone there … 'we think you are the man to expand our interests in the Transvaal. We know your worth.' Now he was being ushered as an equal into the inner sanctum of this extraordinary man, the shrewd eyes smiling as secretaries hurried in with the latest.

'London is slow to react, Leonard. There's selling in Paris and some movement on the Viènna Bourse.'

'Johannesburg?'

'We'll know tomorrow. I thought we might have a little dinner this evening … a celebration.'

'Isn't it a bit soon for that?'

'Call it the birth of your son, just a few close friends.'

'I shall not have any friends tomorrow,' said Penlynne sombrely.

'Not among those dealing for a rise.'

Wernher's eyes moved over family portraits. The beginnings of the family business in Kessel. Wernher's association with Julius Porges the most successful diamond dealer in early Kimberley. 'Politics! I've no time for it, Leonard. It's a fool's business.'

'Barnato's having a party tonight, Julius. I'm invited.'

Wernher made a motion of disdain. 'As you please.'

'It's to launch Barnato Bank in London.'

'Better go before it founders.'

'Who will be there, do you think? City men, bankers, merchants?'

'No one who will count for anything this time next week.'

Barnato had taken a suite in the Savoy. He came through the throng of guests at once and tackled Penlynne. 'That was a fine bloody speech you made to the Worshipful Company of Goldsmiths,' he said with heavy sarcasm. 'Nothing personal, of course, as the farmer said to the fuckin' goose as he cut its throat … I'm surprised you 'ad the cheek to turn up. I'll hold the market up … pound for pound. See if I don't. You're backing the wrong 'orse, Penny old cock.'

Penlynne was suddenly aware of a pool of silence around

them. What a bunch! Over-dressed women with nondescript faces. Fanny Barnato's extravagance of diamonds. His old music hall cronies in hired evening clothes. Waiters serving champagne dressed as bank tellers. At the far end of the room was a model of the Barnato Bank. A fragile masterpiece of the confectioner's art in spun sugar. Golden coins burst from its open doors. Everyone applauded.

'I never lost a fight in my life, Penny. And I won't lose this one.' He stripped off his frock coat and stood with fists up, grinning. It was the old Barnato. The street Arab performer, grinning with impudent amusement at Penlynne's embarrassment.

'This's 'ow we used to settle it in the old days in Joh'burg, eh Penny.' He slipped back into his coat and mingled with the guests.

During the banquet every guest was presented with shares in Barnato Bank. A hundred each. Fifty thousand pounds worth. 'A little demonstration of my confidence, friends,' said the little mountebank, raising his glass to a clamour of cheers and female shrieks.

Penlynne had to admit the man's *chutzpah*. The London press had been sniping at his bank. Warning investors of its gimcrack edifice. 'Those who have placed their money in well-managed companies,' Barnato was saying, 'need have no fear of the future.'

That was when Penlynne rose and left. He began to walk east. He was making, he knew, for the bed-sitter in Bethnal Green. He often remembered that small room with its cheerful fire in the grate and his deep depression at the time. A failure at twenty-eight. Then Wernher's offer to send him to the new gold fields to challenge Rawlinson. 'We know your worth, Leonard.' The letter that changed his life had come to that room.

He had forgotten the size of the city. Its labyrinthine sprawl seemed endless. Streets were growing meaner. He could turn back at any time … hail a cab. No sleep tonight. This time tomorrow the bourses of the world would be panic-stricken. The whole crazy edifice of the Kaffir market collapsing in chaos. He walked on. It had begun to drizzle. Dark figures in doorways. In Johannesburg too, men slumped beside their packs.

Under a pool of gas light he came on a young woman. Shawl

over her head, she was singing a whining song. Over the street came the din of a public house. She pushed a child forward at Penlynne. Pinched, fallen face and skinny arms. He gave her half a sovereign. 'Feed the child,' he ordered. 'Get him bread and milk.' He had hardly turned his back when she was making for the public house. He was seized with a sudden blazing anger. It was for the child, he thought furiously. What right had she to deprive the child. His boy must never suffer. Dorothy's boy.

He hailed a ramshackle cab. 'The Savoy,' he ordered. It stank of damp straw and mouldy leather. The driver was as meagre as his horse. The smell of poverty frightened Penlynne. 'Make haste!' he ordered and the man set the nag at a trot.

Two attempts on his life already. Tomorrow they'd be after his blood. It would all be laid at his door. He thought: I'll go into the country for a day or two ... maybe look for a place to retire. Sussex. Charles Warewood had once hinted that he would sell his country seat and make his future in Africa. Everybody wanted to have a foot in Africa. Well ... first the unholy smash-up. Then the rewards for those with the guts to see it through.

He went into the country next day, missing the evening press. Gigantic bear operation – panic selling in Paris – collapse of Kaffir market – extreme confusion – warnings ignored. Once there, he found the wintry landscape hostile. The bleak skeletons of the elms gave him a feeling of foreboding. He could not stand the harsh and incessant crying of rooks and their sinister plumage.

Back in London he went to the offices of the Secretary of State for Colonies. He had no appointment with Joseph Chamberlain and he was asked to wait. It struck Penlynne as typical that the affairs of Empire were being run in such unpretentious rooms. An atmosphere of an Inns of Court chamber. The moment he saw Chamberlain he knew that the days of the accidental empire were over. This man would drive for what he wanted.

'I am sure sir,' Penlynne ventured, 'you have been kept informed of developments in Johannesburg.'

'Johannesburg can take care of its own affairs, I have no doubt. I have given Rhodes a strip of Bechuanaland for his railway. It will, naturally, require policing. Again, that is his affair. His and Dr Jameson's.'

'May I ask, sir, what degree of commitment we, that is the Reformers, can expect from ....'

'From this office? ... None, Mr Penlynne.'

'It will be hard for us without an assurance.'

'Mr Penlynne, I know that Johannesburg is anxious about reforms in the Transvaal ... and that it will apply some form of pressure. That is Johannesburg's business.' The man was coldly assertive. Almost dismissive. As if he did not want to hear. And yet in his manner there was what Penlynne took to be an unspoken assurance. The British government would support the rising. There was too much at stake for the Colonial Office to have any moral scruples. But it must not be seen to support rebellion. 'I have every confidence that Mr Rhodes will do the right thing ... at the right time,' he said cryptically.

This was the man who had taken over from Sir Henry Loch. Rhodes was committed to the Loch Plan. This was the man who had cautioned Germany not to interfere in the affairs of the Transvaal. 'I am required to ask you, sir ... on behalf of the Reformists ....'

'Say no more, Mr Penlynne ... you are not tied to the apron strings of this office.' With that Chamberlain rose and his secretary who had taken notes throughout, showed Penlynne out. He was faintly disgusted. He could not help wondering if the gulf between them had been more subtle than mere diplomatic caution. Was it personal? Had the man perhaps lost heavily in the crash? As he hesitated on the stairs Chamberlain's secretary approached.

'I am to tell you, Mr Penlynne. The British naval squadron anchored in Delagoa Bay will remain.'

'Alongside the German flotilla?'

'Yes.' He handed Penlynne a copy of the *Times*.

Penlynne felt his spirits soar. That journal had made its feelings clear. And that journal's feelings were the feelings of the Colonial Office. *The time is past,* he read, *when even in South Africa, a helot system of administration can no longer be allowed to resist the force of enlightened opinion.*

For the moment he must be content with that. Yet he could not rid himself of the feeling that he had manoeuvred himself into a cul-de-sac and that the rights of the *uitlander* in the Transvaal, including his own, were unimportant. If anyone burned his fingers it would not be Joseph Chamberlain. I am the catspaw, he thought.

'Where to, guv'nor?' he heard. A cabby's phlegmy croak.

That is a good question, Penlynne thought.

'Whites,' he heard himself saying as he mounted. Why not a good supper and an evening at the tables? He left the club about midnight. He had played with £100 counters on the red and won twelve consecutive coups together with several maximums on the 'seven'. In half an hour he had picked up twelve thousand pounds. Then the table ran out of chips. It seemed a good omen. He went down the marble staircase towards the flunkey, waiting with hat, coat and stick. In the hall he saw Walter Gardiner come in. They were equally astonished. After him came Arthur Crawley and a woman.

'Hold on there, Penlynne,' Gardiner detained him. 'You might have let an old associate in on this operation ... for Christ's sake man, are you trying to ruin us all?'

'You had your opportunity, Walter.'

'Who was that?' he heard the woman say with more than casual interest.

'The biggest bastard unhung.'

Hullo, thought Penlynne. That's the second time I've been threatened with a hanging. Next day he cabled Rhodes from Wernher's office. 'Chamberlain sound in case of interference.' He had to believe it was true, especially if he was ever to hear Her Majesty's voice, 'Arise, Sir Leonard!'

The day before he was to sail he had a surprise visitor. A Mr Edward Fairfield sent up his card. He was a tall man, of ruddy face and something of the style of a serviceman about him, but now in his middle years and unhealthy.

'I am the Africa expert, so-called, of the Colonial Office.' He spoke loudly, like a man hard of hearing. 'Former naval commander.' Deafened by gunfire, perhaps, Penlynne thought. 'I will come to the point,' said Fairfield. 'There is some concern that a hasty act of retaliation for the closing of the drifts might be in the wind. Johannesburg's desire for justice is understood ... but premature action could be disastrous.'

'Premature?' said Penlynne.

'Such an act might start a war. I must tell you in strict confidence that Her Majesty's Government has sent what amounts to an ultimatum to Kruger ... threatening military action if he does not yield and re-open the drifts. We believe he will back down. Do you see my point?'

'Of course. If you were obliged to support a rising and were not yet prepared ... extremely awkward.'

'Quite.'

'Can I take it from this that if a coup were to succeed the British Government would give full support.'

'Personally I have no sympathy for imperialism ... for Mr Rhodes. I believe the whole business of empire a profound mistake.'

'Is this then ... a warning from you.'

'I am merely discharging a duty as a civil servant.'

'In other words ... a coup is a high-level risk.'

'If it fails.' Fairfield's smile was cynical.

'Timing is everything ... is that it?'

'A word to the wise.'

'May I ask by whom you were sent?'

Mr Fairfield appeared to be struck by sudden deafness.

Penlynne cabled Rhodes from Wernher's office: *Friends and investors here will definitely support a successful promotion of new company*.

An enquiry was made by Wernher about Fairfield. He was an under-official who could only advise and hint and try to influence. 'However, in this case, I think we can take it that he was passing on a message from Chamberlain.'

'Chamberlain then, is clean in the event of failure.'

Wernher nodded. 'In the meantime, an atmosphere of uncertainty will increase money market pressure for a major change. Johannesburg must be kept ... simmering.'

Three weeks later Penlynne stood at the Vaal River. Rail traffic was not moving. The drifts crisis was evident in crates and abandoned wagons. Johannesburg was still in limbo. That night he saw his infant son for the first time. Good God, he thought, at first sight of the child, can I have sired a weakling? Puny and milk white. Dorothy had become overly solicitous. He sensed that motherhood had subtly changed her attitude to him. Perhaps, he thought, it was no more than the general atmosphere of uncertainty. Pistol practice on the terrace and the rolling of bandages was hardly conducive to the tranquillity she should be having.

'Well, King Penlynne,' Dorothy exulted. 'You have your little prince.'

'He shall want for nothing ... I promise you.'

Penlynne stood on the platform of the Sons of England Hall and waited for the applause to die down. It was a working class audience. Artisans and clerks. The kind of men who were honestly trying to make a better life here. Yeatsman already had a copy of his address. He saw a blur of faces through a haze of smoke. These were the men who must be persuaded. He spoke for half and hour in dead silence and found himself carried away by his own eloquence.

'... if we had stood up as men, years ago, we would today be respected as men. Now we are faced with closing mines ... a hostile and pitiless autocrat is out to finish us off. Development work has been stopped. The prosperity we brought is being strangled ... deliberately. Kruger's aim is to ruin us and drive us out.'

'What then?' a voice shouted.

'Transfer the suzerainty of England to Germany. We are being pushed to the point where we must become burghers of the Transvaal, abandon all we hold dear ... accept the German Kaiser or get out. But there are men here ... men who will not turn their backs if the call comes ... who will not repudiate the great traditions of their race ... or forget the heroic past.'

The hall thundered with stamping feet. He was cheered and cheered. Someone broke into Rule Britannia and the entire hall rose to sing. Men rushed the stage to pump his hand, tears flowing. He was centre of a surging mass. Only at the last moment did he recognize the livid, bearded face that came close to his. Starched evening shirt. Bared teeth. He saw with a kind of numb disbelief the flash of a blade towards him. So it ends like this...

A woman screamed. Abruptly as it had begun the attacker was wrestled to the floor. Amazingly, the face that his mind focused on at that second was not that of de la Roche ... that came later. It was Christiaan Smit. He staggered into the darkness, groped for a wall and vomited. Dizzily he thought: How damnable ... how absurd. I owe my life to Smit.

'Will you press charges?' Smit asked him.

'No, let him go. He's an ill man.'

'It might be better, considering everything.'

'It has nothing to do with magnanimity.'

'It will make a good impression ... Mr Penlynne forgives his enemy.' Smit was looking at him with a whimsical expression. He refused Penlynne's offer of his flask.

'I expect I must thank you for your intervention.'

'Had I been a moment later ... it would have saved me a great deal of trouble, Mr Penlynne. Think man, there is still time to call off this foolishness ... this capitalist republic you're after.' He was so frank and open that for a moment Penlynne was disarmed.

'I haven't forgotten the Cape train,' he countered.

'You must know how all this will end,' Smit said. 'Mr Rhodes has contrived this crisis. We will bring it to a conclusion.'

They measured each other in silence. Penlynne proffered his flask. This time the Boer accepted.

'How did it go?' Dorothy asked.

He thought it better not to keep the attempt from her.

'But why de la Roche?' she cried.

'He lost heavily in the crash. His Banque Francais de L'Afrique de Sud went under.'

'I'm glad about that,' she said. She was passionate that night. The first time since his return. He milked her full breasts with his lips, astounded at the sweetness. She pushed him away, protesting, laughing. 'He steals his baby's milk ... you are quite shameless. A thief!' The hand that wiped it from his beard was tender and she received him with the utmost pleasure. It was only later that she clung to him. 'I wish it were all over.'

'It will not be long now.'

'I hope you will keep Robert out of it,' she said.

Why was it, he thought, that in moments of great felicity some ugly thing will rise to tarnish it. And yet he knew the thing had lain in wait for them. He'd kept it from her. He'd made a practice of going over to the Pretoria cement factory where he had put her brother to work. One morning he arrived unannounced and found Robert in the drawing office. The young man had made a clumsy attempt to cover a sheet of drawing paper. Penlynne uncovered it. 'Who ordered this ... what is it, a new kiln?'

'I was told to make a full-scale drawing.' It seemed to Penlynne to be the ground plan of some construction, circular in form, with a number of abutments.

'What is it, Robert?'

'I've no idea.'

'Who put you to it?'

'Mr von Trotheim.' Penlynne had agreed to employ the German engineer on the recommendation of de la Roche. He was efficient. He very quickly produced a quality of cement so far impossible. It was selling well to the mines and the Government Engineer had placed considerable orders. Now he knew why. He was looking at the plan of a fortress. He made enquiries. Von Trotheim was a reserve officer of the Prussian army. He'd been brought out to make cement and plan fortresses for the Boers.

'You know what you're drawing, of course. Don't lie, Robert.'

'You sent me here,' said the boy sullenly.

Fair enough, thought Penlynne. And I am making a handsome profit on the cement. Let them carry on. As Rhodes said: it will be over before they finish them. He closed the office door and returned, smiling. 'I don't blame you for what you're doing ... I accept that you don't know what it is. Just carry on but I want you to make an additional copy for head office records in Johannesburg. Say nothing to Herr von Trotheim. Do you understand?'

On the whole he was relieved. It had gone against his patriotic conscience to have a share in a government-sponsored enterprise. He'd done it for the sake of the mines. Or so he rationalized. Now he could square the account. The plans would go to the War Office. He'd had to laugh the way it had turned out. Why should patriotism not be profitable?

'Robert is working quite well,' he said to Dorothy, glad she could not see his face in the dark. 'In fact, he's being rather useful.'

'I felt it all along,' she said complacently.

Penlynne hoped he would never have to undeceive her.

Chapter Nineteen

Charles Warewood rode into Johannesburg on 15th December There was no sign of a city preparing for a military coup The shops were decorating for Christmas. Cottonwool snow and tinsel, artificial fir trees and even, God help us, grubby old men with snuff stains on red dressing gowns. *Othello* was playing at The Globe and *Puss in Boots* at the Empire. There was a wedding at Village Main. Men whooped as they drew the bridal carriage through an arch decorated with paper roses. Shots were fired and charges of dynamite exploded and there was much horseplay by drunken guests.

The arrangement was to meet Leonard Penlynne at the Rand Club. Penlynne was there and welcomed him. 'Good to see you again. Are your horses stabled? Good, come inside.'

Talk at the long bar was of share prices. Race week was coming up. Penlynne saw that Warewood was taken aback by the lack of warlike preparations. And when the soldier asked about the issue of weapons in Johannesburg Penlynne hedged. 'The rifles are still in grease. Mustn't do anything premature, you know.'

'The Maxims?'

'They came up in oil drums fitted with taps to drip oil if anyone checked.'

'What am I to tell Jameson?'

'Problem is ... there's Christmas ... then race week and New Year.'

'Good God, Penlynne. We've been kicking our heels at Pitsani for over a month. Men are deserting already. They're bored stiff with drilling. The professionals are all right but the rest are youngsters and hardcases out for the pay.'

'It will be all right, I assure you.'

'How many rifles arrived?'

'About three thousand.'

'To arm twenty thousand … isn't that the figure you gave?'

Penlynne laughed. He felt uncomfortable with this man whose piercing blue eyes gave an impression of total loyalty. 'Our chaps here will get the rest from the arsenal in Pretoria.'

'You're going to storm the arsenal!'

'It's poorly guarded. One wall is down for repairs. I'm told the guards are in bed by nine.'

'It has all the earmarks of a classic ballsup.'

'The British way, old man.' Penlynne felt uncomfortably Levantine before the scorn of this typical cavalry officer. A combination of ancient blood, stupidity and boneheaded obstinacy. Totally inflexible in his thinking.

'The Boers are moving already, you know. On my way here I saw small parties making for Pretoria. Commando men.'

'It's *nagmaal* … communion. They come into Pretoria for Christmas services.'

'Frankly, Penlynne, I'm appalled. What am I to tell Jameson and Colonel Willoughby?'

Penlynne handed him a bulky envelope. 'He'll be expecting this from us. It's all there, everything he wants to know. How is he?'

'Chafing at the bit.'

'Have they anything to drink?'

'A hundred cases of champagne for one thing.'

'For the officers.' Penlynne laughed. 'Shall we see you for dinner tonight?'

'Thank you … no.'

They shook hands and Charles took the road to Langlaagte, making for the old Rawlinson house. He knew it from rides with Katherine. It was the perfect place to meet her. Secluded and neglected since Muriel's death, its acres of garden and orchard given over to bush. They'd sit together on the stoep, watching the stars. As he rode he felt his depression lifting. He longed to see her. He had dreamed his soldier's dream of this reunion, drilling his sweating men till they were ready to fall from the saddle. There were blinding dust storms but there was water in the Molopo and they bathed there at sundown. His brother officers included a baronet and two honourables. Damned idiots, every one. They played cricket and polo and cursed the flies. It was all too lighthearted for his taste. It was India all over again. Except that this was not the regiment and if it was the Queen's business it did not feel like it to him. Still, these were honourable men and his comrades. Except for one. He had not expected to find himself in company of Major Hamilton, now in charge of the Rhodesian volunteers.

'Last time I saw you, you were on your back with fever, Charlie.' Charles was barely civil with him but Hamilton persisted.

'Riding for Rhodes, eh Charlie ... there'll be good pickings, I hear and some lovely ladies in the gold city.'

In the mess tent Charles heard gossip he did not like the sound of. He refused to believe that Earl Grey had disposed of nearly all his shares in the British South Africa Company. And that Rhodes himself had reduced his holding from 166 057 to 30 000. He'd heard Lord Gifford speaking out in Parliament ... urging it to grant Rhodes the charter to explore and exploit Lobengula's country. Now he was hearing that Grey had kept only a thousand of 10 000 shares.

It had been a worse shock to be told by Jameson that they would not be riding in under the Union Jack. In the hectic atmosphere of heavy drinking the general feeling seemed to be that the whole thing was 'a bit of a lark!'. In India he'd met with officers who did not take soldiering seriously. It was the preserve of gentlemen who saw the army as one long polo game, interrupted by tea with the ladies.

Perhaps because he was dog tired after two days in the saddle he found the road to Langlaagte worse than he remembered. Broken machinery and gaunt structures of windlasses long abandoned, heaps of broken rock and straggling bluegum plantations. Suppose she did not turn up. In a way it was vague and dreamlike. Whirr of the fan in her cabin. Firelight on the ceiling of his bedroom at Warewood ....

Katherine put the key in the lock of the Langlaagte house and stepped into the stifling, unaired hall. Nothing seemed changed. At any moment she might hear her father's step on the stoep. Muriel Ferguson shouting orders in the kitchen.

Charles's letter had warned: *we can't have more than a few hours together but I cannot embark on this venture without seeing your beloved face again.* She sat in the cross-breeze of two windows she'd flung open, his note in her hand. It had been delivered to her two days ago. And this was her second visit to the house. What kept him?

After dark she lit a lamp. The mine was quiet. The *kaffirs* had been deserting in hundreds in the past week. Long processions of them with bundles and sticks, making across the veld. She wondered what they made of the parties of mounted Boers and the digging of trenches by white miners. Alone in the silence she was more than ever aware of her feelings. She did not care what was going on. Let them have their revolution. An hour with Charles meant more to her than anything. She knew nothing except that he was at Pitsani. A hundred miles of scrub country from god-forsaken Mafeking ... where there was nothing but a Resident Officer and a mudbrick barracks. A trooper had ridden in with Charles's note. In the uniform of the Bechuanaland Border Police.

'Is he well, the major?' she asked, giving him her reply. Yes, at Langlaagte. Weeks of separation between them. Only her maid knew what she had gone through waiting to hear from him. Mildred was concerned when she returned twice. 'Oh, madam, take care. It's not safe these days.' Then the long wait for his appearance. And the longer ride home. After the second time Mildred pleaded. 'Oh, ma'am ... he'll never come now.'

'I must be there if he comes.'

That was the Tuesday ... and again Wednesday. Now, as she waited in the rising din of singing insects that might have been the fever in her blood, she was ready to give up again. Then, out in the blackness the figure in tattered clothes, typical of a thousand down and outs. Dangerous and unemployed. A small man, wiry and weaselish. She attempted a composure she did not feel. His soft tongue only made her the more apprehensive.

'Would this be the Rawlinson house then?'

He stank sourly of vagrancy. The accent of a lowland Scot.

'This is a private house. What do you want?'

'A word wi' the housekeeper, Mrs Ferguson.'

'That is not possible.' Her mind in a turmoil.

'Is that a fac',' he said, insinuating himself between her and the door. 'An' I havna seen my guid wife this long time.' He pushed open the door and looked about. Seeing the furniture covered with dust sheets, the obvious unoccupation, the single lamp burning, he became insultingly familiar.

'Is there a drink for a man ... an' it's a fine hoose.' He began to open cupboards.

'I shall call the mine police,' she said, making for the telephone. He cut her off, cornering her. The weasel face was red-eyed in the yellow lamplight, the mouth jammed with ill-assorted teeth.

'Muriel Ferguson is dead,' Katherine said.

'Aye, but she died Rawlinson. You might say we're related ... me and you. I've been six years in yon Pretoria *tronk* and I'm dry. An' I havna seen a woman like you in a' that time. A right bonnie lass.' Coming close, smiling grotesquely.

Oh God! Rather die than be touched by those hands. He had the look and stench of carrion, a reddish-grey stubble sprouted on his face and by his hand he had been at hard labour. To cry out would be futile. She knew she must keep her head. This was Muriel's soldier husband of twenty years back, the deserter from the Majuba battlefield. The older woman had always feared he would turn up. Her life was hanging by a thread ... she knew it. Humour him. Keep him distracted.

Oh God, where was Charles?

'You'd better go at once,' she said calmly. 'My husband is over at the mine, he's coming at any moment. If you need something to help you on your way, there's money in the desk.' She moved and he moved, duplicating each step with horrifying ease so that he was right behind her as she opened the door.

She saw her father's old rolltop desk. The photographs of the early workings on the Star, his riding crop and a white sun helmet. Everything was just as Muriel had left it. She felt the floorboards give in places and thought, incongruously – white ants.

'It's been closed up for years,' she heard him say. 'There's nae husband coming frae the mines, now is there?' His lips lewdly moist. If only the door would open and her father stand there. Sweep her up in his arms. How's my girlie? He had kept a pistol in the third drawer on the right. The same sabre that hung by his side in the wedding photograph was on the wall, gathering dust, its gilt tassels tarnished.

She was icily calm, wary of making a sudden move towards it. First the drawer. But his hand anticipated hers, throwing open

225

the rolltop. Uncanny how Muriel had left it, bundles of father's letters, curled and yellowed. The hands throwing open drawers. No pistol in the third drawer. Dried carcase of a field mouse. The hands scattering papers.

'Where is it, the cash?'

She moved so quickly she had the sabre in her grasp before he could grasp her intention. The curving blade came brown and greased from the scabbard ... sliding out as if her father's hand was on the hilt, drawing it.

'Get out!' she commanded in a voice she did not recognize, advancing the point with instinctive imitation of her father as he did sabre drill in the yard, the steel flashing as he cut and thrust. Vivid memory of girlhood, her childish delight in his splendid figure ... the point at the creature's throat, hand steady. The weasel eyes were bulging, the lips drawn back in an absurd grimace of terror. Ferguson had fled the face of death before, but this time he saw it under the dead-white mask of a woman. She pressed him back but her hands were faltering ... the tarnished tassel on the hilt had disintegrated in dust. She was going to faint ... the point of the sabre falling from the leathery throat.

Wheels were grating and a horse whinnied. 'Charles,' she cried. Ferguson cursed her and fled. Charles caught her. He saw her extreme pallor, the naked blade on the floor ... the ripped front of the dress that exposed the whiteness of her breast.

'It's all right now,' he kept saying. She clung to him and suddenly there was passion in their embrace. The terror was past. Eyes, lips, hands groping for one another, trembling, falling, groaning. When she opened her eyes she saw the shadows of moth wings on the ceiling. Moth eyes glowed as they circled the lamp. They lay still, in a disorder of their clothing, Charles lighting a cigarette. A scorched moth sizzled and curled on the edge of the table, its eyes still fiery.

She touched the place where the blonde hair concealed the fullness of his mouth. 'Please won't you call it off. You don't have to go back there and join them. There's no reason, surely.'

He put it aside lightly. 'It's simply a ride in, a demonstration. It must be done now ... the Boers are arming against us. Johannesburg will rally.'

'You believe that? Leonard Penlynne and his friends? And that rabble. Everyone knows that there's no real organization, no leadership. It's all confusion ... no one knows who to trust.'

'I gave my word, Katherine.'

'It's rebellion.'

'Not so,' he said quickly. 'They have no rights ... no country. They're demanding what they're entitled to have.'

'You don't know the Boers,' she countered. 'None of you. Not Penlynne, not Jameson ... especially not Rhodes. You must tell them they can't succeed.'

'Whatever,' he said, 'I can't let our chaps down. Not now.'

He would ride in with Jameson and Willoughby, no matter what. Lost cause or hopeless chance, it would make no difference. She had a sudden sickening sense of powerlessness in the situation. Whatever protestations of love he made would make no difference. The very thing which gave him the quality of nobility she admired completely blinded him.

'You'll go then,' she said when his silence had become intolerable.

'That's right.'

'You say you love me.'

'You don't understand.'

'Honour, I expect.'

'One doesn't talk of that.' As if explaining etiquette to a savage.

'You mustn't expect me to understand, after all, I was born in Kimberley.'

'Don't let's say goodbye this way, Katherine. Come, we'll ride back together.' He kissed her gently but she turned her face away.

As they brushed through the rank weeds of the garden she had a sudden overwhelming sense of desolation. She knew she would never return to the house in Langlaagte. In their haste to be gone she had not even locked the door. What did it matter anyway if it became a haunt of vagrants and fell into ruin? Everything she cared about was centred on this man who behaved as if her pain and concern were not worth considering.

She leaned against him as he gave the pony its head. He put his arm about her. They were nearing her home. Lights burning and laughter from the servants' quarters.

'When is it to be?' she said as he handed her down. 'Will you at least tell me that?'

'When Jameson gets the signal. Look Katherine,' he said gravely. 'Will you do something for me? Take the children to the coast. You'll hear when it's safe to return.'

'I'll stay,' she said. 'If you go, I must be here.'

'Keep the doors locked and the shutters fastened.'

'You told me it would all be over in a day,' she said, attempting lightness.

Stewart MacDonald woke on New Year's Day with a feeling of foreboding. There had been explosions and shots during the night. Several times he had gone to the bedroom window and looked out. None of the Scots community had come to the door. The traditional first footing that ushered in the New Year at midnight. Impossible to tell if the noise was miners revelling or the start of the uprising.

'What a fool the man is,' Mary said. 'And to think Jameson's a Scot.'

Presently she slept, her tension lessened. Stewart lay awake. He must get them away to Natal without delay on the first available train. Mary had been obstinate. 'There'll be wounded,' she said. 'You'll need help ... they go on as if nobody will get hurt. And the women are as bad as the men.'

It was a miserable business with both sides out to have it their way. Such poisonous and bitter talk that a man hardly knew the right of it.

He was at breakfast when he was called out. A Rand Club messenger was urging, 'Come at once, doctor. It's one of the gentlemen took bad at the club. They've been disputing and arguing for three days, doctor, and there's no saying where it'll end. Telegrams going off to Jameson like homing pigeons ... and nothing coming back. Some are saying he's already on his way.'

It was a seizure. The man lay where he had fallen. Leonard Penlynne was on his knees at the man's side. He looked up with relief on his shrewd dark face. 'Thank God you're here, doctor.' To Stewart the extraordinary thing about the scene was the intimation it seemed to give ... almost a foreshadowing of something worse. The richly appointed inner sanctum where the Reform Committee had been directing events was heavy with cigar smoke and littered with paper, empty glasses and open dispatch cases. It was, he thought, like a board meeting gone mad.

Stewart gave the patient what assistance he could and a cab was called to take him home. Outside the club a boy was crying, 'Newspapers!' He bought *The Oracle*. Boldly displayed was a letter to Dr Jameson from the Reform Committee. *We call upon you to rescue the thousands of unarmed men, women and children of our race who will be at the mercy of well-armed Boers should a revolt break out ... we believe that you and the men under you will not fail ...*

He went back into the club. Penlynne took him aside. 'Doctor, if I may advise you ... and we have been friends for some years now, do not hesitate to get Mrs MacDonald and the children away from here.'

'You mean Dr Jameson has crossed the border?'

'Jameson has left Pitsani, yes. Without our permission. We have telegraphed him to turn back and we have sent messengers. So far no acknowledgement. We are not ready for him in Johannesburg. But he has taken the bit in his teeth. Bloodshed may still be avoided ... I can't vouch for it. Do get your family on that train. The Reform Committee will do what it can to keep order here.'

Penlynne turned back to his companions. Faces Stewart knew. All prominent in the mining and finance world. He had heard them lauded for their stand against Kruger, read their letters and denunciations in the Press. Wherever they went they were slapped on the back. Stout fellows. Now he saw them in a whispering conclave. Outside in the street men were shouting their names and demanding arms.

'I will not deceive you, doctor,' Penlynne said. 'The invitation to Jameson was a pretext ....'

'To confer legitimacy.'

'It was to be acted upon, only on confirmation from us. He has not waited for that and we have been obliged to publish the appeal here ... and in London. We had hoped to bluff our way through this situation, now we have no choice but to support him in arms.'

'Madness,' someone was shouting.

'Gentlemen,' Penlynne was calling to order. 'For those who have no stomach for this, it is time to get out.'

The press of people in the streets was so heavy Stewart had difficulty in reaching Park Halt. Shutters were going up all down

229

Eloff Street. 'What is the news, doctor?' he was asked by men making way for him. He saw a train about to leave. It was besieged by jostling and shouting crowds. They surged ten deep around the telephone. The Hollander station master was shouting in Dutch. He calmed when he recognized Stewart's voice. *Ja,* he would do what he could to reserve a coupé for Mrs Mac-Donald and children on the next train to Durban. They would have to share.

As Stewart was about to hang up he heard a voice on the line. '... there's a rumour the Boers have started to tear up the railway lines ... no one will get away.'

He closed his consulting room. The day's heat had built to a climax. The streets were suffocating with red dust mingled with the pungent odour of horse and oxen dung. To the hurrying doctor, that smell, mingled with the acrid sweat of frightened blacks and whites, remained unforgettable. It seemed to him to be the authentic odour of panic and civil disturbances. Part of his mind was already occupied with the problem of how to cope with wounded. The Boers would carry off their own. It was the *uitlander* mobs he was thinking of ... people whose nationality you had to guess.

At the corner of Bree and De Villiers streets he came on drunken Cornish miners holding chariot races with abandoned rickshas. A patrol of volunteer Scots on bicycles gave him a cheerful wave. Each had a new rifle slung on his shoulder, brave in tam o'shanters. Cab ranks were deserted and there was no sign of the Russian Jew peddlers and bootblacks. Suddenly the streets were swept by a strong wind and a few drops of stinging rain. It stopped as suddenly as it began. His clothes were sticking to his back as he reached his house. He looked back and saw a train pulling away past Braamfontein with a plume of white steam and long afterwards, the scream of the whistle. It seemed to move with intolerable slowness. Unbelievably, from its open windows he saw the coloured scraps of fluttering Union Jacks.

The last hours together in the house were spent covering the furniture with sheets and securing the place. 'I just have a feeling,' Mary said, 'we won't be back in a fortnight.' They made a game of it for little Ruth but when Stewart threw a cover over a mirror on the dressing table Mary snatched it away.

'Don't you know never to cover a looking glass ... and you a doctor.' And suddenly they were in the reality of her putting on her hat and knotting her veil, fussing the children and packing the picnic. He thought then, watching her kneel to the bairns (as she called them) that he had never seen anything so lovely; the dark hair pulled back into the nape of her neck, her bosom pressing against the constraining material ... the children so assured of her love.

The years in Africa had lessened the high colour of girlhood but the raven tresses were as dark as ever and the flesh beneath her clothing was white as the first day he watched her lift her arms to remove her camisole ... creamy white, and beneath her armpits the black hair curled. He had seen many a woman's body. None that affected him as hers.

She was looking up. 'I've a mind not to go, Stewart,' she said, removing hat pins.

'Mary ... it's too late for that.'

'I'll miss our things,' she said wistfully, looking at the prints of highland cattle standing knee-deep in some Scottish ford, at the brass she loved to polish and at the flowered basin and ewer from her mother's house. There was a bedcover of ripe Victoria plums from her own bed as a child, now cut into covers for the children. On an impulse she folded it and put it with the other bundles.

'Let's hurry now,' he said.

'Let's hurry now,' piped little Ruth. Her sweet voice clutched at his heart. Tears burned in his eyes, and he embraced them both.

There were twelve in a first-class compartment for four. And lucky to get it at all, Mary thought. You'd think some folk were moving house the things they brought. At the station there'd been shouting and fighting for seats. A group of Cornish miners pushed the women from one coach and took over. There were cries of 'call yourselves British ... call yourselves men!' At every stop they were on the lookout for drink. No wonder the Dutch despised them.

After four hours, what with the heat and the only toilet jammed, they were all too exhausted to protest any more, falling into a stupored sleep, children's heads on their laps. Half the women spoke no English, making do with smiles, some sharing what they had, others looking after their own comfort. They were in a coach of the Nederlands Railway Company. Mary thought it a poor thing next to the London Midland Scottish. Jostling, swinging, thumping. What a way to spend the New Year. At home, snow was on the ground, thick on tree and hill, the hayricks smothered. Every barn and outhouse was mysteriously transfigured and the familiar paths were strange to the feet.

New Year's Day was a big event at Ferrygate with all the hands being served by the family at the table in the kitchen, the fire roaring in the grate. She was remembering the men's hands, clumsy with unaccustomed cutlery. Some of them were more at home with horn spoons. Stewart's blonde head was down the table with his ploughman father – that was before he went away to medical school and came back a stranger – and she so eager to be walked out and kissed.

At Newcastle the train stopped to take in water. Mary walked with the children, her attention drawn to heavy black clouds ahead and the strangely disfiguring light that seemed to turn faces to yellow wax. How oddly ominous it looked. She heard there were heavy winds ahead and some people were transferring their things to the coaches of the Natal Railways now being coupled up. They looked to her more solid and reliable, more like British stock. It gave her a feeling of security to settle the children.

She heard the English guard saying the Transvaal train had arrived four hours late. 'We'll have to make up the time now.' Well, they were in Natal. In British territory. 'This is better, darling,' she assured Ruth and opened their picnic.

As the train rounded the steep bends in the hills she could sometimes see the locomotive steaming furiously. The railway seemed to cling precariously to the green slopes. Often the coach leaned heavily to one side or the other and the wheels ground noisily. Shortly before they reached Dannhauser, the storm came tearing out of the hills. The coaches swung in gusts of wind but the speed of the train did not slacken. It was as if the iron monster was challenging the elements.

Hail battered on one side. A window shattered. Icy air blew in. Chunks of ice were passed from hand to hand. Was it safe to be travelling at this speed, charging through thick, obscuring rain, whistling furiously, the darkening countryside hurtling past the windows? Did it really matter so much if they arrived a few hours late at Durban? Some were saying they would protest at the next station.

'What station is that?' Mary asked.

'Glencoe.' The word meant nothing to the others but in her Scottish heart it struck as a premonition. It was a woeful word in her country's history. Was it not there the Campbells had slaughtered the MacDonalds in their beds? She held the sleeping child closer.

The locomotive charged into a cutting, whistling fiercely as it tore on in a shower of sparks, the fireman shovelling. At the rear of the train of carriages one of the coaches of the Nederlands Railway left the track, drawing four others with it in a horror of splintering, rending woodwork.

Chapter Twenty

The telegram in Yeatsman's hand read: *Charlestown, Monday afternoon (Special) The down Johannesburg mail passing through at 4 o'clock containing fully 150 women and children met with terrific storm of wind and hail. Many windows broken and one carriage partially unroofed.*

Instinct warned Yeatsman this was not the end of the story but on a day like this it was unlikely to warrant much attention. Everything he believed in was being put to the test. He had supported the Reform Committee's ideals with passionate conviction. The ink was hardly dry on his leading article calling on Johannesburg to rise in support of Jameson.

It is the finest equipped British force yet assembled in the land, he had written, *and it is coming at the request of this city's men, women and children* .... He had been stirred when Penlynne handed the appeal to him with his signature and those of the other leaders. 'Print this now, Stephen ... a special edition if necessary. Give it today's date.' That was yesterday.

There were signs that the Boers were alerted and moving to surround the city. He was exhilarated. When Jameson broke through the Boers and joined hands with the city volunteers ... why, that would be the end of Krugerism. Penlynne and his friends would dictate their terms to the Transvaal. A British Transvaal in a British South Africa. An end to the German threat. There was no other way. On his way to the Rand Club for news of Jameson he was stopped at barriers by armed men with rifles barely out of the grease.

The exodus had been something he would never forget. Trains had been booked six days in advance. Food was at famine prices though hoarding was prohibited. The key to the situation was to break that obstinate old man in Pretoria. That would happen when Jameson rode in and the High Commissioner came up from Cape Town to see the republican flag come down.

As he hurried towards the club he heard a lad running and shouting behind him. He was a prentice from the works waving a telegram. From Glencoe. 'There has been an appalling rail accident near the Glencoe junction. The mail train from Johannesburg with a large number of women and children from the Rand has been derailed. The death toll is believed high.'

'Get this set at once,' he ordered the boy and hurried on. At the last barrier on Commissioner Street he was stopped by a group of men setting up a machine gun to cover the approaches from Krugersdorp.

'Is it true, sir. Has the doctor broken through them?'

Their cycles were leaning against the wall of the Empire Theatre with a poster for *The Yeoman of the Guard* obscured by the word: Closed.

'What word of Jameson?' he heard on all sides as he entered the club. 'Is Kruger ready to back down?' He sent in his name to the committee, apprehensive without knowing why. Was this fear for Jameson and his gallant fellows, or a sense that everything was going to go wrong ... an expectation of disaster aroused by the news of the refugee train? In the committee room he saw a dozen men all known to him, shirt-sleeved and unshaven among plates of half-eaten food and coffee cups. The air was rank.

Leonard Penlynne looked up. He was bleary-eyed with exhaustion but he came towards him like a man who had just been relieved of a great uncertainty. 'You're just in time, Stephen. We have just finished drafting a declaration of allegiance.'

'Support for Jameson.'

'No, the immediate thing is to calm the situation.'

'Allegiance to the Transvaal ... to Kruger.'

'We must show we are reasonable men, Stephen. Already we have proved our point ... without bloodshed. The High Commissioner is on his way to urge reforms, on our terms. We have won, Stephen. This statement will show the Government our good will. It must be printed at once and ....' He broke off seeing Yeatsman's expression.

Why, Yeatsman thought, the man's nothing but a compromiser. It's his business interests that concern him ... what's good for the mines. Penlynne drew him aside. 'If we do not show good will, Stephen, they'll blow up the mines. The truth is, Jameson moved without our instructions. Rhodes has done his damndest to stop him.'

'What about the appeal ...?' He threw the newspaper aside.

'It was a ruse ... it was necessary to prevent the Boers taking over in the city.'

'You never had any intention of using arms?'

'Only a show of force.'

'All this agitation has been for nothing?'

'Not at all ... we have shown our strength.'

'And Jameson ... does he know?'

'We've sent gallopers to turn him back.'

'And if he persists?'

For the first time since he had known him, Stephen saw that Penlynne evaded his direct look. 'I admit it will be a grave embarrassment. You do see the need to convince the Government of our good will?'

Strangely, Yeatsman was at that moment hearing the splintering of wood, metal grinding on metal ... the shocked silent aftermath before the screaming began.

'Don't imagine, Stephen, that I have not believed in the justice of our cause.' He was urging Stephen to take the declaration.

'I would be ashamed to print it.'

'*The Oracle* is mine ... need I remind you.'

'Are you telling me the truth this time, Mr Penlynne? If not, I must resign.'

Penlynne flared up in a way Yeatsman had never seen before.

'I am exhausted trying to do the best for everyone and I believe I have a lot more at stake than your notion of honour.'

'I insist on the truth.'

Penlynne sank into a chair. 'Very well. The High Commissioner is to give an order for all British subjects not to aid us in any way. We are disarmed. There is no way Jameson can prevail against the commandos. Johannesburg will not support us.'

'But the barricades ... the men you've armed?'

'They must lay down their weapons at once. Publish the statement, Stephen. You can save much bloodshed. You do see the necessity?'

Yeatsman felt young, ignorant and deceived as he took the statement. Penlynne was offering his hand. 'Our time will come, never doubt it.' He smiled with that sudden, attractive flash of good teeth against the redness of lip and the blackly curling beard. 'Don't resign yet, Stephen ... as a newsman you wouldn't want to miss publishing the account of my arrest!'

For Stewart MacDonald the summons from Dorothy Penlynne could not have been more badly timed but he got his things together and followed her servant to the waiting carriage. He was surprised to see *Far Horizons* was in a blaze of light. It stood out in the darkness like something that had no need to be there at all, arrogantly perched at the top of the winding pass. There was something almost defiant in this brilliance at that moment when the lights of the mining villages along the reef were blacked out.

When the carriage stopped at the gates he heard the sound of a piano playing at an open window. It broke off abruptly. A man in his late twenties met him at the door. He recognized George Borchard, the architect of *Far Horizons*. Some said he was more than that to Dorothy Penlynne. There was something distraught about him.

'We've been quite distracted not being able to contact Mr Penlynne for the past twenty-four hours or more.'

Dorothy Penlynne lay in the huge bed with its rich drapings on a mass of lace pillows. Very pale. The moment he took her hand he saw that she had been drinking, perhaps no more than normal for one of her set. He could find nothing wrong with the 'twisted ankle'.

'What have you heard, doctor. Has Dr Jameson reached us yet?'

'I've heard nothing, Mrs Penlynne.'

'What if he fails?' Her eyes roved round the room, rested a moment on the Florentine screen and on the vivid canvas above her bed. He did not know it was Firenze's *Madonna and Child*.

'Why did you send for me, Mrs Penlynne?'

'I felt I could trust you. All I hear are rumours and more rumours ... that hideous old man in Pretoria will ruin us all. My husband is deeply involved. I can get no response from him. Will you not see him ... ask him, for pity's sake, to give over now. The house has been watched for days.'

'I expect he will do his duty as he sees it, Mrs Penlynne. I'll telephone you if I hear anything.'

'The exchange is not answering. We are cut off.'

'Perhaps it would be wise to prepare to leave ... pack.' He was thinking of Mary and the children. Thank God he got them on the train in time. He suspected Mrs Penlynne's nervous condition was a symptom that she knew more than she was saying.

'It's too late to leave,' she said. 'Does it not all seem like a frightful dream to you?'

'A difficult time,' Stewart said in his medical voice.

'No doubt,' she resumed in her hostess voice, as if she has found some resolution, 'in time we shall all find it very amusing.'

He had no appetite but he went to Frascati's, forcing himself to order. Frascati served him personally, pouring a glass of chianti. '*Permesso dottore* ... it is a bad thing, no ...*quel disastro,* this Jameson ... everybody is ruin. Now there will be war ... *non e vero?*

'Will you go home, Franco?' Frascati's home was there for all to see in the violent oleographs of Naples. Curious how at a time like this one felt an unease with one's surroundings. He was acutely conscious of severance from his own roots, sitting here discussing events with another alien as cut off as himself.

The dish was oily and he felt nauseous. 'You no' like my gnocci,' Frascati mourned. 'I bring you lasagne.' He had hardly left the table when Stewart picked up an abandoned newspaper at the next table. *Shocking rail accident. Down mail derailed. 7 Killed and 40 injured.* His eye saw it but his mind rejected what he saw. His eyes skipped down the column for names. No names but locust swarms had invaded Natal. Which carriages had been derailed? First or third? Her carriage, or the carriages of women he had seen at the station weeping, clutching their belongings? *Full details not received at time of going to press.* His eyes found the locusts again. *Stripped trees. The swarm extended inland for forty miles and was 26 miles long. Deafening sound of wings. Voracious jaws crunching.*

He found himself running in the direction of *The Oracle* office. Stephen Yeatsman looked up to see him and thought he was drunk.

'The train, man ... what news is there?'

'It's worse than we thought. At least thirty dead.'

'Have you their names?'

'Anyone you know, doctor? I hope not.'

Stewart reading the column for names he was afraid of finding. No one he knew ... so far they were still alive. Reading on. *While negotiating a sharp curve one of the Nederlands Railway coaches left the metals, taking with it four other carriages. 50 to 60 people are still trapped under the debris. There are horrifying scenes. It is believed the engineer was trying to make up for lost time on the Transvaal side of the border. Medical assistance and coffins are on their way from Maritzburg.*

'I must get down there,' Stewart said.

'Doctor ... all trains out of Johannesburg have been stopped.'

'I must get there.'

'Sit down, doctor. I'll let you know when we've got the full list. There's no way of getting there and medical help is on its way up the line from Durban. In any case, doctor, it looks as if you'll be needed here.'

Charles Warewood's troopers unsaddled about midnight. Most of them lay down where they stood. Some pickets were posted. Charles found the men asleep when he went to inspect. It was moonless but not dark. One could distinguish men from rocks and rocks from picketed horses. The Maxims had been sited forward, the gunners sleeping close by them. Further back where the seven-pounders had been unlimbered, there were small fires burning. He could hear the chink of equipment and the stir of restless horseflesh. There was exhaustion on every face. Exhaustion and the strain of tomorrow. No sign of the bantering and high spirits of three days ago. The cheering when Jameson read out the appeal from Johannesburg and called for three cheers for Her Majesty. Hats were tossed in the air when they crossed into the Transvaal. No more of that. It had been a damnable ride and the remounts they had expected to pick up on the way were worthless nags.

Ahead lay the Doornkop ridge. There was about a mile of open ground to cross. He did not find it unnerving, as some did, that the enemy was invisible. The Pathan he'd fought with in India also made skilful use of the rocks ... but someone had to go in and winkle them out. Tomorrow, he thought, we'll breakfast, saddle up and charge into the sun. It will be a fine sight for those watching over the muzzles of the Mausers. He lit one of Mr Rothman's handrolled Balkan Sobrani.

Colonel Willoughby strolled over. He'd been in it from the start and was close to Penlynne. 'Well Charles, all over this time tomorrow. Drinks in the Rand Club and we'll be in good time for the New Year's Handicap. The ridge? They'll melt like snow off a wall when we open fire on it tomorrow. Your chaps all right? Good. Get some sleep.'

Charles had hardly laid down when young Robert Orwell shook him up. 'Sir ... major. There's a lady here, asking for you.' The cloaked figure was unmistakably Katherine.

'What on earth are you doing here?' he said. 'How did you find us?'

'Don't send me away, Charles. I had to be with you.'

She came into his arms and he held her as if to impress her body on his, indelibly. 'You're always with me,' he said, 'but this is madness. You must go at once.'

'If you can be here, so can I.'

'You have children to think of.'

'My place is with you.'

She turned her face up to his, pleading. 'We have a few hours yet.' She had left her house after dark and galloped across the veld on tracks she had ridden for years. Dark figures sprang to their feet as she went by and she heard guttural Boer orders to stop. Everyone knew what was in store for the raiders. For days past, the commandos had been riding in from the farms. Johannesburg was surrounded.

'No one will get out to help you,' she told Charles. 'Even if they wanted to ... and that is doubtful.'

'They are men of honour,' he said.

She made a scornful sound. 'Half Johannesburg says you'll never come ... the other half says who cares and don't interfere with the races. The town's boarded up and the prices of everything gone mad ... every church hall is crammed with women and children brought in to save them from the Boers. It's plain madness. They've set up dressing stations and put guards on food stores but nobody thinks for a moment that Jameson can win. Go back, Charles. Tell them to call it off. It's a lost cause, if ever it was a cause.'

'There's a sporting chance we'll pull it off.'

'How many are you? There's talk of seven hundred.'

'We'll muster about three-fifty tomorrow ... all fit.'

240

'There are thousands against you.'

'We have the Maxims.'

'Oh, you damn fool.'

'We seem to spend our time together disagreeing,' he said mildly.

'I won't weep,' she said. 'But oh God, what a pack of idiots you are.'

They spent the early hours lying together. He beat down the high summer grasses and laid out his saddle blanket. Gradually her body relaxed and it seemed that she slept, the warm shafts of her breathing touching his flesh. Once she sat up abruptly. 'Is it time?'

'Not yet,' he said, gathering her again, looking up at the wheeling march of stars, cold, and utterly indifferent. It grew chilly as the night waned and her hair was wet with dew. 'Not yet,' she kept saying.

'You must go now, Katie dear,' he said at last. She rose stiffly and shook moisture from her skirts. He led her through the lines where men were already stirring and stamping stiffness out of their joints. It seemed to him that they passed among them like a pair of wraiths, unchallenged.

He thought: at least I have had this. He helped her into the saddle and she rode off without a backward glance. He raised his hand as she passed into the obscurity of the pre-dawn light and he imagined he saw a flash of her hand as she turned at the last.

A bugle was blasting its brazen summons and he became at once part of the scene he had spent so much of his life preparing for. The schoolboy chanting of verses that had thrilled … was there a man dismayed? Not though the cannon thundered. Into the valley of death rode the six hundred, the gallant six hundred. At cavalry school he'd thought them a pack of fools. Was there no one there with sense enough to call them off? Saddles empty and girth straps trailing. Horses dragging scarlet coats. A valley thick with gunsmoke. Horses disemboweled and trailing their guts like a bloody steeple chase run amok as they jumped the Russian earthworks to sabre the gunners … and then the long trot back through the fallen.

Well, here goes the last of the Warewoods! It made as much sense as anything else and dammit, there was a chance they'd go right through them. Pity it wouldn't be lances … the bright steel spike that sent the bush pigs squealing and tumbling while the point pulled out clean and you levelled the shaft for the next thrust. This would be close range work with sabre and pistol.

He accepted a mug of bitter coffee laced with whiskey.

Oh Christ, Katherine! he cried with inner anguish.

At that moment the sun touched the rocks of Doornkop. To the rear of the troops forming squadron, the seven pounders flashed and red splashes dotted the ridge. 'We'll give them an hour of it,' he heard Willoughby at his elbow. 'Then you'll go in ... all right, Charles?'

'Right-o!' he heard himself reply.

'Take the centre, Charles ... got it!'

'Right-o!' He had to shout to be heard above the clattering as the Maxims opened fire. Not a shot came from the ridge. It lay under a drifting pall of smoke that clung to the ground, only slowly dispersing. As he signalled the extended order and the trot, he looked back and saw the whole force of horsemen, the toy soldiers serving the guns, the glint of brass and flash of steel. The sun rose rapidly. Tall seed-laden grasses turned golden. It was torn from a childhood storybook. It was like the room upstairs at Warewood where he had shown Katherine's boy Spencer how the Scots Greys took the ridge at Waterloo. Why did it look so unreal now? A boy's game.

'Draw sabres ... canter!' Along the line sabres flashed out.

'Charge!' he heard himself scream and bugles sounding. Thunder of hooves and the first flashes from Doornkop ridge.

Robert Orwell stood sketching the small knot of officers around Jameson. A thunderclap burst almost overhead. A black cloud blossomed out of nowhere and with it a hiss of metal balls and the patter of fragments. He felt no fear, only exhilaration. The officers were watching Charles Warewood's squadron through glasses. The first riderless horses had galloped by. Here and there, among groups of horsemen waiting for the order to support Warewood, a man would suddenly fall. It all seemed quite random and casual. Over there men were galloping at an enemy they could not see ... here they stood about or sat on horseback as if nothing was happening.

He had joined Jameson as a trooper but when his sketches were seen, the little Scot had been delighted. 'Just the thing for the illustrated papers at home,' he cried. Robert made some good sketches of Jameson and one of Sir John Willoughby, the commander. He captured his wispy moustaches and an oddly vacant expression. But then they all looked like that, as if they had no real connection with what was going on. The dead looked equally indifferent, as if the death that had found them had arrived randomly. He began to sketch one boy of his own age, finding himself curiously detached from this face he had seen alive not long ago.

Robert Orwell was eager to do the right thing. For the first time in his life he had made a commitment to something worthwhile. He had written to Penlynne his apologies and regrets but there had been no opportunity to post the letter from Pitsani. Sir John Willoughby made him his personal galloper, but had no idea he was related to Penlynne. The morning they left camp at Pitsani, Willoughby told him to put his dispatch case into the mess wagon.

'Sling it in, Orwell ... if we don't get through we'll all be dead anyway and it don't matter a damn who picks it up.' His casual indifference was characteristic of men he had come to admire ... a nonchalance bred of complete confidence in their superiority. There had been a great deal of drinking – which he imagined to be nothing unusual. As long as a man was capable of sitting in the saddle next day, nothing was said.

'They're a hard lot ... colonials and volunteers. They'll do very well. It's going to be a hard, dry ride and they'll be sober enough when we get there.' Nothing much was said of the men who deserted. 'They'll miss a good show,' was the comment. When they finally left Pitsani the force was under four hundred, riding in three columns without its baggage. The plan was to pick up rations and fresh mounts at pre-arranged stages. It turned out that many remounts weren't fit to ride and the troopers were so exhausted by the cracking pace that they slept rather than ate, and rode on with a tin of bully and biscuit.

Robert made some good sketches of booted men lying in rows, some incapable of going further. Dysentery and foul water. And worse, mutterings. Talk of a fool's errand. Scouts brought in reports of mounted men hanging onto their heels ... small parties which galloped off when a few shots were fired.

Jameson was heard in an angry silence. 'Anyone who falls out now must understand that he is deserting women and children of our race. They have appealed to us ... we cannot fail them.' The advance continued but Robert saw few signs of enthusiasm. They were not his idea of liberators ... but then maybe men going into battle always looked and sounded like this. It wasn't the gay cameraderie he'd expected.

Now they were near Johannesburg ... a mere fourteen miles. A ride through a few mining villages. They'd be cheered as heroes when the mine dumps and headgears came in sight and the men raised in Johannesburg came out to meet them.

The Boers had the range at last. Robert saw with dismay that Major Lord Warewood's squadron was galloping back. Fountains of earth and stones were spouting from the ground. Jameson and his officers were looking for cover. Bullets from unseen marksmen continually hissed and cracked past. Or thumped as they found a mark. The drawing pad was wet under his hand.

'Orwell ... Trooper Orwell!'

Sir John Willoughby beckoned. 'You know this part of the country, Orwell. We're going to have to give over ... the doctor's decision. That dispatch case ... rather compromising. Get a horse and get it away from here ... destroy it. Take the fly ... go boy!'

As he mounted Robert saw the fluttering of a white rag being raised over headquarters. Men were laying down their arms and waiting to be taken prisoner. Jameson slumped in his canvas chair. Robert rode fast, making for the Far West Rand Gold Mine, a desolation of corrugated iron buildings and abandoned machinery. It was eerily deserted. As he dismounted and led the horse he saw fresh horse dung. It should have warned him that the place was occupied.

Boers appeared with levelled rifles. They saw this slightly built, fairheaded young man in uniform and called on him to stand. Instead he lifted something from the fly and made a stumbling run towards the mine shaft. They called on him to stop. He hesitated, then ran on. Several Boers fired together ... the dispatch case flew from his hand and stopped within a yard of the shaft.

The irony was that the attempt to lose it focused the attention of men who might well have scattered its papers. Few of them could read their own language, let alone English. They found his sketchbook in the fly. The faces of Jameson and his officers drew gasps of admiration. There was also a letter addressed to Mr Leonard Penlynne, *Far Horizons*, Johannesburg.

I have been a rotter. I find there is no way out of what I have done but to join up and try to make good the damage. You have always been so decent and generous that I could not tell you about my gambling debts. I was a fool and feel only self-disgust. Treachery is an awful word. I hope to redeem myself in your estimation but whatever happens I shall think of you with gratitude. Can you forgive me for any damage I have done?

Chapter Twenty-One

The Zulu watchman at the gates of *Far Horizons* gave Penlynne the royal salute with his *kierie*. *'Bayete nkos!'* His round, sweating face expressing loyalty. The greeting sounded ironic to the man who had just been smuggled out of the kitchen door of the Rand Club by the hall porter. 'Hurry, Mr Penlynne, I've a cab waiting.' Above the sombre club livery, the man's face shone with the zeal of the British servant. There was no reproach for failure here. It was the angry mob at the front entrance that howled for his blood, smashing windows and attempting to burn the building.

Easy for them to express their anger at the whole fiasco. Rage cost them nothing. There was some balm in the loyalty of his servants. They would not question his good faith. *Far Horizons* had never looked so secure, so settled. Hydrangea cuttings he'd had from Rhodes at *Groote Schuur* were in full bloom on the east side. They had decorated the church at Christmas. Christmas flowers they called them in the Cape. Dorothy had massed them in old Cape copper pots. Blue was so rare a colour in Africa.

His roses were past their best. Would he be here to see their last flowering in the autumn?

He went quickly upstairs to find Dorothy. She had never seemed so stately. Calm, very pale. Her eyes enormous but no tears.

'I've packed some things.'

'All I need is a few hours sleep,' he assured her. He was haggard and his clothing unpressed. She had not noticed at first how exhausted he looked. For some extraordinary reason he was in an ebullient state of mind, almost as if he was buoyed up by the disaster. Everything planned had fallen apart but he seemed far from crushed. 'There are some papers I must take care of.'

'They've been here already.'

It was only when he saw the ransacked study, drawers open,

bookcases with gaps and volumes stacked in heaps that he realized how fast things were moving. 'Smit's men. Did he come with them personally?'

'They seemed pleased ... oh, there's a receipt for it all.'

'We were over-confident, I expect. They might have put the books back.'

'They offered.'

'Very civil of them.'

'They were quite polite.'

He lay down on the chaise and was instantly asleep. She covered him with a travelling rug and sat down to watch him. He had not understood her dismay ... the sense of everything she loved here violated. I hate them, she thought. They will never be anything but uncouth, cunning and barbarous. They despise Johannesburg and those who have built it from nothing. They will never be satisfied until they had destroyed all this.

Unseen by Penlynne, her mask of composure had fallen. She had heard Smit's using the word *konfiskasie* – confiscation of all enemy property. I would burn it to the ground first, she thought. Dear Julius Wernher. He had been so wise. Keep out of politics. Madness to squander half a million on the buying of arms. Rhodes a sick man, his judgement failing.

Dorothy had forgotten her own enthusiasm, her addresses to the Guild of Empire Women, the women's pistol club, her subtle influence on Penlynne at a time when he had no interest in the reform movement. Now there was nothing but this sickening premonition of loss. She looked up as a servant knocked. 'A gentleman to see Mr Penlynne.'

'Impossible.' She went downstairs, head up, determined to show nothing but contempt. It was Baron de la Roche.

'I must see your husband at once.'

'He's sleeping ... exhausted.'

He made a dart at the stairs but she barred his way.

'My dear lady, I've come to show him a way out. He's to be arrested tonight.'

'Wait in the library, please.'

Penlynne came down and she heard raised voices. Then de la Roche emerged. 'He refuses the offer,' he said and left the house. She found Penlynne picking up volumes from the floor.

A Tale of Two Cities, he smiled. 'I'll take it with me.' She did not understand the allusion.

'De la Roche said he could offer a way to escape.'

'You refused. Surely not?'

'He said he had it on high government authority they would not stand in our way ... but it must be now.' He was picking up books with maddening deliberation, putting Barrow's Travels in Southern Africa back with special care. 'Of course the man's mad ... and if there's any truth in it he knew I'd be shot dead on the spot if I ran for it. He has no cause to love me.'

'Of course not ... he tried to kill you.'

'The man's ill ... as good as dead himself.'

'What else ... I feel you're not telling me everything.'

He hesitated. 'A letter from Robert.' Penlynne walked to the window and stood with his back to her, the letter of reconciliation in his pocket where he had put it when de la Roche handed it over. A peacock spread its tail on the lawn and screeched.

'I'm afraid he's dead, Dorothy. I blame myself. He was apparently escaping from Doornkop ... The battlefield. The Boers found his body at the old workings of the Far West Rand Gold Mine, near Krugersdorp.'

'May I read it, please?'

How deep is anyone's complicity in the fate of another, he thought. Had I never done this or that would it have come out differently in the long run? Men pursued their fate with fatal energy. But did Robert deserve to die like that? De la Roche had said the boy's sketches would be part of the evidence against the raiders. Everything the boy touched had the seeds of destruction in it. De la Roche had let him finish the letter, then made the offer. In that instant Penlynne had understood why the offer had been made. How typical of them!

'No thank you, Baron. I know it would be very embarrassing for you and your German friends to have their dirty linen washed in public ... at a trial attended by the Press of the world. I'd be very outspoken. I think that is realized in Pretoria.' He was in control again, if only for the moment.

'You may tell your friends I intend to stay and defend myself before the bar of world opinion.' It sounded tremendous and convincing as he said it.

De la Roche laughed. 'Treason! You'll defend treason?'

They were shouting. Penlynne was noticing the man's agitation, his inability to maintain a flow of his argument and his sudden lapses. 'You fools have brought us all to ruin,' he raved. 'My friends … oh yes, there are elements here who will not stop at a trial … they will wipe Johannesburg off the map, totally!'

Penlynne saw how curiously shrunken he looked in his good clothes, folds of his neck drooping over the silk cravat with the diamond pin. Oddly, his shoelaces trailed, as if he had come in mad haste or did not care.

Only after his carriage sounded on the drive had Penlynne remembered a line from his childhood history book. He had been about seven, sitting with his peers in a council school. *They shall be struck a blow and will not know by whom it is struck.* The line had surfaced in his recollection so vividly that he recalled the smell of that classroom … the apple smell of boys, urine and chalk, wet books and stale crusts in ancient desks. An anonymous letter had been enough to hang Guy Fawkes, after suitably painful extraction of his accomplices' names. Accomplices. It was a nasty word. But this hint of destruction of the city by extremists, was it a possibility or only a figment of the man's diseased brain? Surely the most rabid anglophobe would not go so far? And yet it would not be difficult. It had often crossed his mind when he saw the freight train from the Rietfontein dynamite factory shunting in Braamfontein yards. There was enough dynamite to blow this tin town away in a whirlwind of iron sheets … three thousand cases of the stuff to be offloaded for the mines. Sometimes the trucks stood there in the heat of the sun for several days. Again he found himself pondering this man he loathed. How he ingratiated himself with Johannesburg's society crowd and aspired to be accepted by them through gifts and acts of reckless generosity … the gold cup for the Summer Handicap for one. And yet Penlynne pitied him, not only for the disease he had contracted but for his longing to be treated as an equal.

He left Dorothy to read her brother's letter. In the music room he sat down at his latest extravagance, a Wurlitzer pipe organ. He had meant to master it but so far he had little time. It was here that Dorothy found him, his head over the extravagant woodwork and the ivory keys of an instrument assembled by a German technician only a few weeks ago.

He sounded a note or two. 'I was a little overambitious, perhaps. Would you agree?'

'You've always mastered anything you've attempted.'

'That's right,' he said with sudden energy. 'They'll make terms with me. Now, I think I ought to see the little chap before I report to Advocate Smit at the fort. You did pack my razors? Good girl.'

That was when Dorothy broke down.

At the hour he drove away from *Far Horizons* the afternoon sky broke with pelting rain that bounced off the road, splashing the bellies of the horses with red clay. As suddenly, the shower stopped. Flying ants came streaming from the long grass at the roadside, dragging themselves free of the earth, lifting off into the humid air with a whirring of myriad wings.

'Stop a moment, Williams,' he ordered the driver and sat for a moment to see the creatures fluttering upwards in a frenzy of freedom. 'All right, drive on. The fort!'

As if Williams didn't know his destination.

Dorothy had not had much to do with Katherine Gardiner since the breakup of their husbands' partnership. Katherine had declined to join the pistol club and like her father, had shown herself more pro-republican than English. She was a wealthy woman and there were those who respected her opinions and had nothing to do with the reform movement.

A few days after Penlynne was transferred to the Pretoria gaol, Dorothy was surprised by a visit from Katherine. She received her coolly. She was struck by her beauty and something more ... an evident consciousness of her own worth. A maturity that had come late to one dominated first by her father and then by her husband.

'I have come to offer any help I can,' she said.

'Thank you, I am very touched.'

'I hope you have been allowed to see your husband.'

'They gave us ten minutes ... a dreadful place.'

'I have some influence in Pretoria. It may be possible to arrange for bail.'

'It has been refused.'

'Please let me try.'

Dorothy found herself talking more freely than she had for

days. 'I shall never forget the sight of that horrid prison yard ...
seeing so many men I entertained at my own table ... the
dreadful humiliation of a prison built for *kaffirs*. To see honourable men in those circumstances ... the indescribable odour. I all
but fainted. The idea is to humiliate us all, to reduce our men to
begging for mercy. My husband and his close friends were
sleeping on a mud floor and stretchers covered with *kaffir*
blankets ... only small holes high in the wall for ventilation. In
Pretoria ... in February! *Kaffir* convicts bring their food from the
kitchen on trays and set it down in the middle of the yard. A tin
pannikin of mealie pap at six in the morning ... some dreadful
chunks of beef previously used for soup at twelve. The chief
warder jokes it's not fit for a Boer dog but good fare for traitors.'

Katherine was remembering the immaculate Penlynne.

'As for sanitary arrangements. Unspeakable!' Involuntarily
she raised a handkerchief to her nostrils as if to smother the reek
of carbolic powder sprinkled between the iron lean-to's knocked
up to accommodate some two hundred prisoners.

'How was Mr Penlynne?'

'Cheerful. His courage is wonderful. Imagine ... locked in
from six until the following morning, their only means of
ablution a trickle of water running through the yard.'

Some days later Katherine telephoned. 'Bail has been arranged,' she said. She was short and gave Dorothy the impression that all was not well. Wishing to thank her more fully
for her efforts Dorothy drove over to the house in Valley Road,
the house Josiah Rawlinson had given Katherine as a wedding
present. Katherine came into the drawing room with an air of
anxiety, barely concealed.

'I was glad to speak on your behalf to the State Attorney. You
must remember Mr Smit.'

'Smit!' cried Dorothy, and there sprang into her mind the
defeat of Penlynne by this man in the case Rawlinson brought
against African Gold Recovery.

'He was a good friend of my father's,' Katherine explained.

'He is to prosecute the reformers.'

'Yes, I believe so.'

It seemed strange that this man, destined for high office – or so
everyone said – had been so accommodating about bail. It came
into her mind that with Penlynne free to take an accommodation

in Pretoria until the trial, he would also be unprotected. A target for extremists. The thought was chilling.

Katherine saw her change of expression. 'It has been a terrible time for us all.'

'For you, too … surely not. I mean, the humiliation was awful. The way they marched the prisoners through the streets. Poor Jameson … such a gallant man ….'

'I saw it,' Katherine said.

'You were looking for someone you knew.'

'The man I love.'

'I know of whom you speak … was he also taken to Pretoria?'

Something in the way she looked brought Dorothy to her side. They clasped hands.

'Tell me ….'

'When the news came … the surrender, I thought: Charles will never be taken. He'll make his way here. When he did not turn up I went to town to watch the prisoners brought through … to try to speak to someone. It was impossible. He was not among the officers. I went out to Doornkop … fearing the worst.'

Katherine had found the Boers collecting the wounded. There were more than sixty men lying on straw palliasses in the ox wagon transports. Charles was not among them. None of the wounded had seen him fall. She roamed over the valley, led to the unburied dead by vultures coming in from Aasvogel's Kop. She came on the hastily covered remains of several troopers, saw the glittering heaps of shell cases from the quick-firers, the over-turned and smashed ammunition boxes and, incongruously, a folding table with empty glasses. Empty bottles of Veuve Cliquot lay in the flattened grass where headquarters had been. Dead horses, already blown, lay legs-up to the sun as she follow-ed the debris of the charge towards Doornkop ridge. A fallen sabre … a carbine. A broadbrimmed hat with the insignia of the Bechuanaland Border Police. She was sick with apprehension.

'There were parties of Boers roaming around, looking for loot. They paid no attention to me.'

'Go on, Katherine.'

'The grass was burning in places … but not, thank God, near where I found him. The Boers were very kind. They allowed me to carry him off. They even helped me to put him into the car-riage. I heard the *Veldkoronet* say: "Let the Englishwoman have her man. He's as good as dead." They were in high spirits ... who could blame them? They had lost only one man.'

'Another triumph over the British,' said Dorothy bitterly. 'Where is Lord Charles ... in hospital?'

'He's here, in this house.'

'My dear, is that wise?'

'At least he's not a prisoner.'

'I lost my brother there,' Dorothy said.

'What ... that clever young man. The artist!'

'Lord Charles ... will he live?'

'Doctor MacDonald removed a bullet from his lung. Yes, here. In the kitchen. He was all but gone from loss of blood.' Her composure broke. The image of Charles as she had found him was still strong; pale as a corpse, uniform stiff with dried blood, his pulse imperceptible. His blonde hair soaked in sweat, he grasped the water bottle in a grip of iron, the terrible thirst of his wound the only imperative.

'One hopes ... what else?' she said aloud. Charles lay in a darkened room on the south side of the house, racked by fever and the terrible coughing that brought blood to his lips. His eyes followed her about the room but he did not know her.

'You found time to help my husband,' Dorothy marvelled.

'It's all such a terrible mistake ... we must all do what we can to retrieve the situation.'

'What can I do to help you?'

'We must support one another ... it has helped to talk.'

'You are very brave, Katherine.'

'No, I'm as weak as water.'

They parted with expressions of concern about their children.

The preliminary hearing lasted most of February. Penlynne had briefed Esselyn to appear for him and the other three chief accused. 'How does it look, Esselyn?' Penlynne asked. They were returning to the cottage outside Pretoria rented since bail had been granted, the trap going at a brisk trot through hills still green with late summer rains.

'I don't believe they can sustain a charge of treason,' Esselyn replied. 'You are not burghers of the Transvaal.'

'Then we'll probably walk away with a fine,' cried Penlynne.

'It's a little early for congratulations.'

'Oh, come, Esselyn. You've managed brilliantly so far.'

'Preparations are being made,' said Esselyn sombrely.

'I didn't see a guillotine in the market square.'

'I'm warning you, it will be a show trial.'

Penlynne concealed an inward start, 'Go on then.'

'It means,' said Esselyn in the precise, ponderous way that gave such weight to his arguments, 'that the State will use the event to prove to the world that you and your accomplices ...'

'I prefer associates, Esselyn.'

'... attempted to overthrow the sovereign government of the Transvaal with the assistance of a British army. Much will depend on whether you are judged under the old Roman-Dutch law or the 33 Articles ... that is, the Volksraad's adaptation of the old Dutch form for use here, in South Africa.'

'Explain, please.'

'What we call the *Grondwet* ... the Constitution, was written to suit the Boer temperament and the sense of justice of a frontier community. It is actually very tolerant ... much less severe than the Dutch original on which it is modelled. The burghers would not stand for extreme punishment of the European kind. The kind of punishment the early Dutch settlers imposed on the Cape, for instance ... on the Hottentots and their own people.'

'For instance?' said Penlynne.

'Impalement ... breaking on the wheel.'

'Oh, come, Esselyn. That was two centuries ago.'

'I am merely pointing out, old friend, that it is a severe code and still is, compared with Kruger's.'

'Why should we not be tried under Kruger's law?'

'You are not Transvaal burghers.'

The simplicity of it shocked.

'What is the charge likely to be?'

'I have spoken to Advocate Smit ... you know him, of course.'

'What does he say, Esselyn?'

Esselyn kept silent. As if he were turning over the wisdom of revealing unpalatable facts or perhaps raising hopes too soon. The lawyer knew Smit's methods well from past encounters. Particularly the brilliant way he had snatched victory from Penlynne in the matter of the cyanide process patent. Penlynne again saw the stark vision of MacForrest's naked legs as he hung from the beam in the orange farm.

'What chance of bargaining, Esselyn?'

'It will depend on the charges he frames.'

'Charges ... more than one?'

'Certainly ... it will be a formidable indictment.'

'The British High Commissioner ... we must approach him.'

'They have washed their hands of you.'

'But for God's sake, Esselyn ... the British public!'

Esselyn looked at him dryly. 'Oh yes, you are all heroes over there. Unfortunately what they think will not affect things by one iota ... if anything, the louder they clamour, the more vengeful the charges will be.' The lawyer put his heavy hand on Penlynne's arm. 'They are out for their pound of flesh, *ou kêrel*.'

For friendship's sake he did not add: can you blame them!

'Smit especially.'

'*Ja*, he's sharpening the knife already.'

'But he's a man of honour ... I believe so.'

'Smit will use the law ... and use it scrupulously.'

'There's a certain note of ambiguity in that that I'd prefer to ignore, Esselyn.'

They left the trap in charge of a guard and went on to the *stoep*. Penlynne noted, as always, that the trophies of the hunt mounted on a board were crudely hammered there with horseshoe nails. They looked ... and particularly the skull of an old dog baboon, like criminal's heads fastened to a scaffold as a warning. For the first time since coming here, he felt like getting blind drunk.

The hot dry interior, the rough furniture, the cowdung floor – it was like Kimberley when he was Rawlinson's manager on the diggings. He had a chilling sense of having achieved nothing. That he had never escaped from his bad beginnings. At the rear of the house a few withered corn stalks rustled their dryness in the yard where the baboon's pole and iron chain still stood. He could see how the chain had rubbed and polished the tree stump as the beast circled in its captivity.

This can't be happening to Leonard Penlynne, he thought. The man thay call 'king of Johannesburg'. Chairman of companies, of the Mining Chamber ... the man who gave the Rand deep level mining. The man who had dared when others cut and ran. What was it that trade union fellow had flung at him? 'King of Tin Town!' Now chief accused. By God, he would give them a run for their money yet.

Esselyn stood tamping his meerschaum with a blackened forefinger. 'I was thinking,' Penlynne smiled, 'it's a bit stiff that they'll use the money I made for them to try and hang me.'

Esselyn gave a disapproving glance.

'I do but jest,' said Penlynne, feeling far from humour.

Later that night Esselyn sat down with Penlynne and his three companions. 'I have arranged a meeting with the State Attorney. He will give us the date of the trial and the charges against us. I hope to arrange a *quid pro quo* of some kind. It's in our favour that what is on trial here is not just a number of individuals. We are caught up in issues of enormous complexity ... on an international level.'

'What issues then?'

'The right of a small state, under threat by an imperial power, to manage its own affairs. Kruger's regime will hope to come out of this as a power with a voice of its own. No more bending the knee to England.'

'You mean we've done them a favour.'

'So they may be magnanimous, yes. On the other hand, there are strong voices in Pretoria for the iron hand. They hope that death, banishment or confiscation of property will make room for Hollanders, Germans and Frenchman to take your place.'

'In other words, Esselyn ... they'll do anything to prevent a British occupation?'

'Europe's top brains will be at this trial.'

'I see,' said Penlynne. 'We are but pawns.'

'Yes, in an international game ... surely you saw that all along, gentlemen?'

Penlynne looked across at his associates and saw by their faces it was as inconceivable to them as it was to him. Men of their standing could be swept away. No second chances.

'As you'll recall, gentlemen,' said Esselyn remorselessly, 'not a single German or French company on the Rand was represented among the Reformers. They saw how it would go ... the Kruger Government was not taken in for a moment.'

Penlynne was remembering his cautious approaches to Albu and Goerz. Australians and even Americans had raised men.

How shrewd the Europeans had been ... how calculating! There had never been a chance of success. They had waded into quicksand with their eyes open.

'Were we then so incompetent?' Penlynne asked.

'You still don't see it,' Esselyn said. 'You were tampering with the emotions of a people ... their pride. A revolution is not the flotation of a company. You had nothing to offer your shareholders.'

'We were never against the Boers ... the people. We asked for justice against an intolerable tyranny and were refused.' He was rewarded with a rumble of agreement.

'Mr Penlynne ... gentlemen. Penitence is called for. Tirades against the shortcomings of the Kruger regime will not be acceptable. Humility stands a better chance.'

'We are expected to grovel?'

'Correct.'

There was a low growl round the table. 'Humble pie?'

'Correct.'

'Be damned to them.'

Esselyn took a copy of *Die Volkstem* from his case. He did it with the gesture of a man displaying a straight flush. 'I don't think you read Dutch, gentlemen ... allow me. *The historic gallows from Slagters Nek has been brought to Pretoria. It is the same beam the British Government used in 1816 to hang five patriots. Preserved on a farm at Cookhouse Drift as a memento of the Boer revolt against the British, it is said to have been brought to Pretoria for display.*'

Esselyn saw that his hearers were shocked silent. He laid the paper down. 'What that article is saying, gentlemen, is this. If the court does not hang you, the patriotic burghers of Pretoria will do it themselves.'

'I believe you've made your point, Esselyn,' said Penlynne. 'As Dr Johnstone said in a similar connection: "When a man knows he is to be hanged in a fortnight, it concentrates his mind wonderfully!" '

In the only room she had been able to obtain at the Transvaal Hotel Dorothy had no private sitting room, the bedroom was cramped and the bathroom had to be shared. The somnolent country town had been galvanized by the approaching trial.

257

Many rooms were occupied by visitors from Europe. The market hall was being altered for the trial. Cheerfully whistling carpenters were knocking up a dais for the judge and the barristers. She looked in. The place still stank of a market, a market with two crystal chandeliers suspended from the roof joists. She heard herself pointed out – 'Wife of the chief accused.'

One morning she found a note pushed under the door. It was written in rough Cape Dutch. 'We avenge Slagters Nek with good new rope.' Shocked at first to feel hatred so close, it had the effect of rousing her. She wrote at once to Julius Wernher.

I beg you to see Mr Chamberlain at once. He must be made to understand that these people cannot be judged by civilized European standards. The difficulties and dangers they went through in the wilds, fighting beasts as well as kaffirs, gave them the same qualities as their foes – treachery and cruelty. To take the law into their hands is natural to them. Their policy of exterminating the tribes of the Transvaal has made them more and more callous. Mr Chamberlain must demand that Kruger give an assurance that my husband and other prisoners will be safeguarded from treachery. I have already lost my brother in this cruel affair. I know now that the Boers gave him his horse and told him he was free to go. He was shot in the back. A well-known method of Transvaal Boer assassination.

Later she realized it was pointless and destroyed it. In any case it would take two weeks to reach Wernher. The trial date was already set. She must act on her own initiative.

The British Agent received her grudgingly. 'My dear lady, we must all keep cool heads and not give way.'

'I am perfectly calm,' she said imperiously. 'Surely you see it would suit the Boers very well to be rid of such troublesome prisoners.'

'Come, Mrs Penlynne,' he smiled.

'You do not know these people,' she said passionately.

'I will convey your fears to the High Commissioner.'

She laughed scornfully. 'He has already betrayed my husband.'

He opened the door for her. 'We must not take the law into our own hands, Mrs Penlynne.'

'*Et tu Brute,*' she replied in the tones she usually reserved for tradespeople who had given displeasure.

She was surprised to find Penlynne so cheerful. He had been teaching the guards to play cricket. 'Really, they are not bad fellows,' he assured her.

'How can you be so sanguine?' she said. He took her into the peach orchard, heavy with the odour of fallen fruit.

'I don't believe they have sufficient evidence to convict us of treason, Dorothy.'

'The correspondence between you and Sir Henry?'

'Enough to cast suspicion. Not enough to convict.'

'The cables to Europe ... to the *Times* ... to Fairfield?'

'All in code ... without the codebook, meaningless. Believe me, dear girl, we shall walk away from this with our heads up.'

It was the old, confident Penlynne. She felt the assurance of his strength. How often she had heard him use that tone to turn an argument in his favour. He certainly did not look the prisoner. She saw he was popular with the guards. 'They drink my whiskey,' he laughed.

She grasped at it. 'Could you not get them drunk?'

He turned grave. 'I reproach myself very much for having involved you in this.'

'I am your wife.'

'How is my son?'

He put his arm around her and walked her slowly to the trap.

'Of course it has all been a confounded waste of time ... and money. They will try us but the outcome will be the same in the long run. The attempt was not made for nothing.'

'Please, don't be noble.'

He pressed her close. 'The guards are looking,' she said.

'I lie here at night ... thinking of you,' he whispered in her ear.

'You are making me blush.'

He waved as the trap moved off. A lighthearted gesture. He had whispered to her the same words he used in Kimberley. The swing on the pepper tree, the same ardent look. How far they had come together. An end to it all was inconceivable.

She returned to Johannesburg briefly to attend to some business for Penlynne. He was not allowed contact with the business managers. There was anxiety, too, about the child. There had been one wet nurse after another, none of them suitable until the wife of a Zulu groom thrust her great nipple into his mouth. And for the first time the boy took nourishment.

How strange, she thought; the milk-white face and the rich, dark breasts, the tiny hands grasping. The servant woman crooned softly as the white child milked her. What she sang, Dorothy had no idea ... perhaps about the old Africa. Perhaps the new. Whatever, she was the great mother and her strength was passing into Penlynne's son. It crossed her mind that with Penlynne gone this boy was all she had.

Chapter Twenty-Two

State Attorney Smit and Advocate Esselyn spread their papers. Esselyn as always, obsessively tidy, was perspiring freely. Smit was coldly correct, his pale grey eyes intense. He had a precision about him that was somehow deadly. He was a man who'd never let go, Penlynne thought, humourless and wise beyond his years. Yet the man had stopped outside the door to pick and examine a veld grass and had looked about the ground with a farmer's eye. 'Sweet grass,' he commented to Esselyn. Was he so much in control of himself and his case that a grass could draw his attention, or was it a ploy to distract the opposition?

Penlynne had heard the trap and seen the guards spring to attention. Guttural accents and a sharp rebuke. Then Smit limped onto the *stoep* and removed the wide-brimmed, sweat-stained hat.

'I hope you're reasonably comfortable, Mr Penlynne. The date of your trial has been fixed.'

He did not offer to shake hands this time. This was the man who had said: 'I hope to hang you, Mr Penlynne.' Smiling then. Today his face was inscrutable.

For a few moments the attorneys spoke together, amiably enough, Penlynne thought, for men who had the disposing of his goods and his person. He left them to it and walked outside with his friends. 'Remember,' he warned, 'Smit has nothing to go on. No real evidence. We are a group of men denied our rights who attempted to bring our grievances to the authorities. Hang on to that!'

He winced inwardly at his involuntary use of the word hang.

'Keep your courage up. We are far from done.'

Smit opened his briefcase. Penlynne recognized the papers on the table as his letter to Wernher. Smit had made a good start. What else did he have in there? If this were all, things were not too bad.

'With your approval, gentlemen, I shall read the indictment.'

'Hardly with our approval, Advocate Smit.'

Esselyn frowned at this levity.

'The State,' said Smit coldly, 'will show that the accused invited Dr Starr Jameson to invade the sovereign state of the South African Republic. It will show that the accused incited the people of Johannesburg to assist him. The State will show that the accused distributed arms and ammunition. The State will show that the accused formed and armed its own militia.'

As Smit read it seemed to Penlynne that he was reliving it all, point by point. He had not felt culpable then. He was trying not to feel it now, but some echoes of his public remarks had a tinny sound in his ears, especially the more lurid passages. It sounded like cheap rhetoric – the stuff of last words on the scaffold.

Smit laid down his documents. He spoke without particular emphasis. 'The charges carry the death penalty under Transvaal law. How will you gentlemen plead?'

Penlynne recovered from the shock with a flash of anger. He ignored Esselyn's cautioning look. 'May I say, Advocate Smit, that the State will have a devil of a job proving anything. It will drag on for weeks, with business at a standstill. We would hope, of course, to demonstrate the bad faith of the State. There will be plenty of dirty washing.'

Smit smiled thinly and fingered the file.

'My dear Smit,' Penlynne urged. 'We both know that there is nothing in my correspondence that is not, shall we say, honest indignation. An expression of political views. A little heated, at times, but nothing treasonable.'

Smit was filling his pipe from Esselyn's *twaksak*. He struck a light and drew contemplatively, the dry tobacco crackling. A trapped bluefly buzzed frantically on the window pane. With equal deliberation Smit extinguished the match. A deadly man, Penlynne thought again.

'Gentlemen,' Smit began. 'You have three choices before you. Not so, Mynheer Esselyn?' Esselyn nodded. 'If you choose to plead "not guilty" we shall have a long and costly trial. If you refuse to plead – which is your right, of course, it will make a bad impression on the court. If you plead guilty ... '

Penlynne felt those around him react with shock. Smit held up his hand. 'If you plead guilty, the court may be better disposed to leniency.'

Penlynne pushed back his chair. 'A life sentence, no doubt. We shall instruct Advocate Esselyn to enter a plea of "not guilty" to all charges. And devil take you, Smit! I warn you the Republic will come out of this with its armour badly battered.'

'Hold on there, Mr Penlynne,' said Smit quietly. 'There is something you should consider before you make a final decision.' From the doorway he signalled a man in the trap. 'Please bring Colonel Willoughby's dispatch case.'

Penlynne exchanged a puzzled look with Esselyn. The black leather dispatch box carried the coat of arms of Lord Willoughby in faded gold. By its condition it had been knocked about on many a foreign campaign. Penlynne noted a fresh rip on the leather.

'This was taken near Doornkop, gentlemen. On a mine property.'

Smit was turning out diaries, orders, copies of messages and code books. He noted that Penlynne lost colour but not his composure. The jumble on the table was all too recognizable. 'Your appeal to Jameson ... your signatures you won't dispute. And this is the key to the cypher used in all negotiations.'

'Well, the damned fool,' someone groaned.

'I think you'll agree it's all here, gentlemen. Everything we need, kindly provided by Colonel Willoughby who attempted to have it destroyed. By your brother-in-law, Mr Penlynne.'

Poor boy, thought Penlynne. He failed in that, as he failed in everything. He avoided the faces of his friends. 'Esselyn?'

'We must ask Advocate Smit for the best terms he can offer.'

'A plea of guilty,' said Smit. His lips moved in a slight smile. In the silence the dry tobacco in Esselyn's pipe crackled. Penlynne felt sweat run from his armpits. Someone excused himself from the table. The screen door slammed. They heard footsteps stumble across the yard to the privy.

'If you gentlemen plead guilty,' Smit said, 'the State will withdraw counts two, three and four. Your associates, the other sixty-three men we are holding, will be asked to plead guilty to counts three and four. Purely nominal sentences. If you agree to a plea of guilty, gentlemen, you would not have to offer testimony that would incriminate Dr Jameson – who is still in our hands. You and I have known one another for a long time, Mr Penlynne, you know I have always tried to bridge the gap between us.'

'Yes, I acknowledge that.'

'That is why I must warn you that one of Jameson's officers is willing to give evidence that will implicate you.'

'His name, if I may ask?'

'Captain Hamilton.'

'I don't know him.'

'He has proved helpful ... and I might say, repentant.'

'Repentance is a grace in some men, Mr Smit. In others it is not.'

Smit rose from the table, gathering his material and passing the dispatch case to his man. He showed no sign of triumphing. Esselyn detained him. 'If we should plead guilty ... what sentence can we expect?'

'That I can't say ... it will be up to the judge.'

'Are we to be judged under Transvaal law ... I am speaking of the Amended Articles. Or under Roman-Dutch law as applied in Holland. The difference could be critical.'

'I am aware of the difference.' Smit turned on the *stoep*. 'Think about it, gentlemen. You have a few days to decide.'

Penlynne followed Smit to the trap. 'Be frank. If we plead guilty will you ask for the death penalty. I think you owe us that much to let us know.'

Smit picked up the reins. 'I owe you nothing, Mr Penlynne.' The trap jerked away. Guards at the gate saluted and the trap rattled into the distance. Dust drifted back.

'I am closing the gate, mynheer,' said the guard.

Penlynne thought the inflection of respect in the man's voice was one usually reserved for the condemned.

Stewart MacDonald rose early that morning to get to his rooms in Von Brandis Street. The trap was held up at the rail crossing as a goods train clanked into the Braamfontein siding. Almost mechanically he counted the trucks, eight of them marked *Explosives*. It was by now a scene as familiar as the coal trucks of Ayrshire crossing the green meadows of his homeland. His conscious reaction to what he saw was an annoyance that his study on the effect of explosive fumes and rock dust on lungs had still barely begun. At this rate, years of post mortems lay ahead. He had been continually distracted, most recently by the wounded of the Jameson fiasco. He had often enough seen the effect of explosives undergound; shattered rock ground into mangled tissue, arteries severed and splintered bone. The wounds of the battle showed that the new high-velocity bullet was at its worst at the point of exit. The surgery of machine-gun wounds was something still to be mastered.

By the time he had been called in by Katherine Gardiner the patient was far gone through haemorrhage. He recognized Lord Warewood at once but said nothing. There was prostration and delirium and the stench of sepsis. Katherine did not flinch as he cut away the lacerated and morbid flesh and sutured the wound, leaving a drainage tube from the punctured lung.

'That is all I can do for him now,' he told Katherine. 'I'd advise you to burn his uniform.' He did not press her further. Katherine detained him on the stairway.

'How long before it's safe to move him?'

'Don't even think of it,' he said.

At the trap he saw her anxious glance at the upper room. 'Is it true that they are searching houses?'

'I don't know, Mrs Gardiner ... I do know there was a proclamation to hand in all weapons, even sporting guns.'

'How is your wife?' the young woman asked.

'I want her to remain at the coast until things return to normal.'

'It must be hard for you without her and the children.'

'Thank God, they survived,' he said.

'I'm terrified they'll come here, doctor.'

He thought: how this thing has affected us. People were talking in the wildest way. Almost every hour brought fresh alarms. 'I don't believe half the rumours I hear,' he assured her. 'The Boers are not the kind of folk to shoot wounded men.'

'There are elements here that want us wiped out.'

He disagreed. He believed her sensibilities had been affected by her situation, giving rise to fears that had no factual basis. Most wild talk could be discounted as mischievous. He wondered what had become of Katherine's husband. Had he been one of the plotters?

As if divining his thoughts she said: 'My husband and I separated some time ago.'

'I'll come as often as I can,' he assured her.

Despite the pressures on him he managed to write to Mary.

... people one would not suspect of losing their heads are being affected. There is an atmosphere of fear and suspicion. I was called to Far Horizons *by Dorothy Penlynne, her husband was a prominent reformer and now a prisoner. Mrs Penlynne has a history of neurasthenia and has a highly sensitive temperament. I can only think that this contributed to her extraordinary suggestion to me. She asked me about poisons, how effective they were. Which were the quickest and least painful. When I declined to discuss poisons she spoke of drugs. Would I help her to acquire a supply of morphine? When I asked her why, she told me an escape is being planned. How much morphine would she require to drug her husband's guards? Quite wildly she added: 'I already have four revolvers obtained for me from a trustworthy woman. The High Commissioner disarmed us on behalf of the Boers'.*

In the atmosphere of the drawing room, you know, this all sounded quite lunatic. I tried to dissuade her but she was beyond reasoning. 'I shall get what I need without your help.' And as a parting shot, 'Can chloroform be bought from the chemist?'

What a terrible distortion of patriotism we are witnessing here. Essentially good people are being carried away by violent emotions. I miss you deeply, my love, and our baby, but I fear it is far from finished here ....

Even the rail disaster had been used as a political weapon. The Nederlands Railway Company was blamed on all sides. Its coaches were unsafe ... they had dragged the sturdy British coaches from the line. Newspapers had printed reports of gross Boer indifference. The *Natal Witness* correspondent wrote: *A burly Dutchman laughed when a girl trapped between coaches by her feet and hanging upside down begged him to release her.* This kind of jingo reporting was like a torch to gunpowder at such a time ... as if the scenes of horror were not enough in themselves.

Hardened though he was, he had wept to read of two women found dead, prematurely born infants in their clothing. And Dr Howard ... a man he had often worked beside. The reporter described his injuries. *He shrieked in agony when lifted from the van. Once on a stretcher he became calm and instructed his brother practitioners. The poor fellow died within a few hours in frightful agony.*

Because of Mary, the descriptions that affected him most were of women and children's clothing, parasols, toys, sewing machines, spirit flasks, lamps, bread, fruit and literature, all jumbled with blood-stained garments. And all, all, he thought, to be laid at the door of Jameson and his friends. Thank God he had persuaded Mary to stay in Durban. He had an apprehension of worse to come.

He though of his beloved, her skirts lifted to her knees as she paddled the child in the sea. Mary of the beautiful feet, so sweetly shaped, so white. Had he lost her, nothing he could achieve here would have any meaning for him.

He was about to leave the dispensary when he thought: I should put my dangerous drugs and poisons in some safe place. He began to remove them to his bag. With the chloroform bottle in his grasp he was remembering his experiment in Glasgow ... dropping a few drops on cotton wool and inhaling ... then everything spinning, the walls dissolving. A sensation of pitching headlong into darkness.

Again. Was it happening again? Cupboards and bookcases were falling. A blizzard of papers whirled through a hole in the roof where iron sheets had been ripped away. He had heard nothing. His senses had been overwhelmed by a blow more than his senses could convey. Out of this silence he became aware of a woman wailing. An explosion, he realized. The Boers must be shelling the town. He went into the street to see it blizzard-strewn. Moving creatures were emerging from a storm of red dust. Shops had spewed their goods across the street. Shattered glass glittered. Blood ran from a horse, dead in its traces.

He began to run towards the centre of the explosion. Where the railway siding had been, there was a crater the size of a city block. The shanties of Braamfontein and Fordsburg and slum alleys of the Brickfields had disappeared. A woman hurried past him pushing an empty pram. The acrid stench of explosives pinched his nostrils as it had underground. Blacks and poor whites were already scrabbling among the debris for their belongings and when he looked back towards the commercial centre, he saw the well-built facades of the city's major buildings emerging from the smoke and dust. On the ridges of Parktown and the Berea the windows of the great houses glinted, seemingly untouched.

It was then that he saw a locomotive thrown on its side, steam gushing from fractured pipes and a grotesque tangle of steel and wood that had been explosives trucks ... all at the bottom of this smoking pit. In a daze he picked up a hand to draw the man from under the pinning debris. It came away with the sleeve of the jacket. Now he became aware of cries and groans on all sides. He turned and ran back to the surgery for his equipment, the bottle of chloroform still clenched in his hand.

There seems no doubt, Dorothy Penlynne wrote in her bold hand. *The explosion at Braamfontein railway yard was deliberate. How else could eight freight cars containing three thousand cases of dynamite for the mines have gone up? Attempts have been made to explain it away. The trucks had been standing in the hot sun for three days! We are not so naive as to swallow that. No one dares admit what we all know. Such people will stop at nothing. One does not accuse the moderate Boer, but the extreme element.*

Our women were magnificent, rallying at once, bringing the wounded and homeless into their houses and providing emergency supplies. At such a time, all sectional quarrels are forgotten. Alas, for so short a time. What with our top men in captivity, the lack of water making it difficult for the mines, and the flight of native labour to their kraals, everything is at a standstill.

When I sat in on the preliminary examination in Pretoria in that hideous market hall, it broke my heart to see the best and finest men in the country as prisoners. I am closing Far Horizons *and cancelling all engagements to be near Leonard now that the trial is upon us.*

Dorothy rose from the escritoire and looked down from the window at the roofless walls of *Bloukoppen*. 'That woman', as she always thought of Kitty, had not been in the house at the time. She was in Europe. Looking at it now, a shell, she was remembering how she had first seen it, its walls rising in direct line of her view from the house she was building, and her demand to Penlynne that the plans of *Far Horizons* be altered so that she did not have to see the house that had humiliated her.

No attempt had been made to save it. The speculation was that a burning brand hurled from Braamfontein had fallen there.

Wheels from the freight cars had been found five miles away. Dorothy rode over to see what remained. The reek of burned timbers mingled harshly with garden scents. It was up those steps that Penlynne had come on the morning of her unexpected return from England ... with the Loftus creature hanging on his arm.

Now it was open to the sky. The great oak staircase had fallen in. She remembered how the redheaded woman had paused halfway up and turned, in her fancy dress costume, to challenge the wife of the man she had seduced. Dorothy had thought then: how beautiful. How common!

Now the house of her humiliation was the house of her triumph. Leonard was never more hers than now. She was preparing to leave when a man entered the grounds. Walter Gardiner approached. He was bareheaded and dressed in rumpled whites.

'What brings you here?' he said.

'I might ask the same of you ... every decent man I know is in Pretoria.'

'More fool they.'

'That is contemptible.'

'They wouldn't listen to me.'

'Other Americans were in the movement ... honourable men.'

'Come off your high horse, Dorothy.'

'I suppose you're here to gloat.'

'And you ... would it be regret or remorse that brings you here?'

Gardiner pitched his cigar into the shrubbery and took a gulp at a silver flask. 'I'm fond of Leonard, even if he is a fool. If there's anything I can do to assist, please let me know, Dorothy.'

She saw that he meant it and it softened her. 'I was badly hurt by this place. I'm glad it's gone.'

'It was a fool's palace,' he admitted.

Gardiner mopped the back of his neck. His eyes roamed over the cracked stone and the melted windows. 'I sent her to Europe. I don't expect it would interest you ... she's contracted tuberculosis. They say the air in Switzerland is the best.' He walked inside, disappearing into the gutted interior. That was when she saw something part-black, part-golden in the tall weeds. It was the blackamoor which had stood in the hall that day. Headless.

She was still there when Gardiner came out into the sunlight.

'I hear you're closing *Far Horizons*, Dorothy. That is very wise. No matter what the outcome in Pretoria, this is just the beginning. Leonard's kicked open the ants' nest. You see, there's always Europe for you and America for me, but for the Boers, the Africanders, there's only Africa. They'll never let go of that. They'd rather see all of this destroyed ... I can't say I blame them.'

They were walking slowly round the house and had come to the gazebo. Behind it the *koppie* rose steeply in a series of stony ridges covered with aloes. She could see sunlight on the windows of *Far Horizons*.

'I won't give it up,' she assured him. 'I won't be intimidated.'

'You must be realistic. They will apply the sternest measures of the law, especially to the leaders.'

'Are you suggesting ...?'

He helped her sit down. She remained pale but composed.

'Are you saying they will hang my husband?'

'It is very possible.'

'You offered to help. How sincere are you?'

'At this moment in my life I haven't much to lose.'

'I believe this meeting was Providential. I have a plan.'

'Then you must act while they are still on bail. Are they under guard?'

'Twelve men by day ... six at night. The lieutenant drinks Leonard's whiskey. I have obtained morphine and chloroform. And four revolvers.'

Gardiner was astonished at her resolution. He had always regarded Dorothy as the arch-hostess and socialite, the collector of the right people, totally committed to creating what almost amounted to a kingdom for herself and Penlynne. He had found it both aggravating and amusing ... this queenly dignity she pretended to. Now he was looking at a woman who was proposing something so preposterous that he had to recognize her desperation and admire her spunk.

'How do you propose to get them to him?'

'We are allowed to bring in food. And, of course, Leonard's chef is free to buy supplies in Pretoria.'

'His chef is there, with him? I doubt my chef would do as much for me.'

'Leonard inspires loyalty.'

'You are evidently determined. You know you haven't much time. The trial date has been set.' He took a turn on the flagged path, increasingly intrigued by the turn of events. 'Gregorowski will be trial judge ... I've had brushes with that little weasel. It'd be a pleasure to spoil his fun.'

'Gregorowski! His father was a colleague of my father in Kimberley.'

'That'll cut no ice. He's a tough judge. They could get no one else in Pretoria to bring in the verdict they'll demand. They'll keep a close watch on all the trains. I could arrange fresh horses as far as the Natal border.'

She seized his hand and kissed it.

'Depend on me,' he said, touched in spite of his cynicism.

'When shall I hear from you?'

'As soon as I'm ready.'

'How can I thank you?'

'Let's say I owe it to Penlynne ... for old times sake.'

'Yes,' she said emotionally. 'Without you and without him, there would be none of this.'

Katherine seldom left the side of the wounded man. She feared the silent hours after midnight. She would clench her hands as if to face an enemy. She was aware of every change of breathing. Only hold on, she would plead. If he could hold on till morning they'd have won another day. She had taken every precaution to conceal Charles. Servants who might have talked were given leave. Tradesmen calling for orders were turned away by Mildred who took turns with Katherine at the bedside. Without the maid's help she could not have gone on. Mildred had become closer to her than a sister.

Stewart MacDonald came every day. She let him in by a side door but even with every precaution she could not be sure that the house was not being watched.

Sometimes she woke with a start to find his eyes on her. She longed for a smile of recognition. She had grown fiercely possessive. She alone washed his body and changed the dressings.

One night Katherine wakened to find Mildred shaking her.

'Wake up, wake up!'

'What is it? Is there a change?'

271

The possibility of a change in his condition early in the morning was always with her. Her father had died at that time, before she could get to his bedside, the mine hooters sounding the early morning shift. The grey hour before dawn when the possibility of the soul stealing away seemed most likely while the face on the pillow grew cold. She was rising quickly, almost in panic.

'There's a man at the front door,' said Mildred.

'I'll go down.'

'Oh ma'am. I beg you, don't. We don't know who it might be.'

The sound of heavy, urgent knocking came up.

'We must get Lord Warewood up into the attic.'

'Ma'am … the stairs. It'll kill him.'

Again the thunderous tattoo on the door. Katherine took the lamp and went down. 'Who's there?'

'It's Walter. Open the door.'

'What do you want?'

'For God's sake don't argue, Katherine. Let me in.'

She opened the door on the chain and saw his heavy bulk. He was in evening dress, his shoes thick with red clay. She shot the bolts behind him. He was breathless. .

'Where is he?' he said. 'Where's Charles? The Boers are looking for him. If he's here you'd better move fast and get him away.'

'He can't be moved.'

'Katherine, ugly things have been happening. Men have been put against the wall. They're after anyone who rode with Jameson and got away.' He looked up the stairway to the landing. 'I've a cab at the gate.' He had evidently come from his club. He was sober. 'I've been in a card game till after two.'

She hesitated.

'They think he's here, you know. Trust me. Dammit Katherine, I can't see the fellow shot.' He put a hand on hers. 'Who else is here?'

'Only Mildred. I sent the rest of the staff away.'

He was going ahead of her along the first floor landing, his footsteps muffled in carpeting as he took the stairs to the next floor and passed the children's rooms. She realized he was re-lishing some kind of action … a participation in something he had stood aside from as being none of his concern. As he took the lamp from her hand she saw he was sweating, his eyes puffy and his hand unsteady. But he was still powerful. He greeted Mildred at the bedside. 'Get him dressed,' he ordered.

'Do you want to kill him, Mr Gardiner,' the maid protested.

'Will you have him killed in his bed?' Gardiner said. And it struck him as ironic that the bed had once been his and Katherine's. Now, with the stench of a sick room and the pallor of the wounded man, it had the atmosphere of a deathbed. If the women were right, and Warewood could not be moved from the house, then he must be hidden. The kind of men who were on their way would not hesitate to take their revenge. He had seen their mood when they marched Jameson and his men to the station, the sidewalk crowds either silent or shouting insults. Jameson had marched, head up, as if he saw nothing on either side. He seemed strangely small to have roused such passions. You had to have seen the thousands milling in every street to understand the hostility let loose against the stumbling column. Exhausted and unshaven, they looked a pack of renegades.

Looking at Charles he thought: could they have made it if Johannesburg had kept its word? 'Warewood,' he said. 'We're going to have to move you.' The wounded man reacted, trying to draw himself up, but fell back with a sharp intake of breath.

'The mattress,' Gardiner said. 'We'll lift him on it … get him into the attic.' It proved impossible. 'I'll have to carry him,' Gardiner said. Lights were already moving in the garden. The Zulu nightwatchman went down through the shrubbery to challenge the intruders. His lantern moved among the trees. Then a shot, and the lantern went out. Men were running round the house and there was pounding on the front door.

'I'll go down,' said Gardiner.

Charles reached up a hand. 'Get me on my feet … it's me they're after.' He was struggling to rise.

'Keep this damn fool here,' said Gardiner. He locked the bedroom door on the outside and went past the doors where the children slept, putting aside an impulse to see them. From the side door he heard glass breaking, 'There goes the conservatory,' he thought. Old man Rawlinson used to look at it with scorn. 'What's the sense in growing orchids … there's money in mushrooms.' Why was he doing this? Yet the anger he felt seemed good to him. He had not slaved here to hand his children's inheritance to those goddamn baboons. In the hall he was aware of the silk Ushack underfoot. Gift of an Indian prince. Fleetingly he was realizing there was more of him in this house than he'd remembered, much more than there ever had been in *Bloukoppen*. In the study on the ground floor the old man had kept his collection of *kaffir* weapons, gleaned from the battlefields of the early days. Rawlinson had enjoyed refighting those battles over cigars and brandy, getting out of his chair to brandish a battleaxe or demonstrate the Zulu use of the short stabbing spear that took its name, he explained with relish, from the sucking noise the blade made as it was pulled from the wound.

The front door was splintering. 'Give over!' Gardiner shouted. 'Stand back!' He threw open the door. In the glare of lanterns and torches they saw this giant of a man, the gleam of the white shirt, the debauched face and the immaculate tailoring. Gardiner stood, arms wide and challenged the first man to rush the doorway. Behind him they could see the dim splendour of a house that represented what they hated and hoped to destroy.

'Who's first for shaving!' Gardiner challenged. Behind them he could see the high profile of buildings that had not existed before his work began here. Somewhere, far back in a recess of memory he was reliving the moment when the wedding carriage pulled up at this door and he'd lifted Katherine down, past the domestics, ululating and clapping, and over the threshold. He supposed his face and hers had been as radiant as the photographs recorded.

He charged down the steps, vaguely hoping that what he was doing was for his son ... for Spencer. If this was to be an expiation, then it was what he owed. He was struck by many shots, almost simultaneously. Those who ran away were to remember that when the American fell they felt the ground shake. Or so it had seemed. No one went into the house. The lanterns ebbed away and the sound of horses receded. The shrilling of cicadas rose again.

It was some time before the women came down. 'Wait here, please, Mildred,' Katherine detained the maid. Later, she opened the nursery door and stood gazing at the children. The night light burned steadily at Spencer's bedside. Both he and his sister had flung off the covers and lay, limbs asprawl. Spencer's eyelids fluttered as she bent over him, seeing there the face of the man who had been his father. Walter's bold features still softened by childhood. The girl was slight, so white-skinned as to be almost bloodless. Dark shadows under her eyes, her soft blonde hair glued to her head with sweat.

One day, Katherine thought, she would tell them how their father died and she was glad she would not be ashamed to answer the boy's questions. 'He must have been very brave, my father.'

Several days passed. Dorothy waited for word from Gardiner. Her telephone was cut off. There was an atmosphere of siege. At last she went down to town herself, conscious of many eyes upon her. At the Rand Club she asked the hall porter to call Mr Gardiner.

'Surely you know, madame,' he said gravely. 'Mr Gardiner's funeral's this afternoon. Is there anything I can do, ma'am?' She sent a message of condolence to Katherine from home, now more than ever a prison. Very well, what had to be done she would do herself. She prepared pockets in her skirts to carry the morphine and chloroform. The revolvers would have to go in the basket of provisions. As she made ready she was remembering Robert's criticism of the painting she had bought for the gallery – wild-eyed women storming the Bastille to release husbands, sons and lovers. Now she knew how theatrical the canvas was, she'd have it taken down and put away. The woman reflected in her mirror did not look like one embarking on a journey from which there might be no turning back.

In the train to Pretoria she met women she'd travelled with before. Anxious and burdened by events, fearful of the outcome of the trial, she could not share her secret with them. She was actually fortunate. It had been no problem for Leonard to put up ten thousand pounds in gold. These poor creatures had been unable to raise the two thousand bail demanded of the less important captives. Some of the wives carried food; others medicines against dysentery.

She was recognized. One woman leaned across to her to show her a letter she'd had from her husband. *You must not worry, my dear, the maximum punishment that the law provides is confiscation of property, a fine of about fifty pounds, and banishment, though I fancy they will come down harder on Penlynne and company. Some think as much as a million and a half for damages.*

Yes, Dorothy thought. It could be paid. But was it safe to await the outcome of the trial? 'I don't trust them,' she said.

'It is Rhodes you must blame,' the woman said bitterly.

'What do you mean?'

'Making an excuse for England to go to war with the Republic. Now the Boers are saying they can conquer England and that they will give Chamberlain a hiding. I am a Boer by birth ... a Botha. It is a cruel and wicked thing to split us again. Your husband was fooled into playing Rhodes's game ... all of them were.'

The train stopped and started at halts. It was an interminable journey. She hoped her face showed nothing of her inward quaking. On the platform she was stopped by another woman. 'If it wasn't for your husband none of us would be here. That letter of his!'

'What letter?' said Dorothy stupidly. She was dazed by the woman's violence. 'Already one of them has cut his throat,' she shouted. 'The letter begging Jameson to come in and save us ... from what? And this poor man went into the toilet and did it.'

'Please let me past.'

'He signed it ... your husband.'

Dorothy saw with a contracting of the heart that her husband had become the focus of fault. He had told her nothing of the letter, but if he had, he was no more guilty of complicity than the rest of them. If she had felt guilty about planning for him alone she now felt justified.

Penlynne had told her: 'Never visit without bringing something for the guards.' She loaded the hired trap with fresh food and liquor and set out on that last two miles.

As the house came in sight she was dismayed to see a number of vehicles. She could not think what it meant. The trial did not begin until after the week-end. Surely they were not about to move him back to Pretoria gaol?

'The State Attorney is here,' she was told. The guard gave only a cursory glance at the provisions and passed her through. She saw guards on the stoep. Through the open windows she saw men sitting around a table. Penlynne came out onto the stoep in his shirtsleeves. He had lost weight but it had not diminished his presence. If anything, she was aware of a renewed force as he walked her a few paces away from the house. She was aware of rose briars catching at her skirts and the faintly disturbing scent of oleander. She remembered a warning from childhood. Never touch the oleander. It's poisonous.

Penlynne embraced her lightly. She whispered: 'I have the medicine we discussed.' He walked her a little further. 'You have been very brave, my dearest girl. Are you brave enough to hear what I must tell you now? You reproached me before, because I had not told you the full extent of my involvement. What I have to tell you may shock you.'

'For God's sake, Penny ... keep nothing from me.'

He was supporting her firmly. 'We have made our decision. The four chief prisoners are to plead guilty ... to high treason.'

She pushed him roughly away but he caught her back. 'Hear me out. The evidence against us is too strong to make it worth while disputing the case.' He made a gesture that struck her as very Jewish ... a kind of half-humorous twist of the mouth, and spread his hands.

'It was a fair gamble ... we lost. The Boers showed us Willoughby's dispatch case. It contained not only the key to the ciphers used in all negotiations but a copy of the appeal ... we can't dispute our signatures. Only the date ...' He laughed. 'We left it blank for Jameson to fill in. And of course, he did. In short, the game is up!'

'I will not accept that you committed high treason.'

'Smit has been reasonable. If we enter a plea of guilty he will do his best to obtain the easiest sentences ... something pretty nominal. It is purely a formality ... a *quid pro quo*. They will have their case for breach of their sovereignty. We will have our necks.' He smiled as if it was entirely reasonable.

'You trust them! How can you deceive yourself? It's a trap. They will have their justification and your lives as well. It will be a triumph for them. The Kaiser will send Kruger another telegram of congratulations. I have hired a trap and arranged for fresh horses ...'

He was shaking his head. 'I couldn't leave the others to face it, Dotty. It wouldn't be cricket.'

'What about me ... your child?'

'I care deeply about that.'

'Then prove it … please.'

'Dorothy, this is a matter that concerns our good names, our honour. One of us has already made a mockery of us by hiding under a train seat and getting two women to cover him with their petticoats. You would not have them think that of me, would you?' He laughed.

'My dear, the eyes of the civilized world are on Pretoria. This has become an international *cause célèbre*. You and I have come a long way from the diggings. I have learned much from you … from your standards. You would not have my son learn that his father ran out on his friends.'

'I don't care what they say,' she cried.

'You are most selfish,' he said coldly and walked away. She ran to him. 'I only want to know that you care for me … for us.'

'Keep up your courage,' he said. 'The whole thing is a game. Manoeuvring for advantage. We are far from done.'

She heard the scraping of chairs. He kissed her cheek and went in to join the others. Long afterwards she was to remember how she went away through that scented, tropical garden, weeping bitterly, crushed with the hopelessness of it all. And it was only long after that he told her how the dispatch case fell into Boer hands.

Penlynne watched Dorothy drive away. He felt no particular thrill of nobility at his decision. He was no Sydney Carter. It had been thrust upon him. He had been almost astonished to hear himself saying – and believing – that honourable behaviour was expected of him. If he were hanged he would be … well, he would be dead. But Chamberlain would not forget what he'd done. By his plea of guilty he had saved the Colonial Secretary from a prolonged examination of his part in the reformers' planning. He had, in fact, aborted the possibility of a war between England and Germany. He could almost hear the words of the shrewd and ambitious politician as he addressed the House, the 'hear-hears' as he explained that Britain had had no part in the affair. How damned awkward, he thought, if my neck does for England what Jameson failed to pull off.

On the other hand, if he didn't hang there'd be a knighthood in it. He'd retire to Surrey and buy an estate. Perhaps build a splendid country seat. He'd keep a town house filled with art treasures and at the end of the shooting season in Scotland they'd entertain in their villa on the French Riviera. Friends in society would visit and be entertained. The ruins of ancient Egypt had always fascinated. There would be introductions to Prince Edward ... a sporting man. He might even become a member of parliament. The English were generous to their heroes.

On the other hand there was the gallows from Slagters Nek. Which was it to be? he pondered. The Englishman in him might have a taste for patriotic martyrdom but the Jew in his blood hadn't survived this long to have ceased to love life. The guard saw a flash of gold in the sunlight. The Englishman was spinning a coin. Once ... twice ... it went up. He did not toss it a third time. He put it in his pocket and went inside.

The moment Christiaan Smit rose to make his final address to the court Penlynne knew. He would ask for the death penalty. He saw his knuckle turn white as he gripped the rails in the cage. Smit spoke rapidly in Dutch. Penlynne could not follow it closely but he could not miss the repeated phrase: *hangen by den nek*.

'I demand,' Smit concluded, 'that the accused be punished with the full severity of the law – and the court is well aware what that is.'

Penlynne took a look at Esselyn. The lawyer was deeply shocked. He looked across the court to Dorothy. She sat with her face in her hands. He turned his attention back to Christiaan Smit. He thought: in your position I would have done the same, Christiaan. I am a victim of my own ambiguity, and you have applied that very failing of mine to your demand. You argued very convincingly that the 33 Articles do not need to apply here. The old Dutch law is still valid. You rode your two horses ... just as I have been doing. Believe me, I understand your position very well. A pity we could not have shaken hands.

Yeatsman saw him smile. He imagined that Penlynne could not have fully understood what was being said. His own hands were trembling so he could hardly write. Penlynne was still smiling with that enigmatic expression when Judge Gregorowski adjusted the black cap on his head. Perhaps, Yeatsman thought, he does not believe what he is hearing. Perhaps he is wondering where it all went wrong. Perhaps he even believes it is not finished yet. Perhaps he is right this time.

Three months later Yeatsman was finishing his leader for *The Oracle* when an overseas cable was laid on his desk. *Mr and Mrs Leonard Penlynne and child landed at Southampton this morning from SS* The American. *They are to be guests in London of Mr Julius Wernher. Mr Penlynne, it will be remembered, had his sentence of death commuted by the Transvaal Government. It is believed here that Mr Penlynne will be honoured by Her Majesty with a knighthood. Ends message.*

The London News Agency asked for a local reaction to the news. Yeatsman wrote: *What we are witnessing in this is not the just culmination of events. It is, in fact, a sowing of the seeds of anger. Had the court taken the advice of Advocate Esselyn and made no heroes, things might have gone better for the future. He pleaded then: 'This judgement can be used to cause bitter feeling and a revival of race hatred, or it can be used mercifully and thereby restore to this unhappy land its former peace and happiness. It will do no good to make either heroes or martyrs.'*

That evening Christiaan Smit walked up the steep wagon track to Klapperkop Fort. He could find no consolation in the strength of the German fortifications. A Creusot howitzer was being dragged up the slope in a cradle pulled by twenty oxen. The crate was marked: Battery 7. He sat down and lit his pipe. He had asked for the death sentence to satisfy the State. He had conferred international dignity on his people by asking for its commutal.

I do not want his blood ... the blood of anyone on my hands. You have made a mistake, said a warning voice in his head. Perhaps, he argued. At least the guilt will not be mine. He sat on as the sun went down, smelling the bitter odour of aloe seeds he had crushed in his hand.

JAMES AMBROSE BROWN

THE WHITE LOCUSTS

Johannesburg in the 1880s: a sprawling, brawling town of shacks and shanties, of saloons and whorehouses — and rising above the confusion and squalor, flaunting their owners' wealth, the great mansions of the mining magnates; the men with the Midas touch.

Johannesburg — where men and women struggled for survival and power, for riches and political dominance, a seething society of raw energy, passion, indulgence and ambition.

A Royal Mail service in association with the Book Marketing Council & The Booksellers Association.

Post·A·Book is a Post Office trademark.

NANCY CATO

A DISTANT ISLAND

The fascinating story of Tasmania's famous botanist, Ronald Gunn.

In 1829 young Ronald Gunn, with his wife Eliza and their children, set out on the long voyage to Van Diemen's Land. Life in the new colony brought him family tragedy, great happiness, and a growing interest in the island's unique flora.

Encouraged by the great botanist William Hooker, and with the support of the Governor's wife, Lady Franklin, Gunn devoted himself to exploring the wild interior of Van Diemen's Land and studying and recording its wealth of exotic plants and trees – a lifetime's work which was to make his name famous throughout the botanical world, and lead to the publication of the 'Flora Tasmaniae' of Joseph Hooker.

HODDER AND STOUGHTON PAPERBACKS

NANCY CATO

FOREFATHERS

FOREFATHERS – a tremendous, wide-ranging Australian saga that traces the fortunes, the mishaps, the loves and the hopes of three families through seven generations and a century and a half.

The innocence and wonderment of childhood, the aching turmoil of adolescence, the sensual passions of adulthood flare and burn through their lives. Growing, intermarrying, striking out for pastures new, facing disaster and wresting success out of the often hostile land, these are the people – the farmers, the shearers, the cane-cutters and the miners – who created a new country. Through them we see and feel the whole sweep of Australian landscape and history.

HODDER AND STOUGHTON PAPERBACKS